MID-CONTINENT PUBLIC LIBRARY - BTM

3 0003 01167163 1

MINE IS THE NIGHT

WITHDRAWN
FROM THE RECORDS OF THE
MID-CONTINENT PUBLIC LIBRARY

D1412400

Mid-Continent Public Library
15616 East Highway 24
Independence, MO 64050

This Large Print Book carries the
Seal of Approval of N.A.V.H.

MINE IS THE NIGHT

LIZ CURTIS HIGGS

CHRISTIAN LARGE PRINT
A part of Gale, Cengage Learning

GALE
CENGAGE Learning

Detroit • New York • San Francisco • New Haven, Conn • Waterville, Maine • London

GALE
CENGAGE Learning™

Copyright © 2011 by Liz Curtis Higgs.
Sequel to *Here Burns My Candle.*
All Scripture quotations are taken from the King James Version.
Christian Large Print, a part of Gale, Cengage Learning.

ALL RIGHTS RESERVED
The characters and events in this book are fictional, and any resemblance to actual persons or events is coincidental.
Christian Large Print Originals.
The text of this Large Print edition is unabridged.
Other aspects of the book may vary from the original edition.
Set in 16 pt. Plantin.

LIBRARY OF CONGRESS CATALOGING-IN-PUBLICATION DATA

Higgs, Liz Curtis.
  Mine is the night / by Liz Curtis Higgs.
    p. cm. — (Christian Large Print originals)
    ISBN-13: 978-1-59415-366-2 (pbk.)
    ISBN-10: 1-59415-366-3 (pbk.)
    1. Scotland—Social life and customs—18th century—Fiction.
  2. Large type books. I. Title.
PS3558.I36235M56 2011b
813'.54—dc22   2011003524

Published in 2011 by arrangement with WaterBrook, an imprint of the Crown Publishing Group, a division of Random House, Inc.

Printed in the United States of America
1 2 3 4 5 6 7 15 14 13 12 11

For two special Elizabeths in my life:
Elizabeth Hoagland
and Elizabeth Jeffries,
my dear Louisville friends,
with fond memories of our
Elizabethan lunches.

May the meaning of your name,
"consecrated to God,"
bless your souls
now and forever.

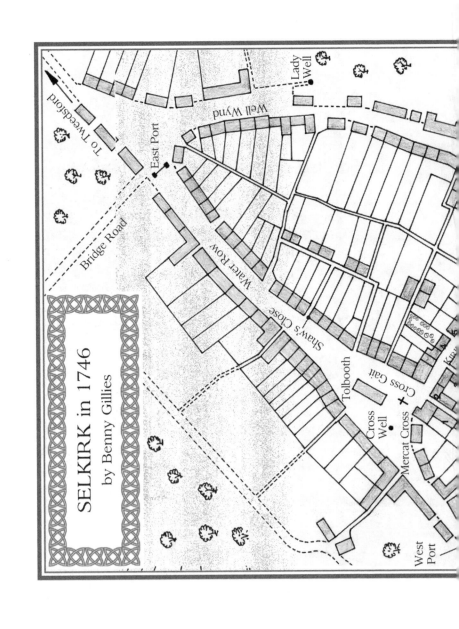

SELKIRK in 1746
by Benny Gillies

To Tweedsford

Bridge Road

East Port

Well Wynd

Lady Well

Water Row

Shaw's Close

Tolbooth

Cross Gait

Cross Well

Mercat Cross

West Port

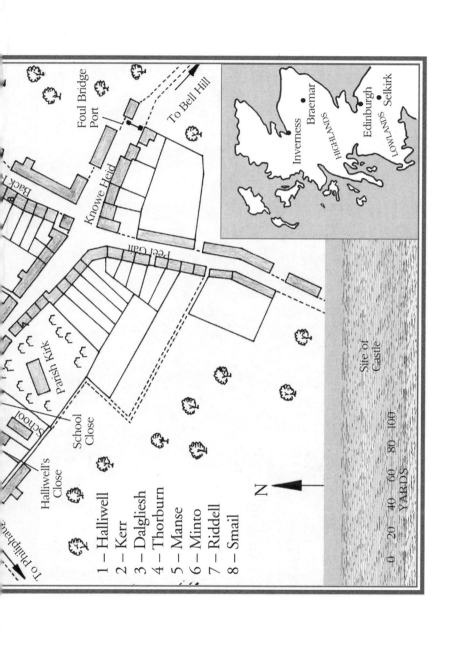

Foul Bridge Port

Knowe Heid

To Bell Hill

Back

Peel Gait

Parish Kirk

School

School Close

Halliwell's Close

To Philiphaugh

1 – Halliwell
2 – Kerr
3 – Dalgliesh
4 – Thorburn
5 – Manse
6 – Minto
7 – Riddell
8 – Smail

N

0   20   40   60   80   100
YARDS

Site of Castle

Inverness
Braemar
HIGHLANDS
Edinburgh
LOWLANDS
Selkirk

Mine is the night,
with all her stars.

EDWARD YOUNG

ONE

Foul whisperings are abroad.

WILLIAM SHAKESPEARE

Selkirkshire
26 April 1746

The distant hoofbeats were growing louder.

Elisabeth Kerr quickly pushed aside the curtain and leaned out the carriage window. A cool spring rain, borne on a blustery wind, stung her cheeks. She could not see the riders on horseback, hidden by the steep hill behind her. But she could hear them galloping hard, closing the gap.

Her mother-in-law seemed unconcerned, her attention drawn to the puddle forming at their feet. A frown creased her brow. "Do you mean for us to arrive in Selkirk even more disheveled than we already are?" Three long days of being jostled about in a cramped and dirty coach had left Marjory Kerr in a mood as foul as the weather.

" 'Tis not the rain that concerns me." Elisabeth resumed her seat, feeling a bit unsteady. "No ordinary traveling party would ride with such haste."

Marjory's breath caught. "Surely you do not think —"

"I do."

Had they not heard the rumors at every inn and coaching halt? King George's men were scouring the countryside for anyone who'd aided bonny Prince Charlie in his disastrous bid to reclaim the British throne for the long-deposed Stuarts. Each whispered account was worse than the last. Wounded rebel soldiers clubbed to death. Houses burned with entire families inside. Wives and daughters ravished by British dragoons.

Help us, Lord. Please. Elisabeth slipped her arm round her mother-in-law's shoulders as she heard the riders crest the hill and bear down on them.

"We were almost home," Marjory fretted.

"The Lord will rescue us," Elisabeth said firmly, and then they were overtaken. A male voice cut through the rain-soaked air, and the carriage jarred to a halt.

Mr. Dewar, their round-bellied coachman, dropped from his perch and landed by the window with a grunt. He rocked back on his heels until he found his balance, then yanked open the carriage door without ceremony. "Beg yer pardon, *leddies*. The captain here would have a *wird* with ye."

Marjory's temper flared. "He cannot expect us to stand in the rain."

"On the contrary, madam." A British dragoon dismounted and rolled into view like a loaded cannon. His shoulders were broad, his legs short, his neck invisible. "I insist upon it. At once, if you please."

With a silent prayer for strength, Elisabeth gathered her hoops and maneuvered through the narrow carriage doorway. She was grateful for Mr. Dewar's hand as she stepped down, trying not to drag her skirts through the mud. Despite the evening gloom, her eyes traced the outline of a hillside town not far south. *Almost home.*

The captain, whom Elisabeth guessed to be about five-and-forty years, watched in stony silence as Marjory disembarked. His scarlet coat was drenched, his cuffed, black boots were covered with filth, and the soggy brim of his cocked hat bore a noticeable wave.

He was also shorter than Elisabeth had first imagined. When she lifted her head, making the most of her long neck, she was fully two inches taller than he. Some days she bemoaned her height but not this day.

By the time Marjory joined her on the roadside, a half-dozen uniformed men had crowded round. Broadswords hung at their sides, yet their scowls were far more menacing.

13

"Come *noo,*" Mr. Dewar said gruffly. "Ye've nae need to frighten my passengers. State yer business, and be done with it. We've little daylight left and less than a mile to travel."

"Selkirk is your destination?" The captain seemed disappointed. "Not many Highland rebels to be found there."

" 'Tis a royal burgh," Marjory told him, her irritation showing. "Our townsfolk have been loyal to the Crown for centuries."

Elisabeth shot her a guarded look. *Have a care, dear Marjory.*

The captain ignored her mother-in-law's comments, all the while studying their plain black gowns, a curious light in his eyes. "In mourning, are we? For husbands, I'll wager." He took a brazen step toward Elisabeth, standing entirely too close. "Tell me, lass. Did your men give their lives in service to King George? At Falkirk perhaps? Or Culloden?"

She could not risk a lie. Yet she could not speak the truth.

Please, Lord, give me the right words.

Elisabeth took a long, slow breath, then spoke from her heart. "Our brave men died at Falkirk honoring the King who has no equal."

He cocked one eyebrow. "Did they now?"

"Aye." She met the captain's gaze without flinching, well aware of which sovereign she had in mind. *I am God, and there is none like*

14

me. She'd not lied. Nor had the dragoon grasped the truth behind her words: by divine right the crown belonged to Prince Charlie.

"No one compares to His Majesty, King George," he said expansively. "Though I am sorry for your loss. No doubt your men died heroes."

Elisabeth merely nodded, praying he'd not ask their names. A list of soldiers killed at Falkirk had circulated round Edinburgh for weeks. The captain might recall that Lord Donald and Andrew Kerr were not named among the royalist casualties. Instead, her handsome husband and his younger brother were counted among the fallen rebels on that stormy January evening.

My sweet Donald. However grievous his sins, however much he'd wounded her, she'd loved him once and mourned him still.

Her courage bolstered by the thought of Donald in his dark blue uniform, Elisabeth squared her shoulders and ignored the rain sluicing down her neck. "My mother-in-law and I are eager to resume our journey. If we are done here —"

"We are not." Still lingering too near, the captain inclined his head, measuring her. "A shame your husband left such a bonny widow. Though if you fancy another soldier in your bed, one of my men will gladly oblige —"

"Sir!" Marjory protested. "How dare you

address a lady in so coarse a manner."

His dragoons quickly closed ranks. "A lady?" one of them grumbled. "She sounds more like a Highlander to my ear."

The captain's expression darkened. "Aye, so she does." Without warning he grasped the belled cuff of Elisabeth's sleeve and turned back the fabric. "Where is it, lass? Where is your silk Jacobite rose?"

"You've no need to look." Elisabeth tried to wrest free of him. "I haven't one."

Ignoring her objections, he roughly examined the other cuff, nearly tearing apart the seam. "The white rose of Scotland was Prince Charlie's favorite, was it not? I've plucked them off many a Highland rebel."

"I imagine you have." Elisabeth freed her sleeve from his grasp. "Are you quite satisfied?"

"Far from it, lass." The captain eyed the neckline of her gown, his mouth twisting into an ugly sneer. "It seems your flower is well hidden. Nevertheless, I mean to have it."

Two

The brave find a home in every land.

OVID

"Stop!" Marjory threw her arm in front of Elisabeth, shielding her from the British dragoon with his ill-mannered words and his insolent gaze. "That is enough, sir." Her heart pounding, her patience long abandoned on the road south, Marjory practically shouted at the man, "If my daughter-in-law says she has no rose, then she has no rose."

"I do not own a single one," Elisabeth said evenly, stepping back.

Marjory lowered her arm but didn't move, still glaring at the captain. Did the scoundrel think she'd simply stand by and watch while he took liberties with her daughter-in-law? *The very idea.*

When the captain did not respond at once, his men grew restless, murmuring among themselves. Finally he offered a careless shrug. "Madam, I did not intend —"

17

"I beg to differ," Marjory retorted. "Your intentions were abundantly clear and wholly dishonorable. Perhaps I should write General Lord Mark Kerr and inform him of your vile behavior." She saw the flicker of fear in his eyes and was secretly pleased.

He shifted his stance. "You are . . . acquainted with his lordship?"

"Very well acquainted." Marjory kept the rest to herself: Lord Mark was not only Honorary Governor of Edinburgh Castle; he was also a distant cousin of her late husband's and a heartless military man who'd done her family many a disservice. She would not correspond with General Lord Mark Kerr if he were the last man on earth.

"We've been delayed long enough," she said, then turned toward the carriage, sensing her bravado beginning to flag. Never in her life had she spoken so boldly to a man, let alone to a dragoon, though he certainly deserved it. Perhaps the Almighty had rescued them just as Elisabeth had said he would.

Marjory held out her hand, amazed to find she was not trembling. "Mr. Dewar?"

"Aye, *mem.*" He guided her into the coach and cast a withering glance over his shoulder. "*Weel,* Captain, 'twould appear ye've met yer match."

The dragoon backed away. "If these women are not Jacobite rebels, I have no use for them." He gestured to his men. "Find your

18

mounts, lads. We're finished here."

A grin spread across Mr. Dewar's ruddy face. "So ye are."

As the dragoons scattered, the coachman helped Elisabeth into her seat, then shut the carriage door with a firm bang. "I'll have ye *hame* afore dark, leddies. Though I doubt either o' ye have *onie* fear o' the *nicht*." He clambered onto his seat, then called out to his pair of horses, while the mounted dragoons galloped down the road, their hoofbeats soon fading.

Both women exhaled and sank back against the worn leather upholstery.

"You were very brave," Elisabeth said at last.

"Or very foolish." Marjory pulled a handkerchief from her sleeve and patted her damp cheeks. "The next soldiers we meet may not be so easily dissuaded."

"Indeed." Elisabeth stretched out her long legs. "Nor so short in stature."

Marjory glanced at her daughter-in-law's gown. "Remind me, where *are* your silk roses?"

"Stitched inside the hem of my petticoat." A smile played at the corners of Elisabeth's mouth. "Had the captain examined me further, he'd have found a whole row of Jacobite rosettes. But I spoke the truth when I said I don't own *one*."

Marjory wagged her head. "My clever Bess."

In years past Marjory had not appreciated her daughter-in-law's ingenuity, thinking her secretive and untrustworthy. How she'd misjudged her! Though Elisabeth was low-born and Highland bred, she'd grown into a gentlewoman by any measure, with courage and tenacity to spare. And the lass was only four-and-twenty!

Marjory sighed inwardly. Had she ever been so young?

" 'Tis good we bade the Hedderwicks farewell in Galashiels," Elisabeth said. "Had they still been with us, they might have talked themselves into an English prison."

"*Might* have?" Marjory scoffed. "I've never known two men who spoke more and said less." The father and son who'd traveled south with them from Edinburgh had boasted endlessly of their Jacobite sympathies, though neither had been willing to bear arms for Prince Charlie.

Unlike my brave sons.

As Marjory tucked her handkerchief inside her sleeve, Donald's parting words echoed in her heart: *May I count on you to look after Elisabeth?* Naturally Marjory had promised to do so, never imagining a day when she'd have no home and no gold. How would she look after Elisabeth now?

Gazing upward, Marjory pictured the small,

20

heavy trunk strapped atop the carriage, bearing the massive family Bible with its comforting words: *They that seek the LORD shall not want any good thing.* Could she trust the Almighty to provide for them? Or would he continue to burden her with further losses? In truth, there was nothing left to take.

When Elisabeth reached out to close the curtain, Marjory stayed her hand. "No need, my dear. The rain has finally stopped."

Beneath the gray evening sky, a dense mist hovered near the ground, rising and falling like a living creature, giving them brief glimpses of the town above them. Stone houses thatched with straw and sod. Windows lit by candle and hearth.

Elisabeth clasped her hands in her lap, her blue eyes glowing. "I've waited a long time to see Selkirk."

"Too long." Marjory opened the curtain on her side of the carriage, ushering in what light remained. "Welcome to your new home, Bess."

Home. Ten years had passed since Marjory had looked upon Selkirk parish. Yet so little had changed. The rolling hills tumbled over one another, forming the grassy banks of the Ettrick Water, swollen from the rain. "More than a thousand souls reside in Selkirk," she said absently. Would any of them remember her? Extend a hand of greeting? Or, once they heard of her disgrace, would they close their doors, shutting her out of all good society?

Nae. This was her childhood home. Surely she'd find sympathy here.

As they crossed a new stone bridge spanning the Ettrick Water below the mill, Elisabeth gazed up at the sprawling burgh. " 'Tis larger than I'd imagined. I do hope Gibson had no difficulty locating Cousin Anne."

"Gibson once lived here," Marjory reminded her. "He knows where Anne resides."

Earlier in the week Marjory had sent ahead their butler, Neil Gibson, bearing a letter for their cousin with an urgent request for lodging. Marjory touched the hanging pocket tied round her waist, knowing very well her purse was empty. Hadn't she bartered her last knife and spoon to purchase their midday meal? They couldn't pay for a bed at the Forest Inn even for one night. Cousin Anne *had* to be home, *had* to make room for them.

The carriage began the precipitous ascent toward the town center, pressing the women back against their seats. Hearing Mr. Dewar urging his team forward, Marjory said, " 'Tis a long pull for the horses."

Elisabeth nodded. "And for Gibson. Do you suppose he arrived yesterday?"

"Or this morn." Marjory felt guiltier with each turn of the carriage wheels. She'd forgotten what a daunting hill this was, especially for a man of sixty after a long journey on foot.

Not many pedestrians were abroad at that hour. A few men in ragged clothes trudged by, walking sticks in hand, dogs at their heels. They glanced in the carriage windows long enough to satisfy their curiosity but didn't acknowledge the Kerrs, only plodded forward.

"Gibson climbed the steep streets of Edinburgh many times a day," Elisabeth reminded her. "We'll find him drinking tea at Cousin Anne's table. I'm certain of it."

But Marjory was not at all certain.

Doubts and fears she'd held at bay the whole of their journey suddenly overwhelmed her. What if Anne had turned Gibson away at the door, unwilling to shelter her tainted relatives? What if she'd married after all these years and moved to a different house in town? Or what if — *heaven forbid* — Anne no longer resided in Selkirkshire?

Nae, nae, nae. Fretting accomplished nothing, Marjory reminded herself. Had she not learned that by now? Determined to put on a brave front, she focused her attention on the changing scenery. "Once through the East Port, we'll not travel far before we reach the marketplace and Halliwell's Close."

Her daughter-in-law inched forward, gripping her seat. "I do hope Anne will be happy to see us."

"Aye." Marjory swallowed. *Let Gibson be there. Let Anne be home. Let all be well.* She

23

sent forth her prayers like winged messengers as she peered ahead through the mist and gloom.

A moment later the coach gingerly maneuvered through the town gate and onto Water Row. Both sides of the main thoroughfare were crowded with houses and shops, just as Marjory remembered. She could still make out the Borderland names painted over each lintel. *Tait. Shaw. Elliot. Murray. Scott. Anderson.*

Clasping the edge of the open window, she pulled herself closer, each familiar landmark tugging at her heart. Mr. Fletcher, the cabinetmaker, lived in a whitewashed cottage hard by the road. Mr. Fairbairn, the merchant, sold his goods beneath a canvas awning not a stone's throw from their carriage wheels.

Unbidden, a distant memory swept over her. Two fair-haired, blue-eyed lads skipping up Water Row, singing out the various trades in a kind of rhyme: *Cooper, souter, tanner, sawyer, dyer, spinner, potter, saddler.* Donald, with his long legs and slender frame, leading the way. Andrew, smaller and frailer, trying his best to keep up.

Had it not always been thus, even to the very end?

My beloved Donald. My precious Andrew.

"Oh, Bess." Marjory sank against the win-

24

dow. "I never . . ." Her voice broke. "I never imagined I'd return home without my family."

THREE

Fear not for the future, weep not for the
past.

PERCY BYSSHE SHELLEY

Elisabeth drew her mother-in-law into a
gentle embrace. "I know 'tis hard," she
whispered, holding Marjory close. "I know."
Other words of consolation leaped to mind
and were discarded. A fine husband lost and
then two sons? Only the Almighty could heal
so deep a wound.

*But you've traveled all this way with her, Bess.
Are you not her family too?*

Elisabeth dismissed her petty complaint
before it took root. *'Tis my duty. And my calling. And my joy.* She'd spoken those words to
Marjory on Thursday morning and meant
them with all her heart. Now she had to prove
it.

When the carriage bounced in and out of a
deep rut, jarring them apart, Elisabeth re-

26

leased her with a firm squeeze. "Our hardest days are behind us, dear Marjory. We're home. And Gibson is waiting for us."

Her mother-in-law nodded, though her troubled expression remained.

The carriage slowed. "Selkirk!" Mr. Dewar called out and eased the horses to a stop.

Her heart pounding beneath her stays, Elisabeth quickly gathered their few belongings — her silk reticule, a small book of poetry, Marjory's linen handkerchiefs — and followed her mother-in-law through the carriage door.

"Not *monie* folk about the *toun* this Sabbath eve," Mr. Dewar observed, helping them step down.

Marjory tightened her cape round her neck. "Have you the time, sir?"

He made a great show of pulling a silver watch from his pocket, the engraved case reflecting the light from his coach lantern. "Just past eight o' the clock, mem. I meant to reach Selkirk afore this, but" — he shrugged his rounded shoulders — "I didna count on three days o' bad weather or a broken carriage wheel."

"Or a party of dragoons," Marjory said dryly.

Elisabeth walked in a slow circle, assessing her new home. The marketplace was indeed deserted. Vendor stalls were locked and windows shuttered for the night. The ancient *mercat* cross was a smaller version of the proud pillar that stood in the midst of Edinburgh's High Street, marking the spot where meat and meal were sold and important events proclaimed.

Two widows are newly arrived from the capital. Elisabeth was certain no one would bother to make such an announcement. The town gossips would spread the news soon enough.

Mr. Dewar jerked his thumb at a foreboding structure at the far end of the fleshmarket. "The *tolbooth*, ye *ken*. Dinna be surprised if ye hear prisoners howling from the thieves' hole." He unloaded their bags, hefting one small trunk onto each shoulder. "After ye, Mrs. Kerr."

Marjory led them toward a row of buildings made of rough whinstone, some with ground-floor shops facing the marketplace. "On Monday the scent of baking bread will come wafting through that doorway," she said, pointing to the corner, "and in the house above it, you'll find a weaver bending over his loom."

Like my father once did. Elisabeth looked up at the weaver's shuttered window. Nights beyond counting she'd fallen asleep to the steady rhythm of her father's treadle raising and lowering the threads of the warp.

Marjory brought them to an arched passageway fitted between two of the buildings.

"And here's Halliwell's Close, where Cousin Anne resides."

Arm in arm the Kerr women ventured within the shadowy close, lit by a single lantern that hung from the stone wall several doors down. The air was dank and smelled of rotting fish. A rat darted past them, its long, thin tail quickly disappearing from sight.

Elisabeth imagined her mother's voice whispering in her ear. *A puir man is glad of a little.* However modest their lodgings, Elisabeth was determined to be grateful. She'd been poor as a child and not minded. She'd been wealthy as a wife yet lived frugally. As a widow she had few needs, and they were shrinking by the hour. Food and shelter would suffice.

Marjory stopped at an unmarked wooden door and made use of the round iron knocker. The hollow sound echoed down the long close.

While they waited, Mr. Dewar deposited their trunks beside them. "I'll fetch the *ither,*" he said, then lumbered off.

After a lengthy silence Elisabeth reached for the knocker. "I don't wish to appear impatient, but . . ." When Marjory nodded, Elisabeth banged the ring against the wood, imagining a warm hearth, a plate of soup, and a snug bed.

But no one came.

Mr. Dewar returned with the last trunk and

placed it at their feet. "D'ye need me to stay with ye, leddies?"

"Our cousin is certain to answer our knock any moment," Elisabeth assured him.

"Then I'm *aff* to the Forest Inn for my supper. I bid ye both a *guid* nicht." He doffed his hat and was gone.

Halliwell's Close was suddenly quiet and, with nightfall upon them, oppressively dark. The lantern illumined their faces but little else.

As they tarried by the door, listening for any sound of movement or voices within, Elisabeth watched Marjory grow increasingly distraught, showing all of her eight-and-forty years. The tender skin beneath her eyes looked bruised, and her mourning gown hung loosely about her shoulders. Most distressing of all were the deep lines etched across Marjory's forehead. Was she worried about Gibson's whereabouts? Or was something else weighing on her mind?

Finally Elisabeth asked, "Are you certain this is Anne's door?"

Marjory looked down, her voice almost too low to be heard. "I am no longer certain of anything."

A knot of apprehension tightened inside her. "Marjory, whatever do you mean?"

"Our cousin once resided here, but" — her mother-in-law lifted her head — "I cannot say she still does. Though I have not heard

30

otherwise," she hastened to add. "Not since Lord John and I moved to Edinburgh."

"But . . . that was ten years ago!" Elisabeth could not hide her dismay. "You've not corresponded with Anne all this time?"

"Nae, I fear I have not. My factor at Tweedsford . . ." Marjory sighed heavily. "That is, Mr. Laidlaw kept me apprised of the news from Selkirk over the years. He never mentioned any change in Cousin Anne's situation."

Elisabeth was speechless. Did her mother-in-law expect a cordial greeting from a relative so long forsaken? From the look of their surroundings, Anne was a woman of lesser means who'd have benefited from the Kerrs' attention. Only a merciful soul could overlook such ill treatment.

Marjory gnawed on her lower lip. "Perhaps she's not at home . . ."

A woman's voice floated down the passageway from the far end. "Who is not at home?"

Marjory spun about, nearly stumbling over the baggage at her feet. "If you please, madam," she called into the darkness. "We are seeking Miss Anne Kerr, my late husband's cousin. Might you know her?"

Elisabeth held her breath. *Please, Lord.*

"*I* am Miss Kerr," the woman announced, quickening her steps.

With a soft cry Marjory clutched Elisa-

31

beth's arm. "We are saved," she whispered.

Their cousin soon appeared, lifting the hem of her blue drugget gown above the wet cobblestones as she hurried toward them, her thin wool cape swinging from her shoulders. Her fair hair and complexion took Elisabeth aback, so closely did her coloring match Donald's. Small in stature, with a trim waist to match, Anne Kerr had a light step, her scuffed leather shoes soundless in the narrow close.

When she reached them, the three women quickly exchanged curtsies.

Marjory spoke first. "Cousin Anne, I cannot tell you how glad we are to have found you."

Anne nodded, though no spark of recognition shone in her light blue eyes. "Did you say your late husband was a cousin of mine?"

"Aye." Marjory took Anne's bare hands in hers. "Lord John Kerr. I feel certain you remember him."

"The late owner of Tweedsford?" Anne's skin grew noticeably paler. "I could hardly forget the gentleman, God rest his soul." She paused, studying Marjory more intently. "But if Lord John was your husband, that means you must be . . ." Her eyes widened. "Nae, you *cannot* be . . . Lady Marjory?"

FOUR

Poverty is a bitter weed to most women, and there are few indeed who can accept it with dignity.

ELIZA LYNN LINTON

Marjory bristled at the shocked expression on Anne's face. *Is it my age? My tattered gown? Or did you think I died too?*

"Do not call me 'Lady,' " Marjory finally told her, disowning the title she'd once loved.

Anne's mouth fell open. "Then you —"

"Call me 'Marjory,' " she insisted. "The king has dealt harshly with me and revoked our family's title, lands, and fortune." She'd not meant to spill out the truth all at once, but there it was.

"King George has done this?" Anne frowned. "There must be some explanation —"

"Treason," Marjory said bluntly. "My sons, Donald and Andrew, fought for the Jacobite

33

cause and died at Falkirk." *There.* She jutted out her chin, if only to keep it from trembling.

Anne slowly pulled her hands from Marjory's grasp. "Ill news indeed, Cousin."

She sensed the aloofness in Anne's tone, the deliberateness of her withdrawal. Nae, this would not do. "Did not our manservant, Gibson, bring a letter to your door?"

"He did not," Anne said evenly. "I've had no correspondence from you —"

"In a very long time," Marjory quickly agreed. "Gibson traveled ahead on foot so we'd not arrive here unexpected."

"And yet you have." Anne took a step backward, putting more distance between them. "What is it you want from me?"

Marjory eyed the woman, a dozen years her junior. Anne Kerr had never married, had never been wealthy or titled, yet she held the upper hand. With a roof over her head and food in her larder, Anne had what they needed but could not afford.

Must I plead with her, Lord? Must I beg? Pride wrapped itself round Marjory's throat, choking back her words.

Then Elisabeth stepped in. "We are rather desperate for lodging," she explained, "and need only the simplest of meals. Might you accommodate us, Miss Kerr?"

Anne turned to Elisabeth with a lift of her brow. "And you are?"

"Donald's widow," she said, offering a

tentative smile. "Elisabeth Kerr."

Anne responded with a slight nod. "Did not Andrew marry as well?"

"He did," Elisabeth said. "This very night his widow, Janet, is returning to her Highland home."

Marjory grimaced at the reminder. During Janet's brief marriage to Andrew, the spoiled, selfish woman had not endeared herself to most of the Kerr household. Before leaving Edinburgh, Marjory had purchased a seat for Janet on a northbound carriage. Janet's halfhearted protest had ended the moment two shillings crossed her gloved palm.

Marjory looked at her younger daughter-in-law now with fond affection. *You should have returned home as well, dear Bess.* But no matter how many times Marjory had entreated her, Elisabeth had refused to leave her side, insisting on traveling with her to Selkirk. She hadn't planned on Elisabeth's company, but Marjory was glad for it all the same.

"Come with me." Anne pushed open her door with a sigh. "I cannot let you sleep out of doors like beggars."

Horrified at the thought, Marjory murmured her thanks, then followed their cousin through the entrance and up a dozen steps to a smaller interior door with even less paint. She'd never visited Anne's house, though Lord John had once described it as cozy and

35

quaint. Whatever awaited them, it was far superior to a cobbled passageway on a chilly April night.

Anne entered first and reached for a candle, then touched the wick to the glowing coals in the hearth and motioned Marjory forward.

The candlelight sent shadows dancing across the low-ceilinged room with its plaster walls and rough wooden floors. Anne's furnishings were neat but alarmingly few: a box bed, plainly draped; a rustic washstand and basin; two upholstered chairs with threadbare arms; a low table covered with sewing items; an oval dining table that would barely seat four; and several mismatched wooden chairs huddled in a corner like gossips exchanging news.

Marjory found her voice at last. "You keep a tidy house, Cousin Anne."

"Easily managed when one owns so little." Anne lit a second tallow candle and placed it on the shelf mounted between her two front windows.

Her only windows, Marjory realized. At least the glazing was clean, and the curtains, surprisingly, were trimmed in lace. An extravagant touch for such mean lodgings. She stepped closer and looked down at the marketplace. "You have a fine view of the town."

"And the town has a fine view of me," Anne said curtly. "If you mean to hide your family's disgrace, Marjory, you've knocked on the wrong door."

She flinched at her harsh words. "Believe me, Cousin, had we anywhere else to go . . ."

Anne had already turned away to poke at the coals in her grate, jabbing them with savage efficiency.

Marjory stared at her cousin's back. A dearth of letters over the years would hardly account for this cold reception. Was it the Kerrs' ill-advised support of Prince Charlie? Or had something else upset Anne?

When Elisabeth crossed the threshold, carrying in the first of their trunks, Anne hurried off to help her, as if glad to escape Marjory's presence. The two younger women disappeared down the stair, leaving Marjory to examine their surroundings and accept the inevitable.

One room. We shall all live in one room.

Disheartened at the prospect, Marjory walked along the front wall, counting her steps. *Eighteen.* Then she measured from the windows to the back wall. *Eighteen.* The supporting wall that ran halfway through the room provided a modicum of privacy between Anne's bed and the rest of her lodging yet made the house feel even smaller.

With a muted groan, Marjory sank onto the nearest chair, wondering what Anne Kerr might serve for supper. Moldy cheese and a stale bannock, she imagined, then chastised herself for judging their cousin so harshly.

Anne had no notice of their arrival, no time to replenish her stores, and limited resources besides.

Hearing voices on the stair, Marjory rose with a guilty start, then watched Anne and Elisabeth struggle through the door, bearing a heavy trunk between them. "You might put it here," Marjory suggested, uncertain how else to assist them.

They dutifully placed the trunk near the foot of Anne's bed and left to fetch the last one, not saying a word.

Like servants, Marjory thought glumly.

Her heart skipped a beat. *Gibson.* How had she forgotten him so quickly?

Appalled, Marjory hastened to the window as if by some miracle she might spot his balding head fringed in silver. Had the rain delayed him? An injury? Illness? Perhaps he'd encountered highwaymen on a lonely road. Or worse, dragoons. Forty miles stretched between Milne Square and Halliwell's Close. Anything might have happened.

By the time the others returned, Marjory was pacing the floor. "However shall we find Gibson?"

"I am worried as well," Elisabeth admitted, heading for the washstand by Anne's bed.

Only then did Marjory notice their faces were red with exertion and their hands soiled.

"We'll consider your manservant shortly." Anne brushed past her. "First, I must attend to our supper. Cousin Marjory, if you might set the table." She gestured toward a low shelf, which held an assortment of trenchers, knot bowls, and carved cups.

Marjory stared at the woodenware, carved in the crudest design. The spoons and forks were gray from years of use, and some of the plates were badly cracked along the grain. This was her future, then. No pewter plates, no crystal goblets, no beeswax tapers gleaming from a polished mahogany sideboard.

Anne called across the room, "Something wrong, Cousin?"

"Nae," Marjory said quickly. She dared not refuse to help, however menial the task. Was she not an interloper of the worst kind? A penniless relation begging for bread with a widowed daughter-in-law in tow and a manservant gone astray among the hills.

Marjory reached for a cluster of wooden utensils, her hands shaking. *How am I to manage, Lord? How are we to live like this?*

FIVE

The night is dark, and I am far from home;
lead Thou me on!

JOHN HENRY NEWMAN

Elisabeth had forgotten the odd sensation of a wooden spoon in her mouth. Once the heat and moisture from a steaming bowl of broth made the wood swell, it felt like a second tongue. She hastily put the spoon down, fearing she might retch.

"Is the broth not seasoned to your liking?" Anne asked. "Too much wild thyme, perhaps."

" 'Tis very flavorful," Elisabeth said, though she edged the bowl of watery broth away from her. "I confess I am more tired than hungry." Not precisely true. She was tired *and* hungry, but she could not bear to offend their cousin.

Anne turned to Marjory, a single candle on the table illuminating the younger woman's sharp features. "This manservant of yours.

He's resourceful?"

"Aye, and brave," Marjory answered, "though not in perfect health. Last winter he suffered from a fever and then a lingering cough."

Elisabeth vividly recalled Marjory assessing Gibson's fever — placing her hand on his brow, on his cheek, on his chest — her demeanor uncommonly tender, her hazel eyes filled with warm regard for the man who'd so faithfully served their family.

"Cousin," Anne said firmly, "you must prepare yourself for the worst. An older servant, still recovering from an illness, traveling on foot in this chilly, rainy weather? Why, the man may never reach Selkirk."

Marjory looked stricken. "Do not say such a thing! I've known Neil Gibson the whole of my married life and all through my widowhood as well."

Elisabeth reached for her hand. "I've no doubt Gibson will arrive in a day or two or send word with a passing carriage."

Marjory squeezed her fingers in response, saying nothing more.

When Anne stood and began gathering their woodenware, Elisabeth leaped up to help her, needing a distraction, wanting to be useful. The two knelt by the fire and washed the dishes with hot water and ragged scraps of linen, then spread out the wooden pieces to dry on the flagstone hearth.

"I've not far to go for water," Anne said. "The Cross Well is in the marketplace, just beyond the mouth of Halliwell's Close."

Elisabeth was already on her feet. "I'll draw some for the morn."

"Oh, but, Cousin Elisabeth —"

"Bess," she said, looking down at her. "Please call me 'Bess.' "

"And I prefer 'Annie,' " she said after a bit. "Still, I cannot have my guests —"

"We are hardly guests," Elisabeth reminded her. "Distant relatives at best. We had no business arriving at your door unannounced, though I do not fault poor Gibson."

"Nor I." Anne glanced at Marjory, by now half asleep in one of the upholstered chairs. When Anne spoke again, her voice was low and taut. "I confess 'tis hard to shelter Lady Kerr beneath my roof. She . . . that is, Lord John . . ." Anne's words faded into silence.

Elisabeth did not press the matter. Perhaps when they knew each other better. Perhaps when Anne trusted her.

"I shan't be a moment," Elisabeth said, then hurried down the stair and into the murky close, blinking until her eyes adjusted. A few more steps and she reached the marketplace, where the square wellhead stood, black as the night itself. She filled the slender-necked stoup in haste, shivering from the clammy mist that swirled round her skirts. Above her the moon and stars were lost

42

behind the clouds, and the three streets that converged to form the triangular marketplace were all bathed in darkness.

Elisabeth looked up at the curtained windows of Anne's house, a growing awareness pressing down on her. *I should not have come.* Anne could not possibly feed them from her paltry stores day after day. And her small house was not meant for three. If Marjory knew what awaited them here in Selkirk, little wonder she'd urged both her daughters-in-law to return to the Highlands.

Janet had honored Marjory's request.

Alas, I did not.

With a heavy heart Elisabeth slipped back up the stair and found Anne waiting beside the enclosed box bed, with its wooden walls and woolen curtains.

"I've a *hurlie* bed stored underneath," Anne told her, "but 'twill take two of us to trundle it about."

After several minutes of tugging and pulling, Elisabeth and Anne managed to free the small hurlie bed from its confines, releasing a plume of dust. They wheeled it into the corner opposite Anne's box bed and swept the mattress clean with a straw broom.

In most homes hurlie beds were meant for children. Or servants. Marjory stared in obvious dismay at the thin mattress stuffed with chaff and the rickety wooden wheels. "Are we expected to share this?"

Anne jerked her chin, a spark of anger in her eyes. " 'Tis the only bed I have to offer you, Cousin."

Elisabeth swiftly intervened. "Marjory, by all means claim the hurlie bed for yourself. I shall sleep by the fire with a *creepie* for my feet." She angled one of the upholstered chairs toward the hearth and pulled up a low wooden footstool. "Annie, if you've a blanket to spare, I'd be grateful."

"But you cannot sleep in a chair," Marjory scolded her.

"Certainly I can." Elisabeth began pulling the pins from her hair. "Highlanders are famous for sleeping on the hills and moors wrapped in naught but their plaids."

"The men, perhaps," her mother-in-law grumbled.

"Nae," Elisabeth assured her, "the women too. I spent many a summer night with my back propped against a tree in the pine woods round Castleton of Braemar."

"You slept in the woods?" Marjory shook her head. "Truly, Bess, you never cease to astound me."

Elisabeth glanced across the room, hoping the trifling exchange had given their cousin's ire time to cool.

But Anne was still frowning. "I've a plaid for each of you," she said, then reached into the recesses of her box bed and pulled out two light wool blankets, woven in muted blues and reds.

"You'll not miss them tonight?" Elisabeth asked, wanting to be certain.

Anne shook her head. "But I'll soon miss my sleep."

They took turns at the washstand, then slipped off their gowns and retired for the night. When Anne blew out the last candle, an awkward silence thicker than any plaid fell across the darkened room.

"Good night," Elisabeth said softly, hoping the others might respond and so end the evening on a sweeter note. But Anne closed her bed curtains without a word, and Marjory exhaled in obvious frustration.

With the Sabbath almost upon them, Elisabeth refused to be discouraged. The light of day and the warmth of society would surely improve things. She quietly arranged her plaid by the faint glow of the coal fire, then closed her eyes and called upon the Almighty.

I remember thee upon my bed, and meditate on thee in the night watches. Since winter she'd consumed the psalms until the words had become her daily bread, feeding her soul, nourishing her mind. When the family Bible was out of reach, or the hour late, or the firelight dim, she could draw upon his holy truth buried inside her.

The words came swiftly, silently, yet surely. *My soul followeth hard after thee.* Her heart stirred at the thought. The Lord had led her

45

to Selkirk, of that she was certain. Now came the harder task: resting in the knowledge that he'd brought her here for some good purpose.

Thy right hand upholdeth me. If the Almighty supported her, might she not support others? Elisabeth lifted her head, buoyed by the realization. Rather than be a burden to Anne, she could provide for their cousin's upkeep by plying her needle. Had she not once earned her living in a tailor's shop? And stitched her own gowns for the sheer pleasure of working with her hands?

She would sew, then, and pray Anne's heart might soften toward them. Sinking deeper into her chair, Elisabeth embraced the gift of sleep and let the Almighty shape her dreams.

Six

There is in every true woman's heart a spark of heavenly fire . . . which kindles up, and beams and blazes in the dark hour of adversity.

WASHINGTON IRVING

Marjory stared into her cup of tea, bleary eyed from a poor night's sleep. Her daughter-in-law had meant well, but the hurlie bed was no prize. The mattress was lumpy, and the wooden frame groaned whenever she tossed and turned.

Even so, you had a bed to yourself, Marjory. And supper before it.

She chafed at the reminder, wishing her conscience were still slumbering. But it was the Sabbath. All of Selkirk would be awake, dressed, and prepared to leave for the parish kirk at the first clang of the bell.

Marjory considered the last bite of her oatcake, then pushed it aside. Her appetite had vanished at the thought of seeing her old

47

neighbors, who would mark her diminished circumstances and quickly learn of her losses. And what would she say to Reverend Brown?

"Come, Marjory." Elisabeth beckoned her toward the window, hairbrush in hand. "Since every eye will be on you this morn, I would have you look your best."

Marjory submitted to her daughter-in-law's ministrations, surprised when her thinning auburn hair turned into a sleek braid, pinned atop her head. Holding up Anne's small looking glass, Marjory pretended not to see the wrinkles outlining her features and admired Elisabeth's handiwork instead.

"Another talent put to good use," Marjory commended her. "Though my gown is frayed, at least my hair is presentable."

"Someday I shall stitch you a new dress," Elisabeth promised, still smoothing a few loose strands of hair in place when the kirk bell began to toll.

Marjory's stomach clenched. *Not yet, not yet.*

"We must away," Anne cautioned, pulling her cape round her shoulders. "The reverend has little patience with stragglers."

Marjory hastily brushed the lint from her skirts, then followed the others down the stair and into the marketplace much too quickly for her comfort. *Help me not be afraid, Lord. Help me not be ashamed.*

The sky was pale blue, and a faint mist hung in the air. Marjory paused at the mouth of the close, taking it all in. Folk streamed past them on foot and on horseback. Dogs and chickens wandered about as they pleased. Pigs rooted through rubbish piled by the sides of houses, and the cobbled streets had no proper drains. Structures that were new in the sixteenth century were showing their age, with broken shutters and ill-fitting doors.

Still, this was home. However common the streets and buildings of Selkirk, the rolling countryside beyond the town gates soothed the eye. Standing in the marketplace, Marjory spotted Harehead Hill to the west and Bell Hill to the east. Her old estate was two miles north, where the waters of the Tweed and Ettrick meet. When their carriage had passed Tweedsford en route, she'd looked away, unable to bear the heartache of seeing the home that was no longer hers.

At Anne's urging they joined the throng flowing up Kirk Wynd, a narrow cobblestone street edged with two- and three-story houses. People crowded them on every side. A woman dressed in rags limped by, followed by two young lads with a barking collie, and a gray-haired man with rheumy eyes.

Elisabeth took Marjory's arm. "Have you spied anyone you know?"

"Not yet," Marjory said, unsure if she was relieved or disappointed. No one had caught

49

her eye. No one had called out her name.

"This way." Anne tugged them toward a humble dwelling on the right, its yawning door an unspoken invitation. "The Mintos will not object if we slip through their house."

Marjory frowned, looking a bit farther up the street. "Has the *pend* leading to the kirk been closed?"

"Oh, the pend is still there," Anne said, "but so is the kirk elder, standing at the mouth of it with his collection plate." She ducked through the doorway of the house, signaling for them to follow.

Marjory felt only a small measure of guilt for avoiding the man. After all, what could she put in his wooden plate? A loose button? A pebble from the street?

When Anne thanked Mr. Minto as they entered, he nodded sagely. "Ye canna give what ye dinna have, leddies."

The Kerrs hastened through one shabby room after another. Marjory politely bobbed her head at various family members, picturing elegant Lady Minto of Cap and Feather Close in Edinburgh with her richly furnished lodgings. If these Mintos were her relatives, her ladyship had sorely neglected them.

The same way you neglected Anne?

Heat flooded Marjory's cheeks. All those years in Edinburgh she'd never inquired about Anne's welfare. Even now Marjory had no notion of how her cousin provided for herself.

"This way." Anne led them through the back door and into the misty kirkyard, not bothering to see if they were behind her.

With Elisabeth by her side, Marjory continued uphill toward the parish kirk, built two centuries past, with a tall, square steeple over the arched entranceway. As they drew closer, her eyes widened. What a dreadful state the preaching house was in! The roof sagged as if prepared to give way, the walls were crumbling, and the main door appeared unhinged.

"Cousin!" Marjory quickened her steps, skirting a row of crooked gravestones. "Is it safe for us to enter?"

Anne paused to look over her shoulder, her expression grim. "You'd best say a prayer, for 'tis far worse within."

Marjory eyed the kirk with dismay. "I fear you are right."

"Come, dear." Elisabeth cupped her elbow, guiding her through the door. "Once we're all seated, 'twill be easier to spot your friends."

"I've few real friends," Marjory confessed in a low voice, "only acquaintances." To her shame, when she was Lady Kerr of Tweedsford, she'd considered herself better than others in her parish. Now she was the least of them. Nae, less than the least.

Marjory scanned the dimly lit sanctuary,

hoping one kind soul might greet her. Was the woman with fading red hair Jane Nicoll? Could the mother with the gaggle of daughters be Katherine Shaw? Names and faces spun through her head. Might that be Christina March? Agnes Walker?

Marjory was so certain an elderly woman was Jean Scott that she spoke her name aloud, expecting her to turn round.

"Jean died two years ago," Anne informed her. "That's her younger sister, Isobel."

Jean, dead? Marjory let the sad news sink in. "What of Margaret Simpson? Or Grisell Lochrie?"

Her cousin shook her head. "Both are gone."

"Then I shall look for their gravestones after services," Marjory said, grieved by the unexpected news. Though she'd not known them well, they were women not much older than she.

As they ventured down the center aisle, Marjory surveyed the interior, her heart sinking further. The woodwork, once impressive, was rotting away. Birds flew about the upper reaches, and straw was scattered across the dirt floor. Some of the walls were out of plumb by a full handbreadth, and the tradesmen's lofts hung at precipitous angles, threatening to collapse.

Was her life not its mirror? Ruined beyond any hope of restoration.

"Do you mean to sit in the Kerr aisle?" Anne nodded toward the north side of the kirk. "Since Lord John's death, it's been sorely neglected."

Marjory stared at the filthy pew and the unstable wall beside it. "Why did Mr. Laidlaw not provide for the upkeep? Surely he paid our rent each Martinmas?"

" 'Twould seem he did not," Anne said as heads began turning. "Nor has he darkened the door of this kirk in many a season."

Marjory moved forward on leaden feet. If Gibson were there, he would see the wooden pew scrubbed clean before they took their seats or remove his coat to spare her gown. But Gibson was lost in the woods or waylaid by some blackguard.

When Marjory turned into the Kerr pew, the voices round them grew louder, rolling up and down the aisles like tenpins.

"It canna be!"

"Leddy Kerr?"

"Surely not . . ."

A middle-aged woman pushed her way through the crowd. "Tell us, Annie! Tell us who yer visitors are."

Visitors? Marjory turned to face them. *Do they not know me at all?* When Elisabeth slipped an arm round her waist, Marjory leaned into her, grateful for her height and her strength. Aye, and her courage.

"These are my cousins," Anne said loudly

enough that all present might hear. "Marjory Kerr, returned from Edinburgh with her daughter-in-law Elisabeth Kerr."

Exclamations rang through the kirk. "Not *Lady* Kerr?" an older woman cried, distress written across her wrinkled features. "But, madam, where are your lads? Where are Donald and Andrew?"

Marjory recognized her at once. "Miss Cranston!" She stretched out her hands toward the former governess who'd once cared for the Kerrs' young sons. "Can it be you?"

"Aye!" Elspeth Cranston hurried forward and briefly clasped her hands in return. She opened her mouth, then closed it again, peering intently at Marjory. "Has something happened, milady? You do not seem . . . yourself."

A murmur of agreement moved through the onlookers as they drew closer.

When Marjory looked up, they were no longer strangers. Here was Martha Ballantyne, who'd oft come to Tweedsford for an afternoon of whist. Behind her stood Douglas Park, with his somber expression and treble chins. Charles Hogg in the next pew had tutored her sons in Latin. Another whist partner, Sarah Chisholm of Broadmeadows, stood nearby, her black hair as thick as a wool bonnet, while John Curror of Whitmuir Hall tarried close behind her.

One after another the townsfolk urged her

to speak, calling out to her.

"*Whatsomever* has happened?"

"Why've ye come hame?"

"*Whaur* are yer sons?"

Marjory's mouth trembled. Nae, her whole body shook while she struggled to find the right words. "I am not . . . as you remember me," she finally said, her voice strained to the breaking point. "When I departed Selkirk, I had a family." She held out her empty hands. "Now I have nothing."

She bowed her head as a wave of anguish washed over her. *Help me, please help me.* Had she not realized this day would come, when all of Selkirk would learn the truth? Once their murmurings finally ebbed, Marjory said what she must. "My husband died seven years ago. But my sons . . . my dear sons died in January. On Falkirk Muir."

"Nae!" Elspeth Cranston fell back a step, her hand pressed to her mouth. "Not the Jacobite battle?" She looked round as if seeking others' counsel. "Forgive us, but . . . we'd not heard of your loss."

Out of the ensuing silence came a gruff voice. "Yer lads bore arms for King George, aye?"

"They're Kerrs," another answered. "*Wha* else would they fight for?"

Marjory looked round, her vision blurring. Must she confess the rest? Or could she tell Reverend Brown in private and let word travel on its own? Nae, there was no honor in that. The Almighty had not brought her home so she might hide.

Thou art with me. Aye, she was certain of it.

Marjory stood taller, lifting her head not with pride but with confidence. "My sons fought for a cause they believed in," she said as bravely as she could. "Prince Charlie's cause, the Stuart cause. Call it what you like, my sons embraced it. And died for it."

A collective gasp filled the sanctuary. Then the shouting began. She'd heard all the words before. *Rebels. Jacobites. Traitors.*

When their angry retorts threatened to drown her response, she held up her hands, praying her voice might remain strong and her courage fast. "The king agrees with you," she assured the crowd, bringing their tirade to a swift end. "On Monday last my late son Donald was declared attainted. Our family title was revoked. And Tweedsford was forfeited to the Crown."

If the walls had toppled onto them, the congregation could not have looked more shocked.

All held their tongues but one. "Noo ye're not so high and *michty,* are ye, Mistress Kerr?"

"I am not," she told the young man who glared at her beneath the brim of his dirty cap.

She knew it was not King George who'd

humbled her. Nae, it was the One who loved her.

With tears spilling down her cheeks, Marjory lifted his sacred words to the farthest reaches of the sanctuary. "The LORD gave, and the LORD hath taken away." She swallowed her pride, her fear, her shame. "Blessed be the name of the LORD."

Seven

Hail, Sabbath! thee I hail, the poor man's day.

JAMES GRAHAME

Elisabeth gazed down at her mother-in-law, her heart near to bursting. *How brave you are, dear Marjory.*

"Shall you preach this morn's sermon, Mrs. Kerr?" a male voice thundered.

They both turned to find the parish minister glaring at them from his lofty pulpit. A tall, stooped man of perhaps seventy years, he wore a plain black robe and a stern expression.

Marjory quickly recovered, drying her tears. "Forgive me, Reverend Brown. I only meant —"

"Oh, I heard every word," he said evenly. "Glory to God, aye. But no respect for our sovereign king." His scowl remained in place as he called forth the precentor to lead the

58

gathering psalm. "We shall speak later in private, Mrs. Kerr," the reverend said, his sharp tone brooking no argument. "You have disrupted the Sabbath enough as it is."

Marjory lowered her gaze, though Elisabeth could see her mother-in-law dreaded the prospect of meeting with the reverend. In a parish with the Duke of Roxburgh for its patron, unswerving loyalty to King George was expected, if not demanded. Might the Kerrs be banished from the kirk? Driven from the parish? Or would the tolbooth in the marketplace, with its irons and stocks, have two new prisoners before the week was out?

Stop it, Bess. She tamped down her fears, reminding herself they served no useful purpose. Had the Lord not kept them safe thus far?

While the congregation moved to their seats, Elisabeth swiftly brushed the debris from the Kerr pew, thinking to spare Anne's moss green gown. Their own black dresses were already soiled.

Soon the precentor appeared. "William Armstrong," Marjory said under her breath, joining Elisabeth on the pew with Anne beside her.

A thin, nervous sort of man with wiry gray hair and spindles for arms, Mr. Armstrong shuffled to the desk where the Psalter lay open and waiting. He shook out the sleeves of his robe, adjusted his spectacles, and

59

peered down at the psalms, translated into a common meter and rhyme for worship.

Elisabeth looked beyond the sagging roof to the heavens above as the precentor duly sang each line, then paused while the congregation responded in unison.

My soul with expectation
depends on God indeed;
My strength and my salvation doth
from him alone proceed.

The truth of those words filled her like a fresh wind. Elisabeth sang out with her whole heart, not caring if heads turned or tongues wagged. She knew the Almighty and was known by him. She trusted him, depended upon him. *Thy faithfulness reacheth unto the clouds.*

To think she'd once found solace in worshiping the moon! Like her Highland mother, grandmother, and great-grandmother before her, Elisabeth had prayed on the sixth day of the moon, recited meaningless words to a nameless god, and clasped a silver ring she no longer owned. Those days were well behind her now. However grim Reverend Brown's countenance, however dour his sermons, this was where she would spend each Sabbath, finding a secret joy in the holy words themselves.

As soon as the closing psalm was sung and

the benediction given, Marjory urged them toward the door. "I've not the strength to face our many neighbors," she admitted.

Elisabeth stayed close by her side. "You are stronger than you know, Marjory. I will gladly speak on your behalf, but 'tis you they wish to see."

"Your daughter-in-law is right," Anne said as they started down the center aisle together. "Let them take a gander at you and be done with it."

The threesome did not travel far. Parishioners of every age and station pressed round them, tugging their sleeves, blocking their path. They were a sober people, dressed in blues, grays, and browns, with little adornment. Some were merely curious, wanting to see what a Jacobite rebel looked like. A few expressed their sympathy or wished them well. Others apparently felt obligated to scold Marjory for her foolish support of the prince.

One elderly fellow wagged his finger at her. "Yer lads were *aye heidie,* demanding their *ain* way. Ye let them do as they pleased and paid dearly for it."

Marjory took their verbal lashing as if it were her due, nodding as they spoke rather than engaging them in further discussion. The naysayers began to wander off, leaving in their wake a cluster of parishioners bent on demonstrating their Christian charity.

Elisabeth answered what questions she

could. "Aye, we are lodging in town with our cousin at the moment." "Nae, my sister-in-law, Janet, will not be moving to Selkirk." "Aye, I was born in the Highlands, then educated in Edinburgh." "Nae, I do not have children." The last was the hardest to answer. Three years of marriage to Donald had produced nothing but a few tarnished memories and a wounded heart, slow to heal.

At least none in the sanctuary had whispered of Donald's unfaithfulness.

One woman with a sleepy child on her hip turned to Marjory and said with a mother's sympathy, "I'm sorry for yer loss, mem. *Verra* sorry."

A red-headed maidservant stormed her way to the front. "And why would ye be kind to a woman who was *niver* kind to ithers?" Her green eyes were hard like gemstones, and her rough, red hands were fisted at her waist.

"Good day to you, Tibbie," Marjory said, her voice steady.

"Nae, 'tis an ill day with ye back in Selkirk." Her gaze narrowed. "Whosoever humbled ye, I'm blithe to see it."

Elisabeth watched Marjory pluck at her skirts, a nervous habit.

"Tibbie Cranshaw worked for me at Tweedsford," Marjory said by way of introduction. "She was one of my best kitchen maids."

Tibbie snorted. "If I was so guid at my *wark,*

62

why did ye send me *awa?*"

"You know the reason," Marjory said.

Tibbie glared at her. "I ken ye're an *ill-kindit* woman. That's what I ken." She turned on her heel and departed the same way she'd come.

Elisabeth inclined her head so Marjory alone would hear her. "I am sorry —"

"Nae," Marjory countered, "she had every right to speak so to me. I sent Tibbie away because she was with child. When she lost her babe a few days later, I refused to take her back." Marjory groaned softly. "I was more than cruel."

"But you're a new woman," Elisabeth said with conviction. "The Almighty has softened you, changed you. Tibbie will see that."

Marjory shook her head. "Too late, I fear. I might have helped Tibbie then. I cannot help her now."

In the wake of Tibbie Cranshaw's outburst, the crowd round them began to disperse.

"Folk are heading home to their Sabbath dinner," Anne said. "We should do the same. I've a slice of mutton for each of us."

"We are truly grateful," Elisabeth hastened to say, "but you cannot continue feeding us, Annie. In the morn I shall offer my needle to a tailor or dressmaker in town and so add to your household coffers."

"A gentlewoman like you?" Anne chided her. "Earning money with her hands?"

"I was once a weaver's daughter." Elisabeth watched her cousin's brows lift in obvious amazement. "You'll find I'm not afraid of hard work."

"Nor am I," was Anne's quick response.

When their eyes met, an understanding sparked between them. Not a budding friendship. Not yet. But a small measure of trust. A beginning.

EIGHT

The secret wound still lives within the breast.

VIRGIL

Elisabeth and the others were nearing the arched entranceway of the kirk when a woman in a striking blue gown swept into view, her ebony hair beautifully styled and her manner regal.

Marjory greeted her at once. "Lady Murray! What a pleasure to see you after all these years."

The gentlewoman slowly turned and regarded Marjory with a look of disdain. "I cannot say I feel the same. After so bold a confession this morn you will be fortunate if anyone of quality receives you."

Seeing the pain reflected in Marjory's eyes, Elisabeth hastened to defend her mother-in-law. "But, madam —"

Lady Murray waved her hand dismissively. "Even so, I suppose I could ask Sir John if he might allow you to call on us at Philiphaugh."

Marjory straightened her shoulders. "Do not trouble yourself, Lady Murray," she said evenly. "I have other friends in Selkirk, not to mention the excellent society of my daughter-in-law Elisabeth Kerr and cousin Anne Kerr."

Elisabeth curtsied briefly, hiding her smile. *Well done, Marjory.*

Deftly put in her place, Lady Murray gave a ladylike shrug. "You know, Mrs. Kerr, you're not the only person of note moving to Selkirk this spring. Have you heard of Lord Jack Buchanan?"

Marjory's brow creased. "I cannot say that I have —"

"Perhaps not, since he is hardly one of your Jacobite rebels," Lady Murray said with a sniff. "Lord Buchanan served under Admiral Anson of the HMS *Centurion* when he circumnavigated the globe. They fought the Spaniards and captured a fortune in gold. Surely you followed the *Centurion*'s triumphant return in 'forty-four?"

"The broadsheets wrote of little else that summer," Elisabeth agreed.

"And no wonder! Thirty-two wagons loaded with treasure chests, delivered to the Tower of London." Her ladyship fluttered her silk fan as if overcome by the thought of such riches. "Lord Buchanan is expected in a fortnight or two. Wealthy as Croesus, they say. An admiral now — and unmarried." She glanced over her shoulder, nodding at a pair of young ladies standing by the door. "Our Clara is too young for him, of course, but Admiral Buchanan would make a fine match for our lovely Rosalind. She'll reach her majority next spring."

Elisabeth took note of the older daughter's glossy black hair and ivory skin, her elegant attire and graceful movements. If this admiral was seeking a wife, Rosalind Murray of Philiphaugh appeared a worthy choice. "But what would bring a British naval officer this far inland?"

"Property." Lady Murray closed her fan with a snap. "I imagine His Majesty rewarded the admiral's efforts with a handsome estate in Selkirkshire."

Elisabeth watched the color drain from her mother-in-law's face. *Not Tweedsford, Lord. Not so soon.*

"I've tarried here long enough." Lady Murray gathered her skirts in hand. "Sir John remained at home this morn. Not feeling well, he said. I'd best see to him." She whirled round and was gone with a whisper of silk.

Elisabeth quietly took her mother-in-law's arm, alarmed at her vacant expression.

"A handsome estate in Selkirkshire." Marjory's voice was thin, devoid of emotion. "King George has awarded this admiral my home. He has given him Tweedsford."

"We cannot be sure," Elisabeth said, realizing it was cold comfort. "Wouldn't Lady Murray have named the property if that were so?"

"You do not know Eleanora Murray." Marjory looked up, resignation in her eyes. "Her ladyship delights in meting out information when and how it suits her, caring little how it may wound others."

Elisabeth glanced at Anne and saw her nodding absently. Lady Murray, it seemed, was no longer a true friend to Marjory, if indeed she ever was.

"You've endured quite enough this Sabbath morn," Elisabeth told her mother-in-law, moving forward. "A light meal and a long nap are in order. If visitors come knocking, I shall see they venture no farther than the foot of the stair."

A soft breeze beckoned the women across the stone threshold and onto the grassy knoll of the kirkyard. The mist was gone, and a wash of pale yellow bathed the landscape. Elisabeth paused to take in her new surroundings. Gently shaped hills undulated round the countryside, covered in the first grass of the season, a bright spring green, and the forest edging the kirkyard was thick with oak and elm, birch and pine, hazel and willow. 'Twas nothing like the vast, treeless moors and glens of the Highlands. Would she ever feel at home here?

"We can use the pend this time," Anne said,

then led them through the narrow passageway to Kirk Wynd. A minute's walk downhill and they were in Halliwell's Close again.

Early afternoon light poured into the small house, warming the air. Anne served their dinner without a word, placing hot tea and cold mutton at each of their places. Marjory had barely finished her meal before she crawled into the hurlie bed with a soft moan. She quickly fell asleep, the sound of her steady breathing an undercurrent flowing through their quiet lodgings.

Elisabeth eyed her leather trunk. "I should unpack my few belongings. That is, if you'll not object . . ."

Anne responded with a faint shrug. "I cannot turn you out. Where else could you stay?"

Nowhere. How hard that was to admit! " 'Twill not always be thus," Elisabeth promised, for her own benefit as well as Anne's.

Kneeling beside the trunk, Elisabeth lifted out a wrinkled linen chemise and several pairs of stockings, all of which required laundering, a task for Monday morning. She owned no jewelry, no silk fans, no fine hats, only a pair of brocade shoes and a handful of accessories. An ivory comb to tuck in her curls and the hairbrush she'd used that morning found a place on the washstand, then she hung her gray wool cape on a hook by the door.

All that remained was a single gown suitable for evening, though not for a widow.

"Lovely," Anne murmured, peering over her shoulder.

Elisabeth held up the rich, lavender-colored satin adorned with silk gauze and gold sequins. "A gift from my late husband."

Anne's breath caught. "Brussels lace?" She reverently touched the broad, creamy swath that draped from each elbow-length sleeve. "You cannot imagine the months women spent creating this."

Elisabeth watched Anne examine the delicate needlework, fingers lightly caressing the tiny buttonhole stitches that formed each lacy flower and stem. "You know something of the craft?"

Anne lifted her head. "Did I not tell you? I am a lace maker." She gestured toward the sewing table between the upholstered chairs. " 'Tis how I support myself. If you open the drawer, you'll find some of my work."

For a dressmaker the invitation was irresistible. Elisabeth eased the silk gown back into her trunk, then moved to the low table and tugged on the drawer. "Oh my." She lifted out a narrow length of lace in the making, taking care not to disturb the many pins holding it in place. "Such delicate knots! Whatever do you call this?"

"Point de neige," Anne said in French, kneeling beside her. "The points are meant to look

70

like snow. Not long before my mother died, she gave me her most treasured possession, a Venetian lace collar. Then I bought a pattern book from a chapman, and . . ." She shrugged.

Elisabeth held Anne's work up to the light, marveling at the intricate pattern. "Surely the gentry pay you handsomely for your labors."

"Aye. Lady Murray once purchased several lace-trimmed handkerchiefs and a jabot for Sir John. I lived on that silver for half a year," Anne told her. "But few in Selkirk can afford such luxury. I depend upon occasional visits from a traveling merchant who purchases my work for a shop in Covent Garden." She carefully retrieved her lace from Elisabeth and placed it back in the drawer. "Unfortunately, he's not come through town in a twelve-month."

Elisabeth gaped at her. "Annie, however do you manage?"

Her thin-lipped smile did not reach her eyes. "I teach lace making to the daughters of local gentry who can spare a shilling a week." She stood and began clearing the dining table. "On Tuesday you'll meet my two pupils, Miss Caldwell and Miss Boyd. Neither of them enjoys needlework, but they've kindly not complained to their mothers. At least not yet."

Elisabeth joined her, collecting the wooden utensils that, by Sabbath law, could not be washed until morning. *Two shillings a week?* Even in rural Selkirk those coins would be quickly spent. "And yet you served us mutton this noontide."

Anne turned to meet her gaze. " 'Tis the one day of the week I have meat."

Elisabeth glanced in the direction of the hurlie bed, then asked in a low voice, "Might your titled cousins not have provided at least a small income for you?"

Anne was slow to answer. "I was not a close relative of Lord John's, nor did I travel in the same social circles." She shrugged, clearly uncomfortable. "When no one asked for my hand in marriage, Lord John took pity on me and quietly arranged a monthly stipend. Lady Marjory was unaware of his generosity. As she was of many things."

Elisabeth merely nodded. Three years of living with her mother-in-law had taught her much about the gentry and their willingness to look the other way when it suited them.

Her cousin went on. "The coins were delivered to my door each month by . . . well, by Lord John's factor, by . . ."

"Mr. Laidlaw?"

"Aye." Color bloomed in Anne's pale cheeks. "When Lord John died, Mr. Laidlaw came to see me." She averted her gaze, her discomfort all too apparent. "He said he would continue bringing silver to my door each month if I opened my . . . if I welcomed his . . . touch."

A dreadful silence hung in the air.

Elisabeth reached for her hand. "Annie, I'm so sorry. Had Marjory known —"

"But she *should* have known." Her cousin drew away from her, a spark of anger in her pale blue eyes. "Mr. Laidlaw made a habit of tormenting her maidservants. He put his hands where they did not belong and took liberties with any lass who gave in to his advances. Ask Tibbie Cranshaw if you don't believe me." Anne's voice dropped to a whisper. "Mr. Laidlaw is a profligate of the worst kind. A virtuous woman like you cannot imagine such a creature."

Elisabeth's heart sank. *Oh, but I can.*

"I refused him twice before he left me alone," Anne said proudly. "No silver is worth such degradation."

"Nae, it is not." Elisabeth looked down at the wooden floor, wishing the heaviness inside her might lift. Could no man be trusted?

She seldom dwelled on Donald's many infidelities and never spoke of them to Marjory. What mother could bear to hear such things? Yet, months after his death, the pain of betrayal lingered and with it a nagging sense of guilt. Perhaps if she'd railed at him, punished him, denied him, her husband might have changed his wanton ways.

Instead, she'd loved him. And forgiven him.

I am more sorry than I can ever say. Aye, Donald was always sorry. What Donald was not was faithful. She could still recall every word on the lover's note she'd found in his glove and the list of paramours he'd confessed in a letter. *Forgive me, lass. For all of it.*

She'd done so. But the heartache remained.

Elisabeth gazed at the door, longing for fresh air and an hour's walk. "What do the kirk elders say if a member of their flock ventures out of doors on a Sabbath afternoon?"

Anne reached for her wool cape. "Nothing is said. Unless they see you."

NINE

And as I turn me home,
My shadow walks before.

ROBERT SEYMOUR BRIDGES

Marjory woke to find sunlight still filtering through the curtains. She'd napped no more than an hour. The house was quiet, empty. She splashed cool water on her face and dried it with a linen towel, then claimed a sheet of stationery from Elisabeth's trunk, telling herself it was but one piece of paper and purchased with her late son's money besides.

Borrowing Anne's quill pen and ink from the shelf, Marjory settled at the dining table and prayed for a steady hand. This would not be a pleasant letter to compose.

To Mr. Roger Laidlaw, Factor
Tweedsford, Selkirkshire

Sunday, 27 April 1746

75

Mr. Laidlaw:

How it irked her to write the man's name! Where was she to begin? No point telling him what he already knew when there was so much else to say.

Marjory inked the quill again.

You have no doubt been told of Tweedsford's new owner. Therefore, I shall not dwell on that unfortunate subject here.

She had yet to speak aloud this admiral's name. Committing it to paper would be even more difficult. Another time she might manage it. For now, Mr. Laidlaw's transgressions were her primary concern.

You have been grossly negligent in your duties, sir, for which you have been well compensated these many years.

Very well compensated. She gripped the quill so tightly the feather shook. Did the man think she would never return to Selkirk and see his carelessness?

This morn I entered the church of my childhood and found the Kerr aisle in an abhorrent state. The wooden pew is decrepit, the floor round it is covered with debris, and the walls are near to collapse.

76

Marjory lifted her pen, struck by a frightening thought. If Mr. Laidlaw was indifferent toward maintaining the house of the Lord, what of Tweedsford?

Images rose before her. Richly paneled walls. An elegant stair with wooden balustrades. Pink marble chimney pieces. Decorative wrought-iron gates. Terraced gardens to the north . . .

Enough, Marjory.

Whatever Tweedsford's condition, it was no longer her home or her responsibility. Her family's corner of the parish kirk, however, mattered very much.

I shall meet with Reverend Brown this week to discuss what must be done as well as to arrange payment for our annual rent, which I am told is in arrears.

Marjory paused, wondering if she was being too harsh. In truth, the whole of the kirk was ruinous. She would soften her tone, if only to be certain Mr. Laidlaw brought her what she wanted.

Ever since Lady Murray of Philiphaugh had hinted at a new owner for Tweedsford, Marjory had thought of the trivial but dear things she'd left behind. According to General Lord Mark Kerr's letter on behalf of the king, the contents of her home were to be seized for payment of fines. If she did not speak up now, these cherished objects would be lost to her forever.

She chose her words with care.

Do locate the following personal effects and deliver them to Anne Kerr's house in Halliwell's Close as soon as ever you can. I assure you, they would mean nothing to your new owner or to His Majesty. You will be breaking no royal decree in doing me this small favor.

Whether or not that was true, Marjory couldn't say. But it certainly *sounded* true.

She made a brief list, describing each item. Lord John's magnifying glass unintentionally left behind. A small bundle of letters from her late brother, Henry Nesbitt, who at seven-and-twenty was killed while hunting in Ettrick Forest. A wooden toy soldier Gibson had carved for Andrew's fourth birthday. *The Famous History of Thomas Thumb,* a chapbook Donald prized when he was a wee lad. And a miniature of Tweedsford she drew as a new bride, done with plumbago on vellum.

Though she wrote as compactly as she could, there was no room for a proper signature. Perhaps that was just as well. Without a title her name carried little weight. She tipped a burning candle over the folded letter, then pressed her thumb into the cooling wax, a poor man's seal.

Marjory was still wiping the ink from Anne's quill when the clatter of hoofbeats drew her to the window. A coach-and-four was emptying its passengers into the marketplace. "North!" the coachman bellowed, prompting two new travelers, a valise in each hand, to quicken their steps toward the carriage. Clearly he was bound for Edinburgh and so would pass Tweedsford en route. Might he deliver her letter this very day? Aye, it was the Sabbath, but if he might be willing . . .

Marjory flew down the stair, her heart racing by the time she reached the coachman, who'd already climbed onto his seat. "Sir!" she called out, holding up her letter as she identified herself. "Would you kindly carry this to Tweedsford?"

He frowned at her, his thick eyebrows drawn tightly together. "I'm certain to be paid?"

"Depend upon it. Mr. Laidlaw or any of the servants at Tweedsford will meet you with coins in hand." She pictured the small drawer in the lobby table where pennies were kept for that purpose. "It is a matter of great urgency," she told him, lifting her letter a bit higher.

"Verra weel," he grumbled, stuffing her correspondence inside his greatcoat. He nodded toward Halliwell's Close. "I ken whaur ye live, mem. If I dinna get my money —"

"Oh but you will," Marjory promised him, stepping back.

He'd lifted the reins, preparing to depart, when she suddenly thought of Gibson.

"Wait!" Marjory stepped forward and grabbed the carriage wheel to keep her balance. "Have you seen or heard of a manservant by the name of Neil Gibson? From an innkeeper perhaps? Or another coachman? Mr. Gibson is traveling alone from Edinburgh on foot. Older fellow, silver hair, with fine posture."

The coachman dragged a hand across his rough beard. "I've not seen such a man on the road. Gibson, ye say?"

"Aye. He has served our family for thirty years." She pointed to Anne's window. "Our name is Kerr. Should you hear of him . . ."

"If I do, I'll get wird to ye *whan* I'm next in Selkirk," he said, then called out to his horses, which responded at once, their iron horseshoes striking the cobblestones.

"Godspeed!" she cried, then hastened withindoors, lest one of the kirk elders spy her in the street.

A moment later Marjory stood before the hearth, catching her breath, pleased to have done something of value that afternoon. Odd, though, to be alone in the house. Wherever had Anne and Elisabeth gone? She was too restless to read, too unsettled to pray — the two pastimes deemed suitable for the Sabbath.

Looking round, she realized Elisabeth had unpacked her few belongings. She could do the same, couldn't she? It wasn't truly work, like washing dishes or laundering clothes. As long as Anne wouldn't think her presumptuous, making herself at home, it seemed a worthy task.

Marjory opened her trunk and placed two pairs of white gloves, her embroidered silk reticule, and a simple black hat on the shelf between the windows. She left her spare whalebone stays, cotton stockings, and embroidered nightgown in her trunk for modesty's sake, then closed the lid, chagrined at how hollow it sounded. She was wearing the only gown she owned, having sold her many satin, silk, brocade, and velvet costumes in Edinburgh, desperate for guineas.

Elisabeth had set the example, selling all her gowns first. Except for the lavender one. The lass might never have an occasion to wear it in Selkirk, but Marjory was glad her daughter-in-law had chosen to keep Donald's gift. Despite his shameful behavior, Elisabeth had loved him while he lived and honored his memory. No daughter-in-law could be more faithful.

Marjory was tucking a pair of damask shoes beneath her bed when she heard voices on the stair. Elisabeth and Anne came strolling

81

through the door, their cheeks bright with color.

"Tea," Anne said without preamble, reaching for clean cups from the shelf by the hearth.

Elisabeth smoothed back the wisps of hair curling round her damp brow. "Forgive us for leaving you, Marjory. We've been walking in the forest near the kirk. I trust you slept well."

"And wrote a letter too," Marjory said, rather proud of herself. "Already on its way to Tweedsford with a short list of personal items I've asked Mr. Laidlaw to bring to me."

A beat of silence followed.

"Mr. Laidlaw?" Elisabeth repeated as if she'd misunderstood.

Anne put down the cups with a dull bang. "You've asked that man to come here? To my house?"

"I'm afraid I did." Marjory stared at them, confused. "Mr. Laidlaw is the only person who can help me retrieve what is rightfully mine before this admiral arrives to claim my property."

The younger women exchanged glances.

"Whatever is the matter?" Marjory demanded, hearing the strain in her voice, the higher pitch.

"Our quarrel is not with you, dear." Elisabeth rested her hand on Marjory's arm. "Annie shared with me something of Mr. Laidlaw's character. He is . . . not what he seems."

"Nae," Anne fumed, "he is precisely what he seems. A lecherous man without scruples."

Marjory stared at her in disbelief. "You cannot mean this!"

"I wish 'twere not so, Cousin. But the maidservants at Tweedsford say otherwise. So do I." The firm line of Anne's mouth and the seriousness of her tone were undeniable.

Marjory sank onto a wooden chair. "The man has worked for our family for fifteen years."

"Then be grateful you are done with him," Anne said with a decisive nod. "Come, let us have our tea, and I shall tell you what I told your daughter-in-law."

A half hour later Marjory was still seated at table, hands wrapped round an empty cup, her heart heavy.

How could she have been so blind to Mr. Laidlaw's devious ways? She'd blamed pregnant Tibbie when it was Sir John's factor who should have been dismissed. Anne, meanwhile, was forced to choose immorality or poverty, all because her wealthy cousin Marjory paid little attention to the needs of others, thinking only of herself.

She sought Anne's gaze across the table. "I should have known —"

"And I should have been long married by now," Anne said abruptly. "So then, what shall we do with this reprobate headed our way?"

Marjory pursed her lips. "If Gibson were here, he would stand up to Roger Laidlaw in our stead."

"Alas, Gibson is *not* here," Elisabeth gently reminded her. "We must prepare to address the man ourselves."

"Indeed we must," Anne echoed.

They looked at one another across the table, determination reflected on each face.

"Agreed," Marjory said at last. "When Mr. Laidlaw knocks on our door, he will find three women who are not afraid to face him."

TEN

The beginning, as the proverb says, is half the whole.

ARISTOTLE

Elisabeth brushed a damp cloth over her mourning gown, wishing she had lemon juice to clean the fabric or fragrant attar of roses to freshen the scent. Tailors were particular about such things.

At least she'd bathed from head to toe with hot water and her last bit of heather soap and cleaned her teeth with a twig of hazel she'd brought home from their forest walk. Her hair was styled, her ivory comb in place, and her prayers whispered across the open pages of the *Buik* earlier that morning.

Elisabeth took a quick peek in Anne's looking glass, then turned toward the door, glad to see a patch of blue sky through the curtains.

"Michael Dalgliesh is the finest tailor in Selkirk," Anne informed her, sweeping the flagstone hearth with quick, sharp movements. "You'll find him a few steps up Kirk Wynd, then down School Close. Call at the first door on the right."

Elisabeth nodded, trying not to stare at Marjory, who was scrubbing the oval dining table. *Dowager Lady Kerr cleaning the house?* A twelvemonth ago Elisabeth could not have imagined her once proud and haughty mother-in-law performing so menial a task. *God giveth grace to the humble.* Indeed he had. Could Marjory see how much she'd changed? How she'd softened yet grown stronger? Become bolder and yet more sensitive?

Elisabeth knew miracles were real because she was looking at one.

Now it was her turn to labor. "Do keep me in your thoughts this morn. Mr. Dalgliesh will not be expecting me."

"See that he pays you a fair wage," Marjory warned. "You are not a common seamstress."

"Why, I'm as common as they come!" Elisabeth protested. "Trained in a Highland cottage. Though my mother was a fine teacher. Pray Mr. Dalgliesh will give me the chance to prove it."

She tied the ribbons of her bonnet under her chin, then started down the stair. The watery tea and toasted bread would keep her stomach from growling, and the hard cheese she'd wrapped in linen and tucked into her pocket would serve for dinner should she find work.

Halliwell's Close was as chilly as a cave, but the late April sun boded well. With such fine weather, Gibson might reach Selkirk before day's end. Elisabeth saw the fear that clouded her mother-in-law's eyes whenever his name was mentioned. *Bring him safely to us, Lord. Soon, if it be your will.*

The moment Elisabeth entered the market-place, a familiar-looking woman came strolling out of the corner bakeshop and into her path. "Miss Cranston," Elisabeth said with a curtsy. "We met briefly at the kirk. You were my husband's governess."

"So I was." The older woman swept her gaze over Elisabeth. "He was a handsome lad, Donald, and an accomplished reader. You have my deepest sympathy, Mrs. Kerr."

Elisabeth murmured her thanks, noticing several others in the marketplace who'd found some reason to linger nearby, curiosity written on their faces. If they each stopped to speak with her, she'd not reach the tailor's shop before noon. But these were her new neighbors. If only for Marjory's sake, she would make an effort.

After Elspeth Cranston continued on her way, a couple in rustic clothing approached, full of questions. "We've niver been to Edin-burgh," the wife said, her eyes round. "Are the *lands* really ten stories high?" A copper-headed woman, bent over with age, reminisced about Lord John, whom she'd known from her youth. "Every lass in Selkirk set her cap for John Kerr, including me," she confessed. Elisabeth moved a few feet up Kirk Wynd, only to be stopped by a young mother holding on to a wriggling charge with each hand. "We're blithe to have a new face in Selkirk," the woman said. "I do hope you've come to stay."

Not all the townsfolk were friendly. One shopkeeper wandered into the street simply to glare at her. Other passersby gave her a wide berth, as if supporting the Jacobites were a contagious disease. Some men stared; more than a few leered.

Elisabeth was relieved when she finally reached School Close and ducked into the chilly passageway, bound for the tailor's shop. She entered through the open doorway, lightly tapping on the wood in passing. "Mr. Dalgliesh?"

Even in the dim interior, the tradesman was easily found, bent over his work, a cluster of candles at his elbow. He was younger than she'd expected: five-and-thirty at most. She'd never seen a brighter redhead nor forearms covered with more freckles.

When he looked up, his blue eyes measured her at once, as if she'd come to him needing a suit of clothes. "What can I do for ye, mem?"

All at once Elisabeth felt rather foolish. Aye, she'd worked for a tailor in Edinburgh, but the late Angus MacPherson had been a family friend. This man seated before her was a stranger. She moistened her lips and braved a smile. "My cousin, Anne Kerr, tells me you are the finest tailor in Selkirk."

"Does she noo?" When he smiled broadly, her apprehension vanished. "Ye must be the young Widow Kerr."

She curtsied. "I am."

"Weel then!" He stood, abandoning his needle and thread. "I am Michael Dalgliesh. *Walcome* to my wee shop. Come, come, have a *leuk*."

His outgoing nature took her by surprise. Anne had not mentioned that.

With expansive gestures and an abundance of words, the tailor guided her round his establishment. "Here's whaur I do my cutting," he said, pointing to the large table dominating the room. "Woolens, linens, broadcloth, serge. Whatsomever folk ask for." Bolts of fabric were stacked high on one end, and muslin patterns were scattered everywhere.

"You seem much engaged," she said, noting the many coats and breeches hanging about. Some clothes were nearly finished; others were marked with chalk, waiting their turn.

"There's aye *meikle* wark to be done." He

shrugged when he said it, but she heard the distress in his voice. No doubt he was overwhelmed by all the tasks at hand. It would have taken Angus MacPherson and his son, Rob, weeks to complete this many pieces.

In the only window, which faced School Close, a plain woolen coat hung on display. "The men o' Selkirk dinna favor velvets, satins, or silk," he explained. "Nor do they like any fancy stitching."

His words gave her pause. In the capital she was known for embellishing waistcoats with intricate embroidery. Would her skills even be needed here? It was time she found out.

"Mr. Dalgliesh," she began, "you must wonder why I've come this morn."

He chuckled, folding his arms across his chest. "I was quite certain ye didna want a greatcoat."

"Nae. But I would be honored to stitch them for your customers." Elisabeth slipped off her gloves, wanting him to see the truth. She no longer had the soft, pale hands of a gentlewoman. Her chapped fingers had wrung out too many wet rags. "I've come to offer my services. As a seamstress."

For the first time since she'd crossed his threshold, Michael Dalgliesh seemed bereft of words. Finally he said, "Ye want . . . to wark for me?"

"I do," she said without apology. "Mr. Mac-

Pherson, a tailor in the Luckenbooths of Edinburgh, kept my needle busy for many seasons."

"Is that so?" His gaze began circling the shop. "Weel, leuk at that!" he exclaimed as if he'd discovered a new island off the Scottish coast. He grabbed a pile of fine cambric, already cut and pinned. "Can ye stitch a man's shirt, Mrs. Kerr?"

"Well, as it happens —"

He'd already thrust the unfinished shirts into her arms. "Not *a'* men are blessed to have a woman in their lives to sew for them." His freckled skin grew ruddier. "I make shirts for Reverend Brown, Daniel Cumming, and James Mitchelhill too. But I'm woefully behind, as ye can see, and would be grateful for those busy hands o' yers."

Elisabeth hardly knew what to say. She'd not been in his shop a quarter hour and already had enough work for a fortnight. But they'd not discussed money. "I wonder, Mr. —"

"I earn ten shillings for *ilka* shirt," he blurted out. "One shilling will be yers."

"One shilling?" she repeated, numbers spinning through her head. If she finished a shirt each day, she could earn six shillings in a week. *Six shillings!* Enough to put meat or fish on the table every night and coins in Anne's pocket for their lodgings.

She clutched the shirts to her chest, trying

hard not to cry.

Mr. Dalgliesh shifted his weight. "I can see I've offended ye, Mrs. Kerr. But after I buy the fabric from a merchant and the thread as weel —"

"Oh! Of course —"

"And my Peter is growing so fast I canna keep him in shoes."

Elisabeth felt a tug at her heart. "You have a son?"

"Aye." He nodded toward the turnpike stair in the corner, leading to a room above the shop. "Peter is seven. Playing with a *freen* just noo."

"And your wife?"

"Jenny." He rubbed the back of his neck, not quite meeting her gaze. "She died whan the lad was four."

Elisabeth looked round, all the pieces falling together. A tailor with too many customers and not enough hours in the day. A father raising his son with no one to help him. A man, starved for company, talking to every stranger who came into his shop. A widower.

"I am sorry for your loss." Such words, however oft spoken, gave little comfort. But they needed to be said.

"Ye've had a loss as weel," he reminded her, lifting his head.

Their eyes met. In the silence a bargain was struck.

"I'll bring you each shirt when it's finished,"

Elisabeth promised.

"And I'll pay ye a shilling whan ye do." He stuck out his hand as if he meant to shake hers, then realized her arms were full. "I may have *mair* wark for ye whan ye're done." He threw up his hands and sighed rather dramatically. "I canna deny, the place is a mess."

Elisabeth smiled. "We'll see what can be done, Mr. Dalgliesh."

Eleven

Whoever fears God, fears to sit at ease.

ELIZABETH BARRETT BROWNING

Marjory balanced the fresh salmon in her hands, impressed by its heft and size, hoping she might do it justice. " 'Tis a fine catch."

"The fishwife said her husband pulled it from the River Tweed this morn." Elisabeth nodded toward the table. "If you're certain you want to do this, Marjory, I've put out all the herbs you'll need."

Anne stepped closer, drying her hands on her apron. "Maybe I should see to our dinner —"

"Nae need," Marjory told her firmly. "I watched Mrs. Edgar prepare court-bouillon many a time." *Well, at least once. Perhaps even twice.*

Her cousin had every right to question her cooking abilities. Did not Marjory doubt them herself? Still, a Scotswoman ought to be able to poach a salmon. "Attend to your own duties," she told them. Then she added in her sternest, Reverend Brown voice, "If any would not work, neither should he eat."

Elisabeth looked up from her sewing and winked. "Then I'll not quit my needle for an instant."

Her daughter-in-law was quickly turning a lapful of cambric into a well-made garment. She'd finished one gentleman's shirt last eve, then collected her first shilling this morning. On the way home Elisabeth had exchanged her silver coin for the salmon, a pound of fresh butter, and a tidy collection of herbs and still had pennies jingling in her pocket. *My prudent Bess.*

For her part Marjory was determined to prepare their meals, having no other talent to offer the household. If Elisabeth might provide some instructions, and Anne a measure of patience, Marjory thought she could manage it.

Cleaning the fish turned out to be a messy, smelly business. When the unpleasant job was finally done to her satisfaction, Marjory scored the sides with Anne's sharpest knife and doused the fish with finely beaten mace, cloves, nutmeg, black pepper, and salt. The spices tickled her nose, threatening to make her sneeze, as she stuffed the notches with butter rolled in flour and tucked a few bay leaves inside the belly of the fish.

"Behold, our seasoned cook," Elisabeth teased her, though Marjory heard approval as well.

"At least it *looks* right," Marjory said, wrapping the fish in linen and binding it with twine. She laid it in a shallow kettle, then added water and vinegar, and swung the kettle over the brightly burning coals.

Anne claimed her knife and wiped it clean. "You cannot have salmon without fresh parsley," she insisted. "Mrs. Thorburn, who lives by the manse, has a goodly supply in her kitchen garden."

Marjory frowned. "She'll not mind if you help yourself?"

Anne pulled a ha'penny from her apron pocket. "Whenever an onion, radish, or lettuce is called for, I pluck what I need and plant a coin in its stead for her children to find. A fair trade, Mrs. Thorburn says. Half the neighborhood does the same."

When Anne hurried off without cape or hat, Marjory reminded herself that the first of May was only two days hence, with a warm Borderland summer just beyond it.

And still no Gibson.

She drew her chair closer to the fire to mind their dinner and stared at the glowing coals, considering the possibilities. However unfriendly Lady Murray's welcome, her husband was Sheriff of Selkirk. Might he send a party of men to look for Gibson? Sir John

96

might think Marjory daft to be so fretful. But she dared not approach Reverend Brown. He'd summon her soon enough. *Too soon.*

After a lengthy silence Elisabeth asked, "Is it Gibson?"

Marjory turned, acknowledging her with a faint smile. "You know me well, Bess."

"And I know Gibson. Whatever has delayed him, he *will* join us."

Marjory nodded absently. "In quiet moments I hear him whisper, 'Ye'll aye be Leddy Kerr to me.' His last words before we parted at Milne Square." Longing to ease her melancholy, she turned back to the work at hand, stirring the boiling potatoes and poking at the salmon. Her former housekeeper, Helen Edgar, had a canny way of knowing when fish was perfectly cooked. Lift it from the water too soon and the texture was like jelly. Too late and the fish was tough. Helen's salmon was always flaky and smooth, like butter in the mouth.

At least Helen was safely at her mother's cottage in Lasswade and not wandering the Moorfoot Hills, injured, lost, taken ill, or worse. *Poor Gibson.*

Marjory bowed her head, the heat from the coals warming her brow. *My soul, wait thou only upon God; for my expectation is from him.* She savored the ancient words, more fragrant than the herbs she'd rubbed between her fingers. A sense of peace began settling round her heart. Elisabeth was right: Gibson would join them in God's good timing. Marjory looked up, her gaze drawn to the window, picturing Neil Gibson striding across the marketplace, his blue gray eyes fixed on Halliwell's Close.

She and Elisabeth both jumped when the door swung open.

"Home again." Anne clasped a bunch of green parsley like a bride with her bouquet. "Still fresh with dew." She held out the leafy herb, her countenance bright as the sun.

"Very fresh." Marjory took the parsley from Anne's hands, studying her closely. Whatever had happened to their sober-minded cousin?

Elisabeth must have seen it too, for she asked, "Who crossed your path, Annie?"

Their cousin flapped her hand, batting away the question. "Oh, many folk are out this noontide."

Marjory and Elisabeth exchanged glances. Anne Kerr had a forthright manner that did not always endear her to others. Whom had she seen on her way to Mrs. Thorburn's garden?

Anne wasted no time washing and chopping the parsley, then sprinkling it onto a flat griddle and holding it over the coals. " 'Twill taste better crisp." When she peered into the fish kettle, her smile faded. "Has the salmon been cooking all the while I've been gone?"

"Aye," Marjory confessed, backing away

from the hearth. Had she spoiled their dinner and wasted Elisabeth's hard-earned shilling?

"Ten minutes to the pound," Anne told her with a note of impatience, then used two wooden spoons to lift the fish from the kettle. "We'll soon know if 'tis ruined."

Marjory carefully unwrapped the salmon, releasing a pungent aroma through the house. "What say you, Anne?"

She poked at the fish. " 'Twill do."

Relieved, Marjory sprinkled the salmon with parsley and served it with butter and potatoes. After the briefest of blessings, all three tucked into their food as if they'd not eaten in a week and quickly finished their dinner.

"Delicious," Elisabeth pronounced, dabbing at her mouth.

"You're certain it was not overdone?" Marjory asked.

Anne nodded at their empty woodenware. "Apparently not, for we ate every bite." She stood, casting her gaze across the dish-strewn table. "My students will arrive shortly . . ."

"Go, both of you," Marjory said with a wave of her hand. "I can take care of this."

Elisabeth offered her thanks and resumed her sewing while Marjory started clearing away the dishes, ignoring the stiffness in her back as she worked. She'd served one tolerable meal at least. The table and hearth were soon set to rights and the house made presentable for Anne's students, who arrived promptly each afternoon at two o' the clock and departed at six.

Yesterday, Marjory had read a book while Elisabeth sewed, both of them seated at the dining table so the girls could claim the upholstered chairs by the windows for their needlework. Today, she imagined, would be no different.

A sharp knock brought all three women to their feet. They pulled off their aprons and smoothed their hair so they might greet the young ladies properly. Anne was bent on polishing her students' manners as well as their skills.

But when she opened the door, Anne froze in place.

"Beg pardon, sir. We were not . . . expecting you."

Twelve

Change, indeed, is painful; yet ever needful.

Thomas Carlyle

A thunderous voice rumbled through the house. "I would see the elder Mrs. Kerr. Alone."

Marjory closed her eyes. *Reverend Brown.* The man who held their future in his hands. As the minister of the parish, he was answerable not only to God but also to King George.

She forced herself to look at him, to move forward, to greet him, then nodded at the others, setting them free. *Do not worry. The Lord is with me.* Elisabeth and Anne curtsied and retreated into the room, leaving Marjory and the minister standing by the door.

He gazed about the small house. "Where . . . , eh, might we converse?"

Marjory was at a loss for an answer. "Our cousin's students are to arrive at any moment. I'm afraid we'll have no privacy here. Perhaps another day —"

"Nae." His permanent frown deepened. "We shall speak at the manse. 'Tis but a short walk up Kirk Wynd."

When she turned to bid the others farewell, their eyes were wide with concern. "I'll not be long," she assured them, praying it might be so.

Her legs a bit unsteady, Marjory followed Reverend Brown down the stair and into the bustling, sunlit marketplace, the blithe atmosphere a strange counterpoint to her fears. The rich aroma of meat pies wafted past her, and the sound of a blacksmith's anvil filled the air. Coaxed from their houses by the warmer weather, Selkirk's residents mingled round the well or the mercat cross, the council room or the tolbooth, with its impressive new steeple. Looking neither left nor right, Marjory remained close on the minister's heels, lest someone step between them and begin chattering away, vexing the reverend further.

Draped in shapeless black clothing, with his shoulders hunched forward and his chin against his chest, David Brown resembled a bird of prey, dark plumed and sharp beaked, pecking his way up the steep wynd. He opened the door of the manse, across from the Mintos' house, and bade Marjory inside.

The interior was less grim than she'd

imagined. Beeswax candles were scattered round the parlor, and a heaping pile of coals glowed in the grate. His furnishings were old but well kept, his burgundy carpet thick. She saw no looking glass — too vain for the minister — but a handsome oil painting of the parish kirk hung over the mantelpiece.

Marjory took the offered seat, a straight-backed wooden chair with the thinnest of cushions, and waited for the minister to begin.

"I've no tea to offer you," he said bluntly, sitting across from her. "On Friday last my manservant flitted to Jedburgh. He should have tarried 'til Whitsun Monday, when I might have easily hired another man. Instead, he took a wife."

Thinking to sympathize with him, Marjory said, "I know how tiresome it can be to find a new servant."

"Do you?" He regarded her at length. "I should think hiring servants is the least of your concerns now, Mrs. Kerr."

If the reverend meant to shame her, he was too late for that.

A dog started barking outside the window, setting off several others, which quickly turned into an ugly, snarling row. Within-doors, the two could do nothing but wait until the noise abated. Marjory tried to appear calm, to seem unaffected, but all the while her heart was racing. When at last the dogs moved on, the silence in the room was palpable.

"So, Mrs. Kerr." The minister's countenance darkened. "What possessed you to support the Stuart claim to the throne? Did your Highland daughters-in-law bewitch you?"

"They did not," Marjory hastened to say, protecting Elisabeth. "Nor did my daughters-in-law coerce their husbands. On the contrary, we begged Donald and Andrew not to enlist. Once they did, we were bound to stand behind them."

He grunted in response. "You gave Prince Charlie money, I suppose."

"I did." *Fifteen hundred pounds.* Unless the reverend inquired further, she would keep the staggering figure to herself.

"The way of a fool is right in his own eyes," he said, beginning to sound as he did in the pulpit. Louder, sterner. "You have lost everything, madam. Your money, your title, your home, even your family." He banged his fist on the table beside him. "Everything!"

She cringed. "Reverend —"

"What am I to do with you, Mrs. Kerr? Banish you from my parish? Deliver you into the hands of the dragoons?"

Nae! Marjory looked down, overwhelmed. "I hoped . . . that is, I prayed you and the elders of the kirk might . . . forgive me."

Her request hung in the air.

"Mercy, is it?" He did not shout this time.

"Aye, mercy." She lifted her head, imploring him with her eyes. "I have nowhere else to go, Reverend Brown. Anne and Elisabeth are all that remain of my family now. Please . . . please do not ask me to leave Selkirk."

The only sound in the room was the creaking of his chair.

Marjory breathed a prayer into the silence, with her eyes open and her heart open and her hands open in her lap like a child waiting for a gift. *Look thou upon me, and be merciful unto me.*

She saw something change in the reverend's eyes. A prick of light.

"Please?" she asked again. Her pride was in tatters, but, thanks be to God, so was her shame.

The minister sat back in his chair, his large hands splayed across his knees. "Some might say you've already suffered the consequences of your folly. For that is what it was, Mrs. Kerr. Sheer foolishness. You broke no commandments —"

"But I did," she protested softly. "Thou shalt have none other gods before me."

He stared at her, aghast. "What god did you worship if not the Almighty?"

"I worshiped . . ." Marjory cast her gaze round the room, trying to find the words. "I worshiped my sons, my possessions, my place in society. All those things you said I lost.

Don't you see? The Lord took them from me." She bent forward as tears spilled down her cheeks. "Because I loved them more than I loved him."

Reverend Brown inched his chair closer to hers. "Mrs. Kerr . . . ," he said gruffly. "Marjory . . ." He lightly rested his hand on her shoulder. "The Lord brought you home empty so he might fill you with himself." He was quiet for a moment, then said, "I see no need for any discipline from the kirk."

Marjory sank beneath the weight of his forgiveness, her damp cheek pressed against her hands.

His voice quavered as he spoke. " 'Tis our task to help you, Mrs. Kerr. To show you God's mercy. And so we shall."

When he paused, Marjory slowly rose and dried her tears. "Thank you," she whispered.

"For the sake of those who will ask, I need you to speak the truth. Are you now loyal to the king?"

Marjory knew what the Lord required of her. *Fear God. Honour the king.* A difficult command after all she'd suffered. Yet Reverend Brown had called her support of the Stuart cause foolish. Had she not come to the same conclusion herself even while her sons lived?

Marjory met the minister's gaze, lest he doubt her conviction. "Aye."

He seemed satisfied, leaning back to fold

his arms across his chest. "So, how will you make your way in society, Mrs. Kerr?"

She dabbed her cheeks with her handkerchief, then answered him honestly. "I will walk through any doors that are opened to me and pray I find friends there."

He nodded thoughtfully. "We are expecting a new resident in Selkirkshire within a fortnight. Admiral Lord Jack Buchanan. Tread lightly in his presence, for he is the king's man, make no mistake. Your family's treason will not sit well with the admiral."

Marjory stiffened. "I'll not seek the company of Tweedsford's new owner."

"What's this?" Reverend Brown looked at her oddly. "Madam, you have been misinformed. Admiral Buchanan is to reside at Bell Hill."

Her mouth fell open. "But I thought the king awarded him —"

"His Majesty had no part in this," he declared. "The admiral bought the property outright from the Duke of Roxburgh. The *Centurion*'s officers sailed into Portsmouth very wealthy men, you'll remember. Since Lord Buchanan's father once resided in Selkirkshire, the admiral chose to settle here."

"But Lady Murray of Philiphaugh suggested —"

"Bah!" he said. "A parish minister is privy to news not commonly known by his flock."

Marjory stared at the wool carpet beneath

her feet, struggling to recall precisely what her ladyship had said. *A handsome estate in Selkirkshire.* Nothing more. "The false assumption was mine," she finally admitted, chastising herself for leaping to conclusions. "Then who is to have Tweedsford?"

"The duke has not apprised me. In the meantime I imagine Mr. Laidlaw will continue to oversee the property."

Mr. Laidlaw. Marjory feared she might deposit her salmon on the minister's fine carpet. Was Reverend Brown aware of the man's vile nature? Perhaps she might test the waters. "I was disappointed not to see my old factor at kirk on the Sabbath," she said, watching for his reaction.

But the reverend spoke without guile, his expression unchanged. "Roger Laidlaw honors the Sabbath at the kirk in Galashiels now. It seems your factor, like my manservant, grew weary of the bachelor life and is courting a widow from the next parish."

"Ah." Marjory was uncertain how to proceed. She'd been wrong about Tweedsford's owner. What if her cousin had overstated Mr. Laidlaw's proposition and the sordid tales about him were unfounded? She would not ruin a man's reputation on hearsay.

But their crumbling pew in the kirk was another matter. "I understand Mr. Laidlaw has not been prompt in paying our rent for the Kerr aisle," Marjory said, on surer footing this time.

"Aye, well . . ." Reverend Brown shifted forward in his chair. "We've not collected pew rents in several years. The kirk session is considering pulling the old kirk down."

"Truly?" Marjory was taken aback by the news. "Our sanctuary has stood for two hundred years."

"Some days I feel I've done the same." The minister rose with considerable effort and started toward the door, candle in hand. "I've kept you long enough, Mrs. Kerr."

Clearly her visit had exhausted him. Marjory trailed after the reverend into the entranceway. "I do hope you find a manservant soon."

"Aye." He tarried with her at the door, one hand resting on the latch.

"As it happens," she said, "our former manservant, Neil Gibson, was to arrive in Selkirk ahead of us. Yet here it is Tuesday, and we've not heard from him." Marjory hesitated but only for an instant. "You'll remember Gibson, I'm sure, from our years at Tweedsford. Might you help us find him, Reverend?"

He did not respond at first, his jaw working as if she'd given him an especially tough cut of meat. Finally he said, "One of the elders, Joseph Haldane, is bound for Middleton in the morn. Suppose I have him inquire at the inn —"

"Would you?" Marjory sank against the wall in relief. Nearly every traveler on the Edinburgh road stopped at the Middleton Inn. "Surely the proprietor will have news for us."

The minister made no such promise. "We shall see when Mr. Haldane returns on Thursday."

Two days. Aye, she could bear two more days.

Reverend Brown regarded her, his wrinkled lips tightly drawn like a calfskin purse. "Change is refreshing," he said, pulling the door open. " 'Tis an old Gaelic proverb your daughter-in-law will know. You may need that reminder in the months to come, Mrs. Kerr. I am certain I will."

She gazed at the aging minister who'd given his best years to their parish. From the pulpit he was intimidating, even frightening. But in person, bathed in the flickering candlelight, his wisdom and mercy shone through.

"God be with you," she said in parting, then stepped into the crowded street, hearing the door close firmly behind her. Each detail of their conversation replayed in her mind as she hastened downhill, ducking round the horses and carts, the fishwives and pie sellers, the tradesmen and laborers who darted in front of her.

She had to get to Anne's house. Had to tell Elisabeth. *We're here to stay. We're home.*

When she turned into Halliwell's Close,

Marjory paused to let her eyes adjust to the dim light, then squinted, uncertain what she was seeing. Was someone at their door? A man of middling size and middling age, no more than a shadow. But as she moved forward, the shadow took shape, and a voice she'd not heard in many seasons spoke her name.

"Leddy Kerr?"

She tried to swallow but could not. "Mr. Laidlaw."

The factor of Tweedsford stood there empty handed, looking precisely as she'd remembered him. Brown, straight hair tied back with a bit of leather, small eyes set rather too close, and a mouth drawn by a firm hand wielding a sharp pen.

But Anne's description was the one she could not forget. *A lecherous man without scruples.* She'd pledged to face Mr. Laidlaw without fear. That hour had come.

He cleared his throat. "I received yer letter —"

"Then where are the items I asked you to bring?" Her words were sharper than she intended, but she could not take them back.

He inclined his head toward the door. "I left them up the stair with the leddies."

"You entered my cousin's house?" Marjory could only imagine Anne's reaction.

"I didna stay but a minute," he quickly explained. "A stranger answered my knock.

Tall, with dark hair. She wouldna let me in."

Elisabeth. Well done, lass.

Roger Laidlaw remained by the door, blocking her way. "Leddy Kerr —"

"I am Mrs. Kerr now, as you well know."

He shifted his stance. "Beg pardon, mem."

Only then did she notice a sad look in his eyes. Still, if the rumors about him were true, he had much to account for. "What have you to say for yourself, Mr. Laidlaw?"

Before he could respond, a trio of maidservants came hurrying up the close and squeezed past, bobbing their white caps in apology. When his gaze followed them down the close, Marjory's control snapped.

"So," she hissed, "I see you've not changed your ways." If indeed he'd misused Tibbie Cranshaw, his actions would not go unpunished. Were there not laws against such behavior? "I've a mind to report you to Tweedsford's new owner," she fumed. "Or ask the Sheriff of Selkirk to charge you in court."

Mr. Laidlaw quickly backed away from her, averting his gaze. "*Mebbe* we might speak *anither* time, mem. Whan ye're not . . . whan 'tis . . ." He turned and fled toward the marketplace, quickly disappearing from sight.

T<small>HIRTEEN</small>

From the manner in which a woman draws
her thread at every stitch of her
needlework, any other woman can surmise
her thoughts.

H<small>ONORÉ DE</small> B<small>ALZAC</small>

Elisabeth glanced at the door. Muffled voices
had floated up the stair for the last few
minutes, too faint to be discerned. Her
mother-in-law was probably speaking with
Reverend Brown, if he'd escorted her home,
or with Mr. Tait, the shoemaker who shared
their entrance off Halliwell's Close.

When she shifted her gaze toward Anne and
her students, Elisabeth was touched by the
lovely tableau. Sunlight gilded their faces as
the threesome bent over their work, speaking
softly in a lace tell, a rhythmic chant used by
lace makers to keep a steady pace.

Nineteen miles to the Isle of Wight,
Shall I get there by candlelight?

Yes, if your fingers go lissome and light,
You'll get there by candlelight.

Their lilting voices were as bonny as they were. Sandy-haired Lesley Boyd had a sweet smile and an effusive personality. Grace Caldwell was long-limbed, dark-haired, and gentler in nature, with eyes that hinted at a fine intellect. Both were six-and-ten, on the cusp of womanhood. Looking at them now, with their fine, smooth complexions, Elisabeth shook her head in disbelief. Had she ever been so young?

"I'll turn five-and-twenty in a fortnight," she'd confessed last evening to Anne, who'd muttered, "At least you were married once." Elisabeth was left not knowing how to respond. One moment Anne seemed content to be unwed, and the next she was miserable.

Then there was Mr. Laidlaw. His brief appearance earlier had all but ruined the start of their quiet afternoon. Anne had blanched at the mere sight of him. With Marjory gone and the young ladies present, Elisabeth hadn't allowed the factor across the threshold, only took the small sack of items from Tweedsford and placed it on Marjory's bed, waiting for her return.

Seated at the empty dining table, Elisabeth had pressed on with her sewing, pulling her needle through the closely woven cambric. A fine French cotton, Mr. Dalgliesh had said proudly. The slight gloss on the right side of the fabric caught the afternoon sunlight pouring across the room. She hoped to deliver another finished shirt before supper. One simple phrase ran through her head as she stitched. *Another shirt, another shilling.* She had never in her life cared about money. But she cared very much about keeping food on their table.

At the sound of footsteps on the stair, Elisabeth quickly put aside her sewing, anxious to hear the details of Marjory's meeting with the reverend. He could make their lives difficult if he chose to. A moment later, when the door creaked open and her mother-in-law appeared, Elisabeth saw at once how upset she was and so feared the worst.

Marjory yanked her handkerchief from her sleeve and pressed it against her brow. "I should have marched him up to the manse," she fumed.

Elisabeth glanced at Anne and her students, who were agog. "Whatever did the reverend say?" Elisabeth asked in a low voice, stepping between Marjory and the others.

Her mother-in-law looked surprised by the question. "The reverend? Oh . . . well . . . we are free to make our home in Selkirk," she told her. "And the admiral will not reside at Tweedsford."

"Oh!" Elisabeth exclaimed. "Good news all round, then."

"Not all." Marjory frowned at the door. "I met Mr. Laidlaw in the close."

At that, Lesley and Grace abandoned their lace making and hurried to Marjory's side. "Who *was* that man?" Grace asked, her eyes aglow with curiosity, while Lesley pleaded, "Can you not tell us anything?"

"He's an old family acquaintance," Anne said offhandedly, then waved them toward the table. "Shall we have tea before resuming your lesson?"

"You'll not put us off so easily," Lesley protested. "We caught a glimpse of the man when he tarried at the threshold. He is *far* below your station, Miss Kerr."

"I am glad you think so," Anne told them. "He was once Mrs. Kerr's factor. And that is all you need to know."

Elisabeth took each girl by the elbow and steered them toward the chairs on the far side of the table. "We have gingerbread cakes," she said, hoping to tempt them, "and fresh milk for your tea. Only promise you'll not ask any more questions about our visitor."

"Very well," Grace said with an exaggerated sigh.

As soon as they were all gathered, her mother-in-law prompted the young ladies, "Tell us something of yourselves." They did so in colorful detail, forgetting all about Anne's mysterious caller, to Elisabeth's great relief.

She'd not liked the look of Mr. Laidlaw from the moment she'd answered the door. Whether it was his too-familiar demeanor or his slouching stance, Elisabeth could not say. Anne's words had marked him with the blackest of ink. *A profligate of the worst kind.* That was all Elisabeth needed to know.

When her teacup was empty and her gingerbread reduced to crumbs, she could not delay her labors any longer. "I have much to do if I'm to finish this shirt before sunset."

As Anne pulled off her apron, an object dropped to the floor with a slight clink. She bent to retrieve it, then held out the small item. "From Michael Dalgliesh."

"For me?" Elisabeth took the silver thimble and slipped it in place. " 'Tis a perfect fit."

"So I see," Anne said evenly.

"When did he give you this?" Elisabeth asked, holding up her thumb.

"Earlier today when I went looking for parsley in Mrs. Thorburn's garden. He was on his way to deliver it. Thought you might find it helpful."

Elisabeth studied the dimpled surface, worn from use. "How kind of him."

Anne offered a faint shrug. " 'Tis only a thimble."

Elisabeth heard the note of irritation in her cousin's voice, but could not press Anne further. Not with her students present and Marjory listening. Later, perhaps.

Once the young ladies took their places round the sewing table, Elisabeth saw that Anne's assessment was correct: Lesley and Grace had little talent for needlework. The girls did one buttonhole stitch to Anne's four. But their manners were refined and their expressions pleasing. If that was all their parents wished for, their shillings were well spent.

Elisabeth's needle soon fell into rhythm with their lace tell.

Betsy Bays and Polly Mays,
They are two bonny lasses;
They built a bower upon the tower,
And covered it with rushes.

When the kirk bell chimed the hour of six, a carriage was already parked at the mouth of the close, and a patient footman stood at the stair door, waiting for the two young ladies. Their families' fine estates were not far from town along the road leading from the West Port.

Anne sent them off with curtsies all round, then closed the door behind them with a heavy sigh. "I accomplish little of my own lace making while they're here," she admitted, then quickly reclaimed her seat and angled it just so, making the most of the late afternoon light. "How are you coming with your shirt, Bess?"

"Finished." She shook out the fabric, then spread it across her skirts. " 'Tis embarrassingly easy. Sleeves, seams, cuffs, and a collar."

Anne picked up one of the sleeves and examined the cuff with a practiced eye. "You have a fine backstitch," she told her. "And the neck gussets are neatly done. Michael must be pleased."

Elisabeth eyed her. "Michael, is it?"

Anne did not blush often, but when she did, her pale skin turned quite rosy. "We attended school together, just down from the shop."

"Then you knew Jenny, his late wife."

Anne's cheeks grew pinker still. "Aye."

When her cousin said nothing more, Elisabeth stood and carefully folded the shirt. More pieces were falling into place. Anne clearly harbored feelings for her old classmate. Whether he returned them was less certain. "I shall give Mr. Dalgliesh your regards and return in time for supper." Elisabeth looked toward the hearth. "Eight o' the clock," she promised her mother-in-law, then hurried down the stair.

The sun bronzed the lower western sky and cast long shadows across the marketplace, less crowded now with nightfall approaching. She clutched the shirt to her bodice lest it slip from her hands onto the dirty cobblestones of Kirk Wynd. Nodding at folk in passing, she realized some faces were beginning

119

to look familiar. A pockmarked lad in dingy clothing, head bent to hide his scars. A barefoot dairymaid who danced when she walked yet never spilled a drop of milk. A crookbacked man with a hazel walking stick, making his way from one shop door to the next. She would learn their names, one by one, until Selkirk was truly home.

A minute later she knocked on the tailor's door.

"Anither shirt?" His look of astonishment melted into a grin. "I suppose ye'll be wanting anither shilling as weel."

" 'Tis our agreement," Elisabeth reminded him, then placed the finished garment on the only uncluttered surface she could find. "Your thimble is to blame, Mr. Dalgliesh." She wiggled her thumb. "Now I can sew even faster."

" 'Twas Jenny's," he said simply. "She sewed a fine shirt too."

Yet you parted with your wife's thimble so easily. Elisabeth found his nonchalance unsettling. Did he care nothing for material possessions? Or have little use for sentiment?

"I am honored to use Jenny's thimble," she finally said, slipping the coin he offered into her hanging pocket. "Bless you for sending it home with Annie."

Some emotion flickered in his blue eyes. Not sorrow, not remorse, but something.

Thinking it prudent to change the subject,

Elisabeth glanced at the turnpike stair. "I was hoping to finally meet Peter."

Mr. Dalgliesh reached for a waistcoat in need of buttons. "His *granmither* in Lindean claimed him for the nicht. She *thocht* it might help me with my wark."

Elisabeth could see how exhausted the tailor was. The lines round his eyes were more pronounced, and his shoulders sagged. "I wonder, have you considered taking a partner?"

His head snapped in her direction. "Whatsomever d'ye mean?"

"Another tailor. Or an apprentice."

She'd not seen him frown before. He was frowning now.

"Anither tailor must be paid, and an apprentice taught." Michael stood, tossing aside the waistcoat. "Jenny and I managed the shop verra weel *thegither.* But it hasna been the same without her."

Regret washed over Elisabeth. Whatever was she thinking? Prying into this man's life, making suggestions. She hastened to his side. "Please forgive me, Mr. Dalgliesh. We have only just met. 'Tis not my place —"

"Nae, nae," he said, his features softening. "Dinna mind my ill-natured self. On the morrow 'twill be three years *syne* I lost my wife. 'Tis a hard time, ye ken?"

Elisabeth nodded, imagining how she might feel come the seventeenth of January. "You

121

are right to mourn her still."

Michael's gaze met hers. "As ye do yer husband, I'll warrant."

"Aye." But it wasn't Donald who came to mind as she stood near the tailor. Elisabeth noted the measuring tape draped round his neck, the chalk poking out of his waistcoat pocket, and the sleeves pushed up to his elbows and thought of Rob MacPherson. A childhood friend from the Highlands, Rob had moved to Edinburgh with his father, Angus, and had worked in his tailoring shop, as she had. Alas, Rob had grown too attached to her, seldom letting her out of his sight. Even now she shuddered, remembering his dark eyes.

"I must away," she told Michael, stepping toward the door. "Perhaps on my next visit I'll have the pleasure of meeting your son."

"He'd like that," Michael agreed.

"Tomorrow eve, then." Elisabeth bade him farewell and made haste for Halliwell's Close, uncertain of the time. The kirk bell did not ring every hour during the week, only at noon and six o' the clock. Her mother-in-law's demanding nature had eased considerably, but Marjory was still particular about a few things. Supper at eight was one of them.

Elisabeth arrived without a moment to spare. The table was set, Anne was seated, and Marjory was ladling her fragrant soup into wooden bowls, carved from knobby burls. Since the grain was whorled rather than straight, the bowls were less likely to crack. Elisabeth helped her serve, then took her place at table next to Marjory, who spoke a brief grace over their meal.

Supper was meager fare — one bowl of soup for each of them and a triangle cut from the large, round bannock — but Elisabeth had silver in her pocket. They would have meat on the morrow and send out the month of April with a flourish. "What shall it be, ladies?" she asked, holding up her coin. "Fish, flesh, or fowl?"

"The cook chooses," Anne told her.

"If the flesher might have a pullet and a pound of veal," Marjory said, "I recall a fine dish Helen Edgar oft served. Though I'll need your help, Elisabeth."

" 'Tis yours," she said, honored to be asked. Growing up as a cottager, Elisabeth had learned a great deal about cooking from sheer necessity. But this was an entirely new venture for her mother-in-law.

Later, when they stood to clear the table, Marjory said to her, "Reverend Brown shared a Highland proverb with me today, one I'd not heard. 'Change is refreshing.' "

The words warmed Elisabeth's heart. "My father loved that one."

"Did he?" Marjory paused, dishes in hand, to look at her. "Bess, what does it sound like in Gaelic?"

Her request stole Elisabeth's breath. Never in their years together at Milne Square had her mother-in-law asked her to speak in her native Highland tongue. In truth, Marjory had always seemed offended when she overheard Gaelic spoken in the street.

Now she was willing, even eager, to hear it. Another miracle.

Elisabeth smiled at her and said, "*Is ùrachadh atharrachadh.* Change *is* refreshing, Marjory." *And you are living proof.*

FOURTEEN

What is so sweet and dear
As a prosperous morn in May?

SIR WILLIAM WATSON

When the first rays of the sun stirred Marjory from her sleep on Thursday, the bedframe groaned at the precise same moment she did. Chagrined, she sat up and rubbed her stiff neck, then her aching knees, then her sore back. Surely there was some remedy for growing older. A sprinkle of morning dew on May Day was said to bring health and happiness for the year ahead. If the dew might also make her more youthful, she would bathe in it from head to toe. Aye, and drink it as well.

On a whim Marjory tiptoed to the casement window and eased it open, enough to slip out her hand and touch the wet sill. She patted her forehead and cheeks with her fingertips, then swiftly closed the window, lest the cool air wake the others. Besides, however would she explain herself? A Christian widow dousing her skin in the Beltane dew like pagans of old. Reverend Brown would have something to say about that. With a rueful smile, Marjory dried her face on the sleeve of her nightgown, reminding herself that come August she'd turn nine-and-forty. Not even the rite of May could make her young again.

Fresh coals on the grate brought a small pot of water to boil. Just as Helen Edgar had done many mornings, Marjory added oatmeal in a thin stream with her left hand while stirring sunwise with her right, using a wooden stick Helen called a *spurtle.* After a bit Marjory swung the pot away from the heat to let the porridge simmer, then quietly dressed herself.

With May Day in mind, she took extra care with her toilette, styling her hair and using a splash of Anne's rosewater. The others were soon awake and dressed, each seeing to her own tasks. When they finished breakfast Marjory retrieved the sack of items Mr. Laidlaw had brought from Tweedsford and brought it to table. "Small things," she confessed, "but precious to me, if you'd like to see them."

After setting aside the letters from her late brother, Marjory drew out the little chapbook. Three inches tall and two dozen pages long, the book was as diminutive as its mischievous hero, Tom. She remembered how alarmed Donald had become when the thumb-sized lad fell into a bowl and was accidentally cooked in a pudding. "I bought it for a penny from a chapman who came through Selkirkshire the summer Donald turned three." Marjory held it out for Elisabeth to peruse.

"Tom Thumb, is it?" Her daughter-in-law's smile was bittersweet. " 'Twas the favorite story of my brother, Simon."

"And your husband's favorite as well." Watching Elisabeth's eyes grow moist as she turned the pages, Marjory thought of young Simon Ferguson dying in service to Prince Charlie at Gladsmuir and the mournful weeks that followed. "Why don't you keep it, Bess?"

She clasped it in her hands. "Truly?"

"Aye," Marjory said, "though I cannot part with this." She showed them Andrew's wooden toy soldier, the paint worn off from years of little hands marching the toy round the nursery. "A wee birthday present for Andrew, carved by Gibson."

Saying their names in tandem brought a lump to Marjory's throat. The darling son who'd always longed to be a soldier now lay in a Falkirk grave. And Gibson had been traveling on foot for ten days, with one shilling in his pocket and a rough leather bag strapped to his back. Though Marjory did not always voice her concerns, she thought of

127

Gibson almost constantly, fearing for his life one moment, counting on his strength the next. Mr. Haldane was expected back from Middleton Inn today. She would visit the manse as early as she dared and beg the reverend for news.

Marjory slipped the toy soldier in her pocket, reminding herself Gibson was not alone. *The LORD will preserve him, and keep him alive.*

Still holding Donald's chapbook, Elisabeth prompted her, "What else did Mr. Laidlaw bring you?"

Marjory lifted out her miniature of Tweedsford, embarrassed to let them see it. "I was a new bride with an indulgent husband," she said with a shrug. "He ordered sticks of plumbago and sheets of fine vellum from a stationer in Edinburgh, and I pretended to be an artist."

Anne examined the framed drawing, no larger than a man's palm. " 'Tis the very likeness of your old home, with four bays across the front."

Marjory was not convinced. "Someday when I feel especially brave, we'll all walk to the estate, and you'll realize what a poor imitation this is."

"I would love to see Tweedsford," Elisabeth admitted.

Marjory was already sorry she'd mentioned the idea. Who knew when she'd be strong enough to face all those memories? It might be months. It might be never.

Thrusting her hand into the cloth sack, she found the last item. "This belonged to Lord John." Marjory held out his splendid magnifying glass, the ivory handle intricately carved, the circular glass edged in silver. She could still picture him with a delicate wildflower in one hand, his glass in the other, marveling at the tiny petals and leaves. Her husband had loved their country property and all the treasures it contained. Alas, she'd insisted Lord John move their family to fashionable Edinburgh, turning her back on everyone and everything they knew.

Some regrets even time could not erase.

Anne patently admired the magnifying glass, then reached for a sample of her lace. "Look, Cousin." She held her work beneath the round lens. "Now you can see it properly. I confess the stitches are so tiny my head begins to ache after a few hours."

Marjory studied Anne's delicate needlepoint lace with its thousands of buttonhole stitches and knew at once what must be done. "Would my husband's magnifying glass be of some use to you?"

With a slight gasp Anne lifted it from her hands. "You cannot imagine how much."

"Then it is yours," Marjory said without hesitation. "To keep."

"But . . ." Anne's face was scarlet. "I meant

only to borrow it."

Marjory leaned forward and cupped Anne's cheeks, feeling their warmth against her cool palms. "Lord John would want you to have it. And *I* want you to have it." Marjory looked deep into her cousin's eyes. "One magnifying glass could never repay your kindness to us. Or begin to make amends for the years I neglected you. Please, dear Annie, . . . may I give you this?"

Anne's mouth began to tremble. "Oh, Cousin." She lowered her gaze. "I fear I misjudged you terribly."

"Nae, you did not. You thought me haughty and prideful and selfish." Marjory wished it were not so, but it was. "I have been all those things and more, especially toward you."

"Years ago, perhaps. Not now." Anne clutched the glass in her hand. "You are a changed woman, Marjory."

She eased back. "With more changes needed, I'm afraid."

"True for us all." Anne traced the carved handle with her fingertip. "Thank you, Marjory." She sighed, then lifted her head. "I shall be at my lace work until the gloaming. Miss Boyd and Miss Caldwell shan't be coming since 'tis May Day."

Elisabeth was already gathering her sewing items. "Perhaps I might complete *two* shirts with the house quiet."

Marjory had other plans. Buoyed by the

sounds from the marketplace below, she announced, "After I call upon Reverend Brown, I am determined to walk the length of Water Row, greeting everyone who meets my gaze and does not turn away."

Elisabeth and Anne both turned to her, clearly taken by surprise.

"Marjory, are you certain?" Elisabeth glanced at her pile of unfinished shirts, then looked up, her expression resolute. "I could join you —"

"Nae, Bess," Marjory said gently. "If I'm to find my place in Selkirk, I must first know who is willing to befriend me." She did not tarry, lest she lose her nerve. *What can man do unto me?* Aye, she would cling to those words and keep walking.

Just as she'd imagined, Halliwell's Close was crowded with folk bringing in the May. Freshly cut hawthorn branches, fragrant with tiny white flowers, were fastened to every doorpost, and the air was filled with merriment. In the marketplace shepherds from the hills mingled with the lasses of the town, circling the mercat cross in an ancient dance while a fiddler spun a lively reel. At least she'd chosen a day when her neighbors might be more charitable.

First, she would learn what she could of Gibson. Anne's words from days past haunted her. *You must prepare yourself for the worst.*

131

But Marjory was not prepared. Nae, she would not even consider it.

She crossed Kirk Wynd and headed for the manse, praying in earnest. *May there be some report of him, Lord, and may it be favorable.* When Reverend Brown yanked open the door before she knocked, her hopes rose. "You've news for me?" Marjory asked, thinking he'd watched her approach from the window.

"As it happens, I am bound for the school to meet with the *dominie,* Daniel Cumming."

"I see." Marjory knew the schoolmaster only by name. "My daughter-in-law sews his shirts," she said without thinking.

The minister's countenance darkened. "I beg your pardon?"

"That is, she is . . . helping Mr. Dalgliesh, the tailor . . ." Marjory stopped before she made a greater fool of herself or, worse, injured Elisabeth's reputation.

To her surprise the minister's expression lightened considerably. "As it happens, the Widow Kerr will also be sewing my shirts. And very skillfully, I'm told. But you've not come to speak of clothing." He crossed the threshold and joined her in the street. "I met with Joseph Haldane this morn."

Marjory almost stood on tiptoe, her heart prepared to soar. "And?"

The reverend shook his head. "No word of Gibson."

Her spirits sank as quickly as they'd risen.

"What am I to do?"

His silence offered little comfort. "None of the coachmen have seen him," he finally said, "and they've traveled the Edinburgh road many times since your arrival. Nor did the proprietor of the Middleton Inn have any inkling of your manservant's whereabouts. I am sorry, Mrs. Kerr, but . . ."

Nae! She closed her eyes, wishing she might shut out the truth. "He cannot be dead," she whispered. "He cannot be."

FIFTEEN

Our real blessings often appear to us in the shape of pains, losses and disappointments; but let us have patience, and we soon shall see them in their proper figures.

JOSEPH ADDISON

Marjory trudged across the marketplace, hardly able to lift her feet. *My dear Gibson, dead. Because of me.*

"We cannot be certain," Reverend Brown had cautioned her before hurrying off to meet with the schoolmaster. "The weather has been milder than usual. As I recall, he's a capable man, your Gibson."

Aye, he was. And loyal. And kind.

Tears stung her eyes. Could Neil Gibson truly be gone from this world?

"I'll reach Selkirk *lang* afore ye do," Gibson had said before bidding her farewell at Milne Square. She'd believed him, convincing

134

herself that no obstacle strewed in Gibson's path could deter him. Though she'd not had a shilling to spare when they'd left Edinburgh, the fact was, if she'd managed to pay for his seat in a carriage, Gibson would be alive now, safe by her side. How could she live with that awful truth?

Forgive me, forgive me. She'd begged that of Lord John when he lay in his grave and then of both her sons when she learned of their deaths. Perhaps she bore some terrible curse, condemning any man she held dear.

Marjory avoided the May Day revelers with their youthful exuberance and aimed her steps toward the East Port. Any plan to greet her neighbors was quickly forsaken. Such banter required a light heart, a kind word, a ready smile. She could produce none of those. Not this day.

Keeping to one side of Water Row, Marjory fixed her gaze on the broad thoroughfare where strangers on horseback trotted into town and the occasional carriage rattled past. She scanned the men's faces, desperate to see a silver fringe of hair, a wrinkled brow. For the journey south Gibson had traded his neatly pressed livery for a plain brown coat and breeches, so she kept an eye out for such clothing among the passersby.

But her search was in vain. Was the whole world no older than forty? And dressed in every color but brown?

Stop it, Marjory. Stop looking for him.

She jutted out her chin to keep it from trembling, brushed away the last of her tears, then spun on her heel. If she could not save Gibson, then she would mourn him in private.

It seemed the whole of Selkirk stood between her and Halliwell's Close. Folk congregated round one another's doors — talking, arguing, laughing — while children skipped about with their hoops and sticks, dogs barking at their heels. Silver flasks were passed from hand to hand, and young girls threw caution to the winds, flirting with lads they would never speak to were it not May Day.

Marjory did not notice a carriage drawing near until a man's voice called down to her in warning, "Have a care, mem!"

As the horses lurched to a stop, she looked over her shoulder and immediately recognized the coachman, with his thick eyebrows and deeply lined face. "Thank you for delivering my letter to Tweedsford," she said, stepping close enough to be heard. "I trust you were paid?"

"Oo aye," he answered in a gruff voice. "Yer man gave me mair than I asked for."

Though Mr. Laidlaw was no longer in her employ, she did not correct the coachman on that point. "I don't imagine you have any news of Neil Gibson, the manservant I described to you on the Sabbath?"

He wagged his head. "Nae, mem. I've yet to hear his name bandied about."

Marjory sighed. Just as she'd feared: more ill news.

But the coachman wasn't finished. "Noo that ye ask, I did pass a man on foot. Balding, did ye say? With a bit o' gray?"

"Aye!" Hope rose inside her. Might it be Gibson?

"I canna say for sure 'twas him," the man cautioned, scratching at his beard. "He was dressed in plain clothing, yet walked like gentry. D'ye ken?" The coachman threw back his shoulders, showing her what he meant. "He's not far *ahint*. Climbing the *brig* road. A man o' sixty years, I'd say."

Gibson.

By the time she reached Shaw's Close, Marjory was running.

She had not run in many years, but she was running now. Past the houses and the tradesmen and the shops, hearing her sons sing out in rhyme: *Cooper, souter, tanner, sawyer, dyer, spinner, potter, saddler.* Soon she could see the arch of the East Port, where several men on horseback were entering the town. Behind them came a lone traveler walking at a brisk pace. A man in brown clothing with the carriage of a gentleman.

She could not see his face, but she did not need to.

"Gibson!"

137

At the sound of her voice, he took off on a run. By the time he reached her, tears were streaming down both their faces.

"Leddy Kerr, Leddy Kerr!" When he held out his arms, she threw herself into his embrace.

"You are safe," she cried. "You are home." He smelled of heather and sweat and earth and stream. His beard was ten days grown and his hair matted to his brow. Marjory did not mind, not for a moment.

When he finally released her, his face was ruddy. "I beg yer pardon, mem. I didna mean . . . I shouldna . . ."

"I was the brazen one," she reminded him, making use of her handkerchief. "And I'll not apologize for a moment."

Gibson smiled. "Aye, mem."

She tried not to stare, yet here he was, her beloved servant, standing before her, healthy and whole.

"We'd best go," he said, "afore the toun folk start to *blether.*"

Marjory drew him to her side and began walking toward the marketplace. "Let them gossip all they wish. The man I thought was dead is alive and well."

"*Bethankit!*" he said, then patted her hand, as he oft did when she took his arm. "I'm only sorry I made ye wait so lang." His step was light, yet she heard the weariness in his voice. "Whan we reach the *hoose,*" he promised, "I'll tell ye what happened to yer *auld* servant."

Marjory gently admonished him, "Neil Gibson, you cannot leave me on tenterhooks. Will you not tell me where you've been all this time?"

"In Edinburgh, mem." His blue gray eyes met hers. "Locked inside the tolbooth, chained to the *wa'.*"

Sixteen

Beware, so long as you live, of judging
men by their outward appearance.

Jean de La Fontaine

Hearing his voice on the stair, Elisabeth could
not cross the room quickly enough. "Hurry,
Cousin!" she cried, flinging open the door.
" 'Tis Gibson!"

Anne was beside her in a trice as Elisabeth
clasped Gibson's hands and pulled him
across the threshold. "At last, at last." She
kissed his cheek, her heart filled to overflowing. "We feared we'd never see you again."

"Aye, weel . . ." Gibson was clearly embarrassed. "I hope ye'll not mind the leuk o' me."

"Mind?" Elisabeth laughed, a mixture of
joy and relief. "After traveling forty miles on
foot, you look surprisingly well." His clothes
were rumpled and torn, but such things were
easily remedied. "What say you to a comfortable chair and a cup of tea?"

Only then did Elisabeth glance at her

mother-in-law, close by his side. Marjory's color was high, and she was smiling, but her eyes bore a strange light. Something had frightened the woman. Nae, terrified her. Had Gibson come bearing grim tidings?

"What is wrong?" Elisabeth murmured as Marjory eased past her.

Her mother-in-law's response was cryptic. "You'll know shortly."

"Come and sit," Anne was saying as she lifted Gibson's leather bag from his shoulders. "You must be exhausted. Can it be ten years since I last saw you? 'Twas at kirk on a Sabbath morn, I'll wager."

Gibson eased into one of the upholstered chairs, and Marjory claimed the other while Elisabeth poured his tea from the kettle on the hearth. She placed the wooden cup in his hands, then perched on the creepie, her mourning gown pooling round her feet. "Please, Gibson," Elisabeth urged him, "tell us what kept you from Annie's door for so long."

A cloud moved across his face. " 'Tis not a bonny tale, but I suppose ye must hear it, as Leddy Kerr already has." Gibson shifted in his seat, taking care not to spill his tea, while Anne drew her wooden chair nearer. "Ye'll remember I left Milne Square on a Tuesday," he began. "Whan I reached the Netherbow Port, the guard wouldna let me through 'til he'd searched my bag. O' course, he found

Leddy Kerr's two letters."

A chill ran down Elisabeth's spine. "Did the porter not see how harmless those letters were? One for our cousin, requesting lodging. And a written character so you might find a position."

"He didna open them," Gibson said evenly. "Instead, a dragoon marched me to the tolbooth on the High Street —"

"Nae!" Elisabeth gasped.

Gibson shrugged in defeat. "They kept me for nigh to a week. Clapped in an iron collar without meat or ale or a fire to keep me warm at nicht."

Elisabeth felt sick. Poor Gibson, locked in that wretched place! Dark, dirty, and dank, filled with murderers and thieves. When she and Marjory had departed Edinburgh, they'd imagined Gibson well ahead of them, but in fact they'd left him behind.

"I am . . . so sorry," she said, ashamed of how inadequate her words sounded. "We were the ones who supported Prince Charlie, not you."

"But I was the one leaving toun on foot and me not garbed as a servant. The soldiers were certain I was a traitor, carrying messages for the Jacobites."

Marjory laid her hand on his. "This was all my fault. If you'd traveled with us —"

"Nae, mem." Gibson shook his head rather vehemently. "Ye're not to blame."

142

Anne's frustration was thinly veiled. "If they'd simply read those letters, you might've been on your way at once."

"Aye, but it took days for the letters to make their way up to Edinburgh Castle, whaur the governor himself read them."

Elisabeth frowned. "General Lord Mark Kerr?" A merciless gentleman, despite being a distant relation on her father-in-law's side. It was Lord Mark who'd penned the terrible missive on behalf of King George, pronouncing their family attainted and their estate forfeited. "But if Lord Mark read the two letters . . ."

Her voice faded as the truth sank in. *He knows where we are.*

Now Elisabeth understood the fear she'd seen in her mother-in-law's eyes, recalling the day a British soldier pounded on their door with the butt of his pistol. What if dragoons appeared at Anne's house by week's end? What if they forced the Kerr women to return to Edinburgh — or, worse, travel to London — to face charges of treason? With the Jacobite Rising all but over, who could say what the government might do?

Calm yourself, Bess. No one had come looking for them, not yet. She'd ruin Gibson's homecoming if she aired such trepidations. "What happened next?"

He exhaled. "Whan they finally set me free, I walked south as fast as ever I could, keep-

143

ing to the hills and awa from the road, lest the dragoons change their minds and come after me."

"My faithful Gibson," Marjory said, patting his arm.

He turned to her, his expression full of apology. "I ken ye needed me here lang afore this, Leddy Kerr. Nae doubt I've disappointed ye."

"You could never disappoint me, Gibson." Marjory rose with surprising grace, then reached for her apron. "How does mutton broth sound to you?"

He smiled, showing off a fine set of teeth. "Like a dish sent from *heiven*."

"I'll make our Beltane bannock," Anne declared, returning her chair to the dining table. "I've flour, milk, and oatmeal for the baking, with eggs and cream to wash over it."

Seeing Gibson's delight at the prospect helped Elisabeth push aside the last of her fears. "You've left me little to do but set the table."

"And finish another shirt for Michael," Anne said pointedly. Their supply of coins was getting low.

Gibson, meanwhile, was admiring his surroundings. "Ye've a fine wee hoose, Miss Kerr."

"With room for another guest," Anne said firmly. "We shall all sleep better with a man under our roof."

Elisabeth shot her a grateful look. "You'll find our Gibson a welcome addition to the household."

"He is not to be treated like a manservant," Marjory cautioned them. "Such days are behind us."

Gibson made a sound of disapproval, low in his throat. "Ye canna serve me, mem."

"Oh?" Marjory, busily cutting up turnips, stopped to gaze over her shoulder. "Submit yourselves one to another," she reminded him. "Or would you argue with the Scriptures?"

"Nae, mem." His voice softened. "Nor with ye."

Elisabeth was touched by their warm exchange. Even without her title or fortune, Marjory was, by society's measure, far above Gibson, who'd been in service the whole of his life and could not read or write. Any public discourse between them would be deeply frowned upon. But within these four walls, their easy banter was further proof of the changes wrought in Marjory's heart by a loving hand.

An hour later, when the foursome joined round the table for their noontide meal, Marjory invited Gibson to speak the blessing. He balked at first, but Marjory would not take no for an answer. "You are seated at the head," she reminded him.

When Gibson bowed to pray, Elisabeth saw

145

the faint brown spots on his balding pate and the wreath of silver hair that circled it and thanked the Lord this good man had been spared.

"*Almichty* God," he began, "*bliss* yer servants wha are gathered here. Bliss the broth and bread and the hands that made them. I thank ye for bringing me hame, and I thank ye for them that made me walcome. The grace o' the Lord Jesus be with ye. Amen, amen."

All four lifted their heads at the same time and smiled. *Home.*

SEVENTEEN

Let us then be up and doing,
With a heart for any fate;
Still achieving, still pursuing,
Learn to labor and to wait.

HENRY WADSWORTH LONGFELLOW

"Is that a'?" Michael Dalgliesh regarded Elisabeth with mock disdain, his red eyebrows arched, his full mouth curled in a most convincing sneer. "I've not clapped eyes on ye syne Wednesday, and ye bring me one shirt?"

Elisabeth laughed, seeing through his broad pretense. "I'd hoped to finish more, but —"

"Yer manservant arrived from Edinburgh."

"Oh, you've heard, then?"

It was the tailor's turn to laugh. " 'Tis a' folk can blether about."

Elisabeth was not surprised. After dining on their broth and bread yesterday afternoon, the Kerr women had gone for a walk, allowing Gibson the privacy needed for his first hot bath in many days. They'd stopped at the reverend's to share the good news and inquired about another impending arrival, that of Admiral Lord Jack Buchanan. The reverend had nothing further to report. For Marjory's sake, Elisabeth was relieved the admiral would not be living at Tweedsford, but she was still wary of having an officer of the Royal Navy two miles from their door.

Wondering what Michael might know of the matter, Elisabeth baited him. "I should think the gossips would find Lord Buchanan a much worthier subject of discussion than our Gibson."

The tailor wagged his finger at her. "Ye'll not tempt me to sin, Mrs. Kerr. Or have ye forgotten? 'Thou shalt not go up and *doon* as a talebearer among thy people.' "

"Nae, I've not forgotten." Elisabeth was sorry she'd broached the subject. Even if Michael Dalgliesh was teasing, he was not wrong.

She grew quiet, letting him finish a buttonhole without distraction. He had nimble fingers for a man, handling his needle and thread with effortless efficiency. According to Anne, Michael had learned his trade from his late father, just as Angus MacPherson had taught his son, Rob, though the two young tailors had little else in common. Michael was outgoing; Rob was taciturn. Michael had a playful nature; Rob was a brooding sort.

Rob had also loved her rather desperately, though she'd not returned his affections. In the end she'd banished him from her door when he shattered Marjory's good opinion of Donald with the ugly truth of her son's infidelities. Elisabeth had not heard from Rob since he'd headed north to take up arms for Prince Charlie. A thousand Highlanders had died in the final battle at Culloden near Inverness. Was Rob MacPherson among them? She feared she would never know.

Needing some fresh air to clear her mind, Elisabeth stepped back. "Perhaps I'd best leave you to your work this morn."

"Wait." Michael jumped to his feet, casting aside his sewing. "Let me find yer shilling afore ye go."

Elisabeth watched him pat his pockets, lift the lids of several wooden boxes, then start tossing fabric about — all in an attempt to locate his leather drawstring purse. She pressed her lips together, lest a laugh slip out. No one could banish a moment of sadness like Michael Dalgliesh. Though the tailor had many skills, keeping track of things was not one of them.

Standing by his cutting table, she smoothed her hand across a length of gray wool, newly chalked, then eyed his scissors, longing to feel the blades glide through the fibers, a part of sewing she sorely missed. Perhaps cutting his fabric was once Jenny's task. And keeping his books. And straightening his shop.

When Elisabeth looked up, Michael was studying her. Rather intently, it seemed. "Chalk isna shears," he said.

She'd heard Angus utter the same proverb many times. "Just because something is begun doesn't mean it will be finished, aye?"

"Weel said." Michael held up the newly found shilling, then pressed the coin into her hand. "I've given some thocht to yer suggestion o' finding a partner."

"For the shop?"

"Aye. And for —"

"Faither." A child's voice sang out from the floor above them. The sound of little footsteps followed, bounding down the turnpike stair. A moment later a curly-haired lad appeared on the landing, wearing clothes he'd all but outgrown, though he was still small for his age. "Wha be the leddy?" he asked, a twinkle in his eye and a dimple in his cheek.

Elisabeth was instantly smitten.

"She is Mrs. Kerr from Halliwell's Close," Michael said, waving the boy forward. "And this is my son, Peter."

Elisabeth looked at them both, astounded. " 'Tis not your son," she protested, "but yourself in miniature." The blue eyes, the bright red hair, the freckled skin, the charming disposition — Peter Dalgliesh was more twin than offspring, though decidedly smaller and with at least two missing teeth. "I am pleased to make your acquaintance, young Peter."

His little brow wrinkled. "Nae, mem. My name isna 'Young.' 'Tis just 'Peter.' "

Michael ruffled his son's hair. "The leddy kens yer name, lad."

Peter's grin returned. " 'Tis mercat day," he said with glee. "Ye'll take me, Faither? Like ye said ye would?"

"Weel . . ." Michael looked round the cluttered room. "Mebbe in a wee while . . ."

"I ken." Peter groaned loudly. "Ye must wark and canna get awa."

Elisabeth's heart went out to the lad. How many times had Peter heard those words? And how hard for his busy father, being forced to say them.

Seeing the sad expressions on both their faces, she made a proposal. "I am bound for the marketplace this morn and would welcome your company, Peter. That is, if your father can spare you. For I am sure you are a great help in his shop."

"Aye," Peter trumpeted, his chest swelling. "I count the buttons."

"Ye're sure ye'll not mind, Mrs. Kerr?" Michael fished something out of his waistcoat pocket. " 'Tis a great kindness." Eyes shining with gratitude, he produced a wrinkled scrap of paper and two shillings.

"What have we here?" Elisabeth eyed the paper, then tucked it in her hanging pocket

151

with his silver coins. "A market list? I am impressed."

He shrugged. "If I dinna write it a' doon, I get hame with half o' what I went for. Jenny could carry it a' in her head, but I've nae gift for it."

"You have other gifts," Elisabeth told him.

The color in his ruddy cheeks deepened. "Ither than holding a needle, I canna think of onie just noo."

"Come now . . . Mr. Dalgliesh." She'd almost called him by his Christian name. Little wonder when she felt so comfortable in his presence. Michael was sincere and genuine and unassuming. She could only imagine how much Jenny Dalgliesh had loved this man. And could only guess what Anne's feelings were for him now.

If propriety allowed, Elisabeth would touch his hand and assure Michael that he was not only a good tailor but also a good father, that it was difficult to do both at once, that he was managing far better than most widowers, that a tidy shop was not the measure of a life well lived. But she could not say or do any of those things. She could only escort his son to market and hope the simple gesture would ease any sense of guilt or regret.

"We'll find everything on your father's list, won't we, Peter?" Elisabeth claimed the large market basket by the door, then wiggled her fingers in the lad's direction, a tacit invitation. He responded at once, fitting his small hand inside hers, artlessly stealing her heart.

"We're aff," Peter announced, tugging her toward the open door.

EIGHTEEN

Children sweeten labors.

SIR FRANCIS BACON

"This way, mem." Peter Dalgliesh pulled her toward the marketplace like a horse-drawn cart, making certain her wheels did not veer left or right. "The chapmen! The chapmen!" the boy cried, stopping at the foot of Kirk Wynd, where the peddlers had their stalls. Standing like tall, vertical tents, the portable stalls were made of wood and canvas, with pegs, hooks, and narrow shelves displaying the varied wares.

Elisabeth consulted Michael's list while his son carefully examined the wooden figures, leather balls, chapbooks, spinning tops, stone marbles, and other treasures. His father's tally included nothing of the kind; lamb shanks, dried fish, oatmeal, and cheese were scribbled on the paper but not one child's plaything.

Reluctantly she bent down and touched Peter's shoulder. "We'll buy what we must first," she told him, "and then see how many pennies are left for a toy." When he didn't argue with her, Elisabeth decided he'd heard this before, a comforting thought. "Come, let's find the meal sellers."

Selkirk, she'd learned, held its market every Friday. Local folk and strangers alike filled the marketplace, elbowing their way about, calling out greetings, and striking bargains. Elisabeth and Peter maneuvered past the souters — the pride of the town — with their handsome men's shoes done in polished leather and fine calfskin. Elisabeth dared not linger over their ladies' shoes, fashioned of worsted damask and brocaded silk in rich shades of blue, green, and brown. Someday she would own a new pair of satin slippers but not when she had one shilling to her name.

Elisabeth held on to Peter as they walked, unwilling to let him dart through the crowd, chasing after the other children. She cherished the feel of his little hand in hers, though she would never say as much and embarrass him. Was this what motherhood might feel like? This enormous sense of responsibility mingled with pride and fear and joy? A chance to see the world afresh through a child's eyes? She looked down at Peter's bright curls, then swallowed hard. How different her life would be if she'd given Donald Kerr a son or daughter.

"Here's the oatmeal!" Peter nudged her toward the tables piled with sacks of milled grain, well in view of the *tron,* where goods were weighed. "This is Mr. Watson, the miller," the lad said, then turned to her and blushed. "I dinna ken her name, Mr. Watson, but she's bonny."

Elisabeth smiled at them both, not offended that Peter had already forgotten. "I am Mrs. Kerr."

The stout miller bobbed his head. "I ken wha ye are. Miss Anne's cousin."

With others crowding round the tables, there was no time for small talk. Elisabeth attended to her shopping, buying small sacks of flour, oats, and barley. Cheese and butter were next, wrapped in cool, wet muslin.

Most of the sellers were polite, some were even kind, but Elisabeth also heard disparaging words muttered in passing and saw several countenances darken at her approach. Peter, too innocent to notice, proudly pulled her along the thoroughfare.

All through the marketplace one name rose above the din: Admiral Lord Jack Buchanan. "Sailing the high seas," a cloth merchant marveled. "Can ye imagine such a life?" A pie seller said with a note of yearning, "Onie man wha's seen the world carries it in his pocket."

Women seemed more interested in the look of the man. A dairymaid said coyly, "I hear he's *braw*," then winked at Elisabeth. "And I hear he's rich," the lass beside her purred.

Elisabeth squeezed Peter's hand and thought of his kind father. Michael Dalgliesh would never be rich. But as long as men needed shirts, breeches, and waistcoats, a tailor would also never be poor.

As to Lord Buchanan, Elisabeth suspected that the reports were too good to be true, that something unseen and unseemly lurked beneath the surface. Not all men were like Donald Kerr, she reminded herself. Not all men had secrets. But a never-married gentleman surely was hiding something, and a British admiral was to be avoided at all costs.

By the time Elisabeth and Peter had given their custom to the flesher on the far side of the tolbooth, their shillings were reduced to pennies, and the basket was growing heavy on her arm.

"Noo may I have a toy?" Peter asked, his tone plaintive, his expression more so.

She felt her pocket. Michael's money was all spent, but she had a few copper ha'pence of her own left. "See if you can find something for a penny or two."

He slipped from her grasp and dashed straight for the chapmen's stalls. By the time she caught up with him, Peter was on his knees, breathlessly examining a soft leather pouch containing a dozen marbles made of polished stones.

The black-haired chapman hovering over Peter was beaming. " 'Tis a fine set," he told the lad. "If ye have eight pence, 'tis yers."

Peter slowly put them back.

"What d'ye think o' these?" The chapman poured out a handful of inferior clay marbles from a rough linen sack. "Only four pence, lad."

This time Peter looked up at her with a hope-filled expression.

Much as she hated doing so, Elisabeth shook her head. "Not today, I'm afraid. Is there something else you want?"

Peter stood. "Nae, mem," he said in a small voice.

Aching for him, Elisabeth took his hand and started toward Kirk Wynd. "I am sorry, Peter. Maybe something could be arranged for your birthday."

He brightened at that. " 'Tis in February."

"Such a long time to wait," she said, squeezing his fingers. "My birthday is in less than a fortnight. Do you suppose we could exchange them?"

Peter was not fond of the idea. "My faither might forget to *gie* me a *praisent*."

Elisabeth was quite certain that would never happen and told Peter so as they turned down School Close.

When they walked into the shop, Michael was waiting on a customer. She quietly moved toward the stair, thinking to carry up their purchases, but Peter was his father's son and swiftly made his presence known.

"How d'ye do, Mr. Mitchelhill?" the lad exclaimed, then pointed to the man's hands, stained the same color as his chestnut brown hair. "He's a tanner."

With a wry smile, the man splayed his fingers. "I canna deny it."

Michael motioned Elisabeth closer. "Here's one o' the men ye've been sewing for, Mrs. Kerr." He patted the stack of shirts on the counter. "And a bonny seamstress ye are."

When she stepped into the candlelight, Mr. Mitchellhill did not hide his admiration. "Aye, verra bonny." He winked, then tossed two guineas on the counter and quit the shop, tipping his hat to her on the way out.

A troubled look crossed Michael's face. "He didna mean to offend ye."

"Truly, he didn't," she assured Michael, placing the market basket on the counter.

He quickly added, "What I meant was, yer sewing is bonny."

"I see." Now she was amused.

"Och!" he stammered, his skin almost matching his bright red hair. "But ye're bonny too, Mrs. Kerr. As *loosome* as they come."

"No need to explain yourself," she assured him, then lifted out her butter, flour, and barley from the basket. She turned her attention to Peter, smiling down at him. "What a fine morn we had."

He grinned back. "Aye, we did."

Elisabeth longed to touch his wee button of a nose or brush aside the loose curls from his small brow. "Shall I see you on the morrow, Peter, when I bring another shirt?"

The boy nodded with his entire body.

Michael laughed. "Weel, young Peter, ye've found a guid freen in Mrs. Kerr. Noo up the stair ye go, and take our oatmeal and such with ye."

Peter did his father's bidding without complaint, carrying the heavy basket up one stair step at a time. *Plunk,* step. *Plunk,* step.

Only when he disappeared from sight could Elisabeth finally tear her gaze away from the child and turn to his father. "He is the dearest of lads." Her throat tightened round the words. "Thank you for sharing him with me."

Michael shrugged, his heightened color having eased. "Feel free to borrow Peter whenever it suits ye. 'Tis guid for him to be . . . , weel, to spend time . . ."

"With a woman," she finished for him. When Michael nodded, she thought to spare him any further embarrassment and so eased toward the door. "Speaking of women, my mother-in-law will be wondering what's kept me so long."

Michael's exaggerated frown was worthy of the stage. "Must ye leave so soon?"

"I am behind on my sewing," she reminded

him, "and you have work to do."

"Aye, aye," he said, sending her on her way.

When she stepped into School Close, Elisabeth decided to plant her ha'pence in Mrs. Thorburn's garden. She hastened across Kirk Wynd and entered the narrow passageway between the manse and Mrs. Thorburn's house. When she reached the kitchen garden in the rear, Elisabeth chose a small head of cabbage, some ripe lettuce, and a few stems of sage, then laid her coins on the ground. Carefully balancing everything, she gathered up her market fare and started for home, her arms full but her pockets empty.

The joy of her outing with Peter had begun to fade into a sobering reality. She could not hope to provide sufficient food for their household on a few shillings a week. Nor could she add to her earnings by laboring with Michael in his shop, much as he needed her help. A widower and a young widow alone for hours at a time? The gossips would never cease their blethering.

Earlier that morning Michael Dalgliesh had hinted at finding a partner. Elisabeth glanced at the heavens. *Does he mean a tailor, Lord? Or does he mean a wife?*

She tripped over a large stone propped against the outer wall of the house, losing her footing for a moment. Righting herself, she wriggled her toe to be sure it wasn't broken, then shook her head. *Mind your step, Bess.*

However trustworthy the tailor might seem, and however dear his son, she could not — nae, would not — risk her heart again. Especially if she might break Anne's heart in the bargain.

NINETEEN

Poverty is the test of civility and the
touchstone of friendship.

WILLIAM HAZLITT

"We've rain on the way." Marjory glanced at
the windows, noting the thick clouds loom-
ing over the empty marketplace on a cool
Saturday morning. "The sooner you're out
the door, Gibson, the better."

"Aye, mem."

He stood patiently while she brushed the
lint from his clothes, borrowed from their
neighbor, Mr. Tait. Though the sleeves were
too short and the breeches too snug, Gibson
certainly looked more presentable than when
he'd arrived on Thursday.

Two nights' sleep had brightened his eyes,
and meat and ale had softened the sharp
contours of his face. A fresh shave with a
razor provided by their landlord and neighbor, Walter Halliwell, had also done wonders.
"Should ye be wanting a periwig, ye ken

whaur to find me," the wigmaker had said affably. Gibson had never worn a wig in his life, but Marjory had thanked Mr. Halliwell nonetheless.

At his own insistence Gibson had slept each night rolled up in a plaid, his body pressed against the bottom seam of the door. "To keep ye safe," he'd said. Gibson was still worried about the British dragoons, especially after Marjory had described their unfortunate encounter on the road to Selkirk. "Bess and I put them in their place," she'd assured him, trying not to sound *too* prideful.

Smoothing the brush along his sleeve, Marjory reminded him, "I sent a note ahead to Reverend Brown, who'll be expecting you at noon. Apprise him of your loyalty to the Kerr family —"

"Aye, mem. I ken what must be said." Gibson's voice was gentle but firm. "Whan Reverend Brown came to the pulpit in 'twenty-six, I'd already been a member o' the kirk for forty years. I've nae fear o' the man, Leddy Kerr."

His confidence pleased her. "I'm beginning to think you're not afraid of anything."

" 'Tis not true." He looked at her askance. "I've a healthy fear o' ye."

Marjory shook her head, certain he did not mean it. "You have my written character, should the reverend need it. Though I fear my name no longer carries much weight."

Anne, bent over her lace work, lifted her head. "*Kerr* will always command respect in the Borderland."

"She's *richt*," Gibson agreed. "Ye can a' be proud o' bearing that name."

Sewing in hand, Elisabeth eyed him. "How handsome you look, Gibson."

He scuffed his foot against the floor, a school lad again. "Weel, as my *mither* aye said, 'At least ye're clean.' "

Elisabeth nodded absently, then returned to her work. After sewing all Friday afternoon and eve, she'd picked up her needle again at dawn, barely stopping for tea and a bannock. Marjory appreciated her diligence, though she hated to see her daughter-in-law working so hard.

"I'm aff," Gibson announced, his posture as straight as a man of thirty years, his head held high.

Marjory opened the door for him — a fitting irony, she thought — and sent him on his way with spoken good wishes and a silent prayer. *With favour wilt thou compass him.* If the minister employed him, the Kerr women might still enjoy his company on occasion. But if Gibson ended up in service at one of the country estates, they would meet only on the Sabbath, if then. Marjory was surprised to find the notion did not sit well with her. Not at all, in fact.

As his footsteps faded down the stair, she

turned to her dinner preparations: fresh brown trout, cooked in butter with sweet herbs. "We're back to broth on the morrow," she warned the other women, "for we cannot make a habit of dining so richly."

"Aye, Mother," Anne chided her.

Elisabeth did not say a word.

Watching her daughter-in-law's needle move in and out of the fabric in a steady rhythm, Marjory vowed never to take Elisabeth's hard-earned shillings for granted. Work easily found could just as easily be lost. Anything might happen. Had they not learned that lesson well in Edinburgh?

She quickly chopped an onion and some herbs, then smeared the pan with butter, leaving the fish off the fire until Gibson returned. Flour from the market meant a rare treat — wheaten bread — which was already rising beside the hearth, made according to Elisabeth's instructions.

Marjory scrubbed her hands at the washbowl, then went looking for Gibson's livery, rolled and stored in his leather traveling bag. He would need his servant garb again soon; she was sure of it.

"Annie," she asked, holding up his badly wrinkled black coat. "Might I use your iron?"

Her cousin's eyebrows shot up. "You'll not mind if I invite the neighbors? For I believe they'd each pay a ha'penny to see Lady Kerr press a servant's coat."

"We could certainly use the money," Marjory said dryly.

"Let me attend to this, Cousin." Anne placed several linen cloths across the dining table, then claimed the flatiron from the trivet by the coal fire. "He must have cleaned his garments before he left," she said, flicking a few drops of water on the broadcloth, then pressing firmly. "Not a spot on them."

"That's Gibson for you," Marjory said fondly. "Always presentable." She shook out his waistcoat, both embarrassed and intrigued to be handling his personal attire, which bore his unique scent; like pepper, she decided, warm and pungent. She'd purchased this livery more than a twelvemonth ago, the usual arrangement with a maid or manservant. Wages were paid at Martinmas and Whitsun, and a new gown or suit of clothing was provided each year.

Anne held up the ironed coat with a satisfied look, then draped it round the wooden chair while the fabric cooled and took the waistcoat from Marjory's hands. "What have we here?" She pinched a round lump between the wool broadcloth and the muslin lining, then smiled. "Shillings, I'll warrant. Sewn in place for safekeeping. Clever man, spreading them out so they wouldn't jingle." Anne ironed round the coins, then pressed his shirt and breeches as well while Marjory did her small part, sprinkling water ahead of the hot iron.

Anne was hanging his finished shirt over a chair when Gibson bounded through the doorway, his face brighter than any candle. "Leddies, ye have afore ye Reverend Brown's new manservant."

"Oh!" Marjory clapped her hands together. "You'll be close to us, then."

"Aye," he agreed, smiling at her, "verra close."

Anne seemed less elated. "The reverend is not known for his generosity," she grumbled. "You might have worked for Lord Jack Buchanan. Once he is in residence, the admiral could surely use a man of your skills, and the wages he'll offer might be more to your liking."

Gibson shook his head. "Reverend Brown suits me verra weel." He started to say something else, then stopped, and glanced toward the hearth. " 'Tis some fine trout ye have in yer pan, Leddy Kerr."

Within the half hour the four of them were gathered round the table, dining on herb-seasoned fish and freshly baked bread. Marjory was secretly amazed at the easy camaraderie among them, despite their marked differences. A Highland weaver's daughter, a *stayed lass* with no prospects, a veteran manservant, and a widow of gentle birth. In no other household would such people sit at the same table and share the same food as if they were truly equal.

But were they not? She'd read the Scripture the whole of her life: *There is neither bond nor free, there is neither male nor female: for ye are all one in Christ Jesus.* Only now, seeing that truth lived out, did she understand. If such equality made her slightly uncomfortable, so be it. At the moment she was glad to have food on her plate and friends by her side.

"When will your service for Reverend Brown begin?" Elisabeth asked him.

"This verra day. Aye, this verra hour." Gibson stood and reached for his clothes on the chair. "I see that a kind soul has pressed my livery."

"Annie did," Marjory was quick to say, "for I've no talent with an iron."

"Ye're a woman o' monie talents, Leddy Kerr." He gazed down at her. "Ye made me walcome and fed me guid meals. Ye brushed my clothes and wrote a fine character. What leddy would have done *ha'* so much for her ain lord, let alone a manservant?"

Taken aback by his praise, Marjory murmured, " 'Twas nothing, Gibson."

His expression said otherwise. "Leddies, if ye'll not mind, 'tis time I dressed for wark." Seeking privacy, he took his livery round the partition, while the women remained at table, speaking of the weather and the Sabbath to come.

Elisabeth sewed as they chatted, soon finishing another shirt. She held it up, examining it with a practiced eye. " 'Twill do," she finally decided, carefully folding the cambric. "Since the rain has eased, I'll take this straight to Mr. Dalgliesh."

"How is Michael these days?" Anne asked. Her tone was nonchalant yet her eyes attentive.

Elisabeth did not look at her, merely answered, "The same as ever, I imagine."

Marjory eyed them both, trying to sort out what was being said. And not said.

Her daughter-in-law was already donning her cape. "I'll not be long," Elisabeth promised and was gone.

Gibson appeared a moment later, looking dapper in his livery, borrowed clothes in hand. "I'll return these to Mr. Tait on my way."

Anne reached for their second loaf of bread, untouched, and dusted off the flour. "Give him this with our thanks," she told Gibson.

"Weel done, mem," he said, bobbing his head.

Marjory's mind was still fixed on Elisabeth. Naturally, her daughter-in-law was still mourning Donald; she was hardly alone in that. But something else seemed to occupy her thoughts of late.

"Our Bess will celebrate her birthday in less than a fortnight," Marjory informed the others, her thoughts turning at a brisk pace. "She will be five-and-twenty. A quarter of a century, if you will."

"So young," Gibson murmured.

"Aye, but not to her," Anne said. "I well remember that birthday, and 'twas not pleasant."

"Suppose we make it a fine day for Bess," Marjory suggested, hoping to cheer her daughter-in-law. "Unfortunately, I've no money of my own and nothing left to sell. If we mean to buy her a present, we'll have to spend her own shillings, which is hardly fair."

"Wait." Anne dove behind the curtains of her bed, then reappeared with a small wooden box. "My jewelry, such as it is." She lifted the lid, revealing her small collection. A single strand of pearls, badly stained. A ribbon choker. A bracelet meant for a child. A small ivory brooch. A pair of earrings made of amber. But what she lifted out was a dainty silver comb that needed only polishing to be as good as new.

"It belonged to my mother." Anne held it in her palm, a wistful expression on her face. "My hair is so pale the comb disappears when I wear it. But in Bess's dark hair . . ."

"It would be lovely," Marjory agreed. "Still, Annie, a great sacrifice."

Anne pointed to the half-dozen books on

her shelf. "Those were my mother's too and are far more dear to me."

Gibson lifted the comb from Anne's open palm. "I ken a silversmith wha can make it shine." He slipped it inside his waistcoat pocket. "If 'twould not be too bold, I'd like to make the young Leddy Kerr a praisent. I've an auld freen in Selkirk, a carpenter wha has a few scraps o' wood he might part with."

Marjory knew at once what would delight Elisabeth most. "Could you fashion a tambour frame for her embroidery? The dragoons broke her mahogany tambour into pieces and tossed it into the fire."

"Weel I remember," Gibson said darkly. "But, aye, 'tis a guid plan."

At a loss for what she might contribute, Marjory scanned the room, hoping for inspiration. Her gaze landed on the hearth and the remnants of their dinner. "I suppose I could cook something for her, though it is hardly a gift —"

"On the contrary," Anne said, her eyes alight. " 'Twill be the perfect gift, if you'll not mind cooking for . . . say, three dozen friends and neighbors."

"Three dozen? However could we afford the food?" Marjory asked.

Gibson smiled and produced four shillings. " 'Tis the balance o' my wages for this term. Ye paid me yerself, Leddy Kerr, on the eleventh o' November."

Marjory stared at the coins, barely recalling their last Martinmas in Edinburgh. "But that's your silver. Newly snipped from the lining of your waistcoat, I'll wager."

"I've nae need o' them." He pressed the shillings into her hand. "Reverend Brown will see to my meat and drink."

Marjory blinked back tears as Gibson folded her fingers round the silver, then wrapped his hands round hers. Though his fingers were callused, they were warm. So very warm.

He winked at her. "Noo ye can have a *foy* worthy o' the lass wha brought ye hame."

TWENTY

A birthday: — and now a day that rose
With much of hope, with meaning rife —
A thoughtful day from dawn to close.

JEAN INGELOW

"You are certain of this, Peter?" Elisabeth eyed his scuffed brown shoes, which looked rather too tight, then pulled the door shut behind her. " 'Tis a long walk to Bell Hill."

"Not for me," Peter said, towing her along Halliwell's Close, his little hand tightly grasping her fingers. "Besides, my faither willna mind if we're *gane* for a lang time."

"I'll not mind either," she confessed, matching his short but determined stride. She'd been working in the house all day without a word from Marjory or Anne about her birthday. A gift was not expected — who could afford even the smallest token? — but she'd have welcomed their good wishes. Perhaps they'd forgotten. Or perhaps they were being kind, knowing how she dreaded turning five-

and-twenty.

Now that the momentous day had arrived, Elisabeth was relieved to discover she felt no different. A stroll with Peter Dalgliesh was just the thing, with no need of a walking stick to keep her balance or spectacles to find her way. At least not this year.

When they emerged into the marketplace, her mood lifted even higher. After days of endless rain and mist, fine weather had returned to the Borderland. The mid-May sky was a brilliant gentian blue, and the late afternoon sun shone like heated gold, warming their shoulders. "What a splendid day!" she exclaimed, squeezing Peter's hand.

"Aye, mem," he said, a mischievous twinkle in his eye.

Michael had sent Peter round to the house with a scribbled note, now folded in her pocket. *Must finish gentleman's coat. Peter underfoot. Are you free?* She could hardly refuse the tailor's request, especially when delivered by a freckle-faced boy with a winsome smile.

In the last fortnight she'd sewn a dozen shirts for his father's shop and earned a dozen shillings, all spent on meat and meal. Stocking the household larder had eased some of her lingering fears. No dragoons had come pounding at their door, nor had the Sheriff of Selkirk had occasion to call. With Gibson serving at the nearby manse, Marjory busy cooking at the hearth, and Anne teaching her lace making students, their lives had settled into a comfortable pattern.

Only her encounters with Michael Dalgliesh left her shaking her head.

Whenever she delivered another finished shirt, Michael found some reason to detain her. Might she cut his newly chalked fabric? Did she have time to read Peter a story? Could she find buttons to match a blue waistcoat? Elisabeth did not mind, of course, but she did wonder. Was it her heart Michael was after? Or did he simply need a willing pair of hands?

Enough, Bess. No use fretting with a handsome lad by her side and a peaceful hour ahead.

She and Peter passed the kirk and were nearing the first rise on the hilly road leading southeast from town when he pointed a stubby finger to the right. "That's whaur Selkirk Castle stood," Peter told her, "by the Haining Loch."

Though Elisabeth craned her head, she could spot no trace of it. "It must be so old it's in ruins."

"Ye're verra auld," Peter reminded her, "and ye're not in ruins."

"But I *am* five-and-twenty," she told him, still getting used to the sound of it.

They paused at the top of the *knowe* and took in the verdant hills surrounding Selkirk like the soft folds of a green velvet gown. "Beautiful," Elisabeth said on a sigh as a gentle breeze, fragrant with spring, stirred the air.

Peter tugged on her hand. "Wait 'til ye see Bell Hill."

When the road began its steep descent, Elisabeth impulsively challenged Peter to a race, flying downhill past rows of cottages, her long legs quickly outpacing his. She eased up by intent, letting him rush past her at the bottom. "You're too fast for me," she called out, stopping to catch her breath.

He turned round to wait. "Ye slowed doon," he said, as forthright and honest as his father. "Should a leddy run like that?"

"Probably not," she admitted, then took his hand once more as they approached the Foul Bridge Port. After walking through the town gate, they crossed the watery ditch, swollen from the rain, and left Selkirk proper behind. All the while Peter's question prodded at her. Was she a lady? Or a seamstress? On this momentous day she might be anything. Elisabeth smiled down at her charge. "We could pretend I am your governess."

He looked up, hope in his eyes. "Or my mither."

The word brought her to a stop. *Mother.* Was this Peter's idea? Or was it . . .

Nae. Michael Dalgliesh was her employer, nothing more.

"You must miss your mother very much," she finally said, touching Peter's cheek, wishing instead she might bend down and gather the boy in her arms.

"Aye." He gnawed on his lip. "I dinna remember her like my faither does."

"Then his memories must serve for both of you, aye?"

Peter merely nodded.

The road grew wider as they climbed, then broadened on either side into meadows blanketed in wildflowers. Elisabeth tarried along the edge of the road, kneeling now and again to show Peter the deep blue speedwell petals, the feathery-leaved yarrow, the sunny yellow primrose.

But the lad was interested in one thing. "Bell Hill!" he cried, pointing ahead. Amid the rolling landscape rose an impressive mound, dotted with sheep. A carriage road turned south toward Hawick, but they took the narrow track that continued straight, climbing past the South Common, where the townsfolk grew their oats, barley, and hay.

With each step upward, Elisabeth felt younger, less encumbered. She sensed her skin growing warmer from the effort and drank in the rain-washed air, feeling light-headed, almost intoxicated.

Near the crest of the hill, Peter tugged on her skirt. "Turn round, Mrs. Kerr."

When she did, all of Selkirkshire lay before

her, a sweeping landscape of fertile pastures and fields nestled against the misty blue hills. "Imagine having such a view," she breathed.

Peter grinned. "Ye'd have to live o'er there." He climbed onto a large boulder by the road, then pointed at the grand house across the way, situated in a handsome park on top of the rise.

Elisabeth stood beside him, eying Bell Hill and the estate that bore its name. The Scotch pines were an impressive size. An old property, then, with the mansion well hidden behind the trees. She caught a few glimpses of gray whinstone walls, of windows dressed in red sandstone, of gardens and orchards stretched behind the house. For a moment she thought she saw a gentleman on horseback trotting round the corner of the mansion, though he might have been a groom exercising the admiral's horses.

The faint sound of the kirk bell ringing in the distance sent Peter scrambling to the ground. "Time to go, Mrs. Kerr!" He grabbed her hand and abruptly took off down the hill.

She nearly tripped trying to keep up with him. "So soon? Surely it isn't time for your evening meal." Elisabeth thought Michael and Peter supped later, not at six o' the clock.

"Come on!" Peter cried, already breathless from dragging her along. "Faither said I was to start doon the hill whan the kirk bell rang."

On the fourteenth of May, when the gloaming stretched past nine o' the clock, there was no need to hurry. Yet Peter seemed most determined. Elisabeth let him escort her to town posthaste, vowing to climb Bell Hill again as soon as ever she could.

When they finally reached School Close, she started to turn left, but Peter shook his head. "Nae, I'm to take ye hame."

She smiled, realizing Michael must be teaching his son proper etiquette. "May I take your arm, then, as a lady should?" Tall as she was, this was no easy feat. Elisabeth bent forward, her hand circling the upper part of his arm, and tried to walk naturally. "Well done, Master Dalgliesh," she said when they entered Halliwell's Close.

The last thing Elisabeth expected when she pushed open the door was to find their stair lined with people. "What has happened?" she cried, fearing the worst.

Then she saw Marjory beaming at her from the top landing.

And their neighbors welcoming her.

And Mr. Tait lifting his cup of cheer. " 'Tis the leddy with the birthday!"

Twenty-One

My birthday! — what a different sound
That word had in my youthful ears.

THOMAS MOORE

Overwhelmed, Elisabeth picked her way up the steps, aiming for Marjory. "You . . . remembered."

Marjory reached for her hands, then pulled her into a tight embrace. "After all you've done for us, dear Bess, how could we forget?" She released her with a tender squeeze, then guided her into the house while Peter darted round them, no doubt looking for his father.

The house was even more crowded than the stair. A cup of punch was pressed into her hands, then Elisabeth was led to the dining table, laden with savory pigeon pies, oat puddings, apple tarts, and plum cakes. "Marjory, how did you manage this?"

Her mother-in-law swept her hand above the serving plates with a flourish. "Annie helped, of course. Whenever you quit the house for an hour or two, we baked something at Mrs. Tait's hearth and stored it in her larder."

"So I see." Elisabeth shook her head, both delighted and dismayed. "But the cost —"

"Wheesht!" Anne scolded her, touching her index finger to her lips. "You have Gibson to thank for that."

Only then did Elisabeth see their old friend standing by the hearth. When she signaled him, Gibson bowed his way past the throng and joined her beside the table. "How may I serve ye, Leddy Kerr?" he asked, a gleam in his eye.

"It seems you've already served me." Elisabeth kissed his cheek, making him blush. "Thank you, Gibson."

His shrug was gallant. "A leddy celebrates her first quarter century but once."

By the snippets of conversation she heard, her age was barely a topic of discussion. Instead, fresh rumors concerning the admiral were on the tips of their tongues. What day would he reach Selkirk? By carriage or astride? With an entourage or alone? Wearing an admiral's uniform or a riding habit?

Elisabeth found their wild speculations amusing. "Our neighbors have come not to toast my birthday but to deal in gossip," she said, shaking her head before drawing her loved ones closer. "As for you three, I know better. You have done this to bless me, and indeed you have."

Gibson raised his eyebrows. " 'Tis not *ower* yet."

"Aye," Anne agreed, her pale face glowing, "there are presents to be opened."

"We shall save those for later," Marjory insisted, "when our neighbors have gone home to their suppers. Come, Bess, and welcome your guests."

Elisabeth wove through the crowd of well-wishers, greeting each one. Though she could not recite all their names by heart, she knew their faces and was beginning to put husband with wife, mother with child, sweetheart with sweetheart.

At last she spied Michael Dalgliesh standing by the window, holding court. Several young women were circled round him, laughing as he told one of his colorful tales. "Glad tidings to ye, Mrs. Kerr," he said when he caught sight of her, then lifted his cup. His expression was positively smug.

By the time Elisabeth reached him, she had Michael all to herself, the others having momentarily deserted him for the punch bowl.

"I suppose your task was to keep me away from the house," she began, trying unsuccessfully to sound miffed. "What of that gentleman's coat you needed to finish?"

He laughed. " 'Tis done. Tell me, did ye have a bonny afternoon with my lad?"

"I certainly did." Elisabeth looked across the room at Peter, who'd apparently visited the plates of sweets more than once and was now covered in sugary crumbs.

"Faither!" Peter cried, dragging Anne in their direction. "Here's a sweetie for ye."

Michael looked up just as a blushing Anne thrust a small tart into his hands. "Verra kind o' ye, Miss Kerr," he said, then popped the apple tart into his mouth without ceremony.

Anne seemed intent on studying her shoes. "It was Peter's idea," she murmured.

"I've nae doubt." Michael tugged on his son's ear. "Can ye find me anither, lad?"

The moment Peter took off, Michael apologized to Anne in a low voice. "Dinna *fash* yerself, lass. We've been freens a' *oor* lives, have we not? If ye bring me a sweetie, none will think ill o' ye."

When Anne slowly raised her head, Elisabeth saw something travel between them as quick as a flash of lightning in the summer sky. *We attended school together.* It seemed a great deal more had been left unsaid.

Elisabeth stepped back, feeling like an intruder.

When Peter dashed past her, tart in hand, she sought an empty chair, needing a moment to recover. The heat of the room, she told herself. The press of bodies. The noisy chatter.

Gibson appeared a moment later, bearing a

steaming cup of tea. "Drink up, Leddy Kerr, for ye have a *dwiny* leuk about ye."

Elisabeth murmured her thanks, then quickly lifted the wooden cup to her lips, consoling herself with the knowledge that she'd not lost her heart. To Peter, perhaps, but not to Michael.

She managed to compose her features by the time Gibson brought Marjory and Anne to her side. "Oor birthday leddy has had enough merriment," Gibson told them. " 'Tis time for folk to find their way hame."

All three women sat round the table and watched Gibson herd their neighbors out the door with efficiency and decorum. "Here's a wee pie to take with ye," he said to one man, nudging him forward, and, "Mind the stair as ye go," he cautioned another.

An hour later candles were lit to dispel the evening gloom, and the house was quiet again, with only the Kerr women and Gibson remaining. Michael had been the last to leave, tarrying at the door, sending folk off with a jovial word or a hearty slap on the shoulder, while Peter drooped about his father's knees, ready for his supper and a warm bed. Finally Michael carried him off, bidding the Kerrs a good night.

Elisabeth did not follow them with her gaze nor let her thoughts dwell on wee Peter. The lad needed a mother, aye, yet it seemed the Lord had another woman in mind. If 'twas

Anne, was that not the best of outcomes?

"Time for yer praisents," Gibson said, grinning as he rubbed his hands together.

Determined to enjoy the balance of her birthday celebration, Elisabeth sat in the upholstered chair where she slept each night, accustomed to its contours and the feel of the fabric against her cheek. Whenever Marjory or Anne suggested they find some other solution — a mattress made of blankets or a cot borrowed from a neighbor — Elisabeth had assured them she slept soundly.

She looked at her small circle of loved ones and confessed, "I'll not be happy if you've spent any of your precious pennies on me."

"Have no fear on that account." Anne held out two ladylike fists. "Choose wisely, for only one holds a present."

Elisabeth eyed one, then the other, looking for a clue. "What happens if I choose poorly?"

"Then I get to keep my gift," Anne said, sounding as if she meant it.

"Your hospitality is gift enough," Elisabeth protested, then was astounded when Anne opened her hand. "Cousin! You cannot give me such a treasure."

" 'Tis done." Anne held out the silver comb, gleaming in the candlelight, then tucked it into Elisabeth's crown of hair with a satisfied nod. "Just as I'd pictured it."

Elisabeth touched the comb in awe. "Oh, Annie. To think you would part with such an heirloom." When their gazes met, Elisabeth prayed her cousin might see what could not be said. *Have no fear of me, dear Annie. You are the wife Michael wants and the mother Peter needs.*

Then she noticed Gibson carrying something across the room, hidden beneath their cousin's woolen shawl.

"This praisent is from me," Gibson said proudly.

"Is it a table?" Elisabeth wondered aloud. He'd not concealed the wooden legs or the crosspiece between them, but she still wasn't certain what it might be. When he lifted the shawl, she gasped with joy. "A tambour! Gibson, wherever did you find it?"

Enthralled, she ran her hands round the double hoop that held the fabric in place and admired the plain but serviceable legs that positioned the hoop at the perfect height. The tambour Donald had purchased for her soon after they married was fashioned of mahogany, richly polished, and ornately carved. This one was made of sturdy oak along simpler lines but a fine tambour nonetheless. She inched it closer, resting her feet on the crosspiece, already imagining what she might embroider first. "Did you find it at Friday's market?"

Gibson confessed, "I made it myself, mem. With scraps from the carpenter."

Trapped in her chair by the tambour frame,

Elisabeth could not leap to her feet and embrace Gibson, but she could pull him down for a peck on the cheek. "Whatever did I do to merit such blessings?"

"Birthdays are like the good Lord's mercy," Marjory told her. "Undeserved yet always celebrated." She reached for her apron, her gaze narrowing as she regarded their house, now in shambles. "We've work to do before supper and bed. And Gibson has brought news from the manse."

He bowed. "The honor is yers, Leddy Kerr."

Marjory struck an aristocratic pose. "Admiral Lord Jack Buchanan is already in Selkirk."

"Ah!" Anne sat up straighter. "I knew it."

"He arrived this morn," Marjory told them, "and has taken up residence at Bell Hill with a handful of servants who traveled with him from London."

"He's at Bell Hill?" Elisabeth's eyes widened. "Then . . . I saw him."

Twenty-Two

If it were not for a goodly supply of rumors,
half true and half false, what would the
gossips do?

THOMAS CHANDLER HALIBURTON

Every eye in the sanctuary was trained on the open door, and every parishioner uttered yet another conjecture. Marjory tried not to turn round in the pew, tried not to listen to their whispering, but it was hard since the admiral had been in Selkirkshire for several days and had yet to make an appearance. Surely Lord Buchanan would ride down from Bell Hill and show himself on the Sabbath.

Katherine Shaw and her four pretty daughters were seated behind the Kerrs, spinning yarns as though they were seated at a treadle wheel. "He's niver taken a wife," Mrs. Shaw was telling her girls, all of a marriageable age.

"Nae wonder," her oldest said softly. "He doesna set foot on land for years at a time. What sort o' husband would a gentleman like that make?"

"A rich one!" the youngest squealed.

"I do hope he'll tarry in Selkirk," one of the middle daughters said with a sigh.

"He's forty years auld," Mrs. Shaw reminded them. "Nae man would buy so fine a hoose and not live there. Mark my wirds, he means to settle doon and start a family." At which the young women all giggled, drawing stares from those round them.

Marjory held her tongue, but she could not still her thoughts. The admiral would hardly marry one of the Shaw girls, however charming their smiles or beguiling their figures. Not when he might choose a lady of high standing from anywhere in the world. Had Lord Buchanan not circled the globe aboard the *Centurion*? Such a man would want a woman with a title of her own and a dowry to match. If and when this wealthy admiral took a wife, he'd not look for her in the wynds and closes of Selkirk.

"Why is Mr. Armstrong not attending to the gathering psalm?" Anne murmured. At the moment the precentor stood near the pulpit counting heads, a satisfied expression on his wizened face. A kirk filled to the rafters boded well for the collection plate.

When Reverend Brown came down the center aisle, all whispering ceased as folk prepared for the start of the service. Gibson trailed a few steps behind his master, pausing at the Kerr pew long enough to exchange a brief nod with Marjory before claiming his seat in the front, where he might serve the reverend at a moment's notice.

Noting his squared shoulders and lifted chin, Marjory could not keep from smiling. Never mind the good admiral; *here* was a man who should have married. More than once Marjory had wondered if Gibson and Helen Edgar might have made each other happy. But though their exchanges were friendly while in her employ in Edinburgh, no true spark had struck between them.

Mr. Armstrong stepped before the Psalter, eying the congregation over his spectacles. When the precentor began to sing the metrical psalm chosen for this morning, Marjory's smile broadened. Admiral Lord Jack Buchanan was not only anticipated; he was expected.

The earth belongs unto the Lord,
and all that it contains;
The world that is inhabited,
and all that there remains.

Who else, other than the Almighty himself, would the precentor have in mind, singing of all the world and all the earth? Marjory considered the psalm a fitting welcome for Selkirk's newest resident. The parishioners must have thought so too, for they sang the next stanza with unaccustomed zeal.

> For the foundations thereof
> he on the seas did lay,
> And he hath it established
> upon the floods to stay.

Marjory almost laughed aloud. The seas and the floods? Why, the admiral might wash through the door any moment! For the next few weeks, she imagined he would sit in the front pew near the pulpit until a proper loft could be built for him. Perhaps in the upper right corner, above the Kerr pew. She would not object to worshiping beneath his shadow.

Eight stanzas later they still had no sign of the man, but Marjory would not give up hope so easily. She continued to sing, stealing glances up and down the pews to see if anyone had spotted an unfamiliar face. Though most parish churches closed their doors once services began, the dim sanctuary in Selkirk, with its narrow, crumbling window openings, needed every bit of light the sky had to offer. Indeed, the admiral could slip through the gaping entrance without a sound.

> Ye gates, lift up your heads, ye doors,
> Doors that do last for aye,
> Be lifted up, that so the King
> Of glory enter may.

A final stanza and their singing ended, the

last notes hanging in the air like dust motes.

When Reverend Brown ascended the pulpit, his gaze scanned the crowded sanctuary — looking for Lord Buchanan, Marjory was certain of it — before the minister began his sermon drawn from Isaiah. "Thus saith the LORD, thy redeemer," he charged them, "I am the LORD that maketh all things." She nodded in approval. If the admiral was a godly man, he would find much to his liking in the parish kirk this day.

Marjory settled against her seat, grateful the floor had been swept and the pew scrubbed. *God bless you, Gibson.* Other pews had been tidied as well, whether by Gibson's own hand or because of his good example. But the sagging walls needed more than a good cleaning. Perhaps the admiral might contribute some of his vast fortune toward the sanctuary's upkeep.

Unless he hoards his gold, as you once did.

Marjory bowed her head, knowing it was true. She'd been blessed with wealth in Edinburgh yet had spared little for their parish kirk beyond the rent for her pew. And here was Elisabeth, who earned only a few shillings a week, quietly slipping one of her silver coins in the collection plate each Sabbath, far more than Reverend Brown would ask of his flock.

The sermon ended as the kirk bell tolled the noon hour. After the closing psalm and the benediction, Marjory stood, a bit stiff from sitting, then turned to survey the congregation.

"I've never seen the kirk so full," Anne confided to her.

Marjory nodded, narrowing her eyes to improve her vision. "Who is that dark-haired man in the back? The one already bound for the door?"

" 'Tis the admiral," Elisabeth said softly. "At least I think so. On my birthday I caught a glimpse of him on horseback."

Marjory did not doubt the man's identity. Heads were turning, and latecomers seated near the entrance were hurrying out of doors. The Kerrs followed them, moving down the aisle with purpose rather than standing about as they had on Sundays past.

Whispered questions quickly escalated into shouts.

"Did ye see the man?"

"Are ye sure 'twas him?"

"Och! Whatsomever did he leuk like?"

By the time Marjory and the others reached the kirkyard, there was no sign of the stranger who'd slipped from their midst. Folk tarried round the gravestones, waiting for more news now that idle rumors had become fact.

"The admiral rode aff on a bonny gray horse," James Mitchelhill was telling them, pointing east.

"How d'ye ken 'twas him?" Robert Watson

demanded to know.

The tanner grinned. "I called *oot* to him, 'Guid day to ye, Lord Buchanan,' and he lifted his hand."

On the heels of Mr. Mitchelhill's report, another chorus of voices filled the air.

"Then it *was* his lordship!"

"Mounted on a gray horse, ye say?"

"I wonder how monie ithers he has in his stables."

Marjory exchanged glances with Elisabeth and Anne, wishing she might read their thoughts. Anne had no reason to fear their new neighbor, but her Jacobite daughter-in-law certainly did. Marjory took them both by the arm, meaning to steer them down the pend toward home, when Elspeth Cranston asked the question foremost in Marjory's mind.

"When will we have the pleasure of meeting his lordship?"

Reverend Brown spoke up from the threshold. "I can answer that."

At once the gathering of parishioners turned toward the doorway, seeking a trustworthy voice amid the uncertain clamor.

"I spoke with the admiral earlier this week," the minister informed them. "Lord Buchanan will be meeting many of you soon enough." He paused, either for effect or to be sure they were listening. "The admiral plans to engage the balance of his household staff a week from the morrow on Whitsun Monday. Nearly two dozen experienced hands will be required."

There was no controlling the crowd now. Cries of glee rang out across the grassy hillside, and maidservants hugged one another.

Marjory well remembered Whitsun Monday at Tweedsford. Servants, gardeners, shepherds, and field workers were hired to labor through the summer and harvest seasons, with their wages to be paid at Martinmas. For those in need of employment, a wealthy newcomer with a large property was cause for celebration.

Out of the corner of her eye, Marjory noticed Tibbie Cranshaw starting toward her. She turned to greet her old maidservant, hoping to make amends. All she had to offer the woman was a heartfelt apology, but she would do so gladly if Tibbie would receive it.

When she drew near, Marjory met her with a smile. "A blessed Sabbath to you."

"Weel, aren't ye the *gracie* one?" Tibbie said, her words laced with sarcasm.

Chagrined, Marjory stepped away from the others so the two might speak privately. "I'm afraid I owe you an apology, Tibbie —"

"Nae!" The woman's green eyes flared. "Ye owe me a great deal mair than that. Ye owe me a guid position." Tibbie nodded toward Bell Hill in the distance. "I've a mind to seek wark there on Monday next. Gie me a written character, and I'll not tell his lordship what sort o' person ye are."

Marjory looked at her, appalled. Was Tibbie making an idle threat? Or would she present herself to the admiral and fill his ear with tales of a heartless former employer who later turned her back on the king? Such accusations would destroy any hope of the Kerrs enjoying the admiral's company and might well bring the dragoons to their door.

"I will do as you ask," Marjory agreed, knowing she had little choice. "You were a fine kitchen maid, Tibbie. 'Twill not grieve me to say so in writing."

Tibbie stepped closer, her words low but sharp edged. "And ye'll make nae mention of the babe?"

"Certainly not," Marjory promised. "Mr. Laidlaw was far more to blame than you in that unfortunate situation."

Tibbie shrank back, her eyes narrowing. "Wha told ye that?"

Marjory had no intention of drawing Anne into their conversation. "What matters, Tibbie, is that you find a position in a household where you'll neither be tempted nor mistreated. Isn't that so?"

Tibbie's features softened a bit. "Aye."

"Then I'll have a letter for you on the Sabbath next," Marjory assured her, after which Tibbie abruptly turned and disappeared into the crowd, her soiled gown dragging across the grass.

Marjory was still watching her departure when Anne moved closer, a frown on her face. "Whatever did she want?"

Marjory hesitated, wondering what her cousin might say to their agreement. "She requested a written character," was all Marjory told her. It was an honest answer without raising Anne's hackles.

"Tibbie wants to work at Bell Hill," her cousin guessed.

Marjory admitted to that much.

"She'll not get through the door without a clean gown and God's mercy," Anne said, then moved toward the pend, waving to Elisabeth to join them. "At least we'll not be among the throng walking up Bell Hill on Monday next. For I have my lace making. And you, Bess, have Michael Dalgliesh."

"Only as long as he requires my needle," Elisabeth hastened to say.

Anne's frown returned. "I've seen the man's shop. He will need you all the days of his life."

Twenty-Three

Friendship is Love, without either flowers or
veil.

AUGUSTUS AND JULIUS HARE

Elisabeth did not darken Michael's door that
week. Not only did it seem prudent with
Anne moping about the house; Elisabeth also
was determined to see an end to the pile of
fabric draped over the back of her chair.

While she sewed well into each evening,
her neighbors spent the long sunlit hours
climbing Bell Hill. They admired Lord Buchanan's gardens and orchards from a polite
distance and hoped to spy the exalted owner
tramping about the grounds. In Edinburgh, a
city accustomed to visits from princes and
kings, the admiral would've arrived unher-
alded; in rural Selkirk he was viewed as roy-
alty.

Elisabeth shared her neighbors' curiosity
but not their ardent enthusiasm. She'd seen
how wealth and a title could twist a man's

soul, convincing him he was above any moral or social constraints. Lord Donald Kerr had looked the part of a gentleman, yet his behavior was often disgraceful. Who was to say Lord Jack Buchanan would not be the same?

Only a man's character mattered. The rest was window dressing.

Though she had to concede, Bell Hill did have very handsome windows.

When Saturday dawned, Elisabeth awakened before the others and tiptoed about as she dressed for the day. Cambric shirt in hand, she moved her chair closer to the window and began stitching the final sleeve, wondering what, if anything, Michael Dalgliesh might have in mind for her next. Would he permit her to sew a gentleman's coat and waistcoat and thereby prove her tailoring skills? She could at least manage buttonholes and hems or prepare the muslin linings, freeing him to do weightier tasks.

Despite the gray, rainy weather that morning, Elisabeth's heart grew lighter as she imagined the possibilities. Someday she hoped to own a dressmaking concern, but until then, working for Michael well suited her — as long as it suited him.

An hour later Anne rose, brushing aside her bed curtains. "Hard at work already?"

"Aye." Elisabeth kept her voice low for Marjory's sake. "I'll be off to Mr. Dalgliesh's by nine o' the clock." She averted her gaze as Anne bathed at the washbowl and slipped on the blue drugget gown she'd worn the night the Kerrs arrived. Though the fabric was an inexpensive wool, roughly woven, the color matched Anne's blue eyes perfectly. " 'Tis my favorite of your gowns," Elisabeth told her.

Anne shrugged as she crossed the room. "Heaven knows I wear it often enough."

Her cool tone suggested Anne was more irritable than usual. "I will gladly stitch you another gown," Elisabeth assured her. "When I earn enough silver to purchase fabric at market —"

"Nae," Anne said, cutting her short. "Your shillings are better spent on food or your own needs, not on a gown for a stayed lass."

Anne seldom spoke of herself so dismissively. Treading with care, Elisabeth asked, "Why should an unmarried woman not be well dressed?"

"Silks and satins are meant for catching husbands," Anne retorted. "I've long abandoned any such expectations." She turned her back on Elisabeth and began filling the coal grate, abruptly ending their conversation.

In the uncomfortable silence that followed, Elisabeth searched her heart for some encouragement to offer. "Six-and-thirty is not so very old —"

"Oh?" Anne looked over her shoulder, her hands black with coal dust. "This spoken by a bonny lass in her twenties who has half the men in town besotted with her."

Now Elisabeth understood.

"Annie." She quickly put aside the shirt she was stitching and knelt by her cousin. "You are dear to many folk in Selkirk, to Marjory, and to me most of all." She slipped her arm round Anne's narrow shoulders, praying her next words would not make things worse. "Though I do believe there is someone else who holds you in high regard."

Anne was still frowning. "Who might that be?"

Elisabeth stood and brought her cousin to her feet, keeping a close watch on her expression. "On the night of my birthday, I saw a wee spark travel between you and Mr. Dalgliesh."

"Michael?" She brushed the coal dust from her hands, clearly flustered. "We've . . . known each other a long time."

Elisabeth saw through her dissembling and gently tried to help Anne put her feelings into words, which did not always come easily to her. "What of you and Michael now? Still just friends?"

When Anne turned her head away, Elisabeth feared she'd pushed too hard or spoken amiss. She waited for a moment, then said, "Forgive me —"

"Nae." Anne looked at her, eyes glistening with tears. "There is nothing to forgive. You simply stated what you saw. But you do not know the rest."

Elisabeth touched her arm in silent acknowledgment. "Tea, first. Then you may tell me whatever you like. Or nothing at all." Minutes later, steaming cups in hand, the two women sat, their chairs pulled close together.

Anne studied her tea for a moment, her flaxen hair loosely gathered at the nape. When she spoke, her voice was low and strained. "From the time I was a wee lass, I was hopelessly in love with Michael Dalgliesh."

Elisabeth could only imagine what a braw lad Michael must have been in his youth. "Did he not return your affections?"

Anne looked up, her face etched with sorrow. "Nae, he did not."

"Oh, Annie." Elisabeth swallowed hard, seeing the cost of that painful admission. "However did you bear it when he married Jenny?"

"I wanted to die," Anne confessed. "You know how young girls are, thinking their lives are over when the man they love is claimed by another."

"I do know," Elisabeth assured her softly. "Yet you and Michael remained friends."

"After a fashion," Anne said with a shrug. "Jenny was a kind soul and dear to me as well. I couldn't blame Michael for adoring her. We all did. When Peter was born, their happiness was contagious. Everyone loved to be in their company. But when Jenny suffered from a terrible malady no doctor could cure . . ." She bowed her head.

Elisabeth waited, giving her cousin time.

When Anne spoke again, her voice was thin. "As one of his oldest friends, I wanted to comfort Michael in his grief. But I was an unmarried woman and could not rightly do so. As it was, the gossips refused to leave me alone . . ." She gripped the wooden cup in her hands. "They said I wanted Michael for myself. That I was . . . glad that Jenny . . ."

"What?" Elisabeth felt sick. "Annie, you could *never* think such a thing."

"Nae, I could not. Least of all about Jenny." She hung her head. "Michael still loves her, you know. And I still love him."

When Elisabeth lightly rested a hand on Anne's shoulder, her cousin shrank away from her, saying in a bitter voice, "Now it seems he cares for you."

"Annie —"

"Nae." She turned her head. " 'Tis true, and you know it."

"It is *not* true," Elisabeth said, tamping down her frustration. "Though I am curious why you sent me to Michael's shop, loving him as you do. There are other tailors in Selkirk who might have put me to work."

Anne didn't answer at first. When she did,

her voice was low. "Michael was desperate for help. And since you were in mourning . . ."

"He could not court me."

Anne finally met her gaze. "Aye."

When Elisabeth saw the anguish in her cousin's eyes, she vowed at once to help her. She did not know Michael's heart and so dared not give Anne false hope. But what she'd seen pass between them at her birthday celebration was not imaginary.

"Annie, when I deliver his shirts today, may I speak with Michael? On your behalf?"

She shot to her feet. "Nae, you mustn't! For he would surely deny having any feelings for me."

Elisabeth stood as well. "Are you certain of that?"

Anne nodded, but Elisabeth saw the longing in her eyes.

Across the room Marjory stirred. "Good morn," she murmured, tossing aside her bedcovers. If she was aware of their conversation, she did not say so.

When Marjory served them fresh porridge and toasted bread with raspberry jam, Anne ate slowly and Elisabeth swiftly, eager to finish the last of her shirts and see the lot of them delivered. As promised, she would say nothing of Anne's feelings. But if Michael Dalgliesh offered a confession of his own, Elisabeth would gladly listen.

Before leaving for the shop, Elisabeth paid particular attention to her toilette, sweeping her hair into a knot of curls, then tucking Anne's lovely silver comb among them. Should Michael recognize the comb, a conversation about Anne might ensue, and who knew where it could lead? Elisabeth had never fancied herself a matchmaker, but she was willing to try. Her face bathed, her gown brushed, Elisabeth gathered the remaining shirts in her arms and hurried out the door.

The rain had ceased, though not for long, she decided. The air was thick with mist, and the sky above was a dull, metallic gray. Picking her way across the slippery cobblestones, she found herself at Michael's threshold before she was fully prepared. Could she keep from blurting out the truth, knowing what she knew?

The door was open as usual. But when she stepped inside, Elisabeth nearly dropped her bundle of shirts.

Twenty-Four

Change is not made without
inconvenience.

RICHARD HOOKER

Elisabeth stared at the freshly swept floor, the sparkling clean window, the neatly trimmed candles. *Michael, what have you done?*

The broad cutting table was free of clutter except for a few bolts of wool, smoothly wrapped and waiting to be cut. Clothing in various stages still hung round the walls but with a clear sense of order. The stray threads and snippets of fabric that once decorated every surface had utterly vanished.

Elisabeth was so taken aback she could say naught but his name. "Mr. Dalgliesh?"

He came thundering down the turnpike stair, red faced by the time he reached the bottom landing. "Mrs. Kerr! I didna expect . . . That is to say, I've not seen ye a' this week."

"I do apologize." She placed his shirts on

the empty table. "I thought it best to bring them all at once rather than bothering you for a shilling each day."

" 'Twas niver a bother to have ye call." He drew closer, though his steps seemed reluctant, and his gaze shifted about the room. "We've cleaned the place a bit."

We? Elisabeth kept her tone light. "You must have a brownie helping you."

Michael pretended to be shocked. "Dinna let the reverend hear ye say that wird! He doesna believe in the shaggy wee men wha help round the hoose in the nicht."

"I don't believe in brownies either," she admitted, looking from one tidy corner of the shop to the other. "But it does appear human hands have been hard at work here."

"Aye, they have." Michael's expression sobered. "I took yer advice, Mrs. Kerr, and hired anither tailor."

"Oh." Elisabeth felt the ground beneath her shift. "Who might that be?"

Michael pointed to a second small worktable, positioned near the window. "He's oot just noo. Thomas Brodie is his name. He came by the shop on Tuesday last, leuking for wark. Used to have his ain place in Melrose. Whan he offered to start richt awa and cleaned the shop in nae time . . ." He averted his gaze. "I couldna say nae. Not whan I need help so badly."

"I am . . . happy for you," she said, trying

to convince herself she meant it. "With Mr. Brodie here, you'll have more time for Peter." She glanced at the stair, longing to feel his little hand in hers. "Is he here?"

"Nae." Michael still could not meet her gaze. "He'll be hame a bit later if ye care to stop by."

He wants me to leave. Elisabeth gripped the nearest table edge, feeling faint. *He has no more work for me.* Dazed, she merely nodded at the shirts. "Those are the last of them. Five in all."

Michael bolted for his purse, now hanging from a hook where he might easily find it. No doubt Mr. Brodie's idea. "And I've five shillings for ye." Michael dropped the silver into her gloved hand, taking pains not to touch her, or so it seemed.

As her fingers tightened round the coins, her throat tightened as well. Unless she found another employer, there would be no more meat at the Kerr table, no more sweets to share with their neighbors, no more coins for the collection plate.

Hard as it was, she had to ask him. "Mr. Dalgliesh, I hope you were pleased with my work."

"Och, Bess," he said roughly, then caught himself. "I mean Mrs. Kerr. O' course I was pleased. Ye did a fine job. But noo . . ." He rubbed the back of his neck. "I've nae mair for ye to do. Not with Mr. Brodie here."

There. He said it. I am dismissed.

When her lower lip began to tremble, Elisabeth bit down hard to keep from crying. "I . . . thank you . . . for the chance . . . for the . . ."

"Mrs. Kerr." He stepped closer. " 'Tis nae fault o' yers. I canna have a bonny lass warking in my shop a' day. D'ye understand?"

She nodded, not trusting herself to speak. Michael had not promised her such a position, so he'd not broken faith. And he was right: an unmarried man and woman could not work side by side within the confines of a shop. Hadn't she always known that? Yet when she'd suggested he find a partner, she'd not imagined things ending like this.

Elisabeth forced herself to meet his gaze. "Will you give me a written character so I might seek employment elsewhere?"

"Och!" he groaned. "Ye ken I will. Richt noo if ye like." Michael sat down at his newly organized desk and reached for paper, quill, and ink, all at hand.

He wasted no time scratching words across the page while Elisabeth watched him, calming her anxious heart, considering what she might do next. Though several tailors resided in Selkirk, she feared none would be so willing or so generous as this man.

When he finished, Michael cast sand across the ink, then presented the letter to her with a sad smile. "Ye'll have nae trouble finding wark. Start with Edward Smail on Back Row. He's a kind man and fair."

Elisabeth carefully folded the letter, hoping Michael had given an honest appraisal of her talents. Better to have a new employer be pleasantly surprised than patently disappointed.

She lowered her gaze, seeking the strength she would need to begin anew. To call on a stranger and ask for his favor. To put her future in the Almighty's hands once more and not be afraid. *Please, Lord. In thee is my trust.*

When she looked up, Michael was studying her, his expression more serious than she'd ever seen it. "I learned something, having ye here," he said. "I learned I shouldna court a woman just because I need help in my shop or a mither for my son."

"Court?" She looked at him quizzically. "But, Mr. Dalgliesh, I am a widow in mourning —"

"*Hoot!* I didna mean ye!" he exclaimed, then his whole face reddened. "That is . . . I had anither woman . . . in mind . . ."

Annie. Elisabeth relaxed for the first time since she'd arrived at Michael's shop that morning. "You are right, Mr. Dalgliesh. You should court a woman for one reason —"

A single knock on the open door was her only warning.

"So!" a man cried, nearly scaring Elisabeth

out of her wits. "Noo I see what ye meant, Mr. Dalgliesh."

Elisabeth stood in place, letting her heart ease its frantic beating, while Michael mouthed an apology. Whether he was sorry for the presence of this newcomer or for the man's loud greeting, she could not say.

He was standing beside Michael now: a gentleman tailor, if ever there was one. His face was clean shaven, his hair smartly gathered at the nape of his neck, his attire immaculate, and his shoes polished. Only the measuring tape round his neck gave away his profession.

"This is . . . Mr. Brownie," Michael began haltingly.

"Brodie. Thomas Brodie," he quickly corrected, then bowed from the waist. When he straightened, Mr. Brodie smiled, showing all his teeth. Sharp teeth at that. "Ye're surely Mrs. Kerr, for I've heard o' none ither but ye a' week."

"You've made quite a difference here," she said evenly.

"Aye, aye." Mr. Brodie clasped his hands behind his back and looked round with obvious satisfaction. "Meikle mair to do, but as my faither aye said, 'A hard beginning is a guid beginning.' "

Elisabeth could see how uncomfortable Michael was with both of them there. Best to quit the shop at once. "I thank you for this," she said, holding up the letter, then tucking it in her reticule. "And for all the ways you've blessed our household this month."

Michael stepped forward. "A wird with ye, if I may?"

She nodded, grateful for a private farewell.

A moment later they stood in School Close. "Ye *will* find a position," Michael assured her. "If not with Mr. Smail, then Charlie Purdie or Hugh Morrison will be pleased to have ye." He paused. "As I was glad to have ye. And so was wee Peter." He stepped back, a look of regret in his eyes. "I wish ye a' the best, Mrs. Kerr."

The moment Michael returned to his shop, Mr. Brodie closed the door, not loudly, but very firmly, shutting her out.

Wounded by his rebuff and more than a little desperate, Elisabeth strode toward Kirk Wynd. She had no work, little money, and only a few hours to resolve the problem before the threatening clouds spilled their contents.

Edward Smail. Though the name was familiar, she could not picture the man. But she had little doubt she'd find him, for no tailor who wanted business lay in hiding. She climbed uphill toward Back Row, the third leg of the triangle of streets that formed Selkirk. When she reached the ridge where Peter had pointed to the castle ruins, she turned left down a cobbled street lined with stone houses and shops.

The names painted across the lintels were helpful. *Fletcher. Waugh. Blackhall. Dunn.* When she found a promising-looking shop with *Smail* over the entrance and a waistcoat hanging on the open door, she stepped inside and let her eyes adjust to the dim interior before seeking out the owner.

Edward Smail spied her first. "Mrs. Kerr?" he asked, stepping into the lantern light.

The moment she laid eyes on the tailor, she remembered seeing him at kirk and at market, though she'd not known his name. Mr. Smail was aptly named, for he was small and round. His nose was flat, his eyes were close together, and his hands seemed to grow out of his elbows.

"Ye've been sewing shirts for Michael Dalgliesh," he said, casting a wary eye over her. "I confess I envy the man his trade. There was a time not so lang syne whan I had mair wark than I could handle. But not noo." He nodded at the many empty shelves. "I've enough to keep my family in meat and meal, but that is a'."

Whether or not Mr. Smail was kind and fair, he assuredly was not prosperous.

"What brings ye to my door?" he asked rather bluntly, offering her the only seat in his shop.

She hesitated, not wanting to put the man in an awkward position. Or was it pride that stilled her tongue? Finally she confessed, "Mr. Dalgliesh has hired another tailor, so my sewing services are no longer needed."

Mr. Smail frowned. "Mair likely he didna want a bonny lass round his door."

His words stung. "I do all my sewing at home," Elisabeth hastened to explain. "Furthermore, Mr. Dalgliesh has given me a written character."

When she reached for her reticule, the tailor stayed her hand. "Niver mind, Mrs. Kerr. I canna afford ye. And my wife wouldna want ye here *oniewise*."

"Then I am sorry to have bothered you," she said, already on her feet. "I bid you good day."

Mortified, she fled into Back Row, uncertain which way to turn. She had no addresses for the other tailors and little courage left to ask directions from the strangers milling about, staring at her like the outlander she was.

She was too angry to cry and too hurt not to admit his rejection stung.

What shall I do, Lord? Where shall I go?

The answer came quickly. *Home.*

She would lick her wounds, then see about Mr. Purdie or Mr. Morrison, though she feared a similar response. Was there no tailor in Selkirk like Angus MacPherson, who'd given her challenging work and didn't care whether she was bonny or not? She could still remember the twinkle in his eye and the index finger he playfully wagged beneath her nose. *Oh, Angus, how I miss you.*

Discouraged, she pointed her feet toward Halliwell's Close. Perhaps if she found an ugly hat or wore her hair in her face or made certain to always frown, perhaps then she might sew for her supper without distracting men from their work. *Foolishness.*

When she turned onto Kirk Wynd, the heavens opened, and rain poured down in sheets, soaking her to the skin before she reached Anne's house. There would be no more interviews this day; her gown would not dry for hours.

Only when she started up the stair did she remember her conversation with Michael Dalgliesh. *I had anither woman in mind.* But he'd not spoken Anne's name. What if he meant someone else entirely?

By the time she reached the door, Elisabeth was certain of her decision: she would say nothing, lest Anne's hopes for the future be crushed as thoroughly as her own.

Twenty-Five

Now we sit close about this taper here
And call in question our necessities.

WILLIAM SHAKESPEARE

Marjory was stirring a pot of sheep's-head broth for their noontide dinner when her daughter-in-law trudged through the door, dripping wet. Sending Anne to fetch clean towels, Marjory wiped her hands on her apron and hurried to Elisabeth's side. "Poor Bess. I hoped you'd be home before this."

"Mmm," was all Elisabeth said, pulling the silver comb from her drooping curls.

Anne produced several linen towels, then helped Elisabeth undress. "I've an old gown of my mother's you might wear."

"No need. I'll wrap myself in a plaid and hang my dress by the fire," Elisabeth said, rubbing her hair dry with more vigor than the task required.

"But my young ladies will be coming at two," Anne reminded her.

"All right, then." Without another word Elisabeth curled up in the upholstered chair and closed her eyes while Anne went about airing the well-worn gown stored beneath her box bed for many seasons.

Marjory returned to the hearth, keeping an eye on Elisabeth. She'd not seen her this discouraged in a very long time. Even in Edinburgh with their many losses, Elisabeth was the one who'd lifted everyone's spirits.

Letting the broth simmer, Marjory sat on the creepie at Elisabeth's feet and clasped her daughter-in-law's long, slender hands. "So cold," Marjory fretted, rubbing until the skin warmed. She touched Elisabeth's forehead as well and was relieved not to find her feverish.

Finally Elisabeth opened her eyes and offered a wan smile.

"I'm behaving like a mother, aren't I?" Marjory asked, keeping her voice light, hoping to engage her in conversation.

"You are the only true mother I have now," Elisabeth murmured almost to herself.

Oh my dear Bess. Marjory blinked, recalling her daughter-in-law's tearful entreaties when they'd prepared to board separate carriages in White Horse Close. *Please, I cannot go home to Castleton. My mother will not have me.* Marjory did not know Fiona Ferguson. Nor did she care to know her. What woman would not gladly claim Elisabeth as her own?

Marjory said softly, "Suppose we get you into some dry clothing and fill you up with a bowl of hot broth."

The gown fit poorly and the mustard color was less than flattering, but for a rainy afternoon withindoors, it would do. After Marjory spoke grace over their meal, she reached for a wooden spoon, still praying silently for Elisabeth. *Comfort her, Lord. Give her strength. Ease whatever burdens she bears.*

Only when their soup bowls were empty did Elisabeth release a lengthy sigh and meet their worried gazes. "I will no longer be sewing for Mr. Dalgliesh," she announced, looking at Anne. "He has hired another tailor to work in the shop, a Mr. Brodie from Melrose."

"Nae!" Marjory cried. "Why would he do such a thing?"

"I am certain Michael wasn't unhappy with you," Anne insisted. "Perhaps he simply needed a sturdy man about the place to move things and wait on his gentlemen customers."

Elisabeth plucked at a loose thread on her sleeve. "Apparently he did."

"There are other tailors," Marjory said, feeling guilty yet again for sending her daughter-in-law out into the world to earn money for them. But what other choice did they have? No more sewing meant no more shillings, a dismal truth left unsaid but understood.

When Anne suggested a tailor named Mr.

Smail, Elisabeth admitted she'd already visited the man, then described their brief exchange. "He told me his wife wouldn't want me there."

Marjory cringed. No wonder Elisabeth had returned home discouraged. "This dreary weather is sufficient to make anyone feel gloomy," she told her, lighting another tallow candle, ignoring the expense. The steady glow of the candlelight brightened their corner of the room, just as she'd hoped. "Now, then, where might we send our dear Bess where she'll be appreciated?"

Anne pursed her lips for a moment. "Mrs. Stoddart is a mantua maker in Well Wynd, but she pays her seamstresses very meager wages."

Elisabeth glanced upward, deep in thought. "Might Lady Murray allow me to design a gown for her?"

"Her ladyship trusts no one to stitch her gowns except a dressmaker in Edinburgh," Anne said, almost apologetically. "Perhaps you know the woman. A Miss Callander in Lady Stair's Close."

Marjory and Elisabeth exchanged glances.

"Aye, we know her," Marjory said, trying not to sound bitter. "Before we left the capital, Miss Callander purchased nearly every gown we owned."

"And paid you well, I hope?" Anne asked.

Marjory did not want to seem ungrateful,

and so she said nothing, which said every-thing.

Their dinner dishes were still scattered across the table when Gibson dropped by unexpectedly. Anne jumped up at once, gathering the woodenware, inviting their friend to sit by the fire. "You'll have a sweet biscuit, won't you? Marjory baked them this morn."

Gibson turned to Marjory, warming her with his smile. "Ye ken I will." Moments later with biscuit and tea in hand, he said, "I canna stay lang, for I'm on an errand for the reverend. But I had a wee bit o' news I thocht ye'd want to hear." He paused, his smile broadening. "I just noo saw Lord Buchanan at the manse."

"Did you?" Anne exclaimed. "Some claim he's a spirit, the way he comes and goes without being seen."

"He's verra real. O' course, I didna speak to the man myself. But I overheard meikle o' what the admiral and the reverend said to each ither." He took a bite of biscuit and chewed it at a leisurely pace. " 'Tis a puir servant's lot to listen whan great folk speak."

"Come, Gibson," Marjory scolded him lightly. "You cannot keep us in suspense. What might you tell us about Lord Bu-chanan?"

"What ye already ken. He's wealthy and weel traveled, with guid speech."

Anne inched her chair closer. "But what does the admiral *look* like?"

Gibson all but shrugged. "He leuks like a man."

Elisabeth almost smiled. "Nae more biscuits for you, Gibson, unless you tell all."

"Weel, he was dressed in a verra braw manner. Fit to ride his horse, ye ken, with bonny black boots in fine leather up ower his knees."

Anne said, "I heard he was quite tall."

"So he is," Gibson agreed, "with dark skin from years at sea."

However honorable or handsome he might be, Marjory still feared the man. "Would you say he is wholly dedicated to God and king?"

"Oo aye." Gibson paused. "But I *jalouse* by his wirds he favors the first mair than the second. We'll soon ken what sort o' man the admiral is whan he hires folk from the toun." His biscuit gone, his cup empty, the manservant stood and bowed. "I must awa. Guid day to ye, leddies, and I thank ye for yer kind walcome."

No sooner had Gibson left than Elisabeth rose, a look of resignation on her face. "I've no choice in the matter. Come Monday I shall present myself at Bell Hill and see if Lord Buchanan might offer me a position as a dressmaker."

"Bess!" Marjory was aghast. "Are you certain that's wise?"

"If he's going to expand his staff," Elisa-

222

beth reasoned, "the maidservants will need new gowns, aye?"

Her logic was sound, but the situation was perilous. Even if Tibbie Cranshaw held her tongue, Lord Buchanan might still learn of Donald's treason and refuse to engage Elisabeth. Or, worse, deliver her to the king to further earn His Majesty's favor. Marjory glanced at Anne, begging for her support. *She cannot do this. Say something. Do something.*

Anne was a quick study. "But his housekeeper will surely require a sample of your work, and you've naught to show her."

Marjory nodded, relieved. *Well done, Annie.* Elisabeth had sold all her creations to Miss Callander. She had nothing in hand to demonstrate her talents.

But Elisabeth was already opening the trunk in which Marjory had stored her stockings and stays. Her daughter-in-law lifted out the cambric nightgown she'd made, beautifully embroidered with deep pink roses round the neckline.

"Helen Edgar cleaned and pressed it before we left Edinburgh," Marjory told her, realizing she could do little to stop Elisabeth once she'd made up her mind. "If you want to carry it to Bell Hill to show to the housekeeper, I'll not object."

Elisabeth crossed the room at once and pressed a kiss to her brow. "Thank you. And

I'll wear Annie's silver comb, so the two people I cherish most will travel up Bell Hill with me. As to my dress" — she gestured toward the black gown dripping beside the hearth — "at least 'tis freshly washed."

Twenty-Six

Fairest and best adorned is she
Whose clothing is humility.

JAMES MONTGOMERY

Elisabeth rose from the breakfast table, grateful Marjory and Anne could not see her knees trembling beneath her gown. "I must go. 'Tis two miles to Bell Hill."

"And only six o' the clock in the morn," Anne reminded her. "Do you think the others will arrive so early?"

Elisabeth shrugged, if only to shake off her nervousness. "You know what the old wives say. 'The *coo* that's first up gets the first o' the dew.'"

"You are not a cow," Anne said pointedly. "And I'd hate for you to appear too eager."

"But I *am* eager," Elisabeth confessed. "Our food stores are dwindling. And Mr. Halliwell expects his shillings today, does he not?" At Whitsuntide rents were paid, debts settled, and new servants hired. Lord willing, she

225

would be counted among the latter. "I've only to gather my sewing things, and I'll be ready."

Last evening she'd washed her hair in rosewater and brushed it until it gleamed, then rubbed her teeth with a hazel twig until her gums ached, hoping a bright smile might please the housekeeper. She'd polished her black shoes with ashes from the grate, while her mourning gown, stiff after drying by the hearth, had been coaxed into soft folds by Anne's skillful ironing.

Elisabeth reached for the small looking glass, chagrined to find a nagging fear reflected in her eyes. What if ten other dressmakers who were far more qualified presented themselves at Bell Hill? Or the housekeeper took one look at her tattered gown and sent her away?

Nae, Bess. Had she already forgotten what she'd read upon waking? *In God I have put my trust.* The time had come to act on those words instead of simply meditating on them.

She collected her sewing basket from the shelf, then tallied her dressmaking tools: a half-dozen spools of silk thread, her best cutting shears, a packet of straight pins, her measuring tape, her pincushion, a handful of shirt buttons, tailor's chalk wrapped in linen, and a small wooden case with her precious needles. Whatever task might be required, she was prepared.

The most valuable tool her basket contained was the written character from Michael Dalgliesh and another one from Reverend Brown, which he'd provided at Marjory's request last evening. Without them she could not hope to be taken seriously as a dressmaker.

Lastly she slipped round her neck a black ribbon from which dangled a slender pair of scissors meant for snipping loose threads and advertising her services. A gentlewoman would never appear in public displaying her scissors, but a dressmaker would.

She started to close the wooden lid of her basket when a glint of silver caught her eye. *Jenny's thimble.* Elisabeth paused, her mind turning. "Annie," she said, keeping her voice light, "might you return this for me?" She lifted out the delicate thimble and placed it in her cousin's hand. "I am sure he meant this as a loan, not a gift, yet it would be awkward for me to visit Mr. Dalgliesh's shop." Elisabeth met her gaze. "You do understand?"

"Consider it done," Anne said with a shrug, dropping the thimble in her apron pocket.

Elisabeth nodded to herself. *The rest is up to you, Michael.*

A moment later she slipped down the stair and into the close, holding her skirts above the muck until she reached the dry cobblestones in Kirk Wynd. Even at that early hour a goodly number of folk were in the street.

Milkmaids and laundresses ducked round her, intent on their duties. Shopkeepers had already thrown open their doors. The street was crowded with livestock as sheep and cattle belonging to the townsfolk were driven to the common grazing land round Selkirk.

Whitsun Monday was well begun.

Elisabeth spied a young woman walking alone, wearing a freshly pressed gown and a timid expression. Molly Easton, a parishioner she'd had occasion to speak with, was a quiet lass, a few years short of her majority. Was she, too, bound for Bell Hill? Thinking a traveling companion might make the journey easier for both of them, Elisabeth quickly caught up with her. "Good day to you, Miss Easton."

She bobbed her brown head. "To ye as weel, Mrs. Kerr."

As they fell into step, Elisabeth asked, "Might you be seeking a position at Bell Hill?"

"I might," Molly answered cryptically. "And ye?"

Elisabeth hesitated. Should she tell all or simply acknowledge the question, as Miss Easton had? Perhaps it was ill luck to voice one's plans on such a day. "I hope to work for the admiral," Elisabeth finally told her, then began speaking of the fine weather, seeing where their conversation might lead.

Alas, it led only to the edge of town, for

Molly Easton was shy in the extreme. She spoke two words to Elisabeth's twenty and offered little about herself other than her age, eight-and-ten, and her favorite month, June. "Because o' the Common Riding," she explained.

Elisabeth had heard the Riding mentioned in passing but knew little more than the name. "I've never seen one."

"Och, Mrs. Kerr!" Like a puppet come to life, Molly began to hop from one foot to the next. " 'Tis held on a Friday in June. When braw men on horseback take to the marches early that morn 'tis a sight to behold." Color had blossomed in her cheeks, and her dark eyes shone like chestnuts. "Afore the day is done, there's music and dancing in the marketplace."

The lass chattered away as they crossed the road to Hawick and began climbing the grassy track toward Bell Hill. While the sun rose higher, bathing the pastures in the soft light of morning, other folk appeared on foot, all aimed in the same direction. Only when they neared the admiral's property did Molly's comments return to the matter at hand. "Will there be onie ithers, d'ye think, who'll want to be parlormaids?"

"I cannot say," Elisabeth told her truthfully, unfamiliar with the ins and outs of domestic service. In the Kerrs' six-room house in Edinburgh, they'd managed with a housekeeper, butler, and maid. But Bell Hill would require dozens of servants, carefully ranked and paid accordingly. Grooms and footmen, cooks and scullery maids, housemaids and dairymaids. Would she be expected to know the duties of each? Or might she be assigned a small sewing room and left to her own devices?

When they started up the long drive, Elisabeth's stomach twisted into a knot and stayed that way as the leafy trees she'd seen from a distance now loomed over her. The gray stone mansion, rising three stories above the ground, seemed loftier and more imposing with each step. Laid out like the letter *L,* the house was older than she'd imagined, with the remnant of a medieval castle joined to a longer section with a bank of windows overlooking the freshly planted gardens.

Molly whispered as if the gables and turrets might hear, "I have niver seen such a place."

Elisabeth had once danced at the Palace of Holyroodhouse, so she could not say the same. But she'd never worked or lived in so fine a house as this. As they turned the corner, bound for the open door, voices floated out to greet them. She and Molly were not among the first arrivals, then. They quickened their steps, the massive carved entranceway beckoning.

When she crossed the threshold, Elisabeth's heart sank. Dozens upon dozens of eager applicants milled round the broad hall, many more folk than would ever be needed or hired. How many other dressmakers might there be among the sea of faces? Molly Easton's dismayed expression mirrored her own.

Standing just inside the doorway was a tall, middle-aged woman with carefully styled hair the shade of a shiny new ha'penny. Though she lifted her voice, the woman never shouted. "Housemaids in the center. Laundry maids under the window. Scullery maids by the far door." Clearly she was Bell Hill's housekeeper, in charge of the female staff. An impressive gentleman, who could only be the butler, stood beside her, giving similar orders to the men as they entered, sending them to various stations on the opposite side of the entrance hall.

"Parlormaids, mem?" Molly asked tentatively.

The housekeeper appraised her with a quick, sharp glance. "With the housemaids, if you please."

As Molly darted off, Elisabeth lifted her chin, hoping to make a good first impression. "Madam, my name is Mrs. Kerr. I have come to offer my services as a dressmaker. Where shall I stand?"

Her steel gray eyes narrowed. "You have never worked in service."

Elisabeth blanched.

"If you had," the woman said curtly, "you would know there are no permanent positions for dressmakers or tailors. They are engaged only when needed and never on Whitsun Monday."

Embarrassment swept over Elisabeth like a wave. *Why did I not ask someone? Why did I make assumptions?* She locked her knees, lest they give way entirely, and found the courage to respond. "You are right when you say I've not been in service. But I have been a seamstress in two tailoring establishments —"

"Still, you've not worked for a gentleman."

"I have not," Elisabeth conceded, "though I did live in a gentleman's house." She swallowed, then said the rest. "As his wife."

The housekeeper abruptly took her by the arm. "Come with me, madam."

TWENTY-SEVEN

The grandest of heroic deeds are those
which are performed within four walls and
in domestic privacy.

JEAN PAUL FRIEDRICH RICHTER

Elisabeth could not guess where the housekeeper was leading her or what she had in
mind. Was an audience with Lord Buchanan
literally round the corner?

"I am Mrs. Pringle," the older woman said,
then ordered one of her maidservants to take
her place at the door. Turning her back on
the busy entrance hall, she escorted Elisabeth
toward the longer wing of the house.
"Whether or not his lordship is prepared to
engage a dressmaker for the servants' gowns,
I cannot say," Mrs. Pringle told her, "though
I shall address the matter when he returns
from Edinburgh."

"He is away?" Elisabeth was both relieved
and disappointed. The admiral had not been
spied at kirk yesterday morning. Now she

233

knew why.

"Lord Buchanan is managing some business for His Majesty," Mrs. Pringle said offhandedly. She withdrew a set of keys from her pocket as they approached a door of immense proportions. "In his stead, Roberts and I are perfectly capable of filling all the household positions."

"Aye, madam," Elisabeth said, not doubting the woman for an instant.

She followed Mrs. Pringle into a vast drawing room, large enough to hold Anne's house and five more like it. They crossed the room in such haste, Elisabeth's view was reduced to a single, breathtaking sweep of deep burgundy and royal blue. Thick carpeting, ornate columns, brocaded silk upholstery, gilded mirrors, fine oil portraits, and opulent velvet draperies all demanded her attention at once.

The effect was staggering, the admiral's wealth beyond imagining. She barely noticed the corner exit, meant to blend into the décor, until the housekeeper slipped her key into a concealed lock and pushed on the broad wall panel.

"My ground floor office, where I handle the affairs of the household," she said, ushering Elisabeth within. The square room, though small, was elegantly appointed. Mrs. Pringle pointed to a high-backed chair near her desk. "If you please."

After the long walk Elisabeth was grateful to rest her feet, though she longed for something to drink, fearing her parched lips might stick together.

Mrs. Pringle tugged a woven cord, then sat. Her desk was exceptionally neat, with a shelf of books at her elbow. The light pouring in from the narrow window shone on the housekeeper's face, revealing an intricate web of lines and creases. Just short of fifty years, Elisabeth decided. *Marjory's age.*

"Mrs. Kerr," the housekeeper began, "you are obviously a woman of quality. Yet you've come to Bell Hill with a pair of scissors draped round your neck, seeking employment. Explain yourself."

"Perhaps these will help." Elisabeth reached into her sewing basket for her written characters. She'd sealed both letters, lest she be tempted to read them, and offered them now for the housekeeper to examine. "Two characters for your perusal."

Mrs. Pringle held up her hand. "I do not wish to know what others think of you. Not yet. I want to know why you're here." Her tone was cool, her demeanor more so.

Elisabeth met Mrs. Pringle's gaze without apology, knowing she had to speak the truth now or spend the rest of her days trying to conceal it. "My late husband, Lord Donald Kerr, died in battle at Falkirk." She paused, steeling herself. "Because of our family's support of Prince Charles Edward Stuart, our title, property, and fortune were lost, leaving my mother-in-law and me without means beyond what my needle can provide."

Mrs. Pringle studied her at length before she spoke. "Your situation is most regrettable," she finally said, her expression softening ever so slightly. "There were also many in London who secretly favored the prince. Am I to assume you've been duly humbled and now support the rightful king?"

A sense of peace settled over Elisabeth. "Of that you can be certain." *For God is the King of all the earth.*

"And you'll not discuss your former Jacobite sympathies with his lordship?"

"Only if he asks me, in which case I am honor-bound to confess the truth." Elisabeth reached for her basket, eager to press on. "May I show you a sample of my work?" She withdrew Marjory's embroidered nightgown and held it out for Mrs. Pringle's inspection. "Though I realize 'tis not nightgowns you'll be needing —"

"I can see that you are accomplished, as any gentlewoman should be." Mrs. Pringle returned the garment, having barely glanced at it. "What I cannot see is how quickly you work."

A knock on the door announced a young, russet-haired maidservant balancing a tea tray. She poured them each a steaming cup, then curtsied, her manners as pleasing as her features. "Will there be anything else, mem?"

"The mending basket," Mrs. Pringle said, then dismissed her with a nod.

If the housekeeper intended to watch her sew, Elisabeth would not be ruffled. Hadn't Rob MacPherson spent many a quiet hour in Edinburgh with his gaze fixed on her while she stitched for his father? This would be no different.

Elisabeth was still adding milk to her tea when the maid reappeared with a large willow basket overflowing with garments.

Mrs. Pringle drained her cup in one long draw, then placed it in the china saucer with a faint clink. "In that basket, Mrs. Kerr, you will find torn seams, missing buttons, dangling pockets, all the usual. Repair them if you can. I shall rejoin you well before the supper hour and see how you've progressed."

Elisabeth stared at the basket. Was she expected to finish all of this by day's end? "Very well, Mrs. Pringle."

The housekeeper stood, dabbing at her mouth. "Sally will take you to the workroom. Meanwhile, I've a household to manage." Mrs. Pringle did not wait for a response but quit her office with a sweep of her skirts.

Elisabeth could not waste a moment. She gulped down her tea, nearly scalding her tongue, then gathered her belongings and followed Sally back through the drawing room and into the broad hallway with its gleaming sconces and fabric-covered walls.

"This way, mem." Still carrying the heavy basket, Sally led her through a side door and down a steep, curving stairway to the servants' domain below. Though plain and unadorned, the service corridor was freshly scrubbed and well lit.

Elisabeth peered through each open door in passing, noting Mrs. Pringle's influence reflected in the tidy shelves, neat rows of chairs, carefully folded linens, and polished brass lanterns. Twenty, perhaps even thirty servants would eventually labor here. The few souls on hand, hard at work that morning, paused long enough to bob their heads and smile at her. Was Lord Buchanan a fair and just employer or a tyrant? By week's end, Lord willing, she would have her answer.

"Here ye are, mem." Sally blushed prettily, holding open the door to a low-ceilinged room. Though it had only one window, and quite a high one at that, the room also had a candle-stool with a circle of chairs round it. "I'll see to the fire," Sally said, lifting the candle from the mantel, then kneeling before the small hearth, where twigs, sticks, and a split log were expertly laid, awaiting the touch of her flame. She also trimmed and lit the wick in the center of the three-legged candle-stool edged with round glass flasks, each filled with water, magnifying the light. One beeswax candle gleamed like a dozen.

"Will this suit ye, mem?" Sally asked as the wood fire began to crackle.

Elisabeth clasped her basket, surveying the room. Though it was chilly now, the fire would soon warm her, and the clever lighting was more than sufficient. If only Angus had kept such a stool in his dimly lit shop! The unknown contents of the willow basket were her main concern. "I'd best begin," she told Sally, who disappeared with a curtsy.

Alone at last, Elisabeth slipped off her light wool cape and hung it by the door, then settled into one of the chairs, placing the mending basket at her feet and her sewing basket on the empty chair next to her. The day was still young. If the Lord smiled on her work, she might finish before the gloaming.

Elisabeth whispered a prayer for quick fingers and a keen eye, then claimed the first item to be mended, a gentleman's shirt. Rather than the coarse muslin of a laborer or the thick linen of a servant, the fabric was a fine cambric: almost certainly Lord Buchanan's.

A nervous shiver danced up her spine as she lifted the garment for a closer inspection. She'd sewn men's shirts for the last month, but this was different. A gentleman who was not her husband, a gentleman she'd never even met, had worn this fabric against his skin. Numerous times, apparently, for cambric lost its sheen after several launderings.

Judging by the length of the sleeves and breadth of the shoulder seams, Lord Buchanan was indeed tall. She would need to look up to meet his gaze and would not easily see round him. A pleasant scent, more like soap than sweat, clung to the fabric, and the clean neckline hinted at a man who bathed often.

Enough, Bess. She blushed, lowering the shirt to her lap. Her task was to mend his clothes, not assess them. She quickly found a lengthy gap along the side seam, easily repaired. After threading her needle, she went to work and finished the last stitch a half hour later. She pressed on to the next item, a waistcoat with three missing buttons, requiring an entirely new set, which she retrieved from her basket. A rather new linen apron needed only a few stitches to reattach the waistband, and a second shirt of a lesser quality was quickly hemmed.

As the morning progressed, she draped each finished piece over the chair beside her, stopping occasionally to poke the fire, stretch her limbs, or step into the hall to listen for voices. She imagined Mrs. Pringle and Roberts in their respective offices above her, interviewing the many candidates. Would Molly Easton find herself a parlormaid before the day ended?

When the sun was high overhead, young

Sally reappeared with a dinner tray. "I thocht ye might be peckish by noo," she said, placing the wooden tray on a side table. "*Cauld* mutton, *het* tea, and Mrs. Tudhope's shortbread."

"They all sound delicious," Elisabeth told her, grateful not only for the food but also for the company. "If you don't mind me asking, Sally, how long have you worked at Bell Hill?"

"A fortnight," the lass said proudly. "My mither is head laundress. We were the first in Selkirk to be hired. Mrs. Pringle and the ithers came from London toun."

"What about Lord Buchanan?" Elisabeth asked, trying not to sound too curious. "Is he a worthy master?"

Sally smiled. "I've niver met a kinder man. He's auld, ye ken. Nigh to forty. And not verra handsome. But he is guid."

Elisabeth nodded, adding the details to her store of knowledge concerning Admiral Lord Jack Buchanan. She could almost picture him now and would certainly recognize him if he walked through the door, which he might at any time. She thanked Sally, dined with haste, then returned to her sewing, the shadows outside her window lengthening with each passing hour.

When she reached the last garment, a sturdy wool waistcoat, Elisabeth counted the buttons and studied the seams, finding nothing wrong. Had the garment landed in the mending basket by mistake? Running her fingers over the fabric in the waning light, she felt more than saw the problem: a slight tear in the fabric, as if a blade had poked through the wool, severing the weave.

Elisabeth frowned, knowing there was little hope of saving the waistcoat. Cotton and silk thread would never do a proper job of it. She inched closer to the candle-stool, examining the spun wool in the flickering light. If her father were here, he would know what might be done. *Think, Bess. How would a weaver repair this?*

Using a flatiron heated by the fire, Elisabeth pressed the damaged area, then picked apart a section of the hem that would not show, carefully removing a few strands of wool. She inserted the strands along the tear, making certain the colors were a perfect match, then rewove the warp and then the weft, using only her fingers and a blunt needle. At last she snipped away the trailing ends, then pressed the fabric once more.

Elisabeth held up the waistcoat, pride welling inside her. Not because of the work she'd done, but because of the father who'd taught her so long ago.

A woman's voice floated through the doorway. "Still sewing, Mrs. Kerr?"

Elisabeth spun round. "Mrs. Pringle! I thought perhaps you'd forgotten me," she said lightly, then hoped the housekeeper would not take offense.

"I am later than I intended to be," she admitted. "Come, let me see your work."

Elisabeth laid aside the waistcoat for a moment and showed her the rest.

Mrs. Pringle seemed taken aback. "You finished all of it?" The housekeeper inspected each item of clothing, her eyebrows lifting incrementally with each one until finally her face was the picture of astonishment. "You've done three days' work in one, Mrs. Kerr." She nodded toward the waistcoat. "Of course, that must be delivered to a tailor or a weaver in Edinburgh with very particular skills. Rather a nasty gash."

"Aye, it was," Elisabeth said, then held out the mended garment. "See if this is any improvement."

Frowning, Mrs. Pringle took the waistcoat and turned it over in her hands. Once, then twice. "But where is it? I distinctly remember —"

" 'Twas here," Elisabeth said, pointing to the spot she'd labored over.

Mrs. Pringle peered at it more closely, then shook her head. "I would not have believed it possible. Where did you learn such a skill?"

"My father was a weaver. And my oldest friend in Edinburgh was a tailor."

"Well." Mrs. Pringle pursed her lips. "I've one more task for you, Mrs. Kerr, and then we shall see about a position for you at Bell Hill."

Elisabeth stole a glance at the window. The last rays of the sun would be gone in an hour, and she'd not had supper. "Will it take very long?" she asked.

"A week, I imagine." The housekeeper plucked the measuring tape from Elisabeth's sewing basket. "If you are to sew gowns for the maidservants of Bell Hill, you'd best start with mine. Take my measurements, if you please."

Elisabeth's hopes soared. Surely this meant Mrs. Pringle was pleased with her work.

"Lord Buchanan purchased the fabric in London," Mrs. Pringle explained. "Bolts upon bolts of a fine charcoal gray broadcloth."

Elisabeth merely nodded as she took the housekeeper's measurements. *Shoulder to elbow, ten inches. Neck to waist, two-and-twenty in the front, twelve in the back. Waist to hem, eight-and-thirty inches.* She was already imagining the gown she would design. Simple, yet flattering, and above all practical.

When she began measuring Mrs. Pringle's slightly thicker waist, the housekeeper murmured, "You'll not tell a soul the number? Mrs. Tudhope is entirely to blame. We've both worked for his lordship since the *Centurion* came into port, and I cannot resist her shortbread."

" 'Twill be our secret," Elisabeth assured her, making a mental note. *One-and-thirty inches.*

"Leave your basket with me, if you like," Mrs. Pringle told her. "I shall expect you at eight in the morn, prepared to work." Her brow darkened a bit. "This is a trial, you understand, with no promise of engagement."

"Then I shall do my best to win your approval and his lordship's as well."

Mrs. Pringle nodded toward the door. "See that you do, Mrs. Kerr."

Twenty-Eight

Prosperity is not without many fears and
distastes; and adversity is not without
comforts and hopes.

Marjory prepared tea for Reverend Brown
even as she kept an eye on the windows,
watching the bright evening sky fade to a rosy
blue. Wherever was Elisabeth? Surely the
admiral did not expect his household staff to
travel home on foot past the gloaming?
Sometimes the gentry could be so inconsider-
ate.

Marjory had been on edge all day, jumping
at every footfall on the stair, every shout from
the marketplace. To make matters worse,
Anne's young ladies had been fidgety from
first hour to last, and Gibson had not found
a moment to visit. Then at seven o' the clock,
the minister had come to the house unexpectedly, asking to meet with her. "Alone," he'd
insisted. Anne had graciously embarked on

an errand, leaving Marjory and the reverend to converse in peace.

However, *peace* was the very last word she would use to describe her feelings at present.

With her back toward the reverend, Marjory closed her eyes and silently prayed where she stood. *Peace be within thy walls, and prosperity within thy palaces.* If peace reigned in Halliwell's Close this evening and prosperity poured forth from Bell Hill, the Kerr women might yet have hope and a future.

Comforted by the thought, Marjory finished slicing the butter cake, poured their tea, and served Reverend Brown at table, where he sat, looking rather ill at ease. He ate the rich cake in a few hurried bites, then gulped down his steaming cupful as if eager to return home.

"Reverend Brown, it is clear you have something to say." Marjory put down her fork, having no appetite at all. "How might I make this easier for you?"

"You already have," he said gruffly, "and I thank you for it." He cleared his throat, then met her gaze. "I've come to speak about Neil Gibson."

"Oh?" Marjory's skin cooled, her imagination running up and down Kirk Wynd. *What is it, Gibson? What has happened?*

The reverend leaned across the table, lowering his voice. "I am certain you are not aware of this, Mrs. Kerr, but Gibson speaks of you in rather too familiar a manner."

"Too . . . familiar?" She frowned, at a loss even to imagine such a thing. "What, may I ask, has Gibson said about me?"

The reverend sat back, studying his hands, perhaps trying to think of an example. Finally he confessed, "He has never spoken of you in my presence. But this morn I overheard him tell the milkmaid that you were a fine lady and a good friend." The reverend spread out his hands, beseeching her. "You must understand my concern."

"Oh, I do," Marjory said to appease him. *A fine lady. A good friend.* She could not remember the last time she'd been so complimented. "Though I would be more troubled if Gibson spoke poorly of me. I was, after all, his employer for thirty years."

"Precisely," the reverend said, banging his fist on the table for emphasis. "The man has forgotten his place. Despite your present circumstances, Mrs. Kerr, you are a lady and must not be spoken of so freely, nor in such glowing terms, by a mere manservant. One might think Neil Gibson had designs on you."

"One might," she agreed, then quickly hid behind her teacup. *Tread with care, dear Gibson. I'll not have you dismissed because of me.* "What would you suggest, Reverend Brown? Gibson is, after all, a friend of our

248

family. I cannot think of making him unwelcome here. 'Twould not be the Christian thing to do."

Reverend Brown nodded, his frown more pronounced. "It is indeed a puzzle, madam. One that requires further consideration. In the meantime, if you will be cautious in your dealings with Gibson and not . . . , well, encourage such . . . , eh, flattery."

"I would never do so," Marjory said smoothly. She did not need to. Neil Gibson was ever generous with his praise. "He served the Kerrs through many seasons, Reverend. I pray he will do the same for you."

"Aye, aye." He stood, looking relieved at having discharged his solemn duty. "I do hope my written character was of use to your daughter-in-law this day."

Marjory glanced at the door, her fears rushing up the steps to greet her anew. "I thank you again for your willingness to help us," she said, then after a few formalities, bade the minister farewell.

Keeping an eye on the darkening sky, she set the table for three and willed her loved ones home. Though Anne was too old to be her natural daughter, Marjory could not help feeling a certain motherly affection toward her. And Elisabeth *was* her daughter now. Had the lass not said so herself? *Hurry home, dear girls.* Whatever their ages, they would always be young to her.

A half hour crawled by while Marjory walked about the room, picking things up and putting them down with no purpose other than occupying her hands and corralling her anxious thoughts. When at last she heard voices at the foot of the stair, she flung open the upper door. "Annie? Bess?"

"Aye," they called in unison, starting up the stair.

Marjory stood back, fighting the urge to hug them both. Her own mother, Lady Joanna Nesbitt, had never embraced her children, not even in private. Marjory could at least clasp their hands and draw them toward the hearth. "Come, warm yourselves while I serve our supper."

They washed their hands first, then stood dutifully by the coal fire. "I'm famished," Elisabeth admitted. "Do forgive me if I eat before describing my day at Bell Hill."

"By all means," Anne said, pouring fresh tea. "We'll save our stories for later."

When all three took their places, Marjory smiled. "Grace before meat, as they say. Though you'll not find meat on your table this night." What she served them was egg pie, one of Helen Edgar's favorite dishes. Cinnamon and nutmeg made it flavorful, cream and butter made it rich, and currants gave them something to chew on.

Marjory was pleased when her family cleaned their plates and even happier when they accepted a second serving. Odd, how satisfying it was to see loved ones enjoy her simple dishes. Lady Nesbitt would not have approved of *that* sentiment either. As for what her late mother might say about Neil Gibson . . . well, some subjects were best left untouched.

"We've waited long enough, Bess," Anne said, folding her hands in her lap.

Marjory put aside her napkin, also eager to hear a full report.

"I do not have a position yet," Elisabeth began, "but I do have work." She went on to describe her long day at Bell Hill, from meeting shy Molly Easton of Shaw's Close to accepting her new assignment from the formidable Mrs. Pringle. "She worked for the admiral in London and arrived in Selkirk only a fortnight ago."

Marjory was relieved to hear it. "Then she knows nothing of your Jacobite ties."

But the look on her daughter-in-law's face and the hesitancy of her response did not bode well. "I told her myself," Elisabeth finally confessed.

"Oh, Bess." Marjory sank back in her chair, undone. "Must you always be so honest?"

Anne arched her brows. "Cousin, I believe *you* were the one who announced your family's support of the Stuarts in front of the entire parish."

With both of them looking at her — and

rather smugly, she thought — Marjory could do nothing but nod in agreement.

"Mrs. Pringle was sure to hear the story from someone," Elisabeth said gently. "I thought it best she hear it from me. And since she insisted I never mention it to his lordship, you can be sure she'll keep the news to herself."

Marjory sighed. "Let us hope Tibbie Cranshaw follows suit."

"It's possible she'll not even be hired," Elisabeth told her. "I imagine we'll know in a day or two. This eve I'll sketch the gown I plan to make, then seek Mrs. Pringle's approval in the morn." Elisabeth winked at their cousin. "I won't need to leave the house quite so early. Not until seven o' the clock."

"You lazy girl," Anne teased her. "The sun will be halfway across the sky."

Marjory thought their cousin looked especially happy and told her so. "Did something blithe happen on your errand this eve?"

Anne shrugged but could not hide her smile. "I went to Michael's shop to return Jenny's thimble."

"So kind of you to do that for me," Elisabeth said.

"For *you?* Oh, aye." Anne's cheeks pinked. "Peter, at least, seemed glad to see me."

"And his father?" Elisabeth prompted her.

She grew pinker still. "The three of us had a wee visit while Mr. Brodie waited on a customer."

Marjory watched Anne with growing interest. What was it about Michael Dalgliesh that affected young women so? The man was handsome enough, in a rough sort of way, and a charming storyteller, as he'd demonstrated at Elisabeth's birthday gathering. Perhaps wee Peter Dalgliesh had run off with Anne's affections, which Marjory certainly understood. Hadn't young Donald and Andrew stolen her heart on a daily basis?

"Tell me how Mr. Brodie is faring," Elisabeth said.

"Poor Michael spends more time up the stair than down," Anne confessed. "He says the shop is entirely too neat for his taste, and he cannot find a thing."

"Indeed, he never could." Elisabeth smiled at Anne across the table. "Though it seems he's found something worth keeping."

Twenty-Nine

A woman sat in unwomanly rags,
Plying her needle and thread —
Stitch! stitch! stitch!

THOMAS HOOD

Elisabeth unrolled the fine wool broadcloth, sweeping her hands across the downy nap. *Like velvet.* That's how the fabric felt, so close was the weave, calendered between heated rollers to make the finish exceptionally smooth. She eyed her chalk and shears, itching to begin.

"Will the table suit your needs?" Mrs. Pringle asked, standing near, hands clasped at her waist. "You'll need to quit this room by noontide so the table may be laid for the servants' dinner at one o' the clock."

Elisabeth assured her she would finish chalking and cutting the fabric within the hour, then tapped the drawing she'd placed on the corner of the borrowed dining table.

"You are quite certain my design pleases you?"

The housekeeper gave it a cursory glance. " 'Twill do," she said dismissively. "Comfort is what concerns me most."

"Naturally," Elisabeth agreed. "We'll do two fittings before your gown is completed."

"By Saturday," the housekeeper said firmly.

"Aye, madam." Elisabeth moistened her lips, parched at the thought of all that lay ahead. "If you will stop by the workroom at three o' the clock, I shall have it pinned and ready for your first fitting."

When Mrs. Pringle reached out to touch the fabric, Elisabeth noticed a slight fraying on the edges of the woman's cuffs. Though her white apron was crisply starched, Mrs. Pringle needed this new gown. The rich charcoal gray fabric would complement her coppery hair far better than the dull brown the housekeeper was currently wearing, though Elisabeth would never mention it.

"While you are here at Bell Hill," Mrs. Pringle said, "you will be addressed as Mrs. Kerr since you are not counted among the household servants."

"Very well," Elisabeth said. She knew she was foreign, in every sense of the word. A Highlander, a Jacobite, a gentlewoman. If the servants took her into their confidence even a little, she'd be grateful.

"In the meantime," Mrs. Pringle continued,

"I've hired fourteen new maidservants, all of whom begin today." She splayed her long, tapered fingers and counted them. "Two kitchen for Mrs. Tudhope, two parlor, two scullery, one stillroom, three upper house, two lower house, and two dairy."

Elisabeth briefly bowed her head. *And one dressmaker come week's end? Please may it be so.* Clearly not everyone who'd applied on Monday had found a position. She'd not seen Molly Easton on the road that morning. Only a grim sky full of low clouds promising rain.

"The new maids are to arrive at nine o' the clock." Mrs. Pringle consulted a gentleman's pocket watch, pulled from the recesses of her apron. "Will there be anything else, Mrs. Kerr?"

She mustered her courage and asked, "When might the master of the house be expected?"

"I know neither the day nor the hour," Mrs. Pringle told her. "The admiral has been at sea for three quarters of his life. He has lodgings in London and Portsmouth but has never owned a proper estate in the country. I imagine it will take Lord Buchanan several months before he considers Bell Hill his true home." After a long pause she asked, "Are you frightened of meeting the admiral because of your late husband's treason?"

The housekeeper's bold question took Elisabeth by surprise. "I am," she admitted.

"Then we must see it is never mentioned." Mrs. Pringle stepped back. "Ply your needle, madam. If you need anything, Sally Craig can assist you." She quit the room, the heels of her shoes marking her confident steps along the flagstone floor of the servants' hall.

With the small dining room to herself, Elisabeth went to work at once, marking the dark fabric with her slender chalk. What she wouldn't have given for Angus MacPherson's old dress form or sufficient time to make a muslin pattern. Sharpened before they'd left Edinburgh, her shears glided through the fine wool like a knife through butter. Sleeves, then sections of the bodice, then numerous skirt panels were set aside until nothing remained but the pinning. And the stitching. And the fitting. And the hemming.

Aye, and the praying.

Elisabeth gathered the fabric and her sewing basket, then hastened down the long hall to the same cozy room where she'd done her mending the day before. A fire was laid, and a fresh candle stood amid the globes of water in the candle-stool. She lit them both, relieved to have warmth and light, then began with the bodice, pinning the six pieces together, seam by seam.

As she worked, lively voices filtered into the servants' hall. Mrs. Pringle's new maids, she imagined. They sounded young, eager, and nervous. She smiled, remembering her first days at Mrs. Sinclair's Boarding School for Young Ladies in Edinburgh. Elisabeth had been all of eight-and-ten and entirely green, knowing nothing of the world. She learned a great deal in the years that followed. Some of it was painful, yet all of it was needful.

What would Effie Sinclair think if she saw her now? Elisabeth considered her ragged mourning gown, her hastily combed hair, and her chapped fingers and knew what her esteemed schoolmistress would say. "Lift your head, Mrs. Kerr. You have a fine mind, a bonny face, skilled hands, and the Lord's favor. Use them well in the service of others, and a full reward will be yours."

Her spirits buoyed, Elisabeth pinned her seams with renewed fervor, paying no attention to the loud noises in the hall or the laughter spilling from the nearby kitchen. The bodice was soon fully pinned, as were the elbow-length sleeves, with only the skirt remaining. Her head was bent over her work, the pins mere inches from her face, when a gray and white paw batted at her nose.

"Oh!" She jumped to her feet, startled out of her wits.

Looking up at her was a round-faced cat. Its smooth fur was the very color of Mrs. Pringle's new gown but with random streaks of white, as if the puss had come too near a pail of whitewash. Its ears were large, its whiskers long, its golden eyes attentive. Nothing would escape this cat's notice, she decided.

"Who might you belong to?" Elisabeth bent down to scratch the animal's head and realized it was purring rather noisily. When she eased onto her chair, the cat put its paws on her knees, stretching up to sniff her. "We must come to some agreement, you and I," she told the furry creature. "I have much work to do and no time for petting." Still, the animal's fur was exceedingly soft, as velvety as the fabric in her lap. The longer she stroked its head, the louder it purred, until she was certain Mrs. Tudhope would come forth from her kitchen, wooden spoon in hand, intent on dispatching the four-legged intruder.

"Ye've been chosen," a lass said from the doorway.

Elisabeth looked up to find Sally studying her, a dinner tray in her hands. "He doesna like monie o' the servants," Sally commented, placing the food atop a tall chest, well out of the cat's reach. "Keeps his ain company whan the master isna here."

Elisabeth blinked. "You mean this cat belongs to Lord Buchanan?" She could not imagine a man of such stature having a cat roaming about the house. Hunting dogs, perhaps, or collies. Cats were usually meant for *byres* and barns, not mansions.

Sally told her, "His lordship said the cat

came aboard in Canton."

"A Chinese cat?" Elisabeth eyed the animal with more interest. "Well, he certainly is friendly."

Sally called over her shoulder as she left. "To ye, mebbe."

THIRTY

For he purrs in thankfulness when God
tells him he's a good Cat.

CHRISTOPHER SMART

Elisabeth's bewhiskered friend was still there,
circling the room, when she claimed her dinner tray. The plate of steaming beef broth,
thick slice of bread, and generous serving of
butter made her mouth water. She spoke a
hasty grace over her meal, then ate at the
small table while the cat settled at her feet,
watching her spoon travel back and forth, its
slanted eyes gleaming in the candlelight.

"I forgot to ask Sally your name," Elisabeth
said, placing her almost-empty plate on the
floor and letting him lick it clean as she
enjoyed her almond pudding. She retrieved
the dish, then put her dinner tray atop the
chest once more, washed her hands in the
bowl of water beneath the window, and
returned to her labors.

Still the cat did not leave, though the door

was ajar and the hall filled with enticing sounds and smells. While she pinned the long side seams of Mrs. Pringle's skirt, the cat stretched out before the hearth, legs extended, showing off his pristine white belly.

"You must see to your own amusement this afternoon," Elisabeth told him, "for I've a fitting at three o' the clock." Mrs. Pringle would surely know the cat's name, if he had one. Perhaps the admiral simply called him *Puss.*

Elisabeth was putting the final pins in the voluminous skirt when Mrs. Pringle appeared, pocket watch in hand. "I am here for my fitting," she announced.

Whether it was the housekeeper's brusque manner or stern voice that spooked him, the cat shot past her skirts and through the door like a trail of gray smoke. "That *cat!*" Mrs. Pringle grumbled under her breath, then closed the door with a decisive bang.

"Nothing is stitched," Elisabeth reminded her, "and the pins are sharp, so do take care while I slip this on you." She made quick work of the fitting. "We can take in the waist a full inch," she declared, which brought a smile to the housekeeper's face just as Elisabeth had hoped, having intentionally made the waistline an inch too big. A wise dressmaker did what she could to please her customers. "I do wish we had a long looking glass," Elisabeth said, "so you might see how well this fabric suits your coloring."

Mrs. Pringle touched her hair. " 'Twas even brighter when I was a girl."

Elisabeth smiled. *At last something personal.* " 'Tis a lovely shade, like a freshly cut orange." The housekeeper looked the other way but not before Elisabeth saw a hint of a smile.

"If we're finished," Mrs. Pringle said, "I have several younger girls who require a bit of coddling." She quickly dressed herself, then met Elisabeth's gaze. "You are made of stronger stuff, Mrs. Kerr. I cannot imagine having to dry your eyes."

Elisabeth pushed a stray pin into the cushion. "Had you been with me in January when I lost my husband, all the handkerchiefs in your linen closet would not have dried my tears."

"Aye, well." Mrs. Pringle began tying her apron strings. "True for us all. Mr. Pringle died of the plague soon after we married."

Elisabeth gasped before she could stop herself. "The *plague?*"

"He and another merchant went to the Isle of Man to purchase trade goods. When ships from Marseilles sailed into port, the rats on board brought the plague with them." Her delivery was matter-of-fact, but the lingering sadness in her eyes was not. She fished in her apron pocket, drew out two shillings, then pressed them into Elisabeth's hand. "For yesterday's mending. Mrs. Craig, the head laundress, said you did exceedingly fine work."

Elisabeth gripped the coins, overcome. "I did not expect this . . ."

Mrs. Pringle had already opened the door before she turned to ask, "You'll not mind being down here alone all week?"

Elisabeth caught a glimpse of a gray tail flicking past the housekeeper's skirts. "I suspect I'll have company." Unbidden, the cat trotted into the room and sat before the hearth, looking very pleased with himself. "Does this animal have a name?"

Mrs. Pringle made a slight face. "The admiral calls him *Charbon*. A French word, apparently."

Of course. Elisabeth smiled at the cat and then at the housekeeper. "It means 'coal.' He is indeed charcoal gray, just like the fabric Lord Buchanan selected. Do you think he meant for his household staff to match his cat?"

"I hardly think so." Mrs. Pringle was not amused. "I may not see you again until Saturday. I trust you have everything required to complete my gown?"

"Aye, madam." Elisabeth slipped the coins into her pocket, thinking of mutton and veal, salmon and beef, for that was surely how her earnings would be spent. She glanced at Charbon, then wondered aloud, "Why a French word, do you suppose?"

"That I do know." Mrs. Pringle stepped into the hall. "Lord Buchanan's father was Scottish. But his mother was French."

Wednesday dawned grayer still. Though the air was mild, a capricious wind blew Elisabeth's skirts about her ankles as she climbed Bell Hill, bound for another day of sewing. In Edinburgh the breeze was often tinged with brine from the North Sea but not so in the Borderland. Would the admiral miss that bracing scent once he settled here for good? Someday she would ask him. When she met him. If she met him.

Taking Sally's advice, Elisabeth used the servants' entrance round the back of the house rather than walk through the grand halls upstairs. Once she was through the door, her workroom was steps away, with the unfinished gown precisely where she'd left it, draped across the chair. It seemed Mrs. Pringle ran her household in the same way an admiral might command his ship, for the floor was swept clean, the fire already burning, the candles lit, and the water pitcher filled, with a clean linen towel beside it.

A breakfast tray, covered with a linen napkin, rested on the table. Elisabeth lifted the cloth, delighted to find a boiled egg, a buttered roll, and a rasher of bacon. No one could have known she'd overslept and not had time for a single bite of food, yet here was a fine repast, waiting for her.

"Guid morn," Sally said from the doorway, holding up her teapot. "May I pour yer tea?"

"Bless you," Elisabeth said, holding out the empty cup and saucer. "I'd forgotten how nice china feels against my lips. At home we drink from wooden cups."

Sally said nothing, though a look of surprise registered in her sea-colored eyes. In a land where the rich and the poor lived side by side yet never shared table or bed, Elisabeth's situation — an educated lady living in poverty yet working for the gentry — must have struck the lass as very strange indeed.

The moment Sally disappeared down the hall, Charbon entered the room, his gray tail like a flag, waving a silent greeting. He inspected her shoes, still damp from the dewy grass, then sniffed at her skirt hem.

"Aye, 'tis the same gown," she told him. She was quite sure Charbon not only heard but also understood her and responded with the appropriate long blinks. "Pick a warm spot by the fire while I enjoy breakfast," she told him. "I promise to save you a wee bite of my bacon and will scratch your head before I see to my needle."

Charbon dutifully took his place, beating his tail against the floor, waiting his turn.

On Saturday Elisabeth began her journey east to Bell Hill with a lighter step. Though the

266

air was still moist, the rain had abated, and the high clouds bore no further threat.

But it wasn't the change in the weather that brightened her outlook: Mrs. Pringle's gown was all but finished. There were buttons to be added, cuffs to be hemmed, sleeves to be pressed, but the hardest work was behind her.

Elisabeth had sewn many garments in her life, yet none mattered more than this one. Mrs. Pringle must be pleased, of course, and Lord Buchanan even more so. But only if the Almighty was satisfied with her labors could Elisabeth sleep well that night.

"What pleases the Lord is faith," her mother-in-law had reminded her over their bowls of porridge. "And you, my dear, have that in abundance."

Elisabeth carried Marjory's assurance with her that morning, through Foul Bridge Port, then across the broad meadow, and up Bell Hill. She chose the front entrance, hoping to gather a bit of news on the way to her workroom. "Shall we see the admiral today?" she asked the footman at the door.

"I cannot say, madam," he replied, though his half smile indicated otherwise.

Crossing the entrance hall, Elisabeth saw maidservants everywhere, dusting, scrubbing, and polishing each surface until it gleamed. As she turned down the long hallway, she discovered two footmen cleaning the sconces and trimming the wicks, while a third hurried past her with an armload of firewood.

Amid the hubbub she heard a familiar voice. "Mrs. Kerr?"

"Good morn, Mrs. Pringle," she said, turning round to greet her.

The housekeeper hurried to catch up with her, clearly flustered. "I know my last fitting was to be at three o' the clock. 'Twill need to be promptly at eleven instead, for I wish to wear it today. You'll be ready for me?"

Elisabeth gulped. "Aye."

"Off you go, then," the housekeeper said and fled in the opposite direction.

Her heart beating at a breathless pace, Elisabeth aimed for the workroom, looking neither left nor right, lest she be distracted. Her list of remaining tasks lengthened with each step. She'd not sewn pockets in the lining yet, meant for fragrant herbs. Nor had she stitched linen patches inside each cuff for the small weights that held the sleeves in place. And the buttonholes required finishing. And the gown needed a row of hooks and eyes.

A children's rhyme skipped through her head as she hastened down the lower hall. *Jack, be nimble! Jack, be quick!* At least her candlestick was already burning and the log in the hearth as well. She was almost relieved no one had left a breakfast tray for her. How could they be bothered when every pair of hands was readying the house for Admiral

Lord Jack Buchanan's return?

Elisabeth was convinced of his arrival now. Nothing else could explain such a whirlwind of activity. *Time you joined them, Bess.*

Forcing herself to breathe, to think, to plan, she started with the final touches that mattered most and worked her way through her mental list. Charbon must have sensed her urgency, for he curled up in the chair opposite hers, demanding nothing more than her presence.

As each hour passed, the noise level in the servants' hall rose another notch, while excitement and hysteria danced a jig round the doors. Pots and pans clanged in the kitchen, and cooking aromas filled the air. Mrs. Tudhope was serving fish, flesh, fowl, and any number of other courses, all undoubtedly chosen to bless their master.

When Mrs. Pringle came rushing in, her face as bright as her hair, Elisabeth begged her to sit for a moment. "Your gown is ready," she assured her, "but the fabric will stick to your skin unless you take a moment to calm yourself." She pressed a cool, wet cloth against the housekeeper's forehead and offered her a saucer of lukewarm tea, which Mrs. Pringle gulped down like an elixir.

After closing the door, Elisabeth helped the housekeeper into her new gown, praying as she did so. *May it be a perfect fit, Lord. May she be satisfied with my work.* Elisabeth adjusted the bodice, then fastened the hooks and eyes as if she were a lady's maid dressing her mistress.

"How does the gown feel to you?" she asked, though Elisabeth could see how neatly it followed the natural curves of her body.

Mrs. Pringle ran her hands over the gown, inspecting each critical seam round her bodice and waist. "The fabric is very fine."

But what of my sewing? What of the gown itself? Elisabeth held her tongue, remembering Marjory's words. *Faith is what pleases the Lord.*

From her sewing basket Elisabeth pulled Anne's looking glass, borrowed for the day. "See what you think," she urged the housekeeper. "I believe you'll find the color and style very becoming."

Mrs. Pringle held the glass as far away as she could, peering at her reflection. In the soft candlelight the lines and creases in her face disappeared except the few that framed her smile. "My, won't he be pleased?"

It was all Elisabeth needed to hear.

"Now, then." The housekeeper handed Elisabeth the glass and straightened her shoulders. "You must stitch the hem at once, Mrs. Kerr, for we've no time left. Lord Buchanan is expected at any moment."

THIRTY-ONE

And last of all an Admiral came.

ROBERT SOUTHEY

"Almost home, milord."

Jack Buchanan fixed his gaze on Bell Hill, less than a mile away. He'd resided there but a fortnight, and half of that he'd spent elsewhere. Could even so grand a house as this one finally tether him to land? In all his forty years he'd not stepped foot in his father's native Scotland. Yet here he was, looking at a hilly green landscape purchased with Spanish gold.

Home? That remained to be seen.

Jack urged his horse forward, calling over his shoulder, "See to your mount, Dickson, or my dinner will be served cold."

"I think not, milord," his valet replied. A decent horseman, Christopher Dickson closed the gap between them as the horses lengthened their strides into a full gallop.

Jack eased his weight forward, lifting slightly

271

off the saddle, holding himself in balance, while his horse thundered toward the stables. He reveled in the fresh wind against his face and the sheer power of the magnificent animal beneath him. After endless years of riding nothing but waves, Jack valued the gray thoroughbred above all his earthly possessions.

The lofty branches of mature oaks, maples, and elms arched above him as he neared the property and slowed the horse with a quick take-and-give on the reins. Moments later horse and rider reached the stables, and Jack reluctantly surrendered the reins to his head coachman.

"Janvier has earned his oats and hay," Jack told dark-haired Timothy Hyslop.

A taciturn man in his thirties, the coachman had few words for two-legged creatures. He led the horse into the cool interior of the stables, murmuring endearments into Janvier's velvety ear, while Dickson dismounted and handed the reins to one of the grooms.

As the two men walked toward the house, Dickson reminded him, "Roberts and Mrs. Pringle will have their new staffs waiting at the front door to greet you."

Jack slowed his gait, giving the shorter man a fair go at keeping up with him. "You mean we cannot slip through the servants' entrance and see to my grooming first?"

Dickson chuckled. "I am afraid not,

milord." Having circled the globe in his service, the valet well knew his master cared little about appearances.

Jack put up with Dickson's fussing only on those occasions when attire truly mattered. On this last day of May he was simply a gentleman returning home from business in Edinburgh. The king's business, to be sure, but nothing that called for velvet or silk.

When Jack rounded the corner, he found his butler, George Roberts, standing at attention near the entrance with servants lining either side of the paved walk. Along with Dickson and Hyslop, Mrs. Pringle and Mrs. Tudhope, Roberts had traveled from London at Jack's bidding. He trusted each one without reservation and had left Bell Hill in their capable hands over Whitsuntide, allowing them to hire the servants they deemed best.

Within the hour he'd know how well the five of them had managed.

The moment Jack stepped onto the paving stones, Roberts announced him. "Lord Jack Buchanan, Admiral of His Majesty's Royal Navy and Master of Bell Hill."

Jack was accustomed to being saluted by his men aboard ship, but two long rows of people bowing and curtsying was almost more than he could bear. None but the Almighty deserved such obeisance. Jack lifted his hat and said blithely, "May the good Lord be with you."

A bright-eyed maidservant took a cautious step forward. "God bliss ye, sir."

When Jack nodded in her direction, pleased at her response, the rest of his servants swiftly followed her example, their hearty blessings wafting through the air like hawthorn petals on May Day.

Amid their greetings Roberts came forward, a tall man of five-and-fifty years, with a full head of light brown hair and a most efficient manner. "Welcome home, sir. If I may introduce your new menservants."

"Very well." It seemed dinner would have to wait.

Roberts presented more than a dozen men of varying ages chosen to serve as footmen, coachmen, and grooms. Jack had protested when Roberts suggested he employ a page. "Too pretentious," he'd told the butler.

Once the menservants were dispatched to their duties, it was the housekeeper's turn. Upon hiring Mary Pringle two years ago, Jack had decided the woman could easily command any quarterdeck in the fleet.

"Good afternoon, Mrs. Pringle," he said, noticing her new gown. "Is that the cloth we brought from London?"

" 'Tis, sir." She curtsied, a spot of color in each cheek. "Come and meet your new maidservants." Mrs. Pringle had penned a list, giving not only their full names in turn but also whence they came and what experience they brought with them. A tedious business, yet each lass seemed grateful to be duly recognized.

When they finished, the maidservants scattered — to the kitchen or the dining hall, Jack hoped. Only then did he notice another woman just inside the doorway. Her tattered black gown spoke of a widow without means, yet she was not included on Mrs. Pringle's list.

The stranger's face was shadowed by the broad open door, but he clearly saw Charbon curled at her feet. Jack could almost hear the cat purring from where he stood.

"Roberts?"

His butler was beside him at once. "Aye, sir."

"Who's the widow by the door?"

"She's a Highlander. Came from Edinburgh with her mother-in-law, a Mrs. Kerr."

Jack frowned. "*Kerr* is hardly a Highland name." By squinting just so, he caught a glimpse of brown hair, almost the color of his own, a slender neck, and pale skin, though he could not make out her features. "How old would you say she is?"

The butler cleared his throat. "One cannot be certain without asking, but five-and-twenty would be my guess."

Young, then. But wasn't everyone when a man reached forty? As Jack watched, she disappeared into the recesses of the house,

Charbon in close pursuit. "Perhaps Mrs. Pringle knows something of her story."

"I believe she does, sir. You may speak with her at any time, of course, but you might prefer to wait 'til after you've enjoyed your dinner."

"Aye," Jack agreed, striding toward the door. "Dinner."

Jack was miserable. On the *Centurion* he'd dined with other officers round the captain's table, always a convivial group. In London he'd taken his meals at the better inns or public houses with a lively gathering of gentlemen, both friends and strangers. But to sit alone at a long table laden with food enough to feed ten hungry souls while Dickson stood behind him, two footmen tarried at the door, and maidservants came and went with eyes averted — well, it might be proper, but it would not do.

He summoned Roberts. "I wonder if you and Hyslop might join me at table now and again. I realize it flies in the face of convention."

The color drained from his face. "Sir . . . we could not possibly . . ."

Jack narrowed his gaze. "Not even if I commanded it?"

"Oh! Well . . . of course, sir, but . . . the others . . ." Roberts spread out his hands, then folded them together: a servant's equivalent of a polite shrug.

Seeing how uncomfortable Roberts was with the notion, Jack offered something less daring. "Reverend Brown provided a list of the gentry in Selkirkshire. Might dinner invitations be extended? Two or three a week perhaps?"

Roberts brightened. "I'll see to it at once."

It was a start, in any case. Jack surveyed his dining table, toying with another idea. "How many people will she seat?"

"Thirty," Roberts said, "though the furniture maker still has a dozen chairs to finish."

"See that he delivers them by the end of June." Jack looked across the empty room, an image forming in his mind. "On the last of each month, I shall invite the entire household to sup at my table." He turned to Roberts. "What say you to that?"

His voice was noticeably weaker. "If it pleases your lordship."

"It does," Jack assured him, already anticipating the evening.

"I must caution you, sir, their table manners —"

"Will be sufficient to move their food from plate to mouth, aye?" Jack smiled at the man charged with overseeing Bell Hill. Roberts was ever prudent and had his best interests at heart but could also be persuaded to do things his way. "The last day of June, then. I shall look forward to it."

Roberts bowed. "Might there be anything else, milord?"

Jack pushed back his chair and stretched his legs. "Kindly fetch Mrs. Pringle. And that Kerr woman."

Thirty-Two

Let honesty be as the breath of thy soul.

BENJAMIN FRANKLIN

"Was his lordship pleased?" Elisabeth asked, her needle darting in and out of the broadcloth. She'd sent the housekeeper upstairs in such haste that the last few inches of Mrs. Pringle's hem were merely pinned in place. "I pray he didn't notice the tiny glint of steel along the hemline."

The housekeeper looked down at her. "You can be sure of it. And though he did not compliment the gown, his expression was praise enough."

Elisabeth had seen that expression. Brows lifted, eyes alight, mouth curved in a faint suggestion of a smile. He was even taller than she'd imagined and broader in the shoulders, his skin weathered by the sun, the jut of his chin hardened from years of being in command.

She recalled Sally Craig's opinion of the

279

admiral. *Not verra handsome.* But Sally was young.

"Mrs. Pringle?" Roberts stood by the open door to the workroom, his gaze shifting from one woman to the other. "His lordship would have a word with you. And bring Mrs. Kerr."

Elisabeth gripped the fabric to keep her hands from trembling, then looked up at the housekeeper. "What will he want to know?"

"The truth," Mrs. Pringle said firmly. "He is not a gentleman to be trifled with. If he asks about your Highland family, you must speak honestly."

"*I* must speak?"

The housekeeper nodded. "I will meet with him first while you wait outside the door." Mrs. Pringle leaned down and lowered her voice. "That is to say, *listen* outside the door."

Elisabeth swallowed. "Is that not . . . dishonorable?"

"Nae, 'tis prudent," the housekeeper insisted. "You'll hear what his lordship and I discuss and will know what else must be said. Come, finish your stitches, for he does not like to be kept waiting."

Elisabeth sewed in haste, her thoughts whirling. *Speak honestly.* How could she rightly do otherwise? *Let the words of my mouth be acceptable in thy sight.* Aye, that would be her prayer while she tarried in the hall. If Gibson was correct and Lord Buchanan was a man who sought to please God, then she would honor them both with the truth.

She knotted her thread with a decisive tug, then stood, shaking the loose clippings from her skirt. "Might I have a moment to freshen up?"

"Be quick," the housekeeper cautioned her.

Elisabeth hurried to the water pitcher, washed her hands and face, then smoothed her hair, wishing she had a brush. Anne's looking glass, pulled from her sewing basket, confirmed Elisabeth's fears: her skin was becoming freckled from her morning walks, the circles beneath her eyes hinted at too little sleep, and her hair was a mass of wisps and curls brought on by the summer's heat.

"You look presentable enough," Mrs. Pringle told her with a note of impatience. "Come, we must away."

Moments later Elisabeth was seated outside the dining room on a chair that Roberts placed very close to the door. He bade her farewell with a solemn wink, then took his leave.

"I will summon you shortly," Mrs. Pringle murmured before sweeping into the room and greeting the admiral. "How may I be of service to you, milord?"

Clasping her hands in her lap, Elisabeth listened, hardly moving, barely breathing.

The admiral's voice floated into the hallway. "I noticed a young woman standing just inside the entrance earlier today when I arrived, yet you did not introduce her."

"Do forgive me," Mrs. Pringle said at once. "Since we've not spoken of engaging a dressmaker, Mrs. Kerr is not yet in your employ. It seemed unwise to include her with the others."

"I see. She is a dressmaker, you say? I can only assume she made your new gown."

"She did, milord."

Elisabeth could not ignore their conversation even if she tried. The chair was too close, their voices too clear. Above all, her livelihood depended upon the questions asked, the answers given, and the mercy his lordship might extend. She would not likely find work elsewhere in Selkirk. Though Michael Dalgliesh had made use of her talents, the other tailors in the parish seemed less inclined to do so.

"I know little about women's clothing," Lord Buchanan was saying, "though I do recognize quality when I see it. When and how did Mrs. Kerr present herself?"

As Elisabeth strained to hear, Mrs. Pringle described her arrival on Whitsun Monday. "She finished an entire basket of mending that very day, working from morn 'til eve, taking her dinner in the workroom, then continuing to labor."

"She is not afraid of hard work, then."

"On the contrary," the housekeeper said

emphatically, "she embraces it."

Elisabeth heard him shift in his chair.

"What else does Mrs. Kerr embrace, pray tell? Is she prone to drink? To gossip? To dally with menservants? To steal the silver from the cabinets? Or is she a devout woman?"

"Oh, very devout," Mrs. Pringle said. "Sally Craig informs me that Mrs. Kerr prays before taking so much as a sip of tea or a bite of meat. More than once in our discussions she has quoted from the psalms, yet I do not think she does so to impress me."

The housekeeper's words gave Elisabeth pause. *Is that true? Or do I secretly wish to gain the approval of others?* At the moment she desperately needed Lord Buchanan's approval. But if she was anything less than genuine, he would surely see through her.

Mrs. Pringle was saying, "It might be best if you spoke with the young woman yourself, milord."

Elisabeth stood, wanting to be sure her knees would support her. 'Twould not do to stumble into his presence. When Mrs. Pringle appeared, not a word was exchanged as together they entered the sumptuously decorated room with its lofty ceilings, enormous glass chandelier, long windows facing south, and a massive mahogany dining table.

Once Elisabeth settled her gaze on Lord Jack Buchanan, the décor ceased to hold much interest. Though she'd glimpsed him earlier from a distance, now she could assess him properly. His brow was lined with a lifetime of experience, and his brown eyes shone with intelligence.

"Milord," she said, then curtsied.

"Mrs. Kerr," he said with a polite nod. "Roberts informs me you are a Highlander." He quit there as if waiting for her to elaborate.

"I was born in Castleton of Braemar in Aberdeenshire," she began, "the only daughter of Fiona and James Ferguson, a weaver."

"And what of your Highland family now?"

"My father is dead, and so is my brother, Simon. My mother has . . . remarried." Elisabeth hoped he would not require further details. Even speaking of Ben Cromar made her ill.

Instead, his lordship changed the subject. "Roberts said you came to Selkirk from Edinburgh."

"From the age of eight-and-ten I was educated in the capital and worked as a seamstress for a tailor in the Lawnmarket."

Lord Buchanan leaned back in his chair. "Might he provide a character for you?"

"Angus MacPherson is dead, milord. And so, I fear, is his son." She looked down for a moment, composing herself.

"You buried your husband as well," the admiral said.

"Alas, I never saw his grave. He was killed

in battle. At Falkirk in January."

Lord Buchanan straightened, his expression more alert. "Your husband was a soldier? And a Highlander as well?"

Elisabeth hesitated but only for a moment. *Speak honestly.* "He was a soldier, aye. But a Lowlander. 'Tis why my mother-in-law returned home to Selkirk."

He gazed at her more intently. "And you came with her even though the Borderland is not your home?"

"She is the only family I have now." Elisabeth spread her hands, searching for the right words. "As it happens, we share more than our name. We both trust the same God."

He slowly rose, never taking his eyes off her. "Madam, everything else you have told me cannot hold a candle to that."

Elisabeth looked up to meet his gaze. "Should you wish to read them, I have written characters from Michael Dalgliesh, a tailor in Selkirk, and from Reverend Brown."

"Leave them with Mrs. Pringle if you like, though I've no need to see them."

Elisabeth's heart sank. Was he not interested in her services after all? "Milord, I truly need this position," she pleaded.

His gaze did not waver. "And I need a dressmaker."

Does he mean . . . Elisabeth moistened her lips, suddenly gone dry. *Am I to be . . .*

"Heaven knows," he continued, "I brought

enough cloth from London to dress half the county. At the moment I'd be satisfied to have all my maidservants arrayed as finely as my housekeeper." When Mrs. Pringle bristled, he quickly amended his words. "Well, not *quite* so finely. Perhaps a simpler design might be best for the others. Shall we say . . . eighteen gowns in all, Mrs. Pringle?"

"That will do," the housekeeper replied, looking smug.

Elisabeth eyed both of them, wanting to be very sure she understood. "Then . . . I am . . . engaged?"

"Most certainly," Lord Buchanan said. "What say you to six months in my employ? From now 'til Saint Andrew's Day?"

The thirtieth of November. She nodded, uncertain if she could speak. *God bless this man.* Her future, as well as Marjory's, was secure — at least for the balance of the year. "However can I thank you?"

"Don't thank me yet," he protested, "for you'll be working very hard." He began to pace before the massive mantelpiece, hands clasped behind his back. "Tell me, is it a long distance for you to travel each day?"

"Not so far. Two miles on foot."

He spun round. "You *walk* to Bell Hill?" When she assured him she did, he suggested, "Perhaps you might prefer to take up residence here."

Elisabeth balked. She could not entertain

the idea, not even for a moment. "Forgive me, milord, but I've promised not only to provide for my mother-in-law but also to care for her. I cannot leave her side, nor would I choose to."

"Admirable," he said, though something did not appear to sit well with him.

Elisabeth exchanged glances with Mrs. Pringle. Might she know what was on his mind?

Finally he said, "If you insist on walking here from Selkirk, then I would ask you to be cautious, traveling only by the light of day and with other women whenever possible. Even here at Bell Hill, see that you remain in the company of my maidservants."

Elisabeth agreed, if only to appease him. "Is there something in particular that concerns you?"

He rubbed his chin, where a shadow of a beard was starting to show. "Although Roberts and Hyslop have chosen their men with virtue in mind, you are a widow, a Highlander, and a beauty. Some men might view such attributes as license to . . . , eh, overstep their bounds, since you have no male relatives to defend your honor."

Her cheeks warmed at the bluntness of his language. "As you wish, milord."

"I will speak to the men myself and make certain you are not ill treated or taken advantage of." He seemed most adamant on that point.

Mrs. Pringle piped up. "You can be sure I will see to Mrs. Kerr's safety."

"Aye, and to her daily meat and drink as well," he added. "As to payment for your labors, rather than holding your wages until Martinmas, Mrs. Pringle will pay you for each gown when it's finished. Shall we say . . . one guinea each?"

Elisabeth swallowed. *A guinea? 'Tis twenty-one shillings!*

Mrs. Pringle said faintly, "But that . . ."

He held up his hand. "Am I not permitted to spend my money as I see fit?"

"Aye, milord." The housekeeper bowed her head, as meek as Elisabeth had ever seen her. "Forgive me."

"You are merely being mindful of my household accounts, Mrs. Pringle, as well you should be. I shall add sufficient guineas to your ledger such that we needn't give up sugar, aye?"

She lifted her coppery head and smiled. "Very good, milord."

Elisabeth simply looked at the man, awed by a generosity she'd seldom known. "Shall I begin on Monday, then?"

"You shall," he agreed, "though, in truth, you've labored all week." The admiral produced a hefty calfskin purse from which he drew a gold coin. "For Mrs. Pringle's gown. The first of many."

288

When he placed the cool guinea in her palm, Elisabeth stared at the coin. "Are you always so generous with strangers?"

"You are no stranger to God," he reminded her. "This is his blessing, not mine."

Elisabeth looked down, overwhelmed. *You have not forgotten us, Lord.*

Then she felt something brush against her foot. "Charbon," she said softly. "How glad you must be to have your master home."

The admiral scowled at his pet. "There you are, you ungrateful creature. Transferring your affections at the first opportunity." He bent down and scooped up Charbon, then tucked the animal under his arm. "You must be very special indeed, Mrs. Kerr, for my cat does not often pay attention to women."

She scratched Charbon along the crooked white streak between his ears, setting off a roaring sort of purr. "He kept me company all week, awaiting your return."

"Well done, puss." He shifted his stance. "Shall I see you at kirk in the morn?"

She curtsied, then met his gaze. "Indeed you shall, milord."

THIRTY-THREE

O day of rest!
How beautiful, how fair.

HENRY WADSWORTH LONGFELLOW

Marjory still could not believe it. A gentleman who'd sailed round the world was seated in her pew, in her kirk. Well, not truly *her* kirk. *The earth is the Lord's, and the fulness thereof.* She knew everything belonged to the Almighty. Still, Lord Jack Buchanan was definitely situated in the Kerr aisle that Sabbath morning.

Furthermore, he'd engaged her daughter-in-law as a dressmaker, a position not without merit, even for a lady. As if that were not enough, his lordship had sent Elisabeth home with a gold guinea. *A guinea!* The three Kerr women had taken turns holding the coin through most of supper.

Our dear Bess, the dressmaker. And our new friend, the admiral.

290

Marjory was trying hard not to be prideful and failing miserably.

True, she was not much pleased when Elisabeth returned home early last evening with the news of Lord Buchanan's offer. He was a bachelor, after all, and had suggested she reside at Bell Hill. A gentlewoman in mourning, sleep beneath his roof? *The very idea.* When her daughter-in-law explained the reason — for her safety — Marjory was willing to give his lordship another chance to earn her good opinion.

He'd done so the moment he'd arrived at kirk that morning, impeccably dressed in a royal blue silk coat and periwig, and had inquired if he might sit at the end of their pew. "Mrs. Kerr," he'd said with a courtly bow, "it would be my great honor to share your aisle this morn if you would allow it."

When a very tall, very polite, very rich man asked for two feet of wood on which to sit, only a foolish woman objected. "Naturally, milord," she'd told him, moving down so he might be seated next to her rather than beside Elisabeth. It seemed prudent.

Marjory looked round the church, beginning to feel at home once more. Providing a written character for Tibbie Cranshaw had turned out to be a wise decision. Tibbie was now engaged as a kitchen maid at Bell Hill and so had honest work and a worthy incentive to keep hidden her unfortunate history.

And mine. And Elisabeth's.

The admiral would hardly be seated next to her if he knew the truth. Perhaps by the time he learned the whole of it — and Marjory had no doubt he eventually would, for Lord Buchanan was a clever man — they would already be friends and such things might be forgiven.

He'd sung the psalms with conviction, she decided, and listened to Reverend Brown's dry discourse on the Midianites with particular attentiveness. Earlier that morning Marjory had enjoyed pleasant exchanges with Sarah Chisholm and Martha Ballantyne in the kirkyard. It was in every respect a commendable Sabbath. As to the weather, the day was clear and bright and mild. Wasn't that like June, to make so sunny an entrance?

With the reverend's stirring benediction still ringing through the sanctuary, Marjory turned to Lord Buchanan, a thousand questions bubbling up inside her. "Will you be constructing a loft here in the kirk?" she asked him. "I'd imagined it hanging just above us."

"I prefer to sit with the congregation," he said. "In the Kerr pew, if I'll not be imposing on you and your household."

"Not at all!" she cried, then wished she'd curbed her enthusiasm a little. People were staring, and not all their expressions were friendly ones. Tibbie Cranshaw had an espe-

292

cially sour look on her face, which Marjory found irksome after all she'd done for the woman.

Composing herself, Marjory said to the admiral, "I am told, milord, that your father was Scottish rather than English."

"Indeed, madam, from the Borderland. Though he too sailed with the Royal Navy and sold his land to the Duke of Roxburgh long before I was born."

Marjory smiled, realization dawning. "You bought it back, didn't you? Bell Hill was once your family's estate."

"So it was." Though the admiral did not smile in return, his brown eyes gleamed ever so slightly.

When he turned to speak with Elisabeth, Marjory gave them a moment's privacy by blocking the Kerr aisle so no one else could interfere. She'd already learned two important bits of information about Lord Buchanan and found them both heartening. He was willing to sit among commoners. And his ancestors hailed from Selkirkshire. However, he still answered to King George, a vital fact not to be forgotten.

"Leddy Kerr?"

She turned round to find Gibson moving in her direction even as the reverend's stern words rose up to scold her. *Be cautious in your dealings with Gibson.* She would do nothing of the sort. Neil Gibson was her oldest friend in Selkirk. Nae, in all the world. Since she could not write letters to a man who could not read, Marjory made the most of their encounters.

"Good day to you, sir," she said, offering her gloved hand.

She meant for him to clasp it briefly in greeting. Instead, Gibson enveloped her hand in his, the centers of his blue gray eyes darkening. "Guid day to ye, milady."

Marjory glanced over her shoulder, hoping Reverend Brown had already moved to the door. "Have a care," she whispered.

Gibson tugged her closer. "I care mair than ye ken."

Flustered, Marjory withdrew her hand. "My, but we're being rather serious this morn."

He stepped back, his expression cooling. "The reverend is bidding me come."

"You must do so," she urged him, not wishing to anger the man on whom Gibson depended for his living. So many masters to be served! Reverend Brown and now Lord Buchanan. Marjory had grown accustomed to owning few possessions and to living under someone else's roof, but she still missed being in charge of her own household. Best not to dwell on a life she would never see again, she reminded herself, then turned to see how Elisabeth was faring with his lordship.

"So the creature jumped onto my bed

without warning," the admiral was saying, "and licked my face. A rude awakening, to say the least."

Marjory thought she might faint.

Elisabeth calmly replied, "Then you must lock your door at night."

"Or send my cat home with you," he grumbled.

A cat. Marjory felt her rapid heartbeat easing.

"I'm afraid Cousin Anne would not be keen on that idea," Elisabeth told him. "My mother-in-law and I are imposition enough without adding a guest with fur."

Anne joined their conversation, having been properly introduced before the admiral was seated. "Lord Buchanan, I would gladly accept anything you wish to send to Halliwell's Close, provided it has no claws."

"Then I cannot send Dickson either," he said, eying his younger valet. "For he has been known to scratch at my door at all hours."

"Only when bidden," Dickson replied dryly, clearly accustomed to such remarks.

Out of the corner of her eye, Marjory noticed Michael Dalgliesh and his lad approaching the Kerr aisle with lowered chins and furtive glances. She motioned the tailor forward. "Lord Buchanan, if I may be so presumptuous as to introduce a friend and neighbor of our family, Mr. Michael Dalgliesh, a tailor, and his son, Peter."

Michael bowed, a rather clumsy effort, but Peter made a fine show of it, bending straight from his waist, one foot to the front.

"What fine manners you have, lad," Lord Buchanan told him.

Marjory saw the softening of his lordship's expression and heard the tenderness in his voice. How odd the man had not married by now and had children of his own. Too many years at sea, she imagined, and no home for a bride. He'd solved both those problems with his move to Selkirkshire. Was a wife next on his list?

"Lord Buchanan, I thank ye for yer custom," Michael Dalgliesh was saying.

The admiral cocked one brow. "*My* custom?"

"Mr. Hyslop, sir," the tailor explained, his ruddy skin growing more so. "He came by the shop last eve, leuking to buy fabric with yer silver."

"Ah." The admiral leaned forward and said in a stage whisper, "Suppose we keep that purchase just between us, aye?"

Michael ducked his head. "Whatsomever ye say, milord."

Marjory found their little exchange most interesting. Elisabeth seemed intrigued as well. If fabric was being purchased, would her daughter-in-law be expected to create something with it?

Straightening, Lord Buchanan caught his valet's eye. "We must away," he said, "or Mrs. Tudhope will be most vexed. She worked hard late last eve preparing my Sabbath dinner and is determined to have it on my table at precisely two o' the clock." A faint smile creased his swarthy countenance. "The fact that it is served cold apparently does not signify."

When the admiral turned to her, Marjory was struck again by his size. Taller even than Donald and broader by far. His unpowdered wig, with its long queue curling down his back, matched his dark brown eyes.

"It has been a pleasure to make your acquaintance, Mrs. Kerr," he said. "And you as well, Miss Kerr." He bowed to Marjory and Anne, then turned to Elisabeth. "As for you, madam, I shall see you early in the morn."

"Not *too* early, milord," Elisabeth responded. "With summer upon us, the sun is peeking over the horizon soon after three."

His scowl seemed largely a pretense. "I'll not have you storming my front door at six bells in the middle watch," he told her. "Eight o' the clock will suffice."

Elisabeth nodded. "Very good, milord."

Only then did Marjory notice the Murrays of Philiphaugh sailing toward them like a British warship, Sir John at the helm with a smiling young lady on each arm.

"Admiral!" he said jovially. "Sir John Murray at your service." The gentlemen exchanged bows before Sir John continued, "If I might introduce my lovely wife and daughters."

Marjory had never felt so invisible. Neither Sir John nor Lady Eleanora even looked at her, giving the admiral their undivided attention.

Rosalind and Clara curtsied as gracefully as they could in a crowded kirk aisle. Clara was still the shy, rather plain girl Marjory remembered from years past. But her older sister had blossomed into a hothouse flower, fragrant and exotic, with sleek black hair and eyes the color of Scottish bluebells.

"Lord Buchanan," Rosalind said, lifting her chin to meet his gaze. "Your fine reputation is introduction enough."

Marjory watched the Murrays fawn over the admiral, their intentions embarrassingly clear: Sir John and Lady Eleanora wanted his lordship for their son-in-law. Marjory could hardly fault them. Had she not once sought a titled, wealthy bride for Andrew? Still, she hoped she'd not been *this* obvious, offering up Rosalind like a juicy pheasant on a silver platter. Lord Buchanan was provided neither bib nor fork, but the Murrays did their best to whet his appetite, praising Rosalind's many accomplishments.

Only when the Murrays took their leave did

Lord Buchanan turn to bid the Kerrs a hasty farewell. "I fear Mrs. Tudhope will not soon forgive my tardiness. Until we meet again."

His bow was brief but polite, Marjory noted, and aimed solely at Elisabeth.

Thirty-Four

Few men have been admired by their own
households.

Michel Eyquem de Montaigne

Jack smoothed his hand along Janvier's neck.
"You've brushed him thoroughly, have you,
lad? And picked out his feet? Before you
sponge him with water, let me use the wisp."

The young groom quickly produced the
tightly woven knot of rope meant to massage
the horse's muscles and stimulate the skin.
Freshly dampened, the hay wisp fit neatly in
Jack's grip. Wherever Janvier's muscles were
firm and flat, Jack vigorously applied the
wisp, following the lay of the coat, feeling his
own muscles straining.

When he finished, he stood back and
rubbed a bare forearm across his damp brow.
"Sponge him, lad, and see to his saddle. I'll
be taking a long ride this morning."

Jack stepped into the coolness of the stables
and bathed his face and hands in a clean

bucket of water, then ran his wet fingers through his close-cropped hair before dropping his peruke back in place. Some days he missed the sea but not on a summer day like this. Before long he was astride Janvier heading for the orchards at an easy trot. Judging by the slant of the sun, the hour was no later than seven o' the clock.

He kept to the edge of the orchard, not wanting to slow the laborers at their tasks or risk injuring Janvier on protruding roots. Jack lifted his hand to greet his head gardener, Gil Richardson, a local man who'd begun work on the property the moment it was purchased. Many of the trees were old, no doubt planted by his grandfather Buchanan, but some were newly added to the orchards and would not produce fruit for several seasons.

Richardson had chosen the varieties with care. The plums were imperial and damask, the apples golden pippin and autumn permain, and the pears, naturally, were red Buchanan. The trees marched along in neat rows, their branches covered with leaves but not yet heavy with fruit. Jack spotted buds of yellow, green, and a rosy amber. By summer's end he'd have freshly picked fruit at table — a luxury few men in the Royal Navy ever knew.

Sensing Janvier growing restless, Jack turned round and began trotting at a good pace along the ridge of Bell Hill. He intended

301

to explore the eastern marches of his property rather than head downhill toward the ribbon of track that ran between his home and Selkirk, where a certain young widow would be walking that very hour.

Elisabeth Kerr was an enigma. For a dressmaker she was exceptionally well educated and well mannered. They'd not discussed literature or history, but he suspected she was well read in those subjects as well as others. Clearly there was more to the young woman than met the eye, though *that* was impressive too.

He urged Janvier into a full gallop, seeking a distraction. While in his employ, Elisabeth Kerr deserved his respect, not his unwelcome attention.

Horse and rider covered the rolling terrain, jumping the occasional stone dyke with ease, then slowing to pick their way through the forested portions of his family's estate. Had his grandfather marveled at the same view on summer mornings long ago? And had his father bothered to look back when he quit Bell Hill, filled with dreams of the sea?

"When I left Scotland," William Buchanan once confessed, "I broke your grandfather's heart."

Remembering his words, Jack grimaced. *And then you broke mine.*

As a captain in the Royal Navy, his father had sailed the world's oceans but seldom came into port, leaving behind his French wife and British son for months at a time until the loyal captain departed this world forever. Jacques Buchanan was seven when he lost his father, fourteen when Renée Buchanan drew her last breath.

Orphaned, he'd remained adrift in northern France until a naval friend of his father's took him aboard the HMS *Britannia* to train at sea as Midshipman Jack Buchanan. He'd moved up the ranks more swiftly than most, unfettered by family responsibilities. His every waking moment was focused on claiming victories at sea and the prizes that inevitably followed.

According to his bankers in London and Edinburgh, his fortune was prodigious. But Jack knew the truth: he had nothing of genuine value. No wife, no son, and, until now, no true home. He'd remedied the last; Lord willing, the others would follow in swift order.

He pulled Janvier's head round rather sharply and aimed toward Bell Hill. "Run, lad," Jack called out, a command his horse knew well. They were soon galloping hard, the fields and pastures a green blur, the stables forgotten. Only when Jack started downhill toward Selkirk did he see Elisabeth Kerr climbing the narrow track. He brought his horse to an abrupt stop just before he reached her.

She looked up, her face shadowed by the brim of her hat. "Good morn, milord."

"And to you, Mrs. Kerr." He dismounted, then took the reins in hand and began walking beside her as she continued uphill. There was no point pretending he'd not hoped for such a rendezvous. A pity he could not think of a single intelligent thing to say.

"You've a fine horse," she commented. "What do you call him?"

"He was foaled in January, so I named him Janvier."

She reached out to touch the animal's neck. "Rather fond of gray, aren't you?"

"I suppose I am." Jack forced himself to look at the cloudless sky, the rolling hills, the sheep in the lower meadow — anything to avoid studying the lovely young woman beside him. The Almighty had called him to provide for her and protect her, not pursue her. In any case, he was nearly old enough to be her father.

After a quiet moment she said, "Lord Buchanan, you expressed some concern about my traveling alone." She waved her hand across the broad expanse. "As you can see, I have the countryside to myself."

"This morn, aye," he said, more sharply than he intended. "But there are shepherds in the commons, farm workers in the fields, dragoons on horseback, chapmen with their goods —"

"Admiral," she said firmly, "I am a High-lander. Even Mrs. Pringle said I am made of stronger stuff. I can run like the wind if I need to and scream quite loudly if I must. I also carry a lethal pair of scissors round my neck." She held them up to prove her point.

He sensed he was losing ground. "So you have no fear of these men who might cross your path?"

"I do not," she said without hesitation. "My only fear this morn is not arriving by eight o' the clock and thereby disappointing my new employer."

"Well, we can't have that," he agreed, lengthening his stride, forcing her to do the same. They climbed the steep hill so briskly they could not converse. By the time they reached the crest, both of them were red-faced and winded.

"Please, Lord Buchanan." Elisabeth stopped to pull out her handkerchief. "If I might have a moment to catch my breath."

"Of course," he murmured.

What an idiot you are, Jack! Did you mean to exhaust the woman?

When they started again, he let her set the pace. By the time they reached the stables, her cheeks were pale again and her breathing steady. "Thank you for your kind attention," she said, then hastened toward the servants' entrance.

He'd meant to tell her to use the main door.

But perhaps this one was closer to her workroom. Had he even visited below stairs at Bell Hill? The kitchen, aye, but no farther. After handing the reins to a waiting groom, Jack strode toward the house, looking forward to a hot bath and a cooked breakfast, in that order.

Dickson was waiting in his second-floor bedchamber, where a copper bathtub sat by the fire, steaming buckets of water at the ready. Jack peeled off his clothes and was up to his chin in soapy water inside a minute. He exhaled, sinking deeper still.

"Do you mean to drown, sir?" Dickson asked.

" 'Twould be no more than I deserve," Jack confessed, not bothering to explain. Rolling his shoulders beneath the bath water, he felt his sore muscles tighten. "Haven't you a wisp or something?" he grumbled.

"I am not a groom," Dickson said, "and you are hardly a thoroughbred."

"Well, I was *once*," Jack shot back, though with no sting in his words. He was undeniably forty and felt every one of those years in his aching body, having ridden harder that morning than he had in many months, then made a fool of himself with his dressmaker.

After a good soak and fresh clothing, Jack's mood improved. Mrs. Tudhope's thick bacon and perfectly poached eggs helped even more. He was almost feeling human again when Roberts and Mrs. Pringle joined him in his study for their daily forenoon meeting.

Jack wasted no time on idle chatter. "Tell me, Roberts, how are the new servants managing?"

His butler gave a promising report, as did his housekeeper.

"And Mrs. Kerr," Jack said, trying to sound nonchalant. "Today she begins sewing a new gown for . . ."

"Mrs. Tudhope," came Mrs. Pringle's quick reply.

"Milord . . ." Roberts looked at Mrs. Pringle as if seeking her approval. "I've been wondering if it might be faster to hire several dressmakers? We could have the household in matching attire within a month."

Jack answered at once. "It would be faster, Roberts, but not wiser. As you know, Mrs. Kerr is supporting herself and her mother-in-law and desperately needs the income that I am able, by God's grace, to provide."

"Of course, milord. But —"

Jack stood, determined to make his point. "We could indeed hire more dressmakers and in short order have all our maidservants wearing gowns made of the same fabric. But they would not be wearing the same gowns, would they, Mrs. Pringle?"

"No indeed," his housekeeper assured him. "Mrs. Kerr has a unique approach to dressmaking. And we've all seen how diligently she works."

"Better to support one woman for six months," Jack insisted, "than six women for one month and send them all struggling to find work come July." He paused, trying not to gloat. Then he remembered these were his servants, who were bound to do his bidding whether he presented a valid argument or not.

"Very good, sir," Roberts said.

"Well done, milord," Mrs. Pringle echoed.

In his heart Jack heard a more truthful assessment. *Honour is not seemly for a fool.*

THIRTY-FIVE

Shall I never feel at home,
Never wholly be at ease?

SIR WILLIAM WATSON

"We'll not be much longer," Elisabeth told the anxious cook, who stood beside her in the servants' vacant dining hall having her measurements taken. "I know Lord Buchanan's dinner is on your mind."

"And in my cooking pot," Mrs. Tudhope fretted. "The duck only stews for a quarter hour."

Elisabeth bent down to measure waist to hem, hiding her smile. The cook herself stewed round the clock if reports from the kitchen could be trusted.

A woman of sixty-odd years, Mrs. Tudhope was a study in silvery gray, from her hair to her eyes to the spectacles perched on her nose. Her measurements were almost Mrs. Pringle's in reverse, for the cook was very short and very round with no discernible waist.

As Elisabeth recorded the numbers on a slate, Mrs. Tudhope peered over her shoulder.

"No one will see those?" she asked, her voice quavering.

"Not a soul," Elisabeth promised her. "By the time you return for a fitting this afternoon, your slate will be wiped clean."

"If only 'twere that easy," Mrs. Tudhope moaned. "Still, if I do not taste the food, how will I know if it's seasoned correctly?"

"I could not agree more," Elisabeth told her, "and you are a marvelous cook."

When Mrs. Tudhope beamed, showing all her teeth, Elisabeth knew what his lordship would be having for dessert: raspberry tart.

"Off you go." She patted the woman's arm. "I shall need you here at three o' the clock."

No sooner did Mrs. Tudhope scurry out the door than Mrs. Pringle appeared, neatly dressed in her charcoal gray gown. The housekeeper frowned over her shoulder. "Will her dress be the same as mine?"

"The same design, aye, but with a few adjustments." Elisabeth quietly covered the slate. "Every woman deserves a gown that flatters her figure."

"Hmm," was all Mrs. Pringle said.

As Charbon investigated the housekeeper's shoes, Elisabeth began to unfold the bolt of fabric across the dining table. "How may I help you this morn?"

"Lord Buchanan wishes to speak with you."

Sighing inwardly, Elisabeth shook the chalk dust from her apron. "Do you imagine this will take long? I told the cook —"

"Mrs. Kerr," the housekeeper said sternly, "all of us who work at Bell Hill have a single priority: his lordship. Is that clear?"

"Aye, madam." Duly chastened, Elisabeth started for the stair with Charbon darting ahead of her, soon out of sight. Mrs. Pringle was right: Lord Buchanan deserved their best service. Not only because he was generous and fair but also because the Buik required it. *Servants, be obedient to them that are your masters.* The truth could not be put more plainly. The next part, though, spoke louder to Elisabeth, describing how such service was to be rendered: *in singleness of your heart, as unto Christ.* If she was sewing for the Lord himself, for her true Master, then every unseen stitch, every hidden buttonhole mattered.

Elisabeth soon reached Lord Buchanan's first-floor study, one of the many rooms she had yet to explore. Crossing the threshold, she paused, overwhelmed by what she saw. Books everywhere. On his desk. On his chairs. On his table. On his shelves.

In the midst of them sat Lord Buchanan with Charbon climbing onto his lap. "Is something wrong, Mrs. Kerr?"

"Not at all," she said, then quickly curtsied. "You have an impressive library."

He looked about the room as if noticing his collection for the first time. "Do you read?"

She stared at him, perplexed. "I both read and write, sir."

He almost smiled. "I meant, do you often read books? For pleasure or enlightenment?"

"I do. For both."

"What are reading now, pray tell?"

An easy question to answer since she and Marjory owned exactly one volume. "James Thomson's *The Seasons*."

"Poetry?" He wrinkled his brow. "I styled you a more adventurous reader. Defoe or Richardson or Fielding."

"I began *Moll Flanders*," Elisabeth admitted, "but I did not care for its heroine."

"Well, she's hardly heroic, our Moll, though she did spend her last days in sincere penitence. And I am a strong believer in forgiveness." Lord Buchanan stood, letting Charbon slip to the floor. "Mrs. Kerr, I have a gift for you." He reached behind his desk, withdrew a mysterious, cloth-wrapped bundle, and placed it in her arms.

Elisabeth knew at once it was fabric. The outer layer was an inexpensive muslin, wrapped in twine. But upon opening it, she discovered an exquisite broadcloth in a deep, rich black. Enough for at least two gowns.

She gazed at it, bewildered. "This is for me?"

"And for your mother-in-law. No widow should be forced to wear the same gown for an entire year of mourning. Those months are difficult enough." He brushed his fingertips across the edge of the broadcloth. "I charged Hyslop to find a fabric of the highest quality. I hope this will do."

Elisabeth swallowed. "You are too kind."

"Nae, I am selfish," he insisted, "for I wish to see all my household well dressed."

She saw through his protest and was touched by his generosity. Again.

"I shall sew them at home in the evenings," she told him. "Our two windows face west, so I'll have sufficient light well into the gloaming."

He looked horrified. "Your *two* windows?"

"Aye." Elisabeth fingered the twine, suddenly aware of how very poor she must seem to so wealthy a gentleman.

When the cat meowed for attention, Elisabeth bent down and began scratching his head. "*You* are the adventurer among us, Charbon, with your Chinese pedigree and your French name." She looked up at Lord Buchanan, hoping to dispel any awkwardness between them. "I believe Mrs. Pringle said your mother was French."

"Did she?" As he stepped back, a shadow moved across his face. "What else did Mrs.

Pringle say?"

Elisabeth stood, unnerved by the coolness in his voice. "That your father was Scottish."

"Nothing else?"

"N-nothing," she stammered.

"Good, because there is nothing to tell." He turned toward his desk, a patent dismissal.

Holding her fabric to her heart, Elisabeth curtsied, then flew out the door, wishing she could take back her careless words.

In the days that followed, Elisabeth saw little of Lord Jack Buchanan. He was either riding with Dickson or working alone in his study or calling on the local gentry — the Murrays in particular. However vital Sir John's role in Selkirk politics, his daughter Rosalind was the likely reason for the admiral's repeated visits to Philiphaugh.

As for Elisabeth, she was lost in fabric.

Sunlit hours now stretched from three in the morning 'til nine at night. Whether at home or at Bell Hill, Elisabeth felt compelled to spend every minute sewing, though her fingers were growing numb, her neck was often tense, and she had a constant headache. Marjory insisted upon buying her another thimble and had her needles sharpened as well, which did help. But nothing made the hours or the stitches go faster.

Charbon kept her company in the work-room, a reminder of the master she had somehow offended. She'd spoken the truth: Mrs. Pringle had not told her anything else about his parents. Yet there must be a great deal to tell, or his lordship would not have reacted as he did.

She looked up when Sally entered the workroom bearing a dinner tray. "Guid day to ye, Mrs. Kerr."

"And to you," Elisabeth said, putting down her fabric, hoping for a moment's conversation. Perhaps Sally knew something of the admiral's upbringing.

But the lass disappeared as quickly as she'd come. "I'll collect yer tray later, Mrs. Kerr."

Once again Elisabeth was left feeling betwixt and between. She was not a servant, yet she didn't hold one of the head positions. She also didn't reside at Bell Hill. Instead, like one of the gardeners, she came and went each day but was not part of the household.

Folk were polite and kind. And each gown earned her a guinea, for which she was grateful. Still, Elisabeth longed for one good friend at Bell Hill. And a place she could truly call home.

Thirty-Six

There are some occasions when a man
must tell half his secret, in order to conceal
the rest.

PHILIP STANHOPE, EARL OF CHESTERFIELD

Charbon was stretched out on a sunny patch
of carpet, tail twitching, while Jack drank his
third cup of tea and gazed out his study
window. *'Tis almost eight o' the clock, Mrs.
Kerr. Will I not see you this morn?*

He'd managed to keep his distance for a
full week — avoiding her in the house, on the
grounds, wherever they might run into each
other — convincing himself it was the wisest
course of action. *Your mother was French.
Your father was Scottish.* Innocent comments,
nothing more. What was he afraid of? That
she might not think well of his heritage?

*Be honest with yourself, man. You're afraid
she might not think well of you.*

When Elisabeth appeared in his sunlit

316

gardens a moment later, Jack watched her bend toward a cluster of blooming roses, then smile, perhaps breathing in their sweet fragrance.

A moment later she looked up and met his gaze. And held it.

Run, lad.

In a trice he was halfway down the corridor, then darted into the narrow turret stair, startling a maidservant. "Beg pardon," he murmured when the curly-haired lass made way for him and nearly dropped her armful of linens as Charbon streaked past. Jack strode down the servants' hall, nodding at the maids who sank into curtsies the moment they saw him.

He followed his cat, thinking Charbon might lead him straight to Elisabeth. When he found himself in a vacant workroom near the back entrance, Jack had no doubt it was her domain. Folds of fabric and pen-and-ink drawings were neatly stacked beside a tidy sewing basket, a reminder that she was a tradeswoman, not a gentlewoman like Rosalind Murray.

When he heard light footsteps approaching, Jack spun round to greet her and instead found a russet-haired maidservant with a lighted candle hurrying into the room.

Her eyes widened. "Milord!" She curtsied, taking care not to tip the candle. "I didna think to find ye here this morn."

"Sorry I frightened you. Sally, isn't it?"

She blushed, then bobbed her head. "Aye."

With a sweep of his arm, he stepped aside. "Come, light the fire for Mrs. Kerr, for it is cooler down here than it is out of doors." He looked round, wondering what the small, low-ceilinged room would feel like in the dead of winter with only a few hours of frozen light filtering through the single high window.

"Good day to you, Lord Buchanan."

He turned at the sound of Elisabeth's voice. "And to you, Mrs. Kerr." He bowed, while Sally made a furtive exit, then said to Elisabeth, "No new mourning gown?"

"Not yet," she said. "But I finished my mother-in-law's last eve. She was so eager to wear it she awakened at four o' the clock, when I did, just so I might dress her. You have blessed us both more than we can say."

How like her, Jack realized, to sew her mother-in-law's gown first. "Then you'll begin making your gown this eve?"

"In a few days," she said, poking at the sluggish fire. "My hands are quite cramped of late. An evening or two of reading, instead of holding my scissors, should take care of it."

"Might I offer something from my library?" By the lift of her brows, it seemed he'd struck the right note. "Feel free to visit my study and choose what you like."

"If 'twill not be an inconvenience."

"Not at all." He drew a steady breath. Now

that he had her attention, there were far more important things to say. "I must apologize, Mrs. Kerr. For ending our conversation so abruptly on Monday last. And then avoiding your company."

She turned to look at his cat, perched on a chair. Or did she simply not wish to look at him? "So that was intentional," she finally said. "I'd feared as much."

" 'Tis common knowledge that my mother was French and that I spent my childhood in France. You breached no trust."

He was relieved when she turned toward him once more. "Lord Buchanan, ours is an unusual relationship. 'Tis a temporary engagement, not a permanent position. We also travel in very different social circles. I do not wish to make assumptions or speak more freely than I ought."

"I appreciate your candor. Still . . ." He exhaled, uncertain, having not charted his course in advance. "Can we not be friends, madam, at least at Bell Hill?" He picked up two wooden chairs, which looked desperately uncomfortable, and placed them close to the hearth. "Come, Mrs. Kerr. Surely you have a few minutes to spare before you begin sewing."

She quietly took a seat. "I am at your bidding, milord."

"If we're to be friends, you must call me Lord Jack." He sat as well, inching closer.

"Only in private, of course."

" 'Twill take some getting used to," she admitted. "Is your real name John?"

"My real name is Jacques." He paused, realizing he'd not confessed as much in years, then shrugged, making light of it. "But 'Jack' seemed better suited to a British naval officer." He leaned against his chair and found the straight wooden back even more ill fitting than the seat. If they were going to meet with any regularity, something would need to be done about the chairs.

"Mrs. Kerr, 'tis only fair you know a bit of my history." Jack pressed his hands on his knees, gathering his thoughts, preparing to show her a canvas of his life. Certain details would be omitted, but there would be enough for a sketch, if not an oil painting. "I was born in Le Havre. My French mother raised me, while my Scottish father sailed the seas with the Royal Navy. I soon followed in his footsteps."

"Were his boots the size of yours?" she asked, glancing down at them.

"Bigger," he confessed, "for I am quite certain I never filled them. I began my life at sea when I was four-and-ten, as a midshipman."

Elisabeth gasped, as he knew she would.

"Some lads were even younger," he admitted. "The army requires its budding officers to purchase a commission. But in the navy, a first post usually comes about because of family connections."

She tipped her head. "Then you've been at sea for . . ."

"Six-and-twenty years." He seldom said the number aloud, finding it rather disheartening, as if he'd wasted the better part of his life. But he'd had no choice. Once his mother succumbed to fever, he had to sail. "I was five-and-thirty," he continued, "when I joined Admiral Anson aboard the *Centurion,* the flagship among six fighting ships. Some four years later we returned to London, bringing home as our prize a Spanish treasure worth eight hundred thousand British pounds."

He let the number sink in — not to impress her, but simply to help her understand his situation. "The officers shared the bulk of the prize, and several were promoted to the admiralty. But we lost more than half the men who sailed with us and all the vessels but one. Not a good bargain, I'd say."

"Nae," she agreed. After a quiet moment she posed the question he'd been asking himself for two years. "What are your plans now?"

Jack exhaled. "I've had enough of life at sea." He did not confess the rest. That he was tired of being alone, of having no family, no wife, no children. "Within a fortnight I shall officially retire from the navy —"

"Retire?" She looked at him aghast. "And

lose your pension?"

He shrugged, almost ashamed. "I've no need of it, Mrs. Kerr."

"Oh. I see."

When Charbon jumped down, Elisabeth stood. Weary of their conversation, no doubt, or appalled at the thought of someone throwing away a perfectly good pension when she had so little money of her own.

"Forgive me, but I must attend to my work," Elisabeth told him.

He was on his feet at once, chastising himself for not rising the moment she did. Had his manners escaped him completely? "Mrs. Kerr, will you be attending the Common Riding on Friday?"

She nodded. "Apparently all of Selkirk turns out for it. And you?"

"As a landowner I'll be inspecting the marches." He tried to sound blasé, but, in truth, the prospect of riding over the hills astride Janvier appealed to him.

"Might you join us for dinner at noontide?" Elisabeth asked. "Our house is a stone's throw from the mercat cross, where the festivities end."

He knew where she lived. Not the sort of place a gentleman of rank was oft seen, but he cared little for social conventions. "I cannot be certain of my duties for the day," he said cautiously, "but I will look for you on Friday. And join you for dinner if I can."

THIRTY-SEVEN

It's no' in steeds, it's no' in speeds,
It's something in the heart abiding;
The kindly customs, words, and deeds,
It's these that make the Common Riding.

ROBERT HUNTER

"Have you ever seen such excitement?" Marjory felt like clapping her hands or spinning round where she stood or throwing her arms in the air. A mature woman did none of those things, of course. But she could *feel* such urges and no one be the wiser.

She had a right to be merry: Admiral Lord Jack Buchanan was dining at their house this day. She could hardly believe their good fortune. Though they'd spent time and coins they could not spare, their efforts would be rewarded by having the most influential man in Selkirk at their table. Elisabeth had insisted she merely wanted to express her gratitude to the admiral, but Marjory hoped to accomplish more than that. An entrée into society for all the Kerr women. A chance to begin anew.

Her heart light, she surveyed the crowded marketplace. Folk had begun gathering just after the midsummer dawn, bedecked in their brightest and best, reserved for weddings and fairs. Colored ribbons streamed from their hats, and the large cockades worn on their coats declared their allegiance to one of the trades. Anne stood on one side of her and Elisabeth on the other, both happy to be free of their needles and pins for the occasion. Only innkeepers and ale sellers were hard at work this day. The rest of Selkirk left their cares behind, prepared to observe the Common Riding.

Though the air was cool, the June sun would warm them soon enough. So would the press of bodies. Marjory reached for the nosegay of roses tucked in her bodice and breathed in their fresh scent — gifts from Lord Buchanan's garden, provided for each of the Kerr women. Such a generous man. And to think she'd once dreaded his move to Selkirk! By noontide he would be dining at their table. She'd left everything simmering, baking, and stewing and so needed to return home shortly. For a few minutes at least, she could enjoy the day.

"Look, 'tis Molly Easton." Elisabeth nodded toward a lass dressed in a sunny yellow gown. "She once told me June was her favorite month because of the Riding."

"Mine too," Marjory confessed. "A shame she didn't find work at Bell Hill."

"Whitmuir Hall needed a parlormaid, so she's well placed." Elisabeth shifted her attention, looking up Kirk Wynd. "When shall we see the riders?"

"Soon," Anne promised.

Marjory heard the drummers growing restless and the fiddlers tuning their strings. Not much longer now. What began centuries ago with the town burgesses riding the marches — seeing that property boundaries were observed and common lands were not encroached upon — had become an annual summer rite, complete with flags and banners, parades and song.

"There's the reverend," Anne said, nodding toward the corner where Kirk Wynd and Cross Gait met.

Marjory followed her gaze, knowing why Anne had pointed out the minister: Gibson was standing beside him. Although not so tall as his employer, Gibson nonetheless had better posture and a far more pleasing countenance. While the reverend's attention was drawn elsewhere, Gibson lifted his hand in greeting.

I care mair than ye ken. Marjory shivered, recalling his words, not entirely certain of his meaning. He was no longer her manservant, but he was still in service.

And what are you, Marjory Kerr? She well knew the answer: an ill-trained, unpaid cook. That a brave and honest man the likes of Neil Gibson might harbor some affection for her was a blessing and nothing short of it.

" 'Tis the admiral!" Elisabeth cried, standing on tiptoe.

Dozens of heads turned in the same direction, including Marjory's. Gibson's too, she noticed.

Coming down Kirk Wynd on a handsome gray thoroughbred, Admiral Lord Jack Buchanan cut a dashing figure. His elegant powdered wig suited his rank, and his tricorne fit like a crown. The dark blue coat flared round his knees, eclipsed only by the rich scarlet waistcoat beneath it. Anne was no doubt enraptured by the froth of lace round his neck and sleeves, but it was the braided trim that stole Marjory's breath. Every pocket, every buttonhole, and every hem was edged in thick gold braid.

Someone shouted over the crowd, making the admiral's horse grow skittish, forcing his lordship to calm the animal. When he rode by without so much as a glance in their direction. Marjory was more than a little miffed. Might the admiral not at least have *looked* toward Halliwell's Close?

"Here come the hammer men to start the parade," Anne said.

Marjory's irritation quickly gave way as she

watched the burgesses and landowners convene on horseback while the freemen, journeymen, and apprentices of the trade guilds mustered in a designated order, swords held high, flags proudly displayed. Since each guild had its own song, the music was deafening, with drums, pipes, trumpets, flutes, and a host of fiddlers.

The men who worked with hammers — masons, blacksmiths, coopers, and wrights — marched off first. Then came the pride of Selkirk — the souters — a loud and boisterous company of shoemakers. When the weavers marched by, plaids draped over their shoulders and kilted round their waists, Elisabeth sighed. "How my father would have loved this."

Among the tailors, Michael and Peter Dalgliesh were easy to spot with their crimson heads and bright smiles. Anne gave everyone round them a start, loudly calling out to Peter, who waved back with bright-eyed enthusiasm. At last came the fleshers, bearing the sharp-edged tools of their trade and signaling the town to follow them.

"You two walk while I cook," Marjory told them as the crowd moved forward: hundreds of folk cheering, shouting, waving, and singing as they escorted the riders to the edge of town.

Marjory added her voice to the throng, tears filling her eyes, as she remembered the years she'd stood with her husband and sons in their place of honor by the mercat cross.

I am here, dear lads. I am home.

THIRTY-EIGHT

Hark! the shrill trumpet sounds to horse!
away!

COLLEY CIBBER

Where are you, lass?

Jack knew Elisabeth Kerr was here in the marketplace. He could feel it in his bones, had almost sensed her gaze pinned on him as he'd ridden into town, though he'd not spied her lovely face.

By necessity he faced forward in the saddle, keeping a firm control over Janvier, having had a bit of trouble earlier. The strange surroundings, the jostling onlookers, the trumpet blasts, all tested the horse's mettle. "Easy, lad," Jack told him, keeping his grip on the reins supple but sure. Though he longed to turn round and look over his shoulder, Janvier would then follow his lead and disrupt the parade marching up Water Row.

Sir John Murray rode up on his right.

"Mind if I join you, Admiral?"

Their horses fell into step as the two men lifted their voices above the melee, discussing the route. Jack was only now realizing how valuable the common lands were to the burgh. Though he didn't require peat for fuel or turf for building, the cottagers of Selkirk certainly did.

"We'll be riding the marches of the North Common this morn," Sir John explained.

Jack nodded, having studied a crude map to learn where the neighboring lairds resided. Some of them were old enough to remember his grandfather Buchanan and so had bidden him a warm welcome.

When the riders passed through the East Port, they left behind the townsfolk, who sent them off with loud cheers and well wishes. For the riding party a light breeze and abundant sunshine promised a grand outing. Thirty strong, they started downhill and were soon fording the Ettrick Water, ignoring a perfectly good bridge in the process.

When Jack frowned, perplexed, Sir John was quick to say, "Tradition, milord. You'll hear that many times this day."

They cantered on to Linglie Glen, where the men paused to check their horses' girths and enjoy a wee drink of water or a sip of whisky or both — the first stop of many, Jack soon discovered. The ancient northern route covered fourteen miles with only a series of natural markers to indicate the perimeter of the North Common. Crests of hills, lines of hedges, clumps of woods, meandering streams, even solitary trees served the purpose along with the occasional march stone planted amid the wild, open country. With so many riders, Jack had only to fall in step while he took in the splendid scenery his father had once described.

They were climbing now, a long pull toward a summit where three immense cairns stood guard over the Borderland. "The Three Brethren," Sir John told him. " 'Tis tradition to add a stone to each pile."

From this vantage point Jack could see for miles in every direction. The Eildon Hills, a cluster of three peaks, overlooked the Tweed Valley, with the Moorfoots to the north and the Lammermuirs to the northeast. When his father, who'd never lost his Scottish burr, had spoken the names aloud, they'd rolled off his tongue like music.

"There's Philiphaugh." Sir John pointed southward. "On the other side of Harehead Hill."

Jack nodded, having been to the Murray estate on several occasions. During his first visit Lady Murray had insisted, "You *must* hear Rosalind play the pianoforte." Then on his second the young lady was urged to converse in French, German, and Italian, all of which she managed easily. By the third visit Sir John was dropping hints of a sizable dowry. "But only for a gentleman truly worthy of her."

Jack had not lived forty years without learning something of the world. They wanted his title, they wanted his money, and they wanted their daughter in his marriage bed.

His needs were more modest: a wife and children. Still, Rosalind Murray would make a bonny bride, and her mother had borne six children, which boded well.

Sir John turned to him now, smiling broadly, the light in his eyes more avarice than affection. "Rosalind hoped you would dine with us after the Riding."

Jack said nothing, recalling another invitation. *Might you join us for dinner?* He'd made no promises to Elisabeth Kerr, and they'd not spoken of it all week. No one would fault him for preferring a fine meal at a wealthy man's table.

When thou makest a feast, call the poor. Not merely his conscience, but the Lord's own words prodded him.

Jack finally said, "I may have . . . other plans, Sir John."

The sheriff frowned. "Lady Murray will be sorely vexed if I do not bring you home with me."

"I'll know by the time we reach the market-place," Jack told him, stalling for time as he started back downhill, following the others.

With the sun well overhead, Jack wished for a lighter coat. And no hat. And no periwig. But the other men had also dressed for the occasion, so at least he had company.

At Dunsdale, not far north of town, the Common Riding party was met by young men on horseback eager to race their steeds, with a goodly number of spectators prepared to do their part. Jack let his horse graze in the rich pasture while he watched men half his age race for nothing more than a kiss from a blushing lass. Why had he not married when he was a young lieutenant, when life was less complicated and a lady's hand easily won?

An hour later, when they'd had their fill of racing, both walkers and riders headed for the mercat cross for the Casting of Colors. " 'Tis the highlight of the event," Sir John assured him as the townsfolk greeted the riding party at the East Port.

Stable lads at the edge of the crowd took the horses so the riders could move to the very center of things, where a broad wooden platform had been erected. A hush fell over the gathering as, one by one, craft guild members stepped onto the stage with their enormous flags, then swept them round at waist level, forming a figure eight.

Sir John said in a low voice, "The tradition goes back two centuries. Selkirk sent eighty well-armed men to the battle of Flodden Field. A lone survivor returned, bearing a captured English banner. He was so overcome with grief he could only swing the flag round like a scythe." Sir John nodded toward the platform as a weaver performed the same motion. " 'Twas his way of showing the townsfolk that all their lads had been cut down."

Sobered by the story, Jack listened as a song of remembrance rose from the crowd while tears were wiped away and heads were bowed. In that quiet moment he glanced toward Halliwell's Close and saw Elisabeth standing beside her cousin and the red-headed tailor.

Jack waited until the last note rang out, then bade Sir John a hasty farewell. "My apologies to Lady Murray, but I must honor a previous engagement," he said, certain he was committing some grave social faux pas.

The townsfolk parted at his approach, ending any pretense of a chance encounter. Elisabeth would see him coming from twenty ells away. By the time he reached her, a small clearing had encircled them. Their eyes met briefly before he bowed and Elisabeth curtsied, then he moved forward, nodding at the crowd, hoping they might go about their business and let him converse with her in private.

A foolish expectation. Every eye and every ear was fixed on the drama at hand.

The admiral from the sea. The dressmaker from the town.

Had someone sold tickets, he'd have made a handsome profit.

"Safe oot and safe in," she offered him in greeting. " 'Tis what the cottagers cried when they sent out the riders."

Jack lifted his brows. "So that's what they were saying."

"Now the feasting begins," her cousin told him. "Each guild has its own fete. The town council also serves food and drink for all, with music and dancing 'til the wee hours of the morn." Her pale blue eyes looked up at him. "But you'll be joining us for dinner, aye, milord?"

Thirty-Nine

Penniless amid great plenty.

HORACE

"Aye." Jack smiled at Elisabeth, certain he'd made the right choice. "A plate of food with the Kerrs would suit me very well."

"Reverend Brown has agreed to join us," Elisabeth said, "along with Mr. Dalgliesh and his son. You remember young Peter."

Jack looked down at the lad, who did not hide behind his father, as most boys would, but stood proudly in front of him. Imagine having such a son! "The Almighty has been most kind to you, Mr. Dalgliesh."

The tailor smiled broadly, planting his hand on Peter's head. "Indeed he has, milord."

"Come, sir!" Peter cried, tugging on Jack's coat.

"Our house is modest, but our welcome is sure." Elisabeth led him down the shadowy close with the others trailing behind, their lively voices echoing against the dank stone walls.

Jack took careful note of his surroundings, troubled by the thought of Elisabeth facing this grim view every day of her life. Only when they reached the door did he remember Janvier. "I've left my horse with one of the stable lads from Bell Hill. He'll be wondering where I've gone."

Mr. Dalgliesh chuckled. "Is he a Selkirk lad?" When Jack assured him that he was, the tailor said, "Then ye've nae need to worry, for he'll be sitting with the ither lads in a shady spot, watching yer mount and drinking punch for hours. He kens ye'll find him whan ye're done."

Elisabeth studied Jack more intently. "Would you prefer we sent someone to tell him of your whereabouts?"

"Nae," Jack said, trusting the tailor's assessment. "After our brief exchange in the marketplace, Mrs. Kerr, a hundred folk could tell him where I've gone." He stood back. "Now, if someone might unlock the door."

Soft laughter rippled through the group.

" 'Tis an outside door and has no lock," Elisabeth explained, pushing it open. A musty smell wafted out. "This isn't London, milord. We've no need for lock and key here."

A moment later he understood why. There was nothing to steal.

Jack had visited many lodging houses in his

time. Never had he seen one so small or so sparsely furnished. He counted only one bed and two fabric-covered chairs, badly worn. And the oval table would hardly seat four, let alone eight. Yet here they were, these amiable companions, making themselves at home in a dwelling not much larger than Elisabeth's workroom.

"Will you sit here by the window?" Elisabeth asked him, patting the high back of an upholstered chair. "Dinner will not be long. We lack only plates, linens, and cutlery, and those will be arriving shortly."

Busy at the hearth, Mrs. Kerr was wearing her new black dress. Elisabeth, alas, was still dressed in her dreary old gown. Had she not begun sewing a new one? Or had Hyslop not purchased sufficient fabric? Jack dared not ask Elisabeth and risk embarrassing her. Nor could he praise the elder Mrs. Kerr's mourning gown without drawing attention to her loss. Sometimes proper manners were a decided nuisance when one needed the truth on a matter.

Reverend Brown and his manservant, Gibson, came knocking a moment later, arms laden with pewter plates, linen napkins, and sterling forks and spoons. "Here we are, ladies," the minister said, depositing his offering on the table. "My late wife would be glad to know these things were put to good use."

With Gibson's help Anne quickly laid the table for four, then stacked the rest of the settings by the hearth. Jack could not imagine how dinner would be served. Would they take turnabout at table? Stand to eat? Dine two to a plate?

His conscience quickly nudged him. *They have given you the best chair and will feed you shortly. Be grateful. Be humble. Be silent.*

Thoroughly chastised, Jack sat quietly in his chair and surveyed the dinner preparations. Though Elisabeth stood at the ready, her mother-in-law evidently had things well in hand. The air was filled with tantalizing aromas. Jack thought of his mother, who'd kept two cooks yet still insisted on doing all her own baking.

While Anne entertained Peter with a chapbook, Reverend Brown settled into the seat next to him and struck up a conversation. "For a man who's circled the globe, riding the marches of our North Common must have seemed a dull journey."

"Not at all, Reverend." Jack related in detail his experiences that morning, his gaze occasionally drifting toward the sagging beams, the bare floor, and the shabby trunks by the box bed.

A half hour later Elisabeth escorted him to table. "If you might take the chair at the head, milord." She also seated Reverend Brown, Mr. Dalgliesh, and her mother-in-law.

Mrs. Kerr eyed her dishes with concern. "I do hope everything is seasoned to your liking, milord."

However small the table, Jack could not deny that the food looked promising. "Rest assured, madam, I will eat every bite."

The question of where the others would sit was soon answered. Anne and Elisabeth took the upholstered chairs, neatly balancing plates in their hands, while Gibson and Peter served as footmen, bringing each course to table. "We ate earlier," Peter announced, the flour on his nose suggesting he'd enjoyed a roll or two.

To Jack's amazement Mrs. Kerr had prepared not only the obligatory courses of fish, flesh, and fowl but vegetables dishes as well. Potted eel was followed by savory veal pie, then stewed chicken with mace. Warm rolls, fragrant with ale yeast, were served next, then pickled beetroot and asparagus with butter. Strawberries and soft cheese arrived as the final course.

Jack would never inform Mrs. Tudhope, but he'd met her equal.

Conversation ensued when their forks were put aside. Michael Dalgliesh, Jack decided, was a clever raconteur posing as a tailor, who regaled the family and guests with amusing stories. The elder Widow Kerr spoke little but, by her speech and manners, was clearly a gentlewoman. He would see what he could learn of her history and Elisabeth's as well.

When it was his turn, Jack shared his adventures aboard the *Centurion,* including visiting exotic ports of call in Brazil, Argentina, China, and the Philippines. Elisabeth and Anne quietly cleared the table, then drew their chairs closer. Wide-eyed Peter sat at his feet until his father invited the boy onto his lap, all the better to listen.

Jack was seldom jealous of any man, but for a moment the sharp pain of envy cut like a knife. However enthralling his years at sea, they had cost him a son like Peter.

When the dinner party finally stood, well sated with food and words, the kirk bell tolled the hour. "It cannot be six o' the clock." Jack consulted his pocket watch, shocked to learn how swiftly the afternoon had passed. "I must find my stable lad before he sells Janvier and sails for the Continent."

"Walk me to the manse first," Reverend Brown said. "I've asked Gibson to tarry here and be of service."

"Well done, sir." Jack looked round the house, still as mean a hovel as ever. But the women certainly ate well. Perhaps they preferred to spend money on food rather than furnishings.

Jack found his hat, expressed his sincere thanks, then took his leave and followed the minister down the stair and into the marketplace, where revelers were dancing in rounds, their feet lifting high above the cobblestones. He escorted the minister home without attempting any conversation over the spirited fiddlers.

A few minutes later the two men stood in the minister's parlor, the sounds of merrymaking held at bay by his solid entrance door.

"Lord Buchanan," the minister began, "how oft do you imagine the Kerr ladies enjoy such a fine table?"

The question caught Jack off guard. "I . . . cannot say, sir."

"I can," he said gruffly. "On the morrow they'll break their fast eating porridge from wooden bowls. Dinner will be a single course from a single pot and supper no more than cheese and bread and whatever they can afford to pluck from Mrs. Thorburn's garden."

Jack felt the rich meal inside him begin to churn. "Then however did they afford . . ."

"The young Widow Kerr invested a fortnight's wages in that meal. Anne, who earns a pittance teaching lace making, scrubbed her wee house from fore to aft. And the elder Mrs. Kerr spent all week planning and preparing each course."

Jack stared at him, appalled. "For one meal?"

"Nae," the reverend said sharply. "For one man."

"Surely . . ." Jack tried again. "Surely this

was not all for *my* sake?"

The minister scowled. "According to Gibson, who heard this from Marjory Kerr, who knows her daughter-in-law better than anyone, Elisabeth Kerr meant to express her gratitude for all you've done for her."

"I see." Jack's mind was racing. Had he missed something? Had she told him that?

"Yet there you sat, dining like a prince, then offering them nothing in return beyond what a dressmaker is paid for her efforts."

Stung by his accusation, Jack protested, "But I provided fabric for new gowns —"

"Aye," Reverend Brown growled, "so Elisabeth Kerr wouldn't sully the appearance of your household. Meanwhile, she walks four miles a day, labors from dawn until dusk, and has no assurance of any position beyond Saint Andrew's Day."

Jack had not been spoken to so harshly since he was a green midshipman. He did not enjoy it then. He enjoyed it less now. But he heard something behind the minister's tongue-lashing: the truth. "What would you have me do, sir?"

Reverend Brown responded without hesitation, "Treat the Kerr widows as peers."

Jack stared at him, confused. "But, sir, they are . . . poor."

"Now, aye, but 'twas not always thus. Lord John Kerr of Tweedsford was a wealthy and respected resident of Selkirk in his day. His son, the late Lord Donald, inherited his father's fortune, title, and lands. Make no mistake, the Kerrs are gentlewomen."

Jack dropped into the nearest seat, the wind knocked out of him. "The young Widow Kerr told me none of this."

"I cannot blame her for hiding her husband's foolishness, for he did not inherit his father's common sense. Lord Donald Kerr threw his life away on the Jacobite cause, sentencing his mother and wife to a life of poverty."

Jack grasped the situation at last. "When her husband died at Falkirk, he fought for Prince Charlie, not King George."

The minister's expression softened. "Now you see the way of it. General Lord Mark Kerr himself penned the letter that sealed the family's fate. Attainted for treason, they lost everything."

Treason. Jack shuddered at the very sound of the word. He'd known more than one navy man who'd paid for his disloyalty to the king with his life. "And the Kerr women . . . they supported Prince Charlie as well?"

Reverend Brown's gray head slowly bobbed up and down. "To their shame, they did. But above all, they supported the men they loved, for which I cannot blame them. Now you'll find them honoring the king, if only because 'tis prudent. Of their faith in the Almighty, however, there can be no doubt. In that realm we are all peers."

Jack stood again, needing to pace. "Why have I not learned of this treason before now?"

"No one wanted to tell you, milord, lest it cost Elisabeth Kerr her position. She could have returned home to the Highlands but instead chose to stay with her mother-in-law and care for her. 'Tis a sacrifice not all would make, milord."

Jack fixed his gaze on a stack of books on the library table, struggling to collect his thoughts. "I must ask you again, Reverend, what would you have me do?"

The minister's answer was swift. "Find ways to provide for their household that won't cause them shame or require some gift in return."

He groaned. "Like today's feast, you mean."

"Just so."

Jack nodded, an idea forming in his mind and heart. "Silver is a cold offering, easily measured. But I have other ways of supplying their needs." He consulted his pocket watch again, then started toward the door. "I must away, sir. Your admonition has not gone unheard."

"I can see that." Reverend Brown, who seldom smiled, made a valiant effort. "Thou shalt open thine hand wide unto thy brother," he reminded Jack, "to thy poor, and to thy needy, in thy land."

"Aye, sir." Jack tipped his hat and was gone, bound for the edge of town where a stable lad and a well-fed thoroughbred waited for their master.

Less than an hour later he was striding through the corridors of Bell Hill in search of Roberts and Mrs. Pringle. His house was emptier than usual, the servants having been given the day off for the Riding. That also meant fewer ears listening in the halls — a blessing, considering what he had planned.

When the two appeared at his study door, Jack beckoned them within.

"What is troubling you, milord?" Roberts inquired. "For I can see you are anxious."

"*Eager* would be closer to the mark." Jack was standing in front of his desk, rather than sitting behind it. All the better to engage their cooperation. And their silence.

The two waited, hands behind their backs, attentive as ever.

"First," Jack said somewhat sternly, "one or both of you owe me an explanation. Did you know that Mrs. Elisabeth Kerr was once married to a Jacobite who fell at Falkirk and was later charged with treason?"

Roberts was clearly shocked. "Indeed not, milord!"

Mrs. Pringle pursed her lips. "I confess, Lord Buchanan, I was well aware of it. Mrs. Kerr told me within a half hour of her arrival here."

"And still you made her welcome in my household." Jack kept his voice even. "You gave her food. Allowed me to clothe her. Made certain I engaged her."

Mrs. Pringle replied without apology, "I did, milord."

He nodded, barely hiding his pleasure. "Well done."

"Sir?" Roberts exclaimed.

Jack clapped a hand on his butler's shoulder. "We are charged to care for the widows in our parish, and that is what Mrs. Pringle wisely arranged. But there is more to be done. Promise me, both of you, that my intentions shall never be discussed outside this room."

When not only their spoken assurances but also their honest gazes convinced him of their fealty, Jack rubbed his hands together like a shipwright preparing to grip his ax. "Now, then. Here is what I have in mind."

FORTY

The road up and the road down is one and the same.

Clasping a linen bundle in one hand and her sewing basket in the other, Elisabeth started downhill toward home, drawn by the toll of the kirk bell floating on the early evening breeze.

Her feet knew the path well by now. In four weeks she'd finished as many gowns, the latest for Sally's mother, Mrs. Craig, the head laundress. For her own entertainment Elisabeth made one small alteration in each gown's design. An extra set of pleats here, an embroidered buttonhole there, a deeper placket to hide the fastenings — nothing Lord Jack would notice or care about.

She'd seen little of him the past week, though he'd sent a thoughtful note on Saturday's dinner tray, thanking the Kerrs for their hospitality. After reading the note to Marjory and Anne, Elisabeth had tucked it into her apron pocket. Later, when no one was looking, she read it again, smoothing her thumb across Lord Jack's signature.

But his spoken words were hidden in her heart. *Can we not be friends, madam, at least at Bell Hill?* What did that mean? That he'd prefer not to be seen with her in public? Or that he was lonely and wished to enjoy her company while she labored beneath his roof?

Of this she was certain: small gifts had begun to appear at her workroom door. Squares of toffee, which quickly appeased Anne's sweet tooth. Two pints of berries. A basketful of roses snipped from the garden. Then today's fresh wheaten rolls, a specialty of the cook. "Mrs. Tudhope baked more than were needed for dinner," Mrs. Pringle had told her earlier, leaving the linen bundle on the mantel, where Charbon couldn't poke at them with his nose.

Elisabeth suspected Lord Buchanan was behind such blessings, meant to look merely like perishables given away rather than thrown away. Whatever the source, whatever the reason, the Kerr women were grateful.

She was walking down the steepest part of the hill when the clip-clop of approaching horses caught her ear. Elisabeth slowed her steps so the riders could pass by.

Instead the horses drew to a stop. "Afternoon, madam."

Elisabeth turned to find Lord Jack gazing down at her, his face framed in blue sky. He was dressed in a black riding coat and breeches, but without a neckcloth or waistcoat — rather scandalous attire for an admiral. She arched her brows. "You are not bound for town, I see."

"Nae, madam. I'm off in search of ancient ruins. Care to join me?" He nodded at the horse beside him, led by one of Bell Hill's grooms. "Belda should suit you. She's well mannered yet with spirit."

Elisabeth eyed the golden mare, with its cream-colored mane and rich leather sidesaddle. "She *is* lovely," Elisabeth confessed, though she'd not ridden in many seasons. Dare she try it?

"Davie will carry your things home for you." He nodded at the groom, who handed the reins to his master, then came round and relieved Elisabeth of her bundle and basket. "Davie, kindly tell Mrs. Kerr in Halliwell's Close that her daughter-in-law will arrive home by sunset, having had her supper."

"Aye, sir." The groom took off at a sprint.

Elisabeth stared after him. "Lord Buchanan, I am . . . not certain . . ."

"You are to call me Lord Jack," he reminded her, dismounting in one graceful move.

"This outing you are suggesting . . ." She turned to look at him. "Is it quite proper for us to travel unescorted?"

"You mean because I'm an old bachelor and you are a young widow?" He cleared his throat. "Madam, I have been closely watched from the moment I entered this parish. I suspect you have been as well. Such scrutiny tends to keep people on their best behavior. I have no plans to misbehave. Do you?"

She laughed. "I do not."

"Good." He offered his hand. "Let me help you mount her, for 'tis not easily managed in a gown."

She stood beside the mare, smoothing a gloved hand along the horse's sleek, warm neck. "Be gentle with me, lass," Elisabeth murmured, taking long, slow breaths to calm her nerves. "The last woman I saw riding sidesaddle was Lady Margaret Murray of Broughton."

"A Jacobite, I believe," he said evenly.

Elisabeth gritted her teeth. Why had she mentioned such a thing? Probably because she was nervous. Was it riding the mare that frightened her? Or riding with the admiral?

Without ceremony, Lord Buchanan fitted his hands round her waist and lifted her onto the saddle with ease, then politely lowered his gaze as she hooked her right knee round the pommel and arranged her skirts.

Firmly seated, Elisabeth took the reins and exhaled the last of her fears. "I'd forgotten how wonderful the world looks from the back of a horse."

" 'Tis even more wonderful facing this direction." He inclined his head, leading them uphill and away from town. "Have you been to Lessudden?"

"The farthest east I've traveled is Bell Hill. And you?"

He smiled. "Canton, China."

Had the admiral been her brother, she would have swatted him.

The farther they climbed, the more stunning the views. Elisabeth caught her breath, taking it all in, as they continued along a high ridge. The land rolled and dipped on either side of them, and the sky felt close enough to touch.

Lord Buchanan pointed ahead. "The Eildon Hills," he said. "Unusual, aren't they?"

Elisabeth gazed at the three distinct hills. Rather than gradual slopes folded into the landscape, the Eildons poked straight up out of the farmland with only bracken and heather to soften their stark, bald appearance. "More unsettling than beautiful," she confessed.

Their route took them downhill once more, through wide open fields and pastures. Sheep, newly shorn, wandered across the narrow track, bleating pitifully, as if in mourning for their wool.

"We've left Selkirkshire behind," the admiral told her. "As promised, here is the village of Lessudden."

She found the thatched cottages charming enough. "But none of them are ancient," she chided him, "and I see no ruins."

"Patience, Mrs. Kerr."

At his leading they rode north of the village along a high, forested path. The sun was still shining low in the sky, but deeper within the woods, twilight had fallen. A thick carpet of dried leaves and pine needles softened the horses' steps, until it seemed they were approaching on tiptoe.

A slight clearing in the woods revealed their destination: the lofty remains of an abbey. Silent, beautiful, mysterious.

"Tell me, Mrs. Kerr," the admiral said in low voice. "Is the twelfth century ancient enough for you?" He quietly dismounted and tethered his horse, then helped her down as if she weighed nothing.

For a moment Elisabeth sensed he might take her hand, then felt foolish when he didn't. She walked ahead of him, lest he spy her warm cheeks. "What do you know of this place?"

"King David the first founded Dryburgh Abbey," the admiral told her, "but, beyond that, I cannot say. One of my gardeners recommended a visit here. Now I see why."

"Aye," she breathed. A wall here, a wall there, nothing like a whole building, yet sacred nevertheless. The arches of the transepts took on a rosy glow in the diminishing light, while the tall, narrow window openings were dark and blank. Gravestones were scattered about, some grand and ornate, others plain and low to the ground and covered with moss and lichen. She peeked through an immense, roundheaded door into an empty chamber with a stone seat stretching along each wall. "The monks met here," she said, then jumped when her voice echoed through the vast interior.

Lord Buchanan continued exploring the pink sandstone ruins with Elisabeth not far behind. "The Tweed," he said, indicating the river encircling the abbey. "Our horses will be glad for some refreshment."

While their mounts drank their fill, then nibbled at the grass round their feet, the admiral and Elisabeth settled on a low stone wall overlooking the placid waters.

"You said I'd return home having eaten my supper," she reminded him.

"Right." He was on his feet at once and unbuckled a leather bag attached to Janvier's saddle. "I could manage only cheese, bread, a flask of cider, and ripe cherries from the orchard. A poor man's meal, I'm afraid."

"Then 'tis well suited for me."

He resumed his seat beside her, his brow furrowed. "Mrs. Kerr, I did not mean to suggest —"

"Nor did you," she assured him, taking the bread from his hands.

They ate little and spoke even less, tearing their bread into crumbs to feed the blackbirds hopping about. She sampled a few cherries, ate a bite of cheese, then took a long drink of cider from the flask before handing it to him. "The rest is yours."

He downed it in a single gulp, then pressed the cork into place, looking at her rather intently. "I brought you here for a reason, Mrs. Kerr —"

"Please call me Bess," she said, hoping they might dispense with such formalities.

The admiral slowly nodded. "I confess it suits you better."

She'd not sat this near to him before. His forehead was lined, but faintly so, and his nose long and planed on the sides. His cheekbones were high and his mouth firm, almost sculpted. But it was his eyes she noticed most. A warm dark brown, like his hair, like his eyebrows, like the hint of a beard on his chin.

Elisabeth turned away, embarrassed to have studied him so closely. "You say you brought me here for a reason, milord."

"Aye, Bess. I need to know where you stand with the Jacobites."

She whirled round. "Whom have you been speaking with?"

"Reverend Brown." He grimaced. "I was a fool not to have realized it from the first. Perhaps I did not wish to know and so avoided the truth. I'm grateful I'm no longer in active service with the navy, or I should be duty bound to report your whereabouts to the king."

Elisabeth stared at the ground, thankful she'd not had much to eat. "And you . . . feel no such duty . . . now?"

"None whatsoever. But I would know where your allegiance lies."

She lifted her head, determined to speak honestly. "My Highland family always supported the Stuart claim to the throne. Because I loved them, I embraced Prince Charlie and his cause. But after losing my brother . . . and then my husband . . . the Jacobite cause is no longer my own."

"So then, if King George should ask me where your loyalty rests?"

"Only with the Almighty," she said plainly, "and with those who bow to him."

He nodded slowly as if weighing her answer. "Aye, that should please him."

Elisabeth almost laughed, so serious was his expression. "Are you planning on discussing me with His Majesty anytime soon?"

"Perhaps," was all he said, then stood, gazing up at the darkening sky. "Come, Bess. I promised your mother-in-law I'd have you home before sunset. Can you ride with some speed?"

She rose, straightening her shoulders. "I can."

Minutes later they were galloping westward, her mare already sensitive to her cues. Once the road straightened, they eased their pace. "Well done, Belda," she crooned, easing back into the saddle.

"You're a natural horsewoman," the admiral commended her. "I insist you take Belda out regularly, for she needs the exercise."

Elisabeth pretended to look shocked. "But, sir, I must sew."

"Sew faster," he charged her and took off again.

They were riding neck and neck, leaning forward in their saddles, eyes fixed on the lights of Bell Hill, when the admiral suddenly eased his pace and motioned for her to do the same. "Dragoons," he muttered.

The two slowed to a stop, breathing hard, the admiral's hand resting on her reins.

Her heart in her throat, Elisabeth peered ahead. Whatever were dragoons doing at Bell Hill? She counted eight men in uniform trotting away from the house. *Please, Lord. Let them not turn this way.* Along with the admiral, she waited and watched as the dragoons neared the road. When the men finally bore right and started downhill toward Selkirk, Elisabeth nearly collapsed onto Belda's mane. *Thanks be to God.*

Jack was quiet for some time, his jaw working. "I don't know what brought them to my door this night, but you can be sure I will find out. In the meantime, Bess, it might be wise if you remained withindoors."

"If you think it best . . ."

"I do. If I am the one they seek, let them come find me. If it is you they are after, I'll do as my mother once did when two English spies appeared at her door." He leaned so close Elisabeth could smell the sweet cider on his breath. "I shall hide you on my roof and dispatch the king's men to the hills."

FORTY-ONE

Friends are much better tried in bad
fortune than in good.

ARISTOTLE

Marjory paced in front of the hearth, the
embers low, the supper dishes scrubbed. A
single candle flickered on the sewing table.
Night had fallen, and still there was no sign
of Elisabeth.

Anne looked up from her book. "You've no
need to fret, Cousin. She is safe with Lord
Buchanan."

"I know," Marjory said absently, moving
toward the open window. She leaned out,
feeling the night wind against her face. The
marketplace appeared deserted. Other than
the usual sounds of barking dogs and lowing
cattle, all was silent.

Or was it?

She closed her eyes, straining to hear. Aye,
she was certain now: hoofbeats from the east.
"They'll be here shortly," she said, then

exhaled in relief. Wanting to look her best for Lord Buchanan, she smoothed her hair, brushed the lint from her gown, and washed her hands in lavender soap, a present from Anne.

Marjory had hoped her Tuesday birthday might slip by unnoticed, but Anne had insisted on a small gathering of friends. Elisabeth had stitched a new linen petticoat for her, Michael and Peter had found a tin ladle at market, and Gibson had carved a fine set of four wooden spoons. No one else in the neighborhood had been informed, at her request. Though Marjory was grateful for every one of her nine-and-forty years, she saw no need to proclaim her age from the mercat cross.

Hearing the noisy clatter of hoofs on the cobblestones, she hastened back to the window, expecting to find Lord Buchanan and Elisabeth approaching. Instead, several horses were coming down Kirk Wynd. She squinted into the darkness. Only when the first rider came within a stone's throw of their house could she see his red coat.

"Annie!" She yanked the casement window closed. "Dragoons!"

Her cousin blew out the candle, then leaped to her side. "In Selkirk? At this hour?" Anne pressed her forehead against the glass, counting under her breath. "Eight men, I'd say. They seem to be looking for something."

Marjory could hardly breathe. *They're looking for us. For Elisabeth, for me.* Had she not always feared a day of reckoning would come?

"Listen." Anne eased open the window without making a sound, then clasped Marjory's hand in silent support.

The men below were grumbling among themselves, loudly enough for the women to hear.

"I say we should've stayed. Waited 'til the admiral returned."

"Who knows when that would have been?"

"His lordship's housekeeper was little help."

"Best find an inn, lads, and see if supper may be had."

Her heart still beating wildly, Marjory watched the dragoons walk their horses along the row of buildings facing the marketplace. She could almost smell their sweat, their anger, their impatience. As they reached the Cross Well, she heard their muffled comments and guessed what they were saying. The Forest Inn stood downhill, beyond the West Port.

When the men disappeared round the corner, Marjory collapsed onto an upholstered chair. "Annie," she moaned, "they will come for us in the morn."

"But your names were not spoken," her cousin protested gently. "More likely they had business with Lord Buchanan. You can be certain he will not point them in your direction." She lit the candle at the hearth, casting shadows round the room.

Shivering, Marjory pulled Elisabeth's plaid round her shoulders, fearing King George would not be satisfied until every Jacobite was dead. Minutes later, when she again heard horses in the street, Marjory did not move. "You look, Annie, for I haven't the strength to stand."

Her cousin glanced out the window, then touched her shoulder. " 'Tis Bess and his lordship."

Marjory sank back against the chair. *At last.*

The two were soon at the door. "Oh, Marjory!" Elisabeth hurried across the room, then knelt beside the chair, her hair reduced to a nest of wispy curls, her eyes filled with fear. "The dragoons —"

"I know," Marjory interrupted. "We saw them in the marketplace. They paused long enough for us to overhear some of their conversation."

Lord Buchanan moved into the room and bowed. "Did the men say why they've come to Selkirk?"

"Nae," Anne replied, "but they did mention having stopped at Bell Hill. Apparently your housekeeper was not very hospitable toward them."

"Mrs. Pringle is not one to be bullied," he agreed. "Since the dragoons were not expected, she'd not have made them welcome.

Had they been sailors, perhaps, but not soldiers. Still, they will no doubt pay me a second visit in the morn." He glanced at Elisabeth. "All the more reason for you to remain at home."

She nodded. "At least I have my sewing basket and can finish my gown."

"I shall look forward to seeing you wear it," he said. "Ladies, forgive me, but I've two horses that need their supper and a good grooming. I shall keep you abreast of any news." He bowed and was gone, pulling the door shut behind him.

Marjory could not read her daughter-in-law's expression as she watched the admiral take his leave. Was Elisabeth developing an attachment for the man? If so, 'twas far too soon. Donald would not have wished Elisabeth to mourn her whole life, but he deserved a twelvemonth.

My son loved you, Bess. And I know you loved him.

Marjory tossed and turned through the night, haunted by dreams of her husband, of her sons, of Tweedsford. By intent she'd not been to the estate since they'd returned to Selkirk. She tried not to think of it, not to walk through the rooms in her mind, not to punish herself with memories.

When the gray light of morning began filtering through the curtains, Marjory rose long enough to add coals to the grate. Tempted to slip back into bed, she glanced out the window and discovered a steady drizzle of rain, the kind that might continue for hours. Good weather for napping but little else.

She eyed her daughter-in-law, well asleep in her chair, her head tucked into the corner where wing and back met. *You deserve a proper bed, lass.* Marjory felt guilty for not taking her daughter-in-law's place. Yet her own back would never bear sitting upright to sleep.

At least today Elisabeth would not have to climb Bell Hill in this dreary rain.

Marjory eased back onto the hurlie bed and wrapped the linen sheet round her. Closing her eyes, she waited for sleep to fall across her like a soft woolen blanket. *Come, come.*

"Marjory!" Elisabeth was bending over her, shaking her gently awake. "Lord Buchanan has brought us news. Terrible news, he says."

Marjory tried to sit up, clutching the sheet round her neck. "Is he . . . here?"

"His lordship is on the stair, waiting for us to dress." Elisabeth practically lifted her from the bed. "I've brushed your gown and have a cup of tea waiting for you at table."

Marjory dressed in haste, feeling disoriented. Was it still morn? *Aye.* Was it still raining? *Aye.* How long had she slept? *Too long.*

When she fastened the last hook, she nodded to Anne, who ushered Lord Buchanan into the house.

"Many apologies, milord," Anne murmured before curtsying.

"Think nothing of it." He bowed, then looked at each of them in turn before sharing the news none of them wanted to hear. "Those dragoons paid me a visit early this morn. The new owner of Tweedsford sent them in advance of his coming."

"Nae!" Marjory cried softly. "It is done, then." She sank onto the chair at table and stared at her tea, already gone cold.

Elisabeth spoke up. "I don't understand, milord. What did this new owner want from you?"

"He assumed that, as a peer in residence, I would have knowledge of any enemies of the king who might live in Selkirk. Dissenters, rebels . . ."

"Jacobites," Elisabeth finished for him.

He nodded grimly. "He seems to think he alone can quash the last vestiges of the rebellion. But remember, you have advocates here, chief among them Reverend Brown. And I will vouch for your loyalty to the king. At the highest level, if necessary."

Marjory lifted her head. *He means before the king himself.* "So who is this new owner?"

Lord Buchanan eased onto the seat beside her, compassion in his eyes. "Someone you well know, I'm afraid, from your days in Edinburgh. General Lord Mark Kerr."

Forty-Two

Though it be honest, it is never good to
bring bad news.

WILLIAM SHAKESPEARE

"Nae." Marjory stared at him. "It cannot be
Lord Mark's. Not my home. It cannot be his."

She rubbed her brow as if trying to erase
the words imprinted there. *You and your sons
were duly warned, madam.* Dreadful words,
horrible words. *I regret to inform you of the
consequences of their treason and yours.*
Words once written by General Lord Mark
Kerr, who would live in her home where
she'd raised her sons. Her darling sons.

"Nae!" Marjory cried, curling her hands
into fists. She banged them, hard, on the
table. "He cannot live there! He cannot!"

"Marjory, dearest, please." Elisabeth bent
round her, laying cool hands over her
clenched fists. "Your home is here with those
who love you."

"I cannot bear it, Bess." Her hands began to uncurl as she sank forward. "He has taken everything."

Elisabeth hovered over her, lightly touching her hair. "When is Lord Mark expected in Selkirk, milord?"

Lord Buchanan's voice was low. "His men gave me no definite day or time but assured me it will be soon."

Soon. Marjory stirred.

"Take me there." She sat up, her eyes wet with tears. "Please, milord. Let me see Tweedsford before it is closed to me forever."

She feared he might refuse or call her foolish. He did neither.

"At once, Mrs. Kerr." The admiral stood and helped her to her feet. "If your daughter-in-law might find a warm blanket and a hot cup of tea, you'll need both this wretched morn."

Anne touched her arm. "Cousin, shall I come too?"

"Aye, aye." Marjory looked round her, trying to gather her thoughts. "If the carriage will hold us all. Oh, and Gibson! Bess, we must take him with us. He served me at Tweedsford all those years." She turned to the admiral, daring to press him further. "Reverend Brown will not mind releasing Gibson from service this morn if *you* request it, milord."

"Whatever you wish, madam. Haste is best,

for I would not care to cross paths with Lord Mark, for your sake."

A sharp intake of air. "Indeed not. Annie, please bring the tea."

The jostling of the carriage and the queasiness in Marjory's stomach made for an uncomfortable hour. But she was seated between Elisabeth and Gibson, the two people whom she cared about most and who cared about her, so she did not complain.

The northbound route from Selkirk, which ran parallel with the Ettrick Water, was a hilly road that hugged the waterside, then veered sharply upward before reaching the River Tweed and the property that stretched along its banks. *Tweedsford*. Soon they would pass through the wrought-iron gates, always left open as a sign of hospitality. Or would they be locked this morning?

"Tell me what you can of Roger Laidlaw," Lord Buchanan was saying. "He will not object to our seeing the property?"

Looking at Anne, Marjory lifted her eyebrows, an unspoken question. *Will Mr. Laidlaw mind? Will you?*

Anne faintly shook her head. " 'Tis hard to say what sort of reception we might find."

Lord Buchanan stared into the rain-drenched countryside "We shall know shortly."

When, a moment later, they rattled through

the gates and across the gravel to the entrance, Marjory confessed, "I do wish you could have seen Tweedsford on a better day, milord."

He climbed out of the carriage, then turned to offer his hand. "A sailor never objects to water, madam."

The Kerr party stood in a small, wet knot while Gibson lifted the brass knocker and banged it upon the imposing front door.

After several agonizing minutes, a young footman answered, his livery neat, his face unfamiliar. When Gibson announced Marjory and the others by name, the lad fell back a step. "Leddy Kerr?"

"Aye." She slowly crossed the threshold, then forced herself to say the words. "This was once my home."

He bowed rather clumsily. "I . . . I ken wha ye are, mem."

Marjory tried to take it all in with one sweeping glance. The polished wood floors shone, even on this gloomy morning. The icy blue silk she'd chosen as a young bride still covered the walls. The grand staircase, rising two floors, dominated the entrance hall, as it always had.

Nothing had changed. Everything had changed.

She cleared her throat. "If I might speak with Mr. Laidlaw."

"Aye . . . aye." The footman turned and

practically ran toward the rear of the house.

Marjory found it hard to breathe, so familiar was the scent of the place. Not merely wood and plaster and silk and satin but also the muddy riverbed and the drooping roses in the garden and the rain itself — all crept through the house, creating a sweet, earthy fragrance she could not fully describe yet could never forget. *Home.*

With a soft moan she bowed her head, memories pressing down on her, flattening her.

Elisabeth lightly touched her shoulder. "I am here, Marjory. We all are."

Footsteps approached. "Leddy Kerr." Roger Laidlaw's voice. "I didna expect ye."

Marjory lifted her head. "I am sorry we've arrived . . . unannounced . . . we . . ."

When her voice faltered, Elisabeth stepped in to explain. "We learned just this morn that General Lord Mark Kerr is to be the new owner of Tweedsford."

"Aye, mem." Mr. Laidlaw bobbed his brown head, his close-set eyes blinking rapidly. "I've been told to leuk for him at noontide."

Soon. A chill ran down Marjory's spine.

"Then we shall make our visit brief," Lord Buchanan told the factor. "You surely understand Mrs. Kerr's desire to see her home once more."

Roger Laidlaw studied her at length before

371

he responded. "Some o' the *sma'* furniture was taken awa to Edinburgh and sold at auction . . . to . . . to pay the fines, ye ken. But, aye, ye can take a leuk."

Apprehensive, Marjory ventured forth, stepping into the high-ceilinged drawing room with its tall windows and thick velvet drapes. Her heart grew heavier with each step. If they'd never left Selkirk for Edinburgh, this would still be her home. Her sons would be alive. She might have grandchildren by now, running through the halls of Tweedsford.

Marjory stood in the center of the room, barely seeing the marble chimneypiece, the painted ceiling, the decorative cornices. She saw only what was missing. Not her furnishings. Her family.

She closed her eyes and began to weep. *Forgive me, forgive me.*

Elisabeth's hand clasped hers.

Gibson moved closer as well and produced a clean linen handkerchief.

" 'Tis my fault." Marjory dabbed her eyes, but the tears would not stop. "We should never have come."

Anne moved round to stand before her, tears glistening in her eyes as well. " 'Tis naught but a house now, dear Cousin. An empty shell. Do not punish yourself."

Marjory quietly blew her nose, then whispered, "How can I not?"

After a long silence Mr. Laidlaw stepped

forward. "Mem, I found some things ye may wish to have. I set them aside, thinking to bring them to ye. Would ye like them noo?"

"Aye." She swallowed. "If you please."

Gibson led her to a small table and chairs where the gentry of Selkirkshire once spent many happy hours playing whist. No sooner had she settled in place than Mr. Laidlaw reappeared with a wooden box.

When she looked inside, Marjory stifled a moan. *Donald's books. Andrew's toys.*

Gibson took away the box at once. "Suppose I put it in the carriage."

Marjory could not look at the admiral. Whatever must he think of her? "Lord Buchanan, I am . . . so very sorry . . ."

He knelt beside her. "Mrs. Kerr, you were brave to come. But unless you truly wish to see the house, I think it best that we leave at once. It will not do to have Lord Mark find you here."

"Nae," she agreed. "The general may be a distant cousin of my late husband's, but he is no friend of mine."

"Nor of mine," Elisabeth said firmly.

The moment Marjory stood, Mr. Laidlaw presented himself. "Mem, I wonder if I might have a wird with ye. In private, if ye'll not mind."

Anne started to protest, but Marjory saw something in the factor's eyes that could not be ignored. "We must do so quickly," she told him, following him into the vacant entrance hall, leaving the others behind.

The two paused before a gilt-edged looking glass. At first Roger Laidlaw said nothing, only looked at his shoes.

"What is it you wish to tell me?" Marjory asked, not bothering to hide her irritation.

"I'll not keep ye lang," he said, his voice low. "But I must ask yer forgiveness."

Marjory stared at him. "*My* forgiveness?" It was the last thing she expected.

He was quiet for a long time. When he looked up, the pain in his eyes was undeniable. "In the past I had a reputation for chasing the lasses. Most were willing, but —"

"My cousin was right, then," Marjory said sharply. "You *are* a reprobate."

He hung his head. "Whatsomever she said, 'tis true."

Marjory eyed the drawing room door, considering summoning the admiral. He would know what was to be done. Should the sheriff be called? Or might the kirk session mete out sufficient punishment?

But Mr. Laidlaw's humble demeanor gave her pause. This was not a man bragging about his conquests. "You said 'in the past,' Mr. Laidlaw. Are you telling me you've changed?"

He looked up at once. "I *have* changed. Ye must believe me, Leddy . . . , eh, Mrs. Kerr."

Marjory wanted to be angry with him, wanted to see justice done. But when a man asked for mercy, he deserved to be heard. "Go on."

"I'm courting a widow in Galashiels noo. Jessie Briggs is her name. She made me see . . . what sort o' man I was. And what I could be."

Marjory frowned. "Does this Jessie know all that you've done?"

"Aye, ilka bit. I've gone round the countryside and tried to make amends —"

"Tibbie Cranshaw?" Marjory pressed him.

He shook his head. "She wouldna let me past her door. I canna say I blame the lass."

Nor can I. "I should never have sent Tibbie away," Marjory admitted, "nor judged her so harshly."

"Then . . . mebbe ye can forgive me?" Roger Laidlaw shifted his weight. " 'Twas a sickness, mem. Finally I am weel." He pulled out a tattered handkerchief and blew his nose. "I canna believe it, but a guid woman *luves* me. Aye, and the guid Lord luves me, though I dinna deserve it."

Marjory's ire was gone, dissipating like smoke from a doused fire. "No one truly deserves his love and mercy. *I* certainly don't."

He sought her gaze in the quiet entrance hall. "Please, mem. I canna say I'm sorry enough."

"Mr. Laidlaw, you don't need —"

"But I *do*." He pulled off his cap and bunched it in his hands. "Nae man wha

375

behaved as I did should walk round thinking it doesna matter."

Something about his confession prodded at a tender place she could not name. Roger Laidlaw spoke the truth: his lust for women was a sickness the Lord alone could heal. "If the Lord has forgiven you, Mr. Laidlaw, I must do the same."

He was silent for a moment, then nodded. "I thank ye, mem."

Marjory glanced at the drawing room. "Anne Kerr was wronged far more than I. Have you sought her pardon?"

"I meant to do so on the day I came to Halliwell's Close, but . . ." His gaze followed hers across the hall. "Might ye help me?"

Forty-Three

Mercy to him that shows it, is the rule.

Elisabeth turned toward the door as her mother-in-law ushered Roger Laidlaw into the drawing room, her tears gone and her demeanor surprisingly calm.

"Gentlemen, if you might give us a moment." Marjory inclined her head toward the entrance hall. "Mr. Laidlaw has something to say to our cousin."

"We cannot tarry much longer," Lord Jack reminded her, then departed with Gibson, closing the door behind them.

The room fell silent, save the sound of the rain pelting the windows.

"Please, Bess," Anne whispered, almost hiding behind her. "I don't wish to speak with him."

Elisabeth looked at the middle-aged man, his eyes downcast, his hat in his hands, and saw nothing to fear. But she was not Anne.

"Marjory and I will not leave your side," she promised, then slipped her arm round Anne's waist and led her toward him, feeling the tension in her cousin's body.

Marjory spoke first. "Mr. Laidlaw has confessed to me that he's a changed man."

A look of incredulity stole across Anne's features. "And you believe him?"

"I do," Marjory said. "When we are not so pressed for time, I shall tell you the whole of it. Until then, please hear him out, Cousin." She nodded at the factor, who moved one step closer, his gaze fixed on Anne.

"Miss Kerr . . ." He rubbed a shaky hand across his mouth. "Whan Lord John died, I had nae richt to speak to ye as I did. To ask ye . . . , weel, to suggest that . . ."

"Enough." Anne's voice was rough edged. "I know exactly what you proposed to me, Mr. Laidlaw."

"I ken ye do, mem." He gripped his cap so tightly that Elisabeth feared the wool might never recover. " 'Tis not the same man ye see standing here," he said. "The Lord has done a guid wark in me."

"Has he?" Anne did not hide her contempt. "I suppose that makes you a good man."

"Och! I would niver say I am guid." He lowered his gaze. "What I did was wrong, Miss Kerr, and I am verra sorry for it. Ye need not forgive me just because I ask. But I do ask."

He looked at each woman in turn, seeking absolution.

Marjory nodded. Anne frowned.

But Elisabeth did not see dark-haired Mr. Laidlaw. She saw fair-haired Donald Kerr. *Forgive me, lass. For all of it.* Did men think they could simply do as they pleased, then beg to be forgiven? Was there no man who was honorable or faithful or true?

Nettled, Elisabeth edged toward the door, taking Anne with her. "Pardon me, Cousin, but we must go."

"Indeed, our business here is finished." Anne lifted her skirts, turning her back on the factor of Tweedsford.

By the time they reached the carriage, Elisabeth regretted their hasty departure, leaving Marjory to bid the man farewell. Mr. Laidlaw's apology seemed most sincere and his desire to lead a new life commendable. Could she not see past her own heartache? Donald Kerr was the one who'd wronged her, not Roger Laidlaw.

With a heavy sigh, Elisabeth took her place on the cushioned leather seat of the carriage, then watched the admiral help Marjory board and climb in after her, having ordered his driver to make haste. Lord Jack removed his hat, but there was still a great deal of him to fit onto the balance of the seat.

"At least the rain has stopped." He settled

beside her. "And we'll be heading south. If Lord Mark is en route, he'll be coming from the north, from Edinburgh. You've nothing to fear, Mrs. Kerr." He looked at Marjory across the carriage interior. "What of your own carriage ride from the capital? Was it exceedingly uncomfortable?"

Elisabeth listened as he engaged first Marjory, then Anne, then Gibson, dispelling the tension in the air with his thoughtful questions and comments. Though she'd seen other sides of the admiral as well — a flash of impatience, a moment of anger — such things were far outweighed by his warm, generous spirit.

Careful, Bess.

She looked down, studying her hands. When a woman began tallying a bachelor's amiable qualities, thoughts of marriage were sure to follow. But she was a widow in mourning. However unfaithful Donald was, she intended to honor his memory for the full twelvemonth society required. To do otherwise would break her mother-in-law's heart.

Her cheeks grew warm. *Is it Marjory's heart that concerns you? Or your own?*

"You've slipped away from us," Lord Jack was saying as Elisabeth lifted her head, hoping to cool her skin.

"Not far," she assured him, glad the admiral could not read her mind.

How foolish even to think her employer might look in her direction, with Rosalind Murray so temptingly near. What gentleman would not choose a wealthy young lady of good breeding over an impoverished widow who might never bear him a child?

His carriage soon began the steep climb toward the East Port. Since she was facing the back of the coach, Elisabeth had to press her feet against the floor to keep from tipping too far forward and landing on Anne's shoes.

But gravity was working against her. At the very moment Elisabeth feared she might slip from her seat, Lord Jack braced her against the cushioned back, his long, muscular arm pressing into her ribs. Mortified, she turned her head.

"We've managed to avoid generals and dragoons this morn," the admiral said smoothly. "Now if we can all remain in our seats, I shall return you home without injury."

The moment the carriage crested the hill, Elisabeth eased back into place. "Thank you," she said softly.

"My pleasure," he said. Even more softly.

She looked out the window as if the tradesmen's cottages were the most interesting sight she'd ever beheld. *Guard your heart, Bess.*

Forty-Four

What say you to such a supper with such a woman?

George Gordon, Lord Byron

Jack could not remember when he'd last sat down. On his dawn ride, perhaps. Even breakfast had been consumed on the run. He'd tasted a summer pear while inspecting the orchards. Then gulped down a cup of tea while discussing last-minute details with Roberts and finally sampled a yeast roll while reviewing Mrs. Tudhope's menu.

He simply did not have time for lolling about. Bell Hill's first household supper was only seven hours hence, and Jack wanted everything to be perfect.

"Your lordship?" Mrs. Pringle appeared at his study door. "Will you be having dinner at two o' the clock, as usual?"

"Dinner?" Hearing the sharp tone in his voice, he swiftly apologized. "I beg your pardon, Mrs. Pringle. At the moment I'm afraid I have no appetite and even less patience."

"I quite understand," she said kindly. "The house is at sixes and sevens with maidservants colliding into one another in the hall and menservants tripping over their own feet in their haste to have everything ready."

Jack sighed. "Perhaps my plan was too ambitious."

"Nae, milord." Mrs. Pringle stepped farther into the room. "We are proud to be part of that plan. To gather at one table and sup with our master as if he were our friend . . ." She looked away for a moment. "I only hope we meet your expectations. Roberts and I have done our best to teach them proper table manners. We will none of us embarrass you this night."

"What a shame," Jack said, hoping to put her at ease. "I was counting on at least two dropped plates, numerous overturned glasses, and a host of rolls being tossed from one end of the dining room to the other."

Mrs. Pringle gave him a grateful smile. "I'll see what can be arranged, milord."

The supper hour was drawing near when Roberts came looking for him. "Your . . . , eh, staff for this eve has arrived. Shall I bring them in, sir?"

Jack moved to the front of his desk, prepared to greet them. "By all means."

He would never have asked the five of them to serve him in any capacity, least of all juggling plates of food and glasses of claret. But on the Sabbath at kirk, when he'd confessed needing several people to serve the meal, they'd all volunteered.

"I'd be honored to help," Marjory Kerr had said. "It is the least I can do after all you've done for my family."

"I'm a servant, milord," Gibson had insisted, "and richt guid at it."

Anne Kerr had also agreed to join them, then recruited Michael and Peter Dalgliesh. A press gang could not have been more persuasive. "We'll serve you well," Anne had vowed.

Jack had protested, of course. Offered to pay them handsomely for their efforts. The elder Widow Kerr in particular was offended. "I cannot be bought, milord. You must accept my service as a gift of thanks. I believe I speak for all of us."

Now here they were, filing into his study, reporting for duty.

Marjory and Anne wore freshly starched aprons and white, round-eared caps. Gibson had on his usual livery, and Michael had stitched up two black waistcoats for the occasion, one of them perfectly fitted to a seven-year-old boy.

"What a fine-looking group," Jack told them. "Gibson will rightly serve as butler and put the rest of you through your paces. If you'll report to Mrs. Tudhope, I'm certain she'll be greatly relieved to see you." He could not resist asking young Peter, "And how will *you* be of service?"

The lad held out his hands, pretending to hold a dish between them. "I'm to carry the food," he said, standing very tall, "but I'm not to go like this." Peter tipped his hands forward, sending imaginary vegetables spilling onto the floor.

"What will you do if that happens?" Jack wanted to know.

Peter stood on tiptoe, waving Jack closer so he might whisper in his ear. "I will cry," Peter said softly. "Then Annie will feel sorry for me and help me clean things up."

"Excellent plan," Jack assured him. He thanked them one by one, then sent them off to the kitchen. Such friends were more precious than rubies.

No sooner had they left than Mrs. Pringle entered his study, looking quite agitated. "You have a visitor, sir. General Lord Mark Kerr of Tweedsford."

One thought was foremost in his mind. *Bess.*

Jack was halfway to the door. "Escort my guest to the drawing room and serve him tea. I shall join him shortly," he said, then bolted into the hall and down the stair. He'd avoided the man for more than a week. Why had he come today of all days?

The moment he crossed the threshold into Elisabeth's workroom, Jack blurted out, "Lord Mark Kerr is here."

She quickly put aside her sewing. "Have you spoken with him yet?"

"Nae." Jack began to walk the perimeter of the room, his fists clenched. "How can I possibly drink tea with a man who so wronged your family?"

"With decorum, milord." Elisabeth stood, her hands clasped behind her back.

Only then did he notice she was wearing her new black gown. "You look wonderful, by the way. That is to say, your gown —"

"I'm glad you are pleased." She moved closer. "I've been saving it for your supper." Elisabeth touched his arm so slightly he might have imagined it. "Do not let Lord Mark ruin the hours to come."

"Indeed I will not," he assured her. "I intend to find out why he is here, tell him nothing, and bid him leave."

Minutes later Jack strode into his drawing room, not bothering to button his coat, his sheathed sword slapping against his boot. "General," he said with a nod.

"Admiral," he replied, nodding back. A man of perhaps sixty, the governor was tall, but not broad, and impeccably dressed. "Forgive me if my visit is poorly timed."

"I am afraid it is." Jack joined him at the

spacious round table where an elaborate tea had been laid, with sweets and savories enough to feed ten military officers. He could trust Mrs. Pringle to see a thing well done. "Our visit must be brief," Jack informed his unwelcome guest. "This eve I am hosting a supper for thirty."

Lord Mark nearly choked on his tea. "Thirty people of rank? You must have imported them, sir, for you'll not find more than a half-dozen peers in Selkirkshire."

Jack held his tongue, remembering his own vow. *Tell him nothing.* "What brings you to Bell Hill, sir?"

"I wish only to make your acquaintance. As you know, I was awarded Tweedsford for my success in defeating the Jacobites."

The man's arrogance was contemptible. "I was not aware you single-handedly routed Prince Charlie and his men," Jack said evenly.

Lord Mark stiffened. "I suppose a navy man cannot be expected to comprehend the dangers of close combat."

"Oh, I've bested enough Spanish steel to understand very well."

Lord Mark smoothed his narrow mustache. "May I trust you also will show no mercy to any Jacobite rebels who cross your path? You'll find them to be cowards, easily dispatched."

Jack shot to his feet, wanting to put an end to things before he thrust his sword through the man's gullet. "Forgive me, but we'll need to resume our discussion some other time. When Roberts escorts you to the door, inform him of a day that might suit you."

Lord Mark abruptly stood. "I've no intention of remaining in Selkirkshire beyond the week. The house is drafty and ill furnished, and the gardens are in shambles. With due respect for His Majesty, Tweedsford is a poor prize. I've other estates, you know, and the Governor's House at Edinburgh Castle is but four years old. I hardly need another residence."

"So Tweedsford will sit empty?"

"I may return now and again." Lord Mark shrugged. "The house has been vacant for a decade. Another ten years would hardly matter."

The men bade each other farewell without crossing swords — a miracle, to Jack's way of thinking. If he never spoke with General Lord Mark Kerr again, so much the better.

Jack walked into his dining room at precisely eight o' the clock and found his household staff standing quietly round the table as the candles shimmered and the sterling silver gleamed. Thirty well-scrubbed faces turned to greet him: thirty souls, entrusted to his care, who daily served him with gladness.

Jack swallowed until the tightness in his throat eased. " 'Tis an honor to have you at my table. Grace be unto you, and peace." He bowed his head, gave thanks for the meal, then invited them to sit, which they did in haste, their eyes as round as the china saucers beneath their teacups.

At the far end of the table sat Elisabeth Kerr, lovely as ever. The candlelight brought out the reddish gold strands in her hair and made her eyes shine like stars.

Jack leaned toward Mrs. Pringle on his left and asked in a low voice, "Why is Mrs. Kerr seated at such a distance?"

The housekeeper was quick to explain, "Because she is at Bell Hill by special appointment, milord, and not a servant. I thought it most appropriate she be seated at the foot of the table, usually reserved for the lady of the house."

"Well done." He gazed past the long row of candles. *You are not mine, Bess. But you are indeed a lady.*

Roberts, seated at his right hand, and Mrs. Pringle each looked down their sides of the table, then lifted their linen napkins and placed them across their laps, their movements slow and deliberate. Much elbowing and whispering ensued until all the servants had done the same.

Meanwhile, Gibson tarried at the door, anticipating his signal. When Jack nodded at him, his volunteer force went into action. Tureens of soup sailed through the door in the hands of people who'd never in their lives served at table. Not a drop was spilled, not a spoon forgotten. Jack was so engrossed he forgot to eat Mrs. Tudhope's flavorful broth until his housekeeper shot him a stern look, and he swiftly emptied his plate.

The second course, a richly seasoned salmon, came and went smoothly, as did the third, an asparagus ragout, followed by a pig in jelly. Though the laughter was a bit loud and the conversation of a common nature, Jack was pleased to see all his guests enjoying themselves, and his unpaid staff even more so. Marjory Kerr was positively glowing, like a grand hostess in a Paris salon. No wonder Gibson never took his eyes off her. The Dalgliesh men moved rather slowly down the table but only because they were busily entertaining folk. Anne Kerr looked the prettiest he'd ever seen her, and the happiest as well, keeping a close eye on young Peter. And on his father.

Jack tasted everything so he might compliment the cook with all sincerity. But his attention was repeatedly drawn to the opposite end of the table. Elisabeth Kerr was simply too far away. Dessert was almost upon them. How might he bid her to come closer?

Ah. He smiled to himself. *Just the thing.*

FORTY-FIVE

A good dinner sharpens wit, while it softens
the heart.

JOHN DORAN

As Elisabeth watched, Lord Buchanan rose
from his chair, saying nothing yet command-
ing every eye. His servants put down their
forks at once and turned in his direction. Did
he see the admiration reflected on their faces,
their genuine affection for him?

"I trust you're enjoying the evening," his
lordship began. "While our plates are cleared
by our able volunteers, I would invite our
dressmaker, Mrs. Kerr, to join me at the head
of the table."

A smattering of applause brought Elisabeth
to her feet. Uncertain of his intentions, Elisabeth moved past the long row of servants,
exchanging glances with Mrs. Pringle. Did
she know what her master had in mind? Apparently not, for the housekeeper shook her
head. Elisabeth turned to Marjory and Anne,

thinking her family might have some clue what was afoot, but their hands were full of plates, and their wide-eyed expressions offered no answers.

When Elisabeth reached the admiral's side, he lifted his glass of claret and invited those gathered round his table to do likewise. She pressed her hands to her waist, if only to keep her stomach from fluttering. *Whatever is this about, milord?*

Still holding his glass aloft, the admiral explained, "In the clubs I once frequented in London, when a gentleman appeared in a new suit of clothing, he would stand before his friends and say, 'Look how well my garments sit upon me.' You know, from *The Tempest.*"

His servants eyed one another, confusion written upon their features.

Elisabeth blinked at him. "Surely, milord, you are not asking me to do the same? To praise my own work?"

"Oh." He lowered his glass. "I suppose that would be immodest." He paused, as if seeking some graceful exit. "Am I to understand that ladies do not have such a custom when they appear in a new gown?"

"We do not, milord," she said as the maidservants laughed behind their hands. "But I'm grateful you noticed. I believe we all saw quite enough of my old gown."

"Hear, hear," Roberts said, standing, then raising his goblet higher. "To Mrs. Kerr and her fine garment."

Chairs were hastily pushed back as the whole assembly followed suit. "To Mrs. Kerr."

Elisabeth was quite certain her skin matched the deep red claret — hairline to neckline — but she couldn't look away and risk hurting their feelings. Instead she smiled as they took polite sips, dutifully noted her new garment, then sat down again.

Before she could do the same, Lord Buchanan lightly captured her by the wrist. "Come, sit with me, madam. Mrs. Pringle will be glad to take your place at the foot of the table."

The housekeeper vacated her chair at once, leaving Elisabeth no choice but to sit at his left hand, which still encircled hers.

"You must have one of Mrs. Tudhope's orange tarts," he said, leaning closer, his thumb rubbing against the inside of her wrist. "Though she'll never confess it, her tarts require a fortnight to make. Something to do with soaking the fruit. And her puff paste is the finest I've ever tasted."

Elisabeth had not felt a man's touch in so long that even his lordship's innocent caress made her lightheaded. "Did you eat such rich fare on the *Centurion?*" she managed to ask.

He laughed, a rich, warm sound. "Our diet

consisted of salted pork, salted beef, and, on Tuesdays and Fridays, salted fish." His lordship gently released her as Anne placed a flaky tart before each of them. He added, "I vowed that when I retired, I would eat well and eat often."

"And so you do," Elisabeth said, looking at her plate, relieved for somewhere else to cast her gaze for a moment.

Anne bent down and whispered in her ear, "I shall expect a full report on the walk home, Bess."

While the fiddlers tuned their instruments, Lord Jack consumed his tart in three or four bites, as did most folk seated at his table. Elisabeth barely tasted hers, still thinking about his touch. Did he, like Donald, find sport in toying with a woman's affections? Or did the admiral not realize what his actions implied?

Without preamble, the fiddlers began a tender air, their two instruments seamlessly blending melody and harmony. Elisabeth's throat tightened as the familiar Highland tune swept her away to Castleton of Braemar. She imagined her father at his loom. Her mother at the hearth. Simon with his whetstone, sharpening his dirk. And in the inglenook, a neighbor with fiddle or flute playing a tune they all loved, "My Love's Bonny When She Smiles on Me."

Just when Elisabeth thought she could not

bear it another moment, she felt a woman's hand on her shoulder. *Marjory.* She alone would understand why the music affected her so. By song's end Elisabeth saw several round the room using their linen napkins as hand-kerchiefs. The fiddlers played a slow waltz next, equally moving.

When a minor-key lament followed, threatening to drown the room in sorrow, Elisabeth motioned Lord Jack closer. "I wonder if you might you ask them to play a jig or a reel. Something more cheerful."

In a low voice the admiral confessed, "Michael Dalgliesh found the lads for me. Old friends from school, apparently. They play only at funerals."

"Oh." Elisabeth leaned back in her seat and tried not to laugh. Or cry.

The tall case clock in Lord Buchanan's study was chiming the hour of ten when the musicians took their final bow. However melancholy their tunes, their playing was superb, and the household's applause enthusiastic.

"Your first supper was a great success, milord," Elisabeth assured him.

He seemed pleased as he bade his servants good night, sending them to their lodgings on the ground floor off the servants' hall. The women resided on the east end of the mansion, the men on the west, with the kitchen and laundry rooms between them. Mrs. Tudhope and Mrs. Craig remained ever vigilant for midnight trysts.

Only one servant among those hired on Whitsun Monday had been dismissed: Tibbie Cranshaw, who'd flirted shamelessly with the head footman and spoken out of turn on too many occasions. Elisabeth had seldom crossed paths with Tibbie, yet was not sorry to see her go.

Once the dining room was empty, Marjory and the others made quick work of clearing the last of the dessert plates. When Elisabeth joined them, gathering the silverware, a frown crossed Lord Buchanan's face.

" 'Tis not beneath me," Elisabeth said gently. "Not if my mother-in-law is willing to do such work."

"As a gift," Marjory reminded him, sallying out with an empty plate in each hand.

With an exasperated sigh, the admiral picked up two wine goblets and followed the others through the hall and down the stair, then deposited the glasses in the hands of a startled young maid. While the rest of the household slept, the scullery maids would be scrubbing the night's dishes, with a promise they could sleep until the forenoon.

Lord Jack escorted his guests down the candlelit servants' hall and through the rear entrance, then started across the grassy expanse, lantern in hand.

"Milord?" Elisabeth hurried to keep up

with his long stride, the others trailing close behind. " 'Twould be better if we went round the other direction. This is hardly the way home."

"Nae, but it *is* the way to the stables. The hour is too late for traveling by foot, and the waning quarter moon will not light your path. I've asked Hyslop to take you home by coach."

"Och!" Michael Dalgliesh scoffed. " 'Tis but two miles, milord, and a' doon hill. We'll be hame afore lang."

"He's richt," Gibson chimed in. "We'll take guid care o' the leddies. Won't we, Peter?"

"Aye." The lad rubbed his eyes, his bedtime long past.

But the admiral would not be dissuaded. "I do not hear the ladies protesting. You've all worked hard this day and deserve a bit of comfort."

When they reached the stables, they found the horses already harnessed and Timothy Hyslop and a footman waiting for them. The weary party was settled in their seats before another complaint, however feeble, might be raised.

Elisabeth was the last to climb in. When she turned to lean out the open window and thank their host, he was standing in a pool of lantern light. His size and strength, his dark coloring and prominent features might be daunting, even alarming to someone who didn't know him. But Lord Jack did not frighten her.

"I shall see you on the morrow, milord."

"Depend upon it," he said with a steady gaze, then stepped back, signaling the driver. "Carry on."

FORTY-SIX

The showers of God's grace fall into lowly
hearts and humble souls.

JOHN WORTHINGTON

Marjory did not see Lord Buchanan again
until the following Sabbath at kirk. Despite
the soggy, rainy weather, the admiral was
dressed in a striking burgundy coat and
waistcoat with nary a splash of mud on his
boots. He greeted each Kerr woman individu-
ally before claiming the vacant seat next to
Elisabeth.

Marjory could hardly object in so public
and sacred a place. Nor could she blame her
daughter-in-law for brightening when his
lordship appeared. Did not her own heart lift
each time they met?

She was turning to address Anne when her
cousin suddenly rose. "Come and sit with us,
Gibson."

"Aye, please do." Marjory patted the seat

next to her. "My cousin won't mind making room."

Gibson bowed as neatly as any gentleman. "Reverend Brown gave me leave to sit with ye." Then he added in a low voice, "I think 'twas the ginger biscuits ye sent on Thursday last."

Marjory smiled. Her plan had worked.

After he settled next to her on the pew, Gibson did a shocking thing: he quietly captured her hand, safely out of view beneath the folds of her skirt. When she didn't pull away, his strong fingers, rough from years of work, tightened round hers.

Oh my dear Gibson.

Marjory could no longer deny her feelings, at least not to herself. *I am falling in love with a servant.* And not just any man in service but her own Gibson, her own dear friend. Nae, he was more than that. His warmth, his scent, his touch stirred something inside her that was well beyond friendship.

Was it wrong, their mutual affection? In God's eyes, in God's Word, was it wrong?

She knew the answer and was comforted by it. But society had its own rules, and they did not stretch this far. Only the very wealthy could afford to do as they pleased.

Marjory lifted her head, gazing past the leaky roof and rotting beams. *Give me wisdom, Lord. And courage.* Aye, especially that.

Hearing a slight commotion, she glanced down the pew and saw Michael and Peter Dalgliesh taking their seats next to Anne. Late as usual, though who could fault a man with a child to dress and no wife or valet to help him? Anne's face glowed like a candle, even as Peter grinned broadly, showing off his latest missing tooth.

Marjory well recalled young Donald on a similar occasion keeping his lips tightly closed, hoping no one would notice the gaps in his teeth, while Andrew ran up and down the kirk aisles, begging everyone to look.

Gibson glanced at Peter, then bent his head toward hers. "Are ye thinking o' yer lads?"

"I am," she confessed. Gibson had been there. He remembered too.

As the precentor sang the first line of the gathering psalm, Gibson squeezed her hand once more, then eased away. Marjory was both saddened and relieved. She could not risk Reverend Brown looking down from on high and noticing their hands joined. Not when he'd expressed such opposition to their growing friendship.

Marjory had rehearsed his words many times. *One might think Neil Gibson had designs on you.* She eyed the black-gowned minister, now waiting to ascend his pulpit. *And what if I have designs on him, Reverend?* Even the thought made her skin warm.

The sermon that *dreich* and dreary Sabbath morning was taken from Zechariah. Speaking slowly, deliberately, and with conviction, Reverend Brown seemed quite adamant that his congregation take heed of his words. "Execute true judgment," he recited from memory. "Show mercy and compassions every man to his brother." His fierce gaze raked across his audience, landing on one parishioner, then another. Folk squirmed in their seats and looked round the sanctuary, but the minister still did not relent.

When he said, "Oppress not the widow, nor the fatherless, the stranger, nor the poor," Marjory was quite certain his eyes were directed at the Kerr pew, where two widows sat, both fatherless and poor. When the sermon finally ended, Marjory stood, anxious to move about, to escape the conflicting thoughts batting about inside her like moths trapped in a clay jar.

Gibson is a servant, yet a fine one. And I am a lady, yet a poor one.

Lord Buchanan announced to those in the Kerr pew, "Mrs. Pringle has sent me with a rather large dinner basket. Since the weather will not suit for a picnic, shall we find a spot with a fine prospect where we might dine together in the dry confines of my carriage? Unless, of course, you have other plans."

Anne chuckled. "Milord, we have cold mutton and stale bread at home. Whatever is in your basket will be most welcome."

Disappointed that Gibson could not join them, Marjory bade him farewell. "I hope I shall see you soon," she murmured, then watched Gibson make his way through the crowd, not far behind the admiral, who was off to summon his carriage.

As Marjory and Elisabeth started down the aisle, Anne walked ahead of them, one hand tucked round the crook of Michael Dalgliesh's elbow, the other firmly clasping Peter's hand. With each step the threesome drew closer together, matching their strides, smiling into one another's faces.

"Did you know about this?" Marjory gestured toward the small family in the making.

"Annie has always cared for him," Elisabeth admitted. "Michael is finally free to return her affections. And Peter adores her, as you can see."

Marjory heard something in her voice. Not regret, not sadness, not envy. Longing, perhaps.

When they all reached Kirk Wynd, freshly dampened by the rain, Lord Buchanan was waiting with his coach, as promised. The six of them were soon seated inside, dry and cozy.

"Hyslop has assured me we'll not be disappointed with the view," Lord Buchanan told them as the carriage jolted forward. "Come, Peter, let me see that new gap in your teeth."

The lad, seated in his father's lap, turned to his lordship and opened wide.

The admiral's frown was exaggerated, the shaking of his head more so. "However shall we fill that? Perhaps I should ask Mrs. Pringle for a china teacup. Mr. Richardson might have a gardening tool that would serve. Or shall your father stitch you a new tooth? One made of black wool would be very dashing."

Peter giggled as only a boy of seven can. "Faither says I'll grow new teeth a' by myself."

Lord Buchanan feigned shock. "Certainly not during the day, when people are watching."

"Nae!" Peter cried. "At nicht while I sleep."

All through their playful exchange, Marjory watched Anne's gaze shift from Michael to Peter and back again, the love in her eyes unmistakable. Only a fool could have missed such a thing. *And you, Marjory Kerr, are certainly that.*

Anne piped up with a question. "Lord Buchanan, will you be needing our services for your next household supper?"

"Nae, madam, for I could not possibly expect all of you to serve me again. I've asked a half-dozen servants from the Philiphaugh estate to join us on the thirty-first."

"And what o' the fiddlers, milord?" Michael asked.

The admiral glanced at Elisabeth. "I've

something different in mind for this month's supper. After our dessert we shall move to the drawing room, where I've arranged for several musicians to play. Once we've banished the furniture, that is."

"For dancing!" Elisabeth's eyes sparkled. "Well done, milord."

He tipped his head. "I believe *you* were the one who called for a reel or a jig."

"Aye, but as a widow, I cannot dance." Her careless shrug belied her feelings.

"I do not care for it myself," Lord Buchanan confessed.

Whether he spoke the truth or meant simply to put Elisabeth at ease Marjory could not tell. She slipped her arm round Elisabeth's shoulders. "Your dancing days are far from over, my dear. Half the year has already slipped through our fingers. Why, autumn is almost upon us. Isn't that so, Admiral?"

He settled his gaze on Elisabeth. "I am counting the days, madam."

FORTY-SEVEN

My lord a-hunting he is gane,
But hounds or hawks wi' him are nane.

ROBERT BURNS

"For you, milord." Roberts placed a slender letter in his hands. Jack broke the thick seal, curious about the contents. "Do we know who it's from?" He'd received little correspondence during his months in Selkirkshire. Once a navy man came ashore, his shipmates soon forgot him. Even the king had been quiet of late, though that sleeping giant could rouse at any moment.

Roberts opened the study curtains farther, bathing Jack's desk in late afternoon sunlight. "Sir John Murray of Philiphaugh," he informed him.

"Aye, here's his signature." Jack smoothed out the creases. "Remind me who is dining with us this eve?"

"The Chisholms of Broadmeadows, milord, with their daughter, Miss Susan Chisholm. If you care to review the menu —"

"I prefer to be surprised," Jack said, already engrossed in reading. "But thank you, Roberts." As the butler quietly departed, Jack settled back in his chair with Sir John's brief letter.

To Admiral Lord Jack Buchanan
Bell Hill, Selkirkshire
Saturday, 2 August 1746

Lord Jack:

Might you care to join me for a fortnight of hunting in the Highlands? August is a fine month for deer stalking and grouse shooting. I can promise heather moorlands and waterfalls, golden eagles and peregrine falcons, and at our dinner table, venison, salmon, and pheasant.

Jack's brows lifted. *Well, sir. You have my attention.* He scanned the rest of the letter, noting the details, all to his liking. A fine hunting lodge. Magnificent scenery. A gamekeeper to guide them. Hours of amiable conversation.

Had he not grown restless on occasion? Longing for the sea, missing his London companions? Having traveled no farther north in Scotland than Edinburgh, Jack knew at once how he'd respond to the man's generous invitation. He dashed off a letter and put it in his butler's hands a quarter hour later. "Have one of the stable lads deliver this for me," he told Roberts, then headed for the turnpike stair leading down to the servants' hall, Sir John's letter in hand.

Jack paused halfway down the steps, a question nagging at him. When he had good or bad news to report, why was Elisabeth Kerr the first person who came to mind? The answer was patently obvious: she was always the first person who came to mind, from the moment he lifted his head each morning until his last waking thought at night.

A moment later Jack strolled through the door of her workroom, waving his letter like an eager schoolboy on his first outing. "I am soon bound for Braemar," he told her. "With any luck I'll bring home a brace of red grouse."

She looked up, Charbon curled at her feet. "Is that so, milord?"

Jack saw at once she was troubled, though by what he could not imagine. He claimed the empty chair beside her, drawing it as near as he dared. "What is it, Bess?"

"No doubt you've forgotten, but Braemar is my home."

He frowned. "I thought it was Castleton . . ." *Well done, Jack. As if Scotland had only one castle town.*

"Castleton of Braemar," she said. "I wonder

if you might . . ." She paused. "If you might deliver a letter to my mother. Unless 'tis an inconvenience. I write her almost every month and know the cost of my posts must be a burden to her."

" 'Twill be my pleasure," he said, glad for any chance to serve her.

"I do wonder if 'tis wise to travel north," she said, "with the Duke of Cumberland still menacing the Highlands."

"The king's son has no quarrel with me," Jack assured her. "In any case, I will have a gun in hand and Dickson by my side. We are to lodge with Sir John and his manservant at the Mar estate, owned by a Mr. Duff."

"William Duff." She sighed pensively. "I suppose you'll be safe enough there."

Any thoughts of red grouse or fresh salmon vanished when he realized she was concerned for his welfare. Emboldened, he took her hand. "You can be sure I'll return in one piece."

"One can never be certain of such things," she said. "I thought my husband would return from war, and he did not."

Lord Donald Kerr. In all their many discussions, they'd shared few words about the man who'd loved her, married her, then left her a widow. Did she love him still? Would she mourn him always? *Is there hope for me?* That was the question Jack most wanted to ask but could not.

"What might you tell me about Lord Donald?" he inquired at last, letting her decide how much, or how little, to reveal about her marriage.

She did not withdraw her hand, though her tone grew cooler. "My husband was everything a gentleman should be. Well read, well traveled, well educated, well mannered. He was also one thing a gentleman should never be."

Jack waited, his heart thudding in his chest. *What is it, Bess?* He sorted through his memories of their conversations. Perhaps she'd hinted at this before. Was Donald Kerr a drunkard? A gambler? A liar? A coward? Thinking to put her at ease, Jack assured her, "Whatever his weakness, I will not think less of the man. Nor of you for marrying him."

She turned her head away as her limp hand slipped from his grasp. "My husband was unfaithful to me. Repeatedly."

Jack stared at her, certain he'd misunderstood. "You do not mean he —"

"Aye."

He shook his head, trying to make sense of it. "It is not possible," he finally said. "No gentleman with you by his side would ever look anywhere else."

"Nonetheless, he did, milord." Elisabeth rose, casting aside her sewing. "He confessed as much to me, both in person and on paper. And I met one of his . . . women. I can assure you, 'tis more than possible." She moved to the hearth, then stood with her back to him, her shoulders bent from the weight of her burden.

Go to her, Jack. Do something, say something.

He was on his feet and walking toward her before he had time to think of what he might say or do. He wanted to kill the man, but Donald Kerr was already dead. He wanted to take Elisabeth in his arms, though for all the wrong reasons. He wanted to —

"Forgive me, milord." She turned round just as he reached her, then, startled, lost her balance and began falling backward toward the fire.

"Bess!" He caught her in his embrace, meaning only to spare her. For an instant he felt her heart beating against his chest and her warm breath on his cheek.

"Pardon me," she murmured, quickly pulling free. "I did not realize you were so close."

Jack looked down at the floor, at his boots, at Charbon. Anything to clear his mind. The last thing Elisabeth Kerr needed was a gentleman making advances toward her, however unintentionally. "Your husband's behavior was unconscionable," he said in a low voice, fighting to control his emotions. "Not all men are unfaithful."

After a long silence she said, "At least my father honored his vows to my mother."

Jack nodded, his anger and frustration beginning to abate. "I would have expected no less from the man who fathered you."

She reclaimed her chair and began sewing again, her needle moving in and out of the fabric. The steady rhythm seemed to calm her. Perhaps his fortnight in the Highlands would be a blessing for Elisabeth. A relief simply to sew and not have a retired admiral seeking her company at every turn.

Watching her, Jack tallied her labors thus far. Nine gowns were finished. Nine gowns remained. *And then what, Lord? Shall I find her more work come Saint Andrew's Day? Or must I bid her farewell?*

No decision was required at the moment. He would go a-hunting in Braemar and perhaps learn something of her family. "I shall depart two days hence," Jack told her, trying to gauge her reaction, "and will return long before month's end."

Elisabeth's hands stilled. "Then you'll not be here for Saint Lawrence Fair."

"I'm afraid not. But with the marketplace below your window, you and your family won't miss a moment."

"Nae, I suppose not." Her needle began moving again. "But we will miss you, milord."

FORTY-EIGHT

Came but for friendship, and took away
love.

THOMAS MOORE

Elisabeth gazed down at the flood of strangers pouring into Selkirk and imagined eight days of eating and drinking, bartering and trading, dancing and merrymaking. Lord Jack was right: they could hardly miss the fair with its colorful sights, pungent smells, and riotous sounds hovering over the town like a low bank of thunderclouds, charging the air with electricity.

Anne joined her at the window, her shoulder pressing against Elisabeth's arm. "The town council threw open the ports at dawn and will not close them again 'til Monday next."

"However will we sleep at night?" Elisabeth wondered.

"With the windows closed," Marjory said firmly, "and wool in our ears." Standing at the hearth, she neatly turned over a barley bannock, despite working with a hot *girdle* and a thin cake the size of a dinner plate.

"I'll not mind the wool," Anne agreed, "but 'tis too warm for closed windows."

Elisabeth moved toward the washstand and away from the fire. She was already over-heated, and the August day had barely begun. They'd not don their gowns until absolutely necessary — one of the advantages of living in a house with three women. Stays, chemises, stockings, and shoes were covering enough for the moment.

As she splashed cool water on her face, Elisabeth thought of Lord Jack doing the same in some sparkling Highland *burn.* He'd already been gone a full week, though it seemed even longer. Bell Hill felt empty without him. So did the kirk yesterday morn-ing. Elisabeth tried not to speak of him, lest someone misunderstand. They were simply friends. Good friends. Very good friends.

The same could not be said of Cousin Anne and Michael Dalgliesh, who'd traded friend-ship for courtship nearly two months past. Michael came calling most evenings, bring-ing Peter along with a treat from the market to add to their supper. A new spice. Honey in a clay jar. A handful of carrots. Five juicy plums. Marjory seemed pleased to have a man at their table and a boy even more so. Peter had grown at least an inch since they'd arrived in Selkirk and would attend the parish school in the fall, just down the close from his father's shop.

Elisabeth looked at Anne pulling out her lace making supplies, her small hands and nimble fingers well suited to the work. Since Michael had begun to court her, a smile was seldom far from Anne's lips. Michael already grinned round the clock, but the heated look in his eyes whenever he took Anne's hand was enough to make Elisabeth blush and turn her head.

Whatever was the man waiting for? Michael was already a successful tailor, and Anne would make him more so. His son adored her, and the lodgings over their shop could easily accommodate another. Elisabeth could think of no impediment to marriage, save one: Michael was afraid of losing a second wife and of Peter's losing a second mother. Elisabeth could not fault the man for his caution. But she could pray.

Let him trust in you, Lord. Let him take a leap of faith.

She smiled, looking across the room at Anne, thinking of them together, certain they were meant for each other. In her heart of hearts, Elisabeth felt only joy and not an ounce of envy. Well, perhaps a tiny bit when it came to Peter. What a charming companion he would be at the fair! If she asked nicely, the wee lad might let her hold his hand again.

"Breakfast," Marjory sang out, pouring

415

three steaming cups of tea.

The women were soon seated at table, enjoying warm bannocks with Michael's gift of honey, fresh from the comb.

"When shall we venture out?" Marjory wanted to know.

"The earlier the better," Anne insisted. "As the day goes on and the whisky flows, 'tis a less sanguine place for a woman on her own."

"But we'll not be alone," Elisabeth reminded her. "The Dalgliesh men will see that we're safe."

Anne winked at her over her teacup. "Too bad a certain admiral is away. There's not a man in Selkirkshire, or any county round, who would challenge Lord Buchanan."

Elisabeth couldn't agree more and said absolutely nothing.

"Odd," Marjory mused, "that the sheriff is off hunting in the Highlands during Saint Lawrence Fair. Should he not be here keeping the peace?"

" 'Tis not necessary," Anne replied as she folded her bannock with care, honey trickling over her fingers. Between dainty bites she explained the rules of the fair. "There are no restrictions on who can trade, and no one is to be arrested, except for some terrible crime, which never happens with so many witnesses."

Elisabeth glanced toward the window, sensing the size of the crowd swelling. "Those are the only rules?"

Anne laughed. "It is rather carefree. One year the fair was canceled, when the plague struck in June, but that was more than a century ago. In my lifetime it's been a grand place to meet folk from neighboring counties. Our fair is proclaimed from all the mercat crosses round. Hawick, Jedburgh, Kelso, Melrose, even as far away as Linlithgow." She downed the last of her tea and stood. "I, for one, am getting dressed."

Elisabeth and Marjory followed her lead, grateful for the light fabric of their gowns on so warm a day. The house was tidied and the table scrubbed before Michael came knocking at ten o' the clock.

"Leuk!" Peter cried, holding up a wooden pinwheel that spun round while he circled the room as fast as his little legs would carry him.

"Easy noo." Michael scooped up the boy and tucked him under his arm. " 'Tis meant for a hill, lad. Not for a hoose."

Undaunted, Peter held out his new toy so the Kerr women could inspect it. " 'Tis from the chapman on the corner," he said with pride.

Elisabeth dutifully looked it over, admiring the wooden stick, the tiny pin, and the curls of stout paper that made it whirl. "If you carry this in one hand, Peter, I wonder if I might hold the other?"

His little features quickly knitted into a frown. "But what about Annie? Wha'll hold her hand?"

Michael parked him on his feet. "I think I can manage it, lad." He took Anne's hand in his to prove it.

"I suppose I'll hold no one's hand," Marjory said with a dramatic sniff.

Elisabeth knew better. On the first day of the fair, Gibson would have the morning free. If he did not appear on their threshold before they left, Marjory would beat a path to the manse and coax him out. Elisabeth was not at all surprised a few minutes later when they walked to the end of Halliwell's Close and found Gibson heading in their direction.

" 'Tis every couple for themselves," Anne declared, as they were swept into the throng.

Elisabeth bent down to be certain Peter heard her clearly. "Promise you will not let go of my hand?"

"I'll be guid!" he said, nodding emphatically, then pulled her toward the chapmen's stalls for another look at the toys.

Elisabeth had expected Saint Lawrence Fair to be a larger version of their market day. But it was far more than that. Booths stretched down every street, including Back Row, with bright flags advertising the wares sold at each stall. Woolen and linen cloth in stacks taller than even Lord Jack beckoned for Elisabeth's silver shillings. But she'd not part with them

418

easily with three mouths to feed and rent to help pay. Saint Andrew's Day, her last in the admiral's employ, had seemed a long way off in May. Not so now.

The meal sellers came next, with ground oats, barley, and wheat. She'd planned to do some shopping but hadn't thought to bring a basket. When she turned toward the house and considered carrying back each purchase, Elisabeth realized how foolish that would be. She could not see the mouth of the close, let alone reach it without weaving through the masses. On the morrow she would shop. Today she and Peter would play.

"What do you want to see next?" she asked him when he finally tired of the chapmen's stalls with their many temptations.

"Swords!" he exclaimed at once, pulling her along Cross Gait, holding up his pinwheel like a standard bearer marching into battle.

Elisabeth followed him, hanging on to his hand as tightly as she could without crushing his little fingers. At the weaponry stall his eyes grew round at the basket-hilted swords, the studded targes, and the slender dirks. She was glad his hands were occupied, lest he touch one of the sharp blades and cut himself. "Might we look at the saddlery next?" she asked, deciding leather was a safer choice than steel.

His interest in saddles and harnesses quickly waned until she reminded him that

419

such things were used on horses. "And they have those for sale here too."

"Och! Can we leuk?"

Down Water Row they went, the street almost unrecognizable with so many merchants selling their goods. At Shaw's Close the wooden stalls gave way to horses, cattle, and sheep with all the neighing, lowing, and bleating a boy could hope for. "Watch where you step," Elisabeth warned him, clutching her skirts in one hand.

Peter touched each animal that would let him near, marveling at the velvety sleekness of the horses, the large eyes blinking at him as he studied the cows, the thick, off-white wool of the sheep.

"They're Cheviots," Elisabeth told him, recognizing their broad, white faces. "A fine breed for weaving."

The barrel-chested seller lifted his eyebrows appreciatively. "You know something of sheep breeding, madam?"

"My father was a weaver," Elisabeth explained, "and very particular about his wool."

"The fleece of a Cheviot is superior for plaids," he agreed, "though the Dartmoor and Leicester breeds have much to recommend them."

As he waxed on about the merits of one breed compared to another, Elisabeth nodded politely, all the while looking for a graceful means of escape. Only then did she realize Peter's hand was no longer in hers. She quickly spun round. "Peter?"

Though a few heads turned, none of them belonged to a little red-haired boy.

"Peter?" She cried louder this time, trying to lift her voice above the din. "Peter Dalgliesh!"

But his cheerful little voice did not respond.

Her heart beginning to pound, Elisabeth started toward the East Port, thinking he might have been drawn to the ringing anvils and glowing forges farther down Water Row. She ignored all the adults and looked only at the children. But there were so many of them! "Red hair, red hair," she reminded herself under her breath, trying not to panic, trying not to imagine the worst.

She kept calling his name, pushing her way through the crowd. When she reached the fiery hot forges, Elisabeth was certain she'd guessed wrongly. He must have gone back toward the marketplace. Toward the fleshers with their lethal knives. Toward the shoemakers with their sharp awls. Toward the swords and the dirks that he'd desperately wanted to touch.

"Peter!" She was screaming now, not caring what people thought of her. Caring only about a little boy who'd slipped from her grasp. *Peter!*

FORTY-NINE

Never think that God's delays are God's
denials.

GEORGES-LOUIS LECLERC, COMTE DE
BUFFON

Please, Lord. Please help me find him.

Elisabeth retraced her steps, struggling to
catch her breath. "Peter Dalgliesh!" she cried,
knowing the lad would never hear her, no
matter how loudly she called his name. The
marketplace was too noisy, too congested. In
the sea of faces, she saw only strangers.

"Peter, where are you?" she moaned, bending down, fixing her gaze a few feet above the
ground, desperately looking for a red-headed
boy in a muslin shirt and brown waistcoat.
All she could think about was how frightened
he must be. *Oh, Peter. I'm so sorry.*

She felt physically ill, her stomach in knots.
Had he returned to the sheep market? Run
down Shaw's Close, curious what he might

find in the narrow passageway? Or had a stranger beckoned him to follow?

When she heard a child crying, Elisabeth elbowed her way through the milling crowd, more concerned with haste than politeness. "Peter? Peter, is that you?" A moment later she reached the sobbing lad. He was the same age and size, but, alas, he was not Peter.

His mother, holding him firmly by the hand, jutted out her chin. "Have ye lost yer *bairn?*"

"He's run off," Elisabeth confessed. "Perhaps you've seen him? Bright red hair and blue eyes."

"Och! Ye'll find plenty o' lads here what fits that."

"Aye," Elisabeth said, fighting tears.

"Noo, lass, dinna *greet.*" Compassion softened the woman's features. "He'll not have gane far. And he'll be leuking for ye as weel. A bairn aye finds its mither."

But I am not his mother. Jenny would never have let go.

Heartsick, Elisabeth pressed on, searching up and down Water Row. Whenever she saw a familiar face from the neighborhood, she hurried to the person's side and asked the same frantic question. "Have you seen little Peter Dalgliesh?"

The answer was always the same: "Nae, Mrs. Kerr."

Distraught, she stood near a display of

fleeces and skins and bowed her head, pleading for divine intervention. *Help me, Lord. Please.* No wonder the Almighty had never entrusted her with a child of her own. How could she have been so careless? How could she have let him slip away?

Then from high above her, a small, excited voice crowed, "I found her!"

Elisabeth's head lifted as quickly as her spirits. "Peter?"

Here he came, riding on his father's shoulders, his legs draped round the tailor's neck, his wee hands clutching Michael's larger ones.

She hurried up to them, awash with relief. "Wherever have you been, lad?"

"Whaur have *ye* been is mair like it," Michael admonished her, giving his son a playful bounce. "Peter spied Annie and me in the crowd, ran o'er to see us, then turned back and couldna find ye. Och, he felt terrible. Made me carry him about 'til we spotted ye. And so we have."

"Oh, so *I* was the one who was lost." Elisabeth reached up and patted the lad's chubby leg. "I'm sorry I gave you a scare, Peter."

"Next time I'll not let ye go," the boy promised.

Anne tapped the brim of Elisabeth's straw bonnet. "Tall as you are, Bess, we could add a peacock feather to your hat and never lose sight of you."

"A fine idea," she agreed, though the way Anne and Michael had locked gazes, keeping an eye on her was clearly the last thing on their minds. "Suppose Peter and I resume our walk," Elisabeth offered, "and let the two of you enjoy the fair."

"Nae," Anne said abruptly, stepping away from Michael's side. "I would take a turn round the marketplace with you, Bess, if you'll not mind." She claimed Elisabeth's arm, then told Michael, "Kindly meet us at the mercat cross in a quarter hour."

"Verra weel, Annie." If his feelings were hurt, Michael didn't show it as he strolled off with Peter riding high above the crowd.

The women, meanwhile, started toward the souters' market stalls, filled with rows of shoes in various sizes, left and right shaped just the same. Elisabeth said playfully, "Is it leather or brocade you're wanting, Cousin?"

"You know very well what I want," Anne said, drawing closer, lest the two be jostled apart and their conversation interrupted. "A future with the man I love."

Elisabeth saw at once how serious she was and lost the teasing note in her voice. "Has Michael broached the subject?"

Anne shrugged. "He's confessed his affection for me. But the word *marriage* has yet to fall from his lips."

Elisabeth studied the faint lines along her cousin's brow, the hint of sadness in her eyes.

"Are you afraid it never will?"

Anne looked up. "Aye. He seems content to simply court me, but we're both too old for that." As Peter and his father faded from view, Anne scuffed her toe across the cobblestones, her expression troubled. "This I know: Peter needs a mother. And if I hope to bear a child of my own, I cannot wait much longer. Before year's end I'll be seven-and-thirty."

Elisabeth said without hesitation, "Then you must propose to Michael."

"Bess!" A flush of color filled her cheeks. "I could never do such a thing."

"Aye, you could." She stepped closer so no one might overhear them. "He loves you, Annie. A wee nudge and the man will fall like Peter's tower of wooden blocks."

Her cousin began to wring her hands. " 'Tis very bold."

"Indeed." Elisabeth tipped her head. "Do you honestly think he'll refuse you?"

"Nae." Anne ceased her fidgeting at once. "I think he might be . . ."

"Relieved," Elisabeth said for her, and they both laughed. "Michael is waiting for you at the mercat cross. A perfect place to announce your intentions. If not to the whole town, at least to your beloved."

Her face filled with resolve, Anne pulled her along. "Come with me so I do not lose my nerve."

Two women on a mission, they ducked round pie sellers, fishwives, street hawkers, and tinkers, their gazes fixed on the upraised pillar at the center of the marketplace, where Michael stood waiting for them, scanning the crowd. As her cousin's footsteps quickened, so did Elisabeth's heart. *Say yes, Michael. Say yes!*

The moment Michael lowered Peter to the ground, the boy ran into Anne's open arms. "I saw ye from a lang way aff!" he boasted.

"I've had my eye on you as well," Anne murmured, lifting him into her embrace, his little legs wrapped round her waist, his arms circling her neck.

Elisabeth smiled down at them, tears stinging her eyes. *Dear, dear Peter.*

"So." Michael folded his arms across his chest. "If ye dinna mind me asking, what have the two o' ye been about?"

Anne shifted Peter onto her hip, then looked up, her eyes clear, her countenance an open book. "Sir, have you plans for the last day of August?"

"The *what?*" Michael's exaggerated frown made them all laugh. "D'ye think I carry a calendar on my person, lass?"

" 'Tis three weeks hence," she told him. "Enough time to have the banns read each Sabbath and plan a wee wedding at the kirk."

His ruddy skin darkened. "And wha *micht* be getting married?"

She slowly lowered Peter to the ground. "A couple that deserves a bit of happiness."

His voice was low. "What are ye saying, Annie?"

"I am saying I love you, Michael Dalgliesh." She lifted her face to his, her hands still resting on Peter's shoulders. "And I want to be your wife."

Elisabeth knew she should turn her attention to the mercat cross, the blue summer sky, the bustling crowd — anything to give the couple a moment's privacy. But she could not tear her gaze away from the tender scene before her as a broad grin stretched across Michael's bright, freckled face.

"Then I'd best marry ye," he said, "for ye ken I luve ye, Annie Kerr." He bent down and kissed her right there in the marketplace while Peter stood between them, looking up, his eyes filled with wonder.

"Will Annie be my mither?" the lad asked, tugging on his father's sleeve.

"Aye, she will," Michael said firmly, kissing her once more. "And there'll be no calling her Annie from noo on."

Anne smoothed Peter's hair, her hand visibly shaking. "Are you certain of this?"

Michael nodded emphatically. " 'Tis what Jenny would want. And what I want."

Anne glanced at Elisabeth, then said, "You're not offended? That I did the asking?"

"Nae, lass." Michael flung his arm round

her shoulder and pulled her to his side. "Honored is what I am." He eyed Elisabeth. "I'll jalouse yer cousin is the one wha gave ye the courage."

"Perhaps," Anne agreed, "but *I* had to say the words."

"So ye did, lass." He brushed a kiss across the top of her head and winked at Elisabeth. "So ye did."

FIFTY

Who would have thought my shrivel'd heart
Could have recovered greenness?

GEORGE HERBERT

Marjory tarried outside Anne's door in Halli-well's Close, grateful for the cool respite from the day's heat and even more pleased to have Gibson's warm hand in hers, discreetly hidden from view. After a few hours she'd had quite enough of the fair, though she never tired of having Gibson by her side.

"You will join us for supper?" she asked him.

"Nae," Gibson said blithely, "for I've anither widow keen for my company this eve."

She arched her brows, going along with his ploy. "And who might that be?"

"Mrs. Scott." Only the twinkle in his eye gave him away. "Mind, the leddy *is* a bit lang in the tooth."

Marjory laughed, knowing full well that Isobel Scott was five-and-eighty. "She is a good

430

friend," she reminded him, "and old enough to be your mother."

He squeezed her hand. "Then I'll settle for a leddy young enough to be my —"

"Hush." She stemmed his words with a touch of her gloved finger. "Less than a dozen years separate us. Hardly worth mentioning."

Gibson smiled down at her. "If ye say so, Leddy Kerr."

Call me Marjory. She looked away, flustered. Whatever was she thinking? Neil Gibson had never, in all their years together, addressed her by her Christian name.

"Cousin?" Anne suddenly appeared at the mouth of the close, clasping Michael Dalgliesh's hand. "We've been looking for you everywhere!" The couple hurried toward them, Elisabeth following with Peter in tow.

"And here we are." Marjory quickly released Gibson's hand with a parting squeeze.

Her face radiant, Anne pushed open the door. "Come inside, for we've much to tell you." Minutes later the six of them were seated round the small house, the noise of the fair muted by doors and windows firmly latched.

Anne spilled out her news like fresh milk from a pail. "Michael and I are to be married on the last of August."

Marjory could not mask her surprise. "So soon?"

Anne laughed, slipping her hand through

the crook in Michael's arm. "We've known each other since we were Peter's age. I see no need to wait now that we're . . ." She looked up at him, her eyes shining with confidence. "Now that we're certain."

Marjory eyed the betrothed couple, sorting through her mixed emotions. She was happy for them, of course. Anne would make a fine tradesman's wife. But she'd sorely miss their fair-haired cousin, especially with Elisabeth off to Bell Hill from dawn until dusk each day. And however would she and Elisabeth handle the rent, let alone furnish the house, once Anne claimed all her possessions?

Her conscience pricked her, sharp as a pin. *You're being selfish, Marjory. And not wholly honest.*

Marjory looked at Gibson, seated on a battered wooden chair, and admitted the truth, if only to herself. *I am jealous, dear Cousin Anne. For you are free to marry whom you choose.*

"What is it, Marjory?" Anne knelt beside her, concern knitting her brow. "Are you displeased?"

Marjory clasped her cousin's small hands, vowing to think only of Anne's happiness. "I could not be more delighted," she assured her, hoping her words rang true. "Tell me what you have in mind for the wedding."

"Well . . ." Anne glanced at Michael. "We plan to marry at the kirk after services three

432

Sabbaths hence. I've a blue gown that will suit, and Michael will see to his own wedding clothes."

"Will I noo?" he said, patently amused. "I dinna suppose ye'll let me choose the fabric."

"Dark blue wool," Anne told him, her tone brooking no discussion.

News of Anne's betrothal traveled swiftly up Water Row, round Back Row, and down Kirk Wynd until the couple could not venture out of doors without a well-wisher stepping forward to rub shoulders with Michael or Anne, hoping to capture a bit of their good fortune, or so the old wives believed. Friends came round the house at all hours, bearing small gifts of kitchen linens and woodenware. As for Anne's students, they were too excited to work on their lace each afternoon, preferring to speak of flowers and veils and handsome bridegrooms.

Elisabeth smiled through it all, her countenance serene, though occasionally Marjory saw a flicker of sadness behind her eyes. Was there something about Anne's impending marriage that weighed on Elisabeth's heart? By Friday curiosity got the better of Marjory. She followed her daughter-in-law out the door, then caught her elbow before she reached the marketplace. "Bess, we've not had a moment alone all week. Is everything quite well?"

Elisabeth turned, her eyes shimmering in the dim interior of the close. "I fear I've done a poor job of hiding my feelings."

Marjory circled her arm round Elisabeth's waist. "You've no need to conceal them from me, dear girl. Not after all we've been through." She stepped forward, taking Elisabeth with her. "Since you're bound for Bell Hill this morn, suppose I walk with you as far as the Foul Bridge Port so we might chat."

Strangers were already pouring into Selkirk for the fifth day of the fair as the women started up Kirk Wynd, arm in arm against the flow. "I'll be glad when 'tis over," Marjory grumbled, "though I know the town's innkeepers are glad for their custom."

Elisabeth nodded, her thoughts clearly elsewhere.

Not wanting to waste a moment, Marjory cast aside small talk and spoke from the heart. "I sense you are not entirely happy for Anne. Did you form . . . an attachment with Mr. Dalgliesh?"

"Nae!" Elisabeth protested. "He is a friend and former employer, nothing more. I wish them both much joy."

Marjory could not doubt her, so clear and direct was Elisabeth's gaze. "Are you unhappy with me, then?" *Because of Gibson?* Marjory dared not say it aloud. Even the thought made her hands grow damp and her heart

434

skip a beat. What if Elisabeth did not approve?

As they reached the top of the knowe, her daughter-in-law slowed her steps, smiling down at her as she said, "If you mean am I unhappy with your own budding romance, I wish you and Gibson a joyous future as well."

Taken aback, Marjory stammered, "Wh-whatever do you mean?"

"The man adores you. And I believe you return his affections."

Marjory could hardly deny the truth. "But he is a servant, Bess, and I am a poor gentlewoman. What future can we possibly have?"

"A bright one, Lord willing." Elisabeth started downhill toward the town gate, tugging her along. "You once told me that faith is what pleases the Almighty."

"Aye," she sighed. "So I did." *If I am to marry Neil Gibson, Lord, you alone will bring it about.* Marjory sent her thoughts heavenward, above the dirty cobblestones and thatched roofs of Selkirk, then took a long, steady breath. "You've still not told me what's bothering you, Bess."

She gave a faint shrug. "Nothing of importance."

Marjory looked at her. "Now 'tis my turn to speak the truth: you miss Lord Buchanan."

"Ah . . . well . . ." Color stained her cheeks. "Bell Hill isn't the same without its owner."

"And *you* are not the same without your

master." Marjory patted her hand, at a loss for what else to say. She could not in good conscience encourage their growing friendship and risk dishonoring Donald's memory. Nor could she deny the admiral's many fine qualities. Very fine, in fact. Exceptional.

A conundrum, to be sure.

They'd reached the town gate, flung open to all who approached from the southeast. Elisabeth released her but not before kissing her cheek. " 'Twas kind of you to keep me company."

Marjory confessed, "I have little else to offer you now but hot meals and a listening ear."

" 'Tis enough." With a faint smile Elisabeth turned and lifted her hand in farewell.

FIFTY-ONE

Who loves
Believes the impossible.

ELIZABETH BARRETT BROWNING

As her daughter-in-law crossed the small footbridge heading east, Marjory started for home, putting aside any thoughts of men or marriage in favor of more pressing concerns: breakfast, dinner, and supper. She touched her pocket to be certain she had a coin or two, then made a mental list of what she needed from the market. *Cheese, butter, eggs, and milk.* Aye, that she could afford.

Weaving between handcarts and pedestrians moving down Kirk Wynd, Marjory slowed as she neared the manse, hoping to catch a glimpse of Gibson through the window. She felt like a lovesick schoolgirl but eyed the house nonetheless, noting the open curtains, the single candle, and the signs of life within-doors.

Certain she had spied his black livery, Marjory paused at the window and smiled, her nose nearly touching the glass. *Good morn, dear Gibson.*

But it was Reverend Brown, dressed in black, who turned and met her gaze.

Startled, she fell back a step. What must the minister think of her, peering into people's houses?

A moment later he was standing in the doorway, waving her inside. "Come, Mrs. Kerr. I have been meaning to speak with you."

Marjory slipped by him as she entered the manse, feeling awkward and ashamed. Gibson, alas, was nowhere in sight. She took the offered seat by the window, keenly aware of how foolish she must have looked tarrying on the other side of the glass.

"Forgive me for intruding," she began, not knowing how else to phrase it.

"Not at all," he said gruffly, taking the chair opposite hers. "If you were looking for Gibson, I sent him on an errand, for I cannot bear to venture out during the fair." He leaned forward, his eyes as sharp as any owl's. "In the meantime I've news of Lord Buchanan that should be of interest to you."

Her thoughts flew immediately to Elisabeth. "Oh?"

"In truth, his lordship may not be aware of the fact I'm about to share, though I shall inform him at the first opportunity."

Marjory inched forward on her chair, her curiosity mounting. "And that fact is?"

"Admiral Lord Jack Buchanan is distantly related to Lord John Kerr."

Marjory swallowed. "To . . . my late husband?"

"Aye. While reviewing our oldest parish records at the request of the presbytery, I stumbled upon the names Buchanan and Kerr in a marriage entry from the late sixteenth century. To call his lordship your distant cousin would be stretching the truth, but your ancient kinsman he most certainly is."

"News indeed," she breathed, trying to grasp what such a connection might mean for her family.

"Madam, I hardly need mention your dire financial needs. Once he is informed of your common ancestry, Lord Buchanan may be moved to . . . , eh, provide for you and your daughter-in-law."

"I see." Marjory pretended to pluck a bit of dust from her black skirts while she searched her conscience. He was a generous man, Lord Buchanan, and would no doubt do his part. But there was more at stake than mere silver or gold. *Oh, Bess. Would such provision please you? Or embarrass you?* Marjory knew the answer.

She lifted her head. "I wonder, Reverend

Brown, if you might delay mentioning this to his lordship."

He frowned. "But you are the one who'll benefit. Can you afford to wait?"

"Aye," Marjory said, "for a few months at least." Elisabeth was promised employment at Bell Hill through Saint Andrew's Day. If they could somehow make ends meet until then, neither Lord Buchanan nor Elisabeth would be thrust into a difficult situation. And who knew where their friendship might lead someday? " 'Tis best left unspoken," Marjory told him.

The minister held up his hands in surrender. "As you wish, madam. Should you change your mind, I will gladly approach his lordship regarding this . . . obligation."

Hearing the word, Marjory was certain of her decision. Friendship and obligation were not well met.

As she prepared to leave, Reverend Brown cleared his throat. "Madam, you and I discussed another matter of some urgency in late May. Perhaps you recall the subject."

Gibson. "Indeed I do, sir."

"May I be so bold as to inquire where things stand with you and my manservant?"

She moistened her parched lips. "Stand?"

"I believe I stated my objections quite clearly. And yet I hear your name pouring from Gibson's lips, and see you sitting together at services, and find you peering through my window, hoping to catch a glimpse of a man who served you for thirty years. Where is this leading, Mrs. Kerr?"

With each phrase his voice had grown more strident. By the time he reached her name, Marjory was on her feet. Trembling, aye, but standing.

She kept her voice at an even pitch, though she longed to match his volume note for note. "May I remind you, sir, I am an independent woman. Of limited means, aye, but beholden to no man. You'll not find the name Kerr on the parish's poor roll nor a beggar's badge pinned to my gown."

"Now, now, Mrs. Kerr," he said, shaking his gray head. "I am merely concerned lest you lose your place in society —"

"My place?" She threw up her hands in frustration. "Reverend Brown, I no longer have a place. What I have are dear friends, who take me as I am." The truth of her words rang inside her like a bell, clear and strong. "You asked me where things stand with Neil Gibson. They stand very well, sir. I thank you for your interest."

Marjory wanted to stride from the room, her skirts slapping about her ankles, but a show of pique would accomplish nothing. Furthermore, Reverend Brown was Gibson's employer and their parish minister and so deserved her respect.

Help me, Lord. Help me do what I must.

Bowing her head, she eased into a curtsy, deeper than required, and did not rise until peace reigned once more in her heart.

When she lifted her head and their eyes met, she found the words she wanted to say. "Reverend Brown, you once promised to show me God's mercy, and indeed you have. Now I ask only for a small measure of happiness, no greater than the widow's farthing."

The minister placed a withered hand on each shoulder. "Mrs. Kerr, I see that your mind is fixed on this course. How you and Mr. Gibson will navigate these waters, I cannot say. But whatever God joins, I'll not put asunder. Go, now, for I've kept you long enough."

"Bless you," she whispered and turned for the door, thinking only of Gibson. Eager to find him. Eager to tell him. *All is well. God is with us.*

A moment later Marjory found herself in Kirk Wynd, still reeling from the minister's unexpected benediction. He seemed willing to admit the Almighty might have brought them together. *Can it be true, Lord? Is this your hand at work? Do you mean for this good man to be mine?*

When she looked up and saw Neil Gibson walking toward her, all her questions were answered. *Aye, aye, aye.* Marjory reached out, beckoning him forward.

He offered a gentleman's bow, then clasped her hands. "Have ye come leuking for me, Leddy Kerr?"

"I've much to tell you," she began, "but we cannot meet at Anne's house, with Peter due for his morning visit."

"And we canna speak at the manse," Gibson said. "Nor may we stand in the mercat place with the whole toun watching."

"To kirk then." Marjory was already starting uphill. "On a Friday 'tis sure to be empty."

They slipped through the narrow pend and across the grassy kirkyard, then pulled open the door, cringing when the rust-covered hinges cried out in protest. Leaving behind the forenoon sun, they stepped inside the shadowy interior, cool and still.

"A bit gloomy," Gibson murmured, "but at least we have it to ourselves." He walked Marjory down the aisle, her hand tucked round his arm, then brushed clean the Kerr pew and seated her like landed gentry come to church.

Marjory waited until he sat down, her heart beating so hard against her stays she was not certain she could breathe, let alone speak. When she turned to him, their knees almost touched. When he took her ungloved hands in his, she thought she might faint.

"Gibson, I —"

"Neil," he said softly, never taking his eyes

off hers. " 'Tis time ye called me by my given name."

Neil, my dear Neil. Could she say it aloud without blushing? "Neil," she finally managed. "And you must call me Marjory."

He smiled at that. "I've called ye Marjory in my heart syne I first clapped eyes on ye in May. Whan ye pressed yer wee head against my neck and told me, 'Ye're hame.' I canna tell ye what that meant to me."

Overcome with emotion, she bowed her head and whispered, "And to me."

He gently lifted her chin. "Dinna hide from me, lass."

"*Lass?* I'm hardly a girl —"

"Wheesht!" he said with a low chuckle. "Ye're a lass from whaur I'm sitting." He lightly kissed the back of her hand, then said, "Noo, what was it ye were so keen to tell me?"

She described her meeting with Reverend Brown, leaving out any mention of Lord Buchanan for the moment, and watched Neil's expressions change with each revelation.

"So, 'tis only a sma' measure o' happiness ye're wanting?" Neil teased her. "Nae mair than a farthing's worth?"

"You know me very well," she reminded him. "Am I a woman who settles for so little?"

"I've niver seen ye do so," he agreed, looking more serious. " 'Tis why I must ask if ye're sure . . . if ye're verra sure . . ."

"That you'll make me happy?" When he

nodded, she looked into his eyes lest she lose her courage. "Neil Gibson, I cannot imagine a future without you at the center of it."

"Och, Marjory." He hung his head, clasping her hands tightly in his as if he might never let go. "Ye ken I have naught to offer ye. Not a hame, nor a horse, nor a purse full o' guineas. And I dare not ask for yer hand 'til I do."

"My dear Gibson . . ." She caught herself. "Neil . . . I have no such expectations."

He lifted his head. "But I do." His eyes shone like candles in the murky sanctuary. "D'ye remember me saying in Edinburgh, 'Ye'll aye be Leddy Kerr to me'?"

"I remember it well." *So very well.*

"A leddy like ye deserves a' the best the world has to offer. I'll not see ye go without because o' me."

When he started to release her, Marjory drew him closer instead. "Listen to me, Neil Gibson. Possessions mean nothing to me now. Surely you, of all people, know that."

"Aye, but —"

"The Buik tells us only faith, hope, and charity truly matter." She lifted his hands, his strong, callused hands, praying as she did. "My faith has been renewed," she assured him, gently kissing one hand. "My hope has been restored," she promised, kissing the other. "And my regard for you is certain."

When he smiled, she caught a glimpse of

the darling boy of ten he'd surely been. And of the strapping lad of twenty, who must have stolen every maidservant's heart. And of the handsome man of forty, who'd served her at Tweedsford. But none could match the mature man who sat beside her now, with love in his eyes and laughter in the curve of his mouth.

"I canna see my way through just noo," he confessed to her, "but if the Almichty means for us to be thegither, then thegither we shall be." He kissed each hand, as she'd kissed his, then slowly stood, drawing her to her feet. " 'Tis time I walked ye hame."

She started up the aisle with him, in no hurry to leave their quiet sanctuary. "I can only imagine what Reverend Brown will say when you return."

After a moment Neil said, "He's a guid man, wha cares about his flock. As it happens, the reverend and I have a surprise for ye, though 'twill have to wait 'til Michaelmas."

"Ah." She smiled. "We've much to look forward to this autumn. Anne and Michael's marriage, of course, and Lord Buchanan's return from the Highlands. I do hope he'll not be delayed. 'Twould be a shame for him to miss Annie's wedding."

Fifty-Two

My heart's in the Highlands, my heart is
not here;
My heart's in the Highlands a-chasing the
deer.

Robert Burns

Jack stared at the small Highland cottage with its thatched roof, crooked chimney, and unglazed windows. The battered wooden shutters, meant to keep out the elements, sagged on their hinges. A few hens pecked their way across the garden, and a pot of dead violets sat by the door. "You are certain this was Elisabeth Kerr's home?"

Rose MacKindlay looked up at him with eyes as green as the grass on the hillocks. "She was a Ferguson then, but, aye, this was whaur Bess lived and whaur her mither lives noo." An elderly woman, Mrs. MacKindlay shifted her weight from one foot to the other, wincing as she did. "Her man is oot just noo, but I ken for a fact Fiona is at hame. She'll

447

be glad to have a letter from Bess."

Jack had come to Braemar parish solely to shoot grouse, or so he'd told himself. But from the hour he'd reached the Mar estate, his thoughts had circled round nearby Castleton, the hamlet where Bess had spent her first eighteen years. Consisting of a ruinous castle and a knot of stone cottages nestled amid a remote mountain fastness, Castleton of Braemar was as far from Edinburgh's high society as Persia was from Paris. Why had Bess left, and how? And who was this woman who'd raised her?

He was curious, no denying it. The letter in his pocket would open a door he very much wished to walk through.

The fine, springlike weather had kept him on the heather moorlands with Sir John for a full week — enough hunting to last Jack many a season. "Male grouse are a randy sort," the gamekeeper had informed them, "with many partners. And they play nae part in raising their young." That alone was sufficient motive for Jack to take deadly aim with his fowling piece.

But on this cool, rainy Saturday, Sir John was content to sip whisky by the fire while Jack explored the parish. He'd come straight to Castleton, sought out a friendly face, and found himself in the company of Mrs. MacKindlay, the parish midwife.

"If you'll not mind an introduction," he

told her, "I would be honored to meet Mrs. Cromar." He tethered Janvier to a trough, where the horse might drink his fill, then joined Mrs. MacKindlay on the muddy slate by the door.

"Fiona!" she sang out. "Ye've a visitor. And a braw lad he is."

Jack had heard the phrase before, a favorite among his maidservants, though usually directed at far younger men.

The door was pulled open. A dark-haired woman of forty-odd years stood before him. Not so tall as Bess, nor so bonny, but unmistakably her mother. She eyed him closely. "Wha is this ye've brought to my door, Rose?"

"Lord Jack Buchanan," Mrs. MacKindlay answered, emphasizing his title. "He's acquainted with yer Bess. Even brought ye a letter from the lass."

Her eyes narrowed. "Is that a fact?"

"Indeed, madam." He doffed his hat and bowed, then presented her with the sealed missive. "Your daughter is employed as a dressmaker at my estate in the Borderland."

"Ye must come in, then," she said, stepping back, holding the letter to her heart.

As the midwife took her leave, Fiona Cromar hurried to the inglenook, where a peat fire burned with a pungent aroma. "Ye'll be wanting tea, I ken."

While she was busy with her preparations,

Jack surveyed the candlelit interior. Bare stone walls with clay and straw for mortar. Thick wooden beams, not far above his head. And a dirt floor, hard packed yet newly swept. However humble, the cottage was tidy, with a fine woolen plaid across the bed. A handful of books were given pride of place on a shelf above the hearth. No doubt Bess had read every one a dozen times.

Fiona seated him at a square pine table, unfinished but well scrubbed. Tea was served in a pottery cup, accompanied by a plate of round sugar biscuits. Fiona joined him, lifting her teacup almost as gracefully as Bess did. She had her daughter's full lips as well as her striking dark brows. But Fiona's eyes did not sparkle, and the skin beneath them looked bruised, as if she'd not slept in a long time.

"I owe you an apology, Mrs. Cromar, for my unexpected visit."

"Not at a'," she insisted. "In the *Hielands* we're glad for outlanders wha bring us news, as lang as they've naught to do with King Geordie doon in London toun." She lowered her cup and leaned a bit closer. "Afore I read her letter, what have ye to say about my Bess? For I've not seen the lass in ever so lang."

"She is in fine health," he assured her, "and in good spirits, considering all she has been through. You already know, I am sure, how she came to live in the Borderland after

Prince Charlie's defeat . . . after Culloden . . ." He paused when she looked away, her distress evident. Better not to dwell on the subject. "Your daughter accompanied her mother-in-law to Selkirk, where they reside with a distant cousin, Anne Kerr."

When Fiona turned to look at him, her eyes were filled with pain. "I didna ken whaur the lass went. For I've not had a letter from Bess syne I married nigh a twelvemonth ago."

Jack stared at her, confused. "How can that be? I was told she wrote you regularly."

She slowly shook her head. "I've had nae letters. But then I didna expect them. Not after what I did with the last one she sent me the day afore my wedding." Fiona could not meet his gaze. "She begged me not to marry Ben Cromar. Said she'd left Castleton because he . . . because he frightened her."

Frightened? The hair on the back of his neck stood up. *Was it something he said, Bess? Or something he did?* Jack nodded at the letter beside her teacup. "Feel free to read it at once, Mrs. Cromar, so you might put your mind at ease."

Jack's own mind was racing down very dark paths. A frightening man. A lass barely old enough to marry, fleeing from her mother's house. Letters posted but never received. Aye, something was amiss. Jack had no intention of leaving Castleton until he uncovered the truth.

451

Her mother, in the meantime, was engrossed, her lips moving as she read silently, her eyes awash with tears. "She luves me still. My sweet, sweet Bess!" She clutched the paper with trembling hands. "September last, when I didna like what she wrote about Mr. Cromar, I tossed her letter in the fire." Her voice dropped to a whisper. "But I should have listened to her. I should have heeded what she said. I didna ken! I didna ken —"

When the door to the cottage flew open, Fiona leaped to her feet, stuffing the letter in her apron pocket. "Ben! Come . . . come meet oor guest from . . . from . . ."

Ben Cromar swaggered across the threshold, then shut the door with a thunderous bang. "Weel, sir. D'ye make a practice o' visiting ither men's wives while their husbands are hard at wark?"

Jack stood, refusing to acknowledge the coarse remark. Instead, he fixed his gaze on the man. "I am Lord Jack Buchanan of Bell Hill in the Borderland."

"Is that so?" Cromar moved forward, his footsteps muffled by the dirt floor. No older than forty, he had the stocky build of a blacksmith, with thick arms and massive thighs and shoulders broad enough to wield a sledgehammer. "What business d'ye have in my hame?"

Jack avoided any mention of the letter hidden in Fiona's pocket. "Your stepdaughter is in my employ. Since I was shooting grouse on the Mar estate, a visit to her mother seemed in order."

"In yer . . . *employ?*" Cromar muttered. "Is that what gentlemen call it noo?"

"Sir, you do her a great disservice." Jack clenched his fists, struggling to keep his temper in check. "Elisabeth Kerr is a virtuous woman and a fine dressmaker."

Fiona found her voice at last. "She was aye guid with a needle."

"Indeed." Jack stood his ground, waiting for Cromar to move one step closer, make one more untoward comment. However muscular, Cromar was decidedly shorter. A half foot, Jack wagered. Though he took no pleasure in fighting a man, if they came to blows, Jack would not hesitate to defend Elisabeth's honor or to protect Fiona from her brute of a husband.

As if sensing his resolve, Ben Cromar edged away from him. "Have ye finished here, then?"

"Not quite," Jack said. *Not even close.* "Mrs. Cromar tells me she's not received a letter from her daughter the whole of your marriage, though they've certainly been written and posted. Might you know anything about that?"

His skin turned a mottled red. "I dinna ken o' such letters."

Jack knew a lie when he heard one. He

453

could easily imagine Cromar intercepting the posts out of sheer cruelty. But without solid proof, he could hardly press the matter.

"Letters dinna aye reach a Jacobite's hoose," Fiona was quick to say.

Whether she spoke the truth or was protecting her husband, Jack could not be certain. He tried another tack. "Perhaps I might carry a letter to Elisabeth on your behalf, Mrs. Cromar?"

"Oo aye!" A moment later she was seated at the pine table, her quill scratching across a thin sheet of paper. She bent over her words, shielding them from view.

Jack watched her even as he kept a wary eye on her husband. *Speak the truth, madam. Your letter is safe with me.*

When she finished, she waved the paper about, drying the ink, then folded it and carefully sealed it with candle wax. "I mean nae offense, using the wax," she said, handing her letter to Jack. "Ye seem a trustworthy gentleman . . ."

"You are wise to use a seal," Jack told her, aiming his remarks at Ben Cromar, who loomed over her, arms folded across his chest. "The only person who should break it open is the one to whom the letter is addressed, aye?" Like an angler with a fly lying on the surface of the water, Jack baited the man, seeing if he might bite.

But Cromar merely glared at him beneath

a flat brow.

In the stony silence Fiona scurried about the cottage, pouring tea for her husband, righting a toppled book, smoothing the bedcovers. Keeping out of Cromar's way, by the look of it. "I wonder, Lord Buchanan . . . ," she finally said. "My daughter had a bonny silver ring. Might she still be wearing it? 'Twas mine once and my mither's afore me."

Jack couldn't recall seeing it and confessed as much. "Perhaps because of her sewing, your daughter finds rings uncomfortable."

"Mebbe," Fiona said softly. " 'Tis not important." Her crestfallen expression said otherwise. "She is making dresses for yer household, then?"

He nodded. "Gowns for my maidservants. And soon, livery for the menservants."

Consternation filled her eyes. "My bonny Bess? Measuring and fitting men's garments?"

Cromar grunted. "I thocht ye prized the leddy's virtue."

"You can be sure I do." Jack looked at them both. Elisabeth had worked in a tailor's shop. Had he erred in assuming she might sew for Roberts and his footmen? It seemed her mother thought so. "I shall remedy the situation the moment I return," Jack promised her. "There are several competent tailors in Selkirk. One in particular I have in mind."

Fiona's expression lightened at once. "Weel

455

done, milord."

"He's done naught but spin wirds," her husband said darkly. "Onie can do that."

Jack had had his fill of Ben Cromar. He moved closer, if only to look down at the man. "As a retired admiral of the Royal Navy, I assure you, my word can be trusted."

The color drained from Ben's face.

"Then ye're . . ." Fiona's voice was barely above a whisper. "Ye're *leal* to . . . King Geordie?"

Before Jack could answer her, Cromar backed away. " 'Tis a trap, woman. He has ithers waiting outside. Waiting to burn doon oor hoose and us with it."

"Nae." Jack strode toward the door, blocking the man's escape. "I've come alone and not on behalf of the king." He sought Fiona's gaze, wanting to assure her. "Your daughter is my only concern here."

Fiona barely touched her husband's sleeve. "Lord Buchanan willna hurt us. He's a guid man."

Jack clearly saw Elisabeth in her mother now. The tender words, the gentle touch. Yet both women had married men who mistreated them. He could not save Fiona, not in a brief morning visit. But he could see to her daughter's future. Aye, he could.

"I thank you for your hospitality," Jack said with a slight bow, "and bid you both farewell."

"Leuk after my sweet Bess," Fiona pleaded with him. "She's a' I have."

"Depend upon it, madam." He quit the cottage and was astride Janvier moments later, riding hard for the Mar estate with rain pelting his face and Fiona's last words beating in his heart.

He found Sir John where he'd left him by the fire, his feet propped on a leather footstool, a dram of whisky in hand.

"Join me, milord," the sheriff said, raising his glass.

Jack shook his head, his thoughts already halfway to Selkirk. "I wonder if we might head south a bit sooner." He couldn't explain his growing uneasiness, nor could he deny it.

Sir John frowned. "Will Thursday next not suit you?"

Jack groaned inwardly. *Five more days.* "I confess I've enough grouse to fill ten of Mrs. Tudhope's roasting pans. Would you object if we departed Monday?" Even that was a sacrifice. Jack was prepared to leave at once, the letter in his pocket adding to his sense of urgency.

His host downed his whisky, then sighed. " 'Twould seem your mind is set, Lord Jack. No doubt you are missing my Rosalind, for I can assure you, she's grieved by your absence." He waved at their menservants playing cards by the window. "I daresay Dickson and Grahame will be glad to sleep in their

457

own beds."

"As will I," Jack agreed, tamping down his impatience. *Rosalind Murray?* He'd barely thought of the lady since leaving Selkirk. Nae, another woman had occupied his mind from dawn until dusk and into his dreams.

Soon, Bess. Saturday next, Lord willing.

FIFTY-THREE

O woman! thou knowest the hour when the
goodman of the house will return.

WASHINGTON IRVING

Elisabeth had just stitched in place the last
hook on a maidservant's gown when Mrs.
Pringle tapped on the open workroom door.
"A post for you, Mrs. Kerr."

"Delivered here? How very odd." Elisabeth
put aside her finished gown, then studied the
postmark with some trepidation. *Edinburgh.*
Who in the capital knew she was employed at
Bell Hill?

The moment she saw the signature, her
fears vanished. " 'Tis from the admiral," she
said, smiling down at his bold hand.

To Mrs. Elisabeth Kerr
Bell Hill, Selkirkshire
Wednesday, 20 August 1746

My dear Mrs. Kerr,

She paused at the word *dear,* wondering what it might signify, then pressed on, convincing herself the salutation was nothing more than a polite gesture. His lordship might just as easily have written "My dear Mrs. Pringle."

Your Highlands were quite as beautiful as you described them, the stark contours of the landscape softened by occasional wooded areas of Scotch pine. The weather was exceedingly fine, except for two days of rain, and our host made us warmly welcome. Nonetheless, our hunting party will be returning to Selkirk sooner than expected, at my request.

Elisabeth's breath caught. *Are you ill, milord? Or simply restless?* She dared not entertain the thought that he missed her company, though she certainly longed to see him.

Look for us to arrive late in the afternoon on Saturday the twenty-third, if all goes according to plan. I am posting this from Edinburgh, hoping it might arrive ahead of us, lest we catch the household unprepared.

"He is to arrive in a few hours," Elisabeth declared, trying not to let her anticipation show.

Mrs. Pringle hastened to the door, calling

over her shoulder, "I must tell Roberts and Mrs. Tudhope at once."

Left alone, Elisabeth traced his signature with her fingertip. Three times the size of the other lines of text, with a decidedly forward slant, each letter was clearly drawn rather than a violent slash of ink across the page. Here was a man with nothing to hide.

Below it a brief postscript left her even more anxious for his return.

I delivered the letter to your mother as requested. She sent me home with one for you as well. I will have much to share when we see each other.

Whatever he had found in Braemar, she would know by day's end. Some comfort, that.

Elisabeth read his letter again, tucked it in her sewing basket, then gazed down at Charbon curled up at her feet. "Your master will soon appear," she told the cat, scratching him behind the ears as she looked toward the window, left open to welcome the cool morning air.

Hurry home, milord.

One hour dragged by, then two, then four. Her dinner tray came and went, untouched. Focusing instead on her work, she'd begun measuring Kate, the stillroom maid, glad for the distraction the charming lass provided.

"I've niver had a new gown," Kate confided, keeping her posture straight even as her gaze lighted on the sleeping cat, the wool rug, the new chairs. "Clever bit o' business, that," she said, nodding at the candle-stool. "Ye've a richt cozy place, Mrs. Kerr. Leuks like his lordship has taken a fancy to ye."

Elisabeth pretended not to hear her as she busily stretched the measuring tape from waist to hem, then recorded the figure with chalk and slate. When Kate moved on to another topic — all the lads she'd danced with at the Saint Lawrence Fair — Elisabeth finished her task without further questions. Had the whole household come to the same conclusion regarding Lord Buchanan?

When Sally appeared with her afternoon tea tray, her countenance beamed like the sun. "His lordship is hame!" She put down the tray with a noisy clatter, then took off with Kate close on her heels.

Elisabeth watched them go, uncertain of what was expected of her. Would the household line up at the door to formally greet him, as they had when he last returned from a journey? And if so, would she be expected to join them? "Better done than not," she told Charbon, then quickly attended to face, hands, and hair before hurrying out the door and up the stair, the gray cat darting ahead.

Admit it, Bess. You cannot wait to see him.

The truth of it made her heart quicken and her steps along with it.

Bell Hill's staff was indeed standing on either side of the front door, Dickson having ridden ahead to announce his lordship's arrival. All were red cheeked and damp with sweat beneath the hot August sun as Lord Buchanan dismounted, then passed the reins to a stable lad.

"May the good Lord be with you," he called out, as was his custom.

"And with you!" was his household's enthusiastic reply.

Elisabeth watched him greet each one by name and receive a swift bow or curtsy in response. For a moment she thought he'd glanced her way, but perhaps she'd only wished it so. In due time he reached his front door, where she stood beside Mrs. Pringle.

"Your chamber is ready for you, milord, and your hot bath as well," the older woman assured him, then dispatched the household to their duties.

"No man could hope for a better housekeeper. Or a finer dressmaker," he added, nodding at the maidservants as they passed by. More than half of them wore Elisabeth's creations now. "I see you've been busy while I was away, Mrs. Kerr."

Elisabeth felt the warmth of his gaze. "Aye, milord."

The corners of his mouth twitched. "Perhaps I should leave my country estate more often, as some landowners do. Spend six months in London. Take the grand tour."

"Your lordship has already sailed the world," Elisabeth reminded him. "And I do believe the grand tour is meant for . . . well . . ."

"Young gentlemen half my age," the admiral finished for her. "I suppose you're right. If you'll kindly find my cane, I'll hobble off to my study, where I may gum my supper in peace."

Elisabeth smiled. "You're speaking of a gentleman twice your age, milord. You are hardly old and infirm."

"I'm glad you think so, madam."

The two of them were left standing alone on the threshold. Only Charbon tarried behind, curling round their legs.

Lord Jack stepped closer, the earthy scent of horse and rider filling her nostrils. Any sense of levity vanished from his countenance. "I've a letter from your mother." He produced it at once and pressed it into her hands. "Meet me at five o' the clock in my study, and I shall tell you more of what I found at Castleton."

Elisabeth had already broken the seal and unfolded the letter before she reached her workroom. She'd not had news from home since September last, delivered by her brother. *My dear Simon.*

Her throat tightened when she saw the familiar handwriting in Gaelic, the few words scrawled across the page as if written in haste.

Saturday, 16 August 1746

My beloved Bess,

You were right, and I was so very wrong. Please, please forgive me. Lord Buchanan will tell you what I cannot say here.
 I will love you always.

Your mother

The words began to swim. *What has happened, Mother?* She touched the paper, taking care not to let a tear fall on the ink and wash away Fiona's words.

Lord Buchanan will tell you. Elisabeth looked at the sunlight pouring through her window, judging the hour by the slant of the rays. Might it be five o' the clock soon? She started to drink the lukewarm tea Sally had left for her earlier, tried to mark the fabric for Kate's gown, but concentrating proved difficult. Finally Elisabeth abandoned her tailor's chalk and climbed the servants' stair, unable to wait a moment longer.

Lord Jack was seated at his desk when she arrived. He waved her in at once and sent the footman on an errand. "Leave the door open," he told the young man.

"Aye, milord," he said and was gone.

Elisabeth sat across from the admiral, hands folded in her lap, her heart in her throat. "What did you find in Castleton?"

He'd never looked more serious. "Your mother is frightened, and for good reason."

"Ben Cromar," she whispered. *Oh my sweet mother.* When Lord Jack related their discussion, Elisabeth heard her mother's voice. *I should have listened. I should have heeded. I didna ken.* "Is there nothing that can be done?"

"With your permission, I shall speak with Sir John. As sheriff, he surely has a counterpart in Aberdeenshire who might intervene. Though beneath a man's own roof . . ." Lord Jack shook his head. "The law favors the husband in such matters."

Elisabeth knew the Braemar parish minister would offer no assistance. Her mother had kept her distance from the kirk, worshiping the moon instead. "What else did she say?"

"She was very grateful for your letter," Lord Jack assured her. "Said it was the first she'd had since marrying Mr. Cromar."

"But —"

"I know. You wrote her monthly. But your letters were either intercepted by the government en route —"

"Or opened by Cromar." Elisabeth stared at the floor, sickened at the thought of him reading her posts. "How could he be so cruel?"

The admiral stood, walked to the window, and gazed out onto the sunlit gardens. "Some men have no kindness left in them."

She lifted her head. "And some have an abundance."

After a lengthy silence, he turned back and shifted to another subject. "Your mother voiced a strong objection to having you sew livery for my footmen, so I promised her I'd hire a tailor."

"But . . ." Elisabeth shared a concern of her own. "I'll not have enough work to last until Saint Andrew's Day."

He looked down at her. "Bess, we had an agreement, which I intend to honor. Even if that means you'll be tarrying about the house, talking to Charbon for hours on end while a tailor dresses my menservants." When she started to protest, he cut her short. "Michael Dalgliesh. I thought he might be the man for the task."

"He is a fine tailor," Elisabeth agreed, "and would no doubt welcome the business. But Mr. Dalgliesh is already quite . . . engaged at the moment."

"Engaged? By whom?"

"Betrothed, if you will. To my cousin Anne. They intend to wed on the last of August."

His eyebrows rose. "Truly? Then you are quite right. The man can hardly sew for me while preparing to begin a new life with Miss Kerr." He reclaimed his chair, then tossed down a cup of lukewarm tea. "I'll seek some solution come Monday. There must be other tailors in Selkirk."

"There are," she said, though she'd not recommend narrow-minded Mr. Smail.

"Speaking of weddings," Jack continued, "your mother asked about a silver ring she thought you might still be wearing. Something handed down from your grandmother."

"And my great-grandmother Nessa before her." Elisabeth glanced at her right hand, where an engraved silver band had lived for many years. *Measure the moon, circle the silver.* A sacred symbol of the pagan rituals she'd once embraced, then discarded for a greater, truer Love.

"I no longer have it," she confessed, recalling how she'd deposited the silver ring, and her wedding ring as well, into Mr. Dewar's waiting hand to pay for her carriage ride south. "I do hope my mother will forgive me."

His steady gaze met hers. "A ring can be replaced, Bess. A daughter cannot."

FIFTY-FOUR

We often give our enemies the means for
our own destruction.

AESOP

Jack strode through the quiet halls of Bell
Hill, glad to be home. Not sailing the high
seas, not calling at foreign ports, not climbing the rugged Highland hills. *Home.*

Even the rainy Sabbath afternoon could not
dampen his mood. He'd been welcomed back
by many at kirk that morning and had rubbed
shoulders with Michael Dalgliesh, assured of
much luck in love. A foolish custom, aye, but
harmless.

Sitting beside Elisabeth, he'd almost rubbed
shoulders with her too, so crowded was the
pew. Mrs. Kerr and Gibson did little to hide
their regard for each other, all but holding
hands throughout the service. An odd pair-
ing, Jack thought, but who was he to say
where love might lead? As for Elisabeth, she
was equally kind to all who crossed her path,

which both pleased and disappointed him. Might she not shower a bit more attention on him?

Selfish, Jack. And thoughtless. She is a widow in mourning, remember?

Jack paused at the door to his dining room, with its long windows facing the garden, then he squinted, peering through the rain. Was someone approaching the house? Jack could barely make out the shape of a man dressed in dark colors, head bent against the blustery storm. The fellow was limping, Jack realized. He started toward the front door, intending to greet him. Was the man injured perhaps? Or merely seeking shelter from the elements?

Upon reaching the entrance hall, Jack pulled the bell cord, summoning Roberts from his private quarters. His butler appeared moments later, straightening his coat.

"Sorry, milord. Taking a wee Sunday nap . . ."

"No matter. We've a stranger about to knock on our door," Jack told him. "See to his needs. Dry clothes, warm food, and a chair by the fire."

"Very good, sir." Roberts pulled open the great oak door, startling their visitor in the process.

"Lord Buchanan?" the man asked, looking over the butler's shoulder.

"Indeed, sir." Jack stepped forward, making a quick assessment. Thirty years of age perhaps, the dark-haired, dark-eyed man was not quite so tall or broad as he but a sizable figure nonetheless. His club foot explained the limp. The bundle under his arm was a mystery.

"Come, come," Jack urged him, beckoning his visitor inside. " 'Tis miserable to be out of doors in such weather."

The younger man walked across the marble floor, trying in vain to hide his deformity. Jack could hardly blame him. Would he not do the same?

"I thank ye for yer kindness," the stranger began. For a large man, he was uncommonly soft spoken, though the Highland lilt in his voice was easily detected. "I was sent here by Fiona Ferguson . . . , eh, Cromar."

"Mrs. Cromar?" Jack echoed, staring at the man. "From Castleton of Braemar?"

"Aye, milord. The verra same." He unbuttoned the dripping wool cape round his thick neck, then removed it with a gallant sweep. "Micht this be hung by the hearth for a wee bit?"

Roberts claimed the garment at once, then led the two men into the drawing room, where a crackling wood fire held the damp air at bay.

By now Mrs. Pringle had been alerted and stood in the doorway, awaiting orders.

"Will hot tea do?" Jack asked his guest. "Or is whisky more to your liking?"

"Tea," the man said firmly, though he eyed the glass decanters, their amber contents sparkling in the firelight.

Jack nodded at his housekeeper, then directed his guest to a leather chair well suited for wet clothing. "You say Mrs. Cromar sent you?"

"In a manner o' speaking." The man untied his bundle, wrapped in calfskin, and produced a card advertising a tailoring shop in Edinburgh. "This is whaur I warked," he explained, "and these are some o' the garments I stitched."

Jack barely looked at the neat stack of clothing. "Am I to understand you are . . . a tailor?"

"Aye, milord." He smiled, though it did not soften his features. "Mrs. Cromar told me ye had need o' my services."

Jack shook his head in disbelief. "But all I require is livery for a few footmen. A month's work at most. You cannot have traveled all the way from Braemar for so temporary a position."

"A month o' wark will suit me verra weel," the younger man said. "I was already bound for London toun and thocht I might earn a bit o' silver on my way."

Still shaking his head, Jack began examining the offered garments. He saw at once the man was quite skilled with a needle and told him so.

"I learned a' I ken from my faither," he said proudly. "O' course, he's gane noo, and so is my mither."

Jack studied the card from the shop on Edinburgh's High Street. It appeared to be a worthy establishment. "You could lodge here at Bell Hill," Jack said, thinking aloud, "then be on your way to London by Michaelmas."

"Aye, so I could, milord."

Jack would be pleased to have his footmen newly attired in time for the household supper at next month's end. And Elisabeth's mother surely trusted this young man, or she'd never have recommended him.

"Sir, your timing is . . . providential," Jack told him. The truth was, he felt sorry for the younger man with no steady work and both parents gone. Elisabeth might appreciate having another Highlander in the house, and a friend of her mother's at that.

"I can pay you a guinea for each suit of clothing," Jack told him. "If we're agreed, you may start on the morrow. We've a vacant workroom on the men's side of the servant hall that should suit."

That grim smile again. "Aye, 'twill do."

Jack consulted the card once more. "Your name is MacPherson."

" 'Tis, milord." He eyed the steaming cup of tea Mrs. Pringle had just poured for him. "Robert is my proper Christian name, though my freens a' call me Rob."

"I hope you'll soon be among friends here as well." Jack shook the man's hand, taken aback at the strength of his grip. "Rob Mac-Pherson, welcome to Bell Hill."

FIFTY-FIVE

It is easy to say how we love new
friends . . . but words can never trace out
all the fibers that knit us to the old.

GEORGE ELIOT

Elisabeth flew across the stable yard, her gaze
fixed on the servants' entrance. Had the clock
in the drawing room already struck eight?
She'd slept later than she'd intended, then
spilled tea on her white linen chemise. After
soaking the fabric in hot water, she'd
scrubbed the stain with lemon and salt. "I'll
dry it in the sun for you," Anne had promised,
sending Elisabeth on her way. A poor use for
an expensive lemon, but it could not be
helped.

She slipped into her workroom at Bell Hill
unnoticed, then paused by the window, letting her heart ease its pace. Kate was due for
her fitting later that morning. But Elisabeth
had yet to finish chalking the fabric, let alone
cutting and pinning it. If she started at once,

she might be ready for the lass by eleven o' the clock, provided she had no interruptions.

"Mrs. Kerr?"

When she turned to find Mrs. Pringle walking through the door, pocket watch in hand, Elisabeth apologized at once. "Do forgive my late arrival."

The housekeeper smiled. "I've come not to scold you but to summon you. His lordship has hired a tailor to sew for the menservants and thought you'd want to meet him."

"But . . ." Elisabeth tried to fathom how Lord Jack had found a man so quickly. "His lordship made no mention of him at kirk yesterday morn."

Mrs. Pringle stepped farther into the room, glancing over her shoulder. "According to Roberts, the tradesman arrived yesterday afternoon, drenched from head to toe, and was hired within the hour. Come, his lordship is waiting." She added in a low voice, "The man is a Highlander, as you'll soon see."

Elisabeth followed her down the servants' hall, feeling rather dazed. A tailor from the Highlands when skilled tradesmen could be found in Selkirk? She hastened up the stair to Lord Jack's study, then paused at the door, waiting for the footman to announce her.

Standing behind his desk, the admiral waved her into the room. "There you are, Mrs. Kerr. Do come in, for I've an introduction to make."

She slowly entered, gazing not at her employer but at the man seated in a wooden chair with his back facing the door. Even from this view he looked familiar. His black hair was thick and springy like wool. His dark green coat was expertly tailored. His shoulders were broad, yet he sat at an awkward angle with his foot tucked to the side.

When he stood, her heart began to pound. *It cannot be. Nae, it cannot.*

He turned as Lord Jack announced, "Mrs. Kerr, I'd like you to meet —"

"Rob MacPherson." Elisabeth stared at the man she'd known since childhood. "I thought you . . ." *I thought you were dead.* Grasping for something, anything she might say, she blurted out, "However did you find your way to Bell Hill?"

His dark gaze met hers. "Yer mither sent me here. To leuk for wark."

Or to look for me?

She swallowed. "It is . . . good to see you again."

"Ye've not changed at a'," he told her, his voice lower than she'd remembered.

She turned toward the admiral, knowing he deserved an explanation. "Mr. MacPherson and I grew up together. His father was the tailor who employed me in Edinburgh." She hesitated, wondering how much Rob had told him. "I've not seen Mr. MacPherson since before his father's death. You can imagine how . . . surprised I am to see him again. Here, of all places."

"Indeed," Lord Jack said evenly, "of all places. I imagine you two will wish to renew your friendship in the weeks to come."

"Aye." Rob gave her a sidelong glance, his black eyes gleaming. "That we will."

Nae, Rob. We will not.

The tension in the room was more than Elisabeth could bear.

"I must attend to my sewing," she said, easing toward the open door. "If you will excuse me, gentlemen." She curtsied, then fled for the stair, sorry to have left Lord Jack with a scowl on his face. By the time she reached her workroom, she was wound as tightly as thread round a spool. *Why are you here, Rob? What is it you want from me?*

Sally was waiting for her, eyes like saucers. "Did ye meet the new tailor?"

"As it happens, I know him." Elisabeth briefly told her of their connection, imagining how often her words would be repeated once news of Mr. MacPherson's arrival traveled through the house and then through the town.

Rob would seek her out before long. Until then, she would keep her mind on her work and remember her parting words to him in Edinburgh. *I was never yours. I belong to God.*

When a male visitor darkened her doorway that afternoon, he was not a tailor but an admiral. "Mrs. Kerr, if I might have a moment of your time."

She heard the coolness in his tone, the formality of his address, and vowed to put him at ease. "Lord Jack," she said warmly, laying Kate's unfinished sleeve across her lap. "I'm glad you've come." She nodded at the empty chair beside her, with its cushioned seat and broad arms. "These chairs are far more comfortable than their predecessors. A wonderful provision, milord."

Though he merely inclined his head, she could see her words pleased him.

He sat next to her and said in an offhanded way, "Tell me about Mr. MacPherson."

Elisabeth studied his calm expression, the subtle arch of his brows, the thin line of his mouth. However relaxed he might seem, she knew better. Like Charbon, who often appeared to be sleeping yet was fully alert, Lord Jack was watching her intently.

"He is an excellent tailor," she began. "His father, God rest his soul, declared there was not a finer hand with a needle in Edinburgh."

The admiral grimaced. "I've no quarrel with his talent. 'Tis his motive for coming to Bell Hill that concerns me."

"Ah." She trod with care, wanting to be fair to both men. "He certainly needs the position and will work diligently for your guineas. How long have you engaged him?"

" 'Til Michaelmas." He did not sound pleased at the prospect. "The man is a Jacobite, I presume?"

"He is," Elisabeth said, "though I know you'll not betray him to the king."

"And how do you know that?"

"Because, milord, you did not betray me."

He lowered his gaze. "I would never betray you, Bess. But I would know the nature of your relationship with Mr. MacPherson."

"We are friends. Nothing more."

He looked up. "In the same way you and I are friends?"

"Nae, 'tis not the same," she quickly said. "Though I have known Rob longer, I believe my friendship with you is . . ." *Deeper?* Nae, she was not ready to confess that, however true it might be.

"Is . . . what?" he prompted her.

"More pleasing to the Almighty," she finally said. A proper answer, and honest, but not perhaps the one Lord Jack was looking for.

Nonetheless, he nodded and rose, then took a step toward the door before pausing to say, "I am glad, Bess."

She longed to ask him why, longed to know his true feelings. But in guarding her heart, she'd locked his closed as well. "I am glad too," she said softly as he turned to go.

Elisabeth was laboring over the bodice of Kate's gown when a second visitor appeared at her door. His knock was tentative, but his entrance was not.

"I dinna ken what to call ye," Rob admitted, dropping into the chair beside her, "but 'twill not be Mrs. Kerr."

She kept sewing, hiding her warm cheeks. Lord Jack had sat in the same chair not an hour earlier. Now here was Rob MacPherson, come to turn her life upside down. "All of Bell Hill addresses me as Mrs. Kerr," she explained. "So do the townsfolk."

He scoffed at that. "They've kenned ye but a few months. I've kenned ye a' my life. Aye, and luved ye for most of it."

Mortified, she hastily put down her needle. "Rob, you must not say such things."

He leaned back in the chair, his thick arms folded across his chest. "Why, whan 'tis the truth?"

Elisabeth hesitated, but only for a moment. "I am very glad to see you alive, but you well know I do not return your affections." She hated to speak so bluntly, but Rob MacPherson was not a man who dealt in subtleties. "Selkirk is a small town yet with a good number of gossips. As a widow in mourning, I cannot have my name linked with any man."

His dark eyes narrowed. "Not even his lordship?"

"Not even him."

Rob sighed heavily. "I thocht to find a warmer walcome, Bess."

The disappointment in his voice weighed on her heart. "Mr. MacPherson . . . Rob . . . you must understand. I've begun a new life."

"Can I not do the same?" He kept his voice down, closely watching the open door. "I've laid low a' these months, hiding from King Geordie's men. Ye canna fathom what 'tis like noo in the Hielands." He shook his head. " 'Tis a terrible place. Full o' death."

She thought of her mother and confessed, "I am grieved to hear it."

A moment passed before he said, "I was sorry whan ye didna come to my faither's grave."

Guilt washed over her. "Oh, Rob, I am the one who is sorry. Our landlord in Edinburgh neglected to deliver your letter for several days. I was heartsick when I learned I'd missed Angus's funeral. And the chance to bid you farewell."

"So that was the way of it." He wagged his head, his voice rough with emotion. "I stood alone in Greyfriars Kirkyard and leuked for ye to come. But ye didna."

"Forgive me." She lightly touched his arm, the woven fabric rough beneath her fingertips. "I would have been there by your side," she assured him, "if only I'd known."

When she heard voices in the hall, Elisabeth quickly straightened and picked up her sewing. It would not do for Rob to be found alone with her. "You must go," she whispered.

He stood with obvious reluctance. "I dinna expect ye've found monie Jacobites in Selkirk."

"Not with dragoons patrolling the hills." She lowered her voice to a whisper. "They'll mark you as a Highlander the moment you speak. You'll not be safe here for long."

" 'Til Michaelmas is a' I need. Once his lordship's guineas are in my pocket, I've anither plan in mind." Rob looked down, pinning her with his dark gaze. "And ye, Bess, are at the heart o' that plan."

FIFTY-SIX

A day of worry is more exhausting than a
day of work.

JOHN LUBBOCK, LORD AVEBURY

Marjory woke with a dull ache beneath her
brow, just as she had every morning that
week. She trudged to the hearth, then prepared breakfast by rote, the clamor of another
Friday market assailing her ears.

Anne was still asleep after another night of
tossing and turning in her box bed. Too
excited about her upcoming marriage, Marjory decided. Anne's dark blue gown hung
from her bed curtains, well away from the
hearth. The gown was older but newly aired
and pressed, and the delicate lace trim across
the square neckline was the work of Anne's
own hands.

Michael's needle had been busy as well.
Last evening Anne had burst through the
door, her expression jubilant. "Oh, Cousins!
Wait until you see Michael's handsome blue

coat," she'd crowed, practically skipping through the house. "And he's sewn Peter a waistcoat to match." Anne had dropped into a chair with a happy sigh. "Come the Sabbath, the two lads I love will welcome me into their home."

And the one man I love will not.

Marjory pushed away the selfish thought, reminding herself that Anne had waited a long time to marry. Could she not wait as well until God provided or Neil Gibson relented?

Better is a dinner of herbs where love is.

Marjory held the proverb close to her heart, intending to share it with Neil when the time was right. They could wait, aye, but not forever.

She glanced toward the partition, hearing noises from the box bed. A moment later her cousin appeared, squinting round the room. "Where's Bess?"

"She left before dawn," Marjory told her. "Said she had a maid's gown to finish in time for the admiral's monthly supper on the morrow."

"I suppose Lord Buchanan has already arranged for servants," Anne said wistfully. "I don't know when I've had a better time than his first supper in June."

Marjory agreed. "A memorable occasion. Just like your wedding will be."

Anne studied Marjory more closely. "Is that

what's been troubling you of late? My marriage to Michael?"

"Nae," Marjory assured her, sidestepping any mention of Gibson. " 'Tis Rob MacPherson," she confessed. "He's dangerous, that one."

"Dangerous?" Anne's snort was ladylike but still a snort. "Have you forgotten that Lord Buchanan is in residence? A gentleman who commanded hundreds of sailors can surely manage one Highlander."

"Oh, Mr. MacPherson would never hurt Bess," Marjory was quick to say. "Quite the contrary. He was besotted with her in Edinburgh."

Anne's eyes widened. "Is that why he came to Selkirk?"

"I fear so, though Bess has not said as much." As Marjory ladled steaming porridge into their bowls, an idea sprang to mind. "Suppose we pay a visit to Bell Hill this forenoon and see what we can learn? If the walk does not ease my headache, 'twill at least ease my heart."

A light breeze wafted over the Selkirk Hills as the two women headed east on foot, the late August sun warm on their shoulders. Though Marjory was breathless by the time they reached the summit of Bell Hill, the view was worth the effort. Even after several days without rain, the grass shone emerald green.

Bright red berries covered the pair of rowan trees at the entrance gate, and blooming heather turned the distant hillsides a dusky purple.

Greeted at the door by a fair-haired young footman, Marjory and Anne were soon ushered into Elisabeth's small workroom below stairs.

"Why, look who's come to Bell Hill!" Elisabeth said, making them welcome. "Mr. Mac-Pherson, you remember my mother-in-law."

"Verra weel," the tailor said with a low bow. " 'Tis guid to see ye again, Mrs. Kerr."

"And you." Marjory reminded herself of the many kindnesses Rob MacPherson had done for their family in Edinburgh, even as she tried to forget his last visit to Milne Square, when he'd accused Donald of being unfaithful to Elisabeth. *Your son demeaned her well enough.* Even though his charge was true, Rob had no right to speak ill of her dead son.

Marjory gazed at her daughter-in-law, recalling how she'd shown Rob the door that evening in no uncertain terms. *Please, Bess. Do the same now. For all our sakes.*

"Mr. MacPherson has finished sewing his first livery," Elisabeth was saying, "and brought Roberts along to show me his finished handiwork."

The butler stood before the hearth, tall and

proud in his well-fitted black coat and trousers, with a crisp white linen shirt and neckcloth.

"A fine suit of clothing," Marjory begrudgingly agreed.

"I've meikle mair to do at Bell Hill," Rob said, "though I'm in nae hurry to bid farewell to my bonny Bess."

Marjory hastened to correct him. "Mrs. Kerr, you mean."

He shrugged. "She's Bess to me, mem."

When the butler took his leave, Marjory hoped he might drag the Highlander with him. But Rob tarried in the workroom, standing entirely too close to Elisabeth.

"I hear ye've a wedding in the family," he said, glancing at Anne. "Would that be ye, lass?" Belated introductions were made, then Rob finally moved toward the door. "Ye ken whaur I wark if ye need me, Bess."

Marjory watched him depart, bristling at his familiar manner. "Does he visit you here often?"

"Once a day," Elisabeth admitted. "Perhaps twice. His workroom is a mirror of mine on the other side of the kitchen, where the menservants reside."

" 'Tis where he belongs," Marjory said, any charitable thoughts toward Rob well quashed. "You'll forgive me, Bess, but I do not trust him."

"Nor do I," she said, surprising her. "He's

not the man we knew in Edinburgh. The prince's defeat at Culloden changed him, I fear, and not for the better." With a sigh she added, "I'll be relieved when his time at Bell Hill is done."

"Then why not tell Lord Buchanan how you feel?" Anne urged her. "He'd send the man packing in a trice." A thread of impatience ran through her words. "Truly, Bess, you need not suffer Mr. MacPherson's company for another month."

Elisabeth bent forward in her chair, absently petting the gray cat winding round her feet. "I cannot treat an old friend so harshly, Annie. However bold he may seem, inside he's a broken man, without home or family or silver. As you say, Rob will be gone by Michaelmas. And you, dear Cousin, will soon be a married woman."

"So I will," Anne said, brightening.

Marjory looked away. *But I will not.*

FIFTY-SEVEN

I can make a lord, but only God Almighty
can make a gentleman.

JAMES VI OF SCOTLAND

Lord Buchanan gazed down the length of his crowded dining room table, wishing not for the first time he'd sought Elisabeth's counsel before engaging Rob MacPherson. Why had he acted in such haste? He could dismiss the tailor, of course, but justice demanded a cause, and he had none. At least, nothing that was honorable.

I do not like the man. Nae, that was not the issue.

I do not like the way he looks at Bess. Closer to the mark.

Rob MacPherson was simply not worthy of the woman. Not because of his station, but because of his character. What Jack had first perceived as meekness or humility, he now realized was a quiet sort of cunning. And whatever story Mr. MacPherson had invented to explain his appearance, it was clear why he'd come to Bell Hill: to seek the company of Elisabeth Kerr. To capture her heart, perhaps even her hand in marriage when her time of mourning ended.

A pity Jack could not fault the man's tailoring skills. Roberts was the talk of the household in his new livery. If only the tailor might sew faster — much faster — and finish in a fortnight. Still, they'd struck hands on the bargain. Jack was obliged to see things through, however much it grieved him.

He'd at least made certain Rob MacPherson was placed at the far end of the table for their household supper that evening, while Elisabeth was where she belonged: here, close by his side.

Jack smiled at her. "You've done something different with your hair." He lightly touched a wispy curl that trailed down her neck. Her long, graceful neck. "I believe the sun has added a bit of color to your cheeks."

More color appeared, a rosy tint.

He pulled back at once. "I beg your pardon."

"No need to apologize," she murmured. "I blush rather easily."

While she sipped her claret, Jack studied her profile. The generous mouth, the patrician nose, the large, luminous eyes. If he could be certain of Elisabeth's present feelings regarding Mr. MacPherson, the month ahead might be easier. She'd convinced him there was no romantic attachment. "Not on my part," she'd said, and Jack believed her. But the two Highlanders had a long history together. Shared experiences often tipped the scale.

Then throw something on there, Jack, and tip it in your direction.

Prodded by his conscience, Jack knew what needed to be done. It would cost him his pride, but what better way to spend it than procuring Elisabeth's undivided attention? He couldn't put things in motion this night. But he would do so come Monday.

The candles were burning low and the dessert plates already cleared when Jack stood, drawing every eye in his direction. "You are invited to retire to the drawing room," he announced. "Our musicians await us for a night of dancing."

With a gleeful cry the entire household was on its collective feet and bound for the hallway, any sense of decorum left in their wake. Linen napkins were tossed about at whim and chairs left higgledy-piggledy round the room. General Lord Mark Kerr might not approve, but Jack found their abandon refreshing.

"Mrs. Kerr?" He offered his arm, noting with perverse satisfaction Rob MacPherson glowering at him from the doorway. "May I escort you to the drawing room?"

Elisabeth rested her hand in the crook of his elbow, then followed him through the gilded doors, down the hallway, and into the candlelit drawing room, where the carpet was rolled back and a small band of musicians gathered in a circle, tuning their instruments. Amid much giggling and blushing, partners were found and lines were formed in anticipation of the first note.

"How I'd love to dance," Elisabeth said on a sigh. "Just as well I'm not yet permitted to do so since you do not care for dancing. Isn't that so, milord?"

"Quite right, madam."

Not care for dancing? He loathed it. Too many years at sea without any good reason to acquire that particular social skill had left him with no knowledge of the necessary steps and little confidence in learning them. One hardly engaged a dancing master at forty years of age. Unless, of course, one wished to dance with a certain young woman.

When a lively reel filled the air, the polished oak floor almost disappeared beneath swirling skirts and dancing feet. Elisabeth stood, her toe tapping in time to the music, her shoulders faintly swaying as couples moved forward, backward, and round, following the intricate patterns of a country dance.

Jack watched their feet, discouraged at the thought of trying to keep up with them. Was it step to the right, then turn? Or turn to the right, then step? His only consolation was that Rob MacPherson wasn't dancing either, though the tailor had a valid reason.

Standing as close as propriety allowed, Jack remained by Elisabeth's side all evening. She described each dance to him as if she were privy to his musings on the subject, applauded the musicians whenever appropriate, and smiled each time an opportunity presented itself. Elisabeth was, in truth, the perfect companion.

Even if she was once a Jacobite rebel?

Aye, even then.

Of this Jack was certain: any expression of affection would have to wait. Through Michaelmas and Hallowmas, through Martinmas and Christmas, until the seventeenth of January, when all of society, and Marjory Kerr especially, would permit his deep regard for Elisabeth to take its natural course.

Five months was a very long time, even for a patient man.

Jack was not a patient man. Nor, he feared, was Rob MacPherson.

"She'll make a lovely bride, milord," Roberts said, nodding at Anne Kerr, who tarried outside the open kirk door, awaiting her cue.

"Indeed she will," Jack agreed, all the while gazing at Elisabeth.

The kirk was nearly full, only a few parishioners having departed at the end of the morning service, the Murrays of Philiphaugh among them. Jack had spoken briefly to Rosalind and her family beforehand, if only to be polite, then was relieved to see them make a hasty exit. Sabbath weddings were more subdued than most since the kirk frowned on any sort of merrymaking. But curiosity alone had kept most folk in their pews, eager to see two neighbors joined in marriage.

When a fiddler in the kirkyard struck up a familiar tune, Anne stepped through the door, a bouquet of Michaelmas daisies in hand. Jack had to admit she made a bonny bride with her fair hair curled high on top of her head.

Escorting her down the aisle was Peter Dalgliesh, smartly dressed for a wee lad and beaming at the crowd. "This is my new mither!" he announced proudly, delivering Anne to his father's side. The groom looked surprisingly calm, Jack thought, and decidedly happy, standing before the congregation, his red hair bright against the dull gray walls of the kirk. The moment the fiddler ended his tune with a flourish, Reverend Brown stepped forward to do his part.

The minister's expression was stern, his tone of voice more so. "We are gathered here to join Anne Kerr of Halliwell's Close and Michael Dalgliesh of School Close in holy matrimony. Stand for a reading from the

Book of Common Order."

The congregation rose to hear the familiar words, followed by a lengthy prayer, and the necessary question. "Is there any impediment to this marriage?" Reverend Brown asked the crowd of witnesses. "Any reason why these two people should not be joined together as husband and wife?"

When no objection was offered, the minister proceeded with the vows.

But it was not the voice of Reverend Brown that Jack heard. Nae, it was King George shouting in his head. *Admiral Buchanan, you cannot woo a traitor. For what fellowship hath righteousness with unrighteousness? And what communion hath light with darkness? Put her aside, Buchanan, and marry a woman loyal to her sovereign.*

While the ceremony continued, Jack argued with the king in his head. *Can you not see what a good woman Bess is, Your Majesty? Can you not look beyond her Highland past?* 'Twould be no easy thing to tell King George one of his admirals intended to marry the widow of an attainted rebel. But tell him Jack would, when the time came. Not because the king required it, but because the king's blessing would keep Elisabeth safe forever.

"Even so," Anne was saying, her voice clear, "I take him before God and in the presence of his people."

Looking down at Elisabeth, Jack imagined her saying those words. Imagined their hands joined together. Imagined a benediction being spoken over them. Imagined the kiss that would seal their vows. As if sensing his thoughts, she turned to meet his gaze and smiled. "Isn't it a lovely wedding?" she whispered.

"Aye," he whispered back. "Most assuredly."

FIFTY-EIGHT

I saw old Autumn in the misty morn
Stand shadowless like silence, listening
To silence.

THOMAS HOOD

Elisabeth could not recall a lovelier first of September. The morning air was mild, the mist was lifting, and dew sparkled on every flower in Lord Jack's garden. With a few minutes to spare before the start of her workday, she approached the sprawling shrub of roses blooming in colorful profusion, eager for a closer look.

"Autumn damask?" she asked the gardener's assistant, who stepped back, bobbing his head. She leaned toward the pale pink blossoms and inhaled their sweet perfume. "Too delicate for my mother's Highland garden, I'm afraid, but they manage very well here in the Borderland."

"Aye, mem," the young lad said, then offered her a pair of gardening shears. "His lordship willna mind if ye cut a few."

"You are certain?" She eyed the shears.

Another hand reached round her and snatched them instead. "O' course he doesna mind." Rob MacPherson cut off a fresh bloom with a careless snip of the blades, leaving a stem too short for any vase.

When he handed her the flower, she buried her nose in its velvety petals, vowing to find a small cup that might support it rather than let the beautiful rose go to waste. "One bloom is all I need," she assured the lad, plucking the shears from Rob's grasp and returning them to their rightful owner. "Do thank Mr. Richardson for me," she said as the boy hurried off to attend to his duties elsewhere.

"And wha might that be?" Rob grumbled. Once she told him Gil Richardson was the head gardener and well married, Rob's frown eased.

Were you prepared to be jealous of him too? Elisabeth held her tongue, continuing her early morning stroll round the garden. She felt sorry for Rob, so slavish was his devotion — nae, his obsession. During his first week at Bell Hill, he'd found endless excuses to visit her workroom, glared at every man she spoke with, and reminded her how much he'd done for her, how much he cared for her, how much he needed her.

Even now, he was too close on her heels, throwing his broad shadow across her path as she paused to look up at Lord Jack's study and see if she might catch a glimpse of him standing at the window, as he did some mornings. Not this one, it seemed.

Rob touched the small of her back. "He doesna luve ye as I do."

She closed her eyes, feeling almost sick. "Mr. MacPherson, please . . ."

When she started toward the house, he quickly caught up, this time snagging her elbow. "Bess, what must I do to win ye?"

Pulling free of his grasp, she turned to face him, then told him in Gaelic, lest they be overheard, "I am not a game to be won, sir."

After a long pause Rob responded in kind, his words soft and low. "I feared our language was lost to you."

Elisabeth looked down at her damask rose, her throat tightening. "Never," she whispered. She'd not heard their Highland tongue for many months, nor spoken it except for the single proverb she'd recited for Marjory.

Rob stepped closer. "Please forgive me, lass. I meant no offense."

How could she speak unkindly to such a man? And yet she had to tell him the truth.

"I am the one who must ask your forgiveness," she confessed. "For I do not and cannot love you." She forced herself to meet his gaze, knowing the pain she would find in those black depths. "I am grateful for the friendship we had as children. But we have grown into two very different people."

The lines across his brow deepened as he shifted back to English. "Is it money ye're wanting? A rich husband, not a tailor?"

"Nae." She shook her head, certain of her answer. "I want only to honor the vow I made to my mother-in-law and to the Lord. If the Almighty has a husband for me, I will marry again someday. But 'twill not be soon."

"So ye say," he growled, then quit the garden in a huff.

Elisabeth managed to avoid Rob the rest of Monday by tarrying in her workroom. A handful of gowns remained to be sewn: two for upper housemaids, three for lower housemaids, all of whom were most anxious to match their peers. Elisabeth spent the day measuring the five of them, hoping she might speed the process for their sakes and enjoy their company in the bargain.

Mrs. Pringle had trained her staff well. Each young woman was polite and quiet in demeanor, clean and neat in appearance. A maid named Biddy, all arms and legs, was grateful Elisabeth could lengthen her cuffs, making her arms appear less spindly. Elsie was a good deal rounder than the others and so asked, "Might ye add a wee trim about my neck so folk will leuk at my face and not my form?" Elisabeth assured her such a thing was easily done.

Ada, with her ivory complexion and wheat-colored hair, was relieved her gown would feature a line of pearl buttons to brighten the charcoal gray fabric against her pale skin. Nessie was the youngest and smallest and so earned a dainty ruffle along the square neckline. And Muriel, who said no more than five words — "Aye," "Nae," and "Thank ye, mem" — was elated to know a row of pleats across the bodice would give the impression of fullness where there was none.

When Sally swept into the room with her tea tray late in the afternoon, Elisabeth was surrounded with slates full of numbers and notations. Sally deposited her repast on the table, then smoothed her hands over her gown. "Mine is the bonniest," she confided. "My ain mither says so."

Elisabeth smiled as the maidservant poured her tea. "I'm glad you're pleased. A few more gowns, and I'll be finished."

"But, Mrs. Kerr, ye canna leave us!" the lass cried, nearly filling the cup to overflowing. "Ye belong at Bell Hill."

"That will depend on his lordship." Elisabeth rescued her cup, then took a sip, trying not to burn her lips. "If there's sewing to be done, I shall be glad to stay."

Sally rolled her eyes. "If ye think his lordship wants ye for yer needle, ye're not so canny as I thocht."

Elisabeth tried not to smile. "You know very

well I cannot entertain such a notion, and neither can Lord Buchanan."

The lass tossed her russet hair, making her cap dance about. "Say what ye will, ye'll be married afore lang. And not to the Hielander wha's sewing for the lads."

"Nae," Elisabeth agreed, "though I'm curious why you say so."

Sally's voice dropped a notch. "At oor supper on Saturday last, the tailor didna take his eyes aff ye. But ye niver once leuked at him."

Elisabeth could hardly argue with so keen an observation.

"Is he the reason ye've not stepped oot yer door a' day?" Sally asked. When Elisabeth nodded, the bonny maidservant added, "If I see Mr. MacPherson walking doon this hall, I'll tell him ye're busy. Which ye are." She winked, then quit the workroom with a skip in her step, leaving Elisabeth with her chalk-marked slates and her scattered thoughts.

Only when the distant kirk bell began tolling the hour of six did Sally reappear, bearing a note in her hand and a rueful expression. "Mr. MacPherson bade me gie ye this, so I couldna say nae."

"Of course." Elisabeth tucked it inside her pocket to read on the way home. "A good eve to you, Sally."

The maidservant eyed her pocket. "And to ye, mem."

Elisabeth did not open the letter until she

was halfway down Bell Hill, well out of anyone's sight, Rob's in particular. Just as Sally had said, Elisabeth felt his eyes on her all the time, watching her come and go.

She paused at a wide spot on the road and broke the beeswax seal. The letter was brief, the paper inexpensive, but the Gaelic words chilled her heart.

Monday, 1 September 1746

Madam,

You say you do not love me, but I know you better than you know yourself.

Elisabeth's heart sank. *Oh, Rob.* He did not know her at all. Nor did he listen to her. *Cannot love you.* That was what she'd said.

When I spoke our Highland tongue this morn, your eyes rose to meet mine, and I saw the truth.

What truth, Rob? He saw only what he wanted to see.

As you did, Bess, with Donald? She winced, stung by the realization. Aye, she had lied to herself, denied the truth of her husband's affairs, pretended he was a changed man when he was not. She knew about looking into a

504

beloved's eyes and imagining what she found there.

No Lowlander will ever make you happy. But I can.

She shook her head, saddened by Rob's conviction. Would he never accept her refusal?

When Michaelmas comes, I shall sail to the Americas. My father left a small inheritance, enough to buy passage for two. Come with me, Bess. We can make a future together.

Nae, Rob. We have no future. Not together.
She folded the letter, intending to slip it in the coal grate the moment she reached Anne's house. 'Twas best if no one else knew of Rob's delusion. She would handle this herself and spare her old friend any more embarrassment than necessary.

Elisabeth looked across the western sky, where the sun had all but disappeared, leaving only a faint wash of orange glowing behind the hills. However uncertain the days to come, she knew the Lord had not forgotten her. Anne had thought herself a stayed lass, yet Michael had come round with his heart in his hands. Marjory had given up ever knowing the love of another man, yet Gibson had stepped forward with God's leading and the minister's blessing. Though the two had no definite plans, their love for each other shone clear and bright upon their faces.

Might the Lord not have a future in mind for her as well? Elisabeth hoped so. Nae, she prayed so. She continued downhill, quickening her steps now that night was falling. One name beat inside her, warming her through, carrying her home.

FIFTY-NINE

Our patience will achieve more than our
force.

EDMUND BURKE

Jack paused outside the open door to Rob
MacPherson's workroom, watching the man
labor over a pair of trousers. His movements
were swift and efficient, his expression intent,
his finished work exemplary. Were it not for
the Highlander's preoccupation with Elisabeth, Rob would make a fine addition to Bell
Hill's staff.

Jack knocked just before he entered. "Good
morn to you, Mr. MacPherson."

The man turned toward the door, his
features unchanging. "Milord."

A shiver ran down Jack's spine. Aye, the air
was cool and the furnishings sterile, with
none of the warmth and coziness of Elisabeth's workroom. But it was more than that.
Rob MacPherson was like a block of ice cut
from a northern loch in the dead of winter.

Cold, hard, impenetrable. Jack drew up a chair, determined to find a way in.

"Working on another livery, I see," Jack began. "For one of the footmen?"

Rob nodded his dark, bushy head. "A tall lad by the name o' Gregor." He held up the trousers, the fabric draping onto the flagstones. "He'll be newly dressed by Friday."

"Very good." Jack shifted in his seat, hearing a faint jingle from the extra guineas in his waistcoat pocket. He'd come prepared to dismiss Mr. MacPherson if it came to it. To pay him for work he'd not yet performed and send him whence he'd come. None could fault a master who rewarded a servant in full.

But the idea did not sit well with Jack. He would hear out Rob MacPherson before deciding the man's future at Bell Hill.

"I was sorry not to see you in kirk on Sunday morn," Jack said, keeping his tone light.

Rob shrugged. "I didna ken if I'd be welcome."

"We'd be more than glad to have you." Jack almost clapped him on the shoulder as a friendly gesture, then thought better of it. "I shall save a place for you in the Kerr aisle next Sabbath," he promised, to which Rob offered no response. Was the man ungodly? A pagan? Jack knew almost nothing of Rob's history. Only that he was born and raised in Braemar parish. *Like Bess.*

"Did you settle in Castleton after leaving Edinburgh?" Jack asked him. An innocent question, he thought.

Rob's eyes narrowed. "Why d'ye care whaur I lived?"

" 'Tis Mrs. Cromar I have in mind," Jack explained. "If you spent the summer in Castleton, you must have seen her on several occasions. Mrs. Kerr is concerned about her mother's welfare, as am I, having met her husband."

Rob abruptly stood, casting aside cloth and needle. "Ye've no richt to speak ill o' Ben Cromar."

"He's a friend of yours, then?" Jack rose and faced him directly, not in the least intimidated by the man, however fierce his countenance.

Rob finally admitted, "Cromar's a freen, aye."

"Would you say he's a good husband?"

He frowned at that. "What d'ye mean by guid?"

"Does he protect her, provide for her, care for her?" Jack felt his voice rising and his temper with it. "Is Mrs. Cromar safe in his company?"

"O' course she's safe," Rob said with an ugly sneer. "He's her husband."

Jack grit his teeth, his patience dwindling. "Let us be clear on this, Mr. MacPherson. You've never seen Cromar strike her?"

"Nae," Rob said firmly.

"Never noticed any marks on her? Bruises, gashes?"

This response came more slowly. "She once told me she bruised easily."

Before Rob averted his gaze, Jack saw the truth in his eyes.

He turned on his heels and began pacing the room, sorting out his options, which were few. Sir John Murray had already informed him that the Sheriff of Aberdeen would not likely get involved. "Not for a few bruises," Sir John had said. Would no one come to this woman's rescue until she was bloodied and beaten? Or would her death alone bring the law to her cottage door?

Rob spoke up. "If ye're finished here, milord, I've wark to do."

"Work, is it?" He jerked round and felt the coins in his pocket shift. "Was it work that brought you to Bell Hill? Or was it Elisabeth Kerr?"

When Rob did not respond quickly enough to suit him, Jack took a step closer. "As your employer, I've a right to know." Well, he did, didn't he?

"I told ye why I came." Rob sat down and reached for the fabric with its many sharp pins. "Mrs. Cromar kenned ye needed a tailor and wanted a man she could trust round her daughter."

Jack stared at him. *But does her daughter*

trust you? Only Elisabeth could answer that question. "We'll finish this discussion another time, Mr. MacPherson."

Vexed, Jack headed for the workroom on the opposite side of the ground floor, hoping his ire might cool as he strode through the servants' halls. He'd not spoken with Elisabeth on Monday and felt her absence keenly. Perhaps they might go riding together in the afternoon if the weather held.

Jack rounded the corner and found her busy with her chalk. "Mrs. Kerr." He felt better at once, just seeing her. "Might I have a word?"

"Aye." She was quieter than usual, though glad enough for his company, it seemed. "You're here on a mission," she said, perceptive as ever.

Only then did he notice the slates scattered round the room. "What's this?"

"Measurements for the remaining gowns."

So few. An ache spread across his chest. "Are you in a hurry to leave Bell Hill?"

Her blue eyes widened. "Not at all, milord. The lasses are eager for their gowns, so I spent most of yesterday measuring each one."

Jack told her the truth to see where it might lead. "I hoped you were avoiding Rob MacPherson."

"Aye, that too." She pressed her lips together as if reluctant to say more on the subject.

He took a seat. "I spoke with Mr. Mac-Pherson just now. We discussed your mother."

Her hands stilled. "And?"

Jack related their conversation, withholding nothing, though it pained him to see Elisabeth's skin grow pale and her eyes fill with sorrow. "This is not the end of it," he promised her. "I cannot by law remove a woman from her husband's home. But I can send a trustworthy man north to watch over her."

"You would do that?"

He nodded, wishing he might clasp her hand or touch her cheek. Anything to comfort her. "What good is money if it cannot be spent on a worthy cause?"

"But you give so freely," she said, shaking her head as if confused.

"I'll not be thought of as generous, Bess." He leaned forward, determined to make himself understood. "Just as I said on the day we met, anything you receive from me is God's blessing, not mine."

She wasn't quite satisfied. "It still passes through your hands."

"Then I have only to leave them open so the Almighty may do as he pleases." Jack held out his hands, palms up, meaning only to il-lustrate his point.

But Elisabeth slowly placed her hands in his.

He dared not move or breathe or speak, lest he frighten her away.

When she bowed her head, he did the same, closing his eyes, reveling in her gentle touch.

"Almighty God," she whispered, "protect and provide for those I love. Whatever is to come, Lord, I know 'twill come from you."

Jack longed to draw her closer, to hold her in his embrace. Instead, he lifted his head and honored the One who'd brought her into his life. "Trust him, Bess."

"Always," she promised, her hands still resting in his.

Sixty

The motions of his spirit are dull as night,
And his affections dark . . .
Let no such man be trusted.

WILLIAM SHAKESPEARE

Elisabeth woke at dawn on Wednesday morning, having slept poorly. All through the night she'd shifted about in her chair, seeking a more comfortable position, trying to escape her troubling dreams. Rob MacPherson appeared in most of them: a brooding figure wearing shapeless attire and a permanent scowl.

"Is he still convinced you'll marry him someday?" Marjory inquired over their bowls of porridge. "He may be a dozen years younger than Lord Buchanan, but I fear Rob has nothing else to recommend him."

Elisabeth winced at her mother-in-law's heartless assessment. "Mr. MacPherson was a good friend to us in Edinburgh."

"Michael Dalgliesh has befriended the Kerr

514

family as well," Marjory said, "but 'tis not why Anne married the man."

After finishing the last spoonful of porridge, Elisabeth gulped down her tea, mindful of the hour. The sun rose a little later each day, yet she was still expected at eight o' the clock. "Anne is joining us for supper, aye? I should be home earlier than usual since Lord Buchanan has invited guests to share his table, and so will not likely detain me. Sir John and Lady Murray are bringing their daughters."

Marjory made a slight face. "I suppose the sheriff is hoping Lord Buchanan will offer for Rosalind, even though she's half his age."

"You were eight-and-ten when *you* married," Elisabeth reminded her gently. "And Lord John was more than twenty years older than you." She leaned across the table and clasped Marjory's hand. "Of course, Gibson is far younger than that. Handsome, too, if you'll not mind my saying so."

A smile found its way to Marjory's face. "He *is* fine looking. And kind. And attentive."

Elisabeth wished she too might speak of the man who'd captured her heart. But Lord Jack was not a manservant; he was a peer of the realm, who deserved someone like Rosalind Murray. Even though he seldom mentioned her, Elisabeth had watched Lady Murray's relentless campaign unfold all summer. What gentleman with eyes in his head could resist such a prize?

515

After the breakfast dishes were cleared Elisabeth left for Bell Hill and stopped by Walter Halliwell's shop to deliver a plate of fresh ginger biscuits. "Mrs. Kerr made an extra dozen," she told their landlord, "thinking you might enjoy them."

"Most kind," the wigmaker said, popping a small biscuit into his mouth. A moment later, still chewing, he asked, "Are ye bound for Bell Hill? Might I trouble ye to deliver a wig to his lordship?"

When he handed her a gentleman's peruke wrapped in a cloth bag, Elisabeth had little choice but to take it. She had no objection to the errand, only to the rather personal nature of the item. Bidding the wigmaker farewell, she stepped out of his tidy shop and into the close that bore his name, hoping she might deliver the peruke to Roberts or Dickson and so avoid any embarrassment.

But it was not to be.

As she reached the gates leading to the mansion, Lord Jack trotted up on Janvier. Taking his morning ride, it seemed, without coat or hat, the full sleeves of his shirt ruffling in the breeze. "What have you there?" he asked, his gaze resting on her round bundle. "Balls of yarn to amuse my cat?"

"Nae, 'tis something for you," she said, holding it up. "From Mr. Halliwell."

"Ah." He claimed the bag at once. "Shame on Walter for turning my talented dressmaker into an errand boy." As Janvier pawed at the ground, clearly eager to stretch his legs, his lordship surprised her with an invitation. "Might you join me for dinner at two o' the clock?"

"If it pleases you," she said, thinking of someone who would not be at all pleased.

Even without a watch like Mrs. Pringle's in her apron pocket, Elisabeth knew the dinner hour was approaching. The nearby kitchen was in a frenzy, with Mrs. Tudhope at the center of it.

'Tis time, Bess. She bathed her hands, prayed for a calm spirit, and started toward the stair, greeting everyone she passed, hoping to dispel any rumors.

It was not a sin to share a meal with her employer, she told herself. Footmen and maidservants would be in and out of the dining room from one course to the next. The two would never be alone. In an hour dinner would be over, and she could return to her sewing, her only regret a too-full stomach.

"Bess?" A whisper, nothing more.

She turned at the foot of the stair and discovered Rob moving toward her. "What is it?" she asked, certain he meant to speak of his letter, of his plans for the Americas.

His voice was low, yet his tone harsh, strident. "D'ye not ken what they're saying,

Bess? From one end o' the hoose to the ither?"

"Please, Mr. —"

"They're calling ye his leddy. D'ye ken my meaning?"

His mistress. She swallowed. "I do understand, but 'tis not true."

He inched closer. "Can ye say there is naught *atween* ye? Nae luve at a'?"

Elisabeth straightened, meeting his gaze without apology. "Whatever may be in our hearts, you can be very sure our behavior has been utterly chaste. Lord Buchanan honors the Lord at all times, and I hope I do as well." She took her skirts in hand, her thoughts halfway up the turnpike stair. "You must forgive me, but his lordship is expecting me this very moment."

"We'll speak o' this again, Bess," he said, more warning than assurance.

She fled up the steps, praying she was being honest with herself and with the Almighty. *My thoughts are honorable, Lord, yet I do care for Lord Jack. Very much.*

By the time Elisabeth reached the dining room, she was breathless, not from exertion, but from anticipation. "Milord," she said, offering him a low curtsy, if only to calm herself. She was soon seated facing a window overlooking Bell Hill's gardens, then was served a glass of claret, which she politely declined.

"None for me either," Lord Jack told the footman, then settled into his chair at the head of the table, the carved wooden back arching above him at a regal height. " 'Tis the middle of the day, and I would have my wits about me."

"As would I," she agreed.

They smiled at each other across the table while dishes came and went in a steady flow. He told her stories of his years on the *Centurion.* Of tumultuous seas and fearsome storms. Of torn sails and lost trade winds.

"Were you ever frightened, milord?"

He paused, his water glass halfway to his lips. "If I say nae, I'll appear proud. If I say yes, a coward." Lord Jack took a long sip, then admitted, "Aye, there was a moment when I feared our ship might founder on the shoals near Tinion. But God is faithful and came to our rescue with a stout wind that pushed us out to sea." He put down his empty water glass, swiftly replenished by a silent footman. "What frightens you, Mrs. Kerr? Not poverty, it seems. Nor hard work."

"Nae." She dabbed at her mouth, unable to eat another bite. "As the Buik says, I have learned to be content."

He nodded, a thoughtful expression on his face. "You've too many friends to ever fear loneliness."

"Friends, aye," she said softly.

"What of Mr. MacPherson?"

His question caught her off guard. "Milord?"

"Is he a trustworthy man, this Highland tailor? For I must say, if there is anyone or anything you seem afraid of, 'tis him."

Afraid of Rob? She shook her head. "He would never hurt me. As for trusting him . . ." She paused, not wishing to cast doubt unfairly. "In all our dealings in Edinburgh, he always honored his promises."

By the look on his face, Lord Jack saw through her careful wording, but he did not press the matter. "Are you quite sated?" he asked, eying her dessert plate, where only a smudge of lemon cream remained.

She smiled. "I'll not need supper, if that's what you mean."

"Nor will I," he admitted, "though it seems I'll have guests at my table this eve."

Elisabeth waited, hoping he might say something about Rosalind Murray. That he abhorred her, that he adored her — anything to put the subject to rest. On second thought, Elisabeth did *not* want to hear the latter. Nae, she did not.

When she started to rise, the admiral quickly did the same. "A fine meal, milord," she told him.

He offered her a courtly bow. "With even finer company."

Only then did she happen to gaze out the window and notice an abrupt change in the weather. Low, gray clouds were scuttling across the heavens, and a sharp wind lashed the tree branches against the outer walls of the house.

"We'll have rain before nightfall," he said, looking over his shoulder. "Let me have the carriage brought round for you at six o' the clock."

Elisabeth hesitated, tempted by his generosity, yet not wanting to give the household more fodder for their gossip. "Nae," she said at last, "for 'tis an easy walk and all downhill."

"You are certain, Mrs. Kerr?"

She stole another glance out the window. "Aye."

SIXTY-ONE

My day is closed! the gloom of night is
come!

JOANNA BAILLIE

Before the kirk bell tolled the hour of six,
Elisabeth flew out the servants' entrance,
anxious to reach home. The skies were black
with clouds, the sun had all but disappeared
below the horizon, and the temperature had
plummeted since she'd left Halliwell's Close
that morning. A storm was coming hard and
fast from the west.

Why had she refused his lordship's kind offer of a coach? Too late now, for she did not
care to interrupt him with the Murrays
expected. Rain was merely water, she reminded herself.

Elisabeth hastened across the lawn, clutching her hat in one hand and her sewing basket
in the other. She'd promised to alter one of
Anne's gowns that evening after supper and
would not disappoint her. Then she looked

down and realized her scissors weren't dangling round her neck. *Nae!*

She spun about, thinking to return to her workroom, until she remembered Anne's small lace making scissors. Aye, those would do. Elisabeth started for home once more, practically running by the time she reached the road leading west toward town.

Dark, dark. And in the distance a roll of thunder.

Though she had no lantern, the lights of Selkirk beckoned her forward. Elisabeth well knew the steep, narrow track, having traveled it twice daily throughout the long summer. She started downhill, hair blowing in her face, her steps cautious. She could see her outstretched hand, but no farther. The air had a hollow sound as more thunder rumbled overhead.

At the first broad curve rested an enormous boulder the size of his lordship's carriage. She'd nearly reached the other side of it when a large man stepped into her path.

"Oh!" She exhaled, bending forward as if she'd been punched. "Goodness, Rob, you startled me."

The tailor took her arm rather firmly and led her round the boulder to a small patch of grass where clumps of spiny gorse stood guard and Rob's small traveling bundle lay waiting. "I couldna speak with ye at the hoose, so I thocht to do so here."

"Here?" She stared at Rob, his eyes blacker than the sky. "But the storm —"

"Sit with me, Bess," he said, almost as if he'd not heard her.

Elisabeth was not afraid, but she was confused as she gingerly sat on the cool ground. Rob joined her, grunting slightly. Whether on purpose or by accident, he sat on her gown, pinning her in place.

When he spoke again, he looked straight ahead, his voice low but sharp. "Whatsomever were ye thinking dining with his lordship?"

Is that what this is about? "Rob, it was a meal. We were surrounded by servants —"

"I see the way he leuks at ye. I ken what's on his mind."

"You misjudge him," she insisted. "Lord Buchanan is a good man, a righteous man —"

"Then ye mean to marry him."

"Marry? Have you forgotten I'm in mourning?"

"Nae." He turned to her. "But *ye* have." His hand circled her forearm, drawing her closer. "I've waited a lang time for ye, Bess. I'll not lose ye to anither."

When she saw the hardness in his features, the darkness in his eyes, fear began seeping into her heart as surely as the cold had begun seeping through her skirts. Yet she clung to her resolve. "If I'm to marry again, the

Almighty will choose my husband."

"Micht he not choose me?"

"I've never seen you in kirk," she reminded him even as he tightened his grip on her. "Not on all the Sundays we lived in Edinburgh."

He snorted. "This from a lass wha hails the moon."

"Not anymore," she said fervently. "I belong to God."

"Nae, Bess." He pulled her against his chest and held her there. "Ye belong to me."

She tried to wriggle free from his rough embrace. "Rob, please . . ."

But he was too strong for her. He pushed her back against the ground, the weight of his body almost more than she could bear. She could not move. She could not breathe.

"Stop it, Rob!" she cried, her voice thin, pinched.

Then his mouth was on hers, demanding a response.

Help me, Lord! Please, please. With great effort she finally escaped Rob's brutal kiss, her skin burning as her cheek scraped against the stubble of his beard.

But Rob did not relent. With his breath warming her ear, he made clear his intentions. "Ye'll not deny me, Bess. I've luved ye too lang and kenned ye too weel." He kissed the curve of her neck, hard, without tenderness or affection, then reached for her skirts.

"Nae, Rob!" She bucked against him, lifting her shoulders, trying to throw him off balance. "You do not . . . mean . . . this . . ."

"Aye, but I do," he growled, holding her down by the sheer bulk of him. "If I canna marry ye, then I'll have ye just the same."

"Please, Rob," she begged him, beginning to weep as he forced her knees apart. "Please . . . don't . . ."

He was no longer listening. He no longer cared.

But God was listening and cared very much. "Father!" she cried. "Father, don't let him hurt me . . ."

Rob cut her off. "Yer faither is *deid.*"

She drew a ragged breath. "But my heavenly Father is not."

Neither of them moved, though the wind roared and the thunder bore down on them.

Then, with his head turned, Rob finally released her and rose to his knees and then to his feet, while she hastily rearranged her gown, her hands trembling.

Rob stood with his back to her now. His rage appeared to be spent. Even in the darkness she could see the sloped line of his shoulders.

Standing, Elisabeth touched her face, her neck, certain she would find bruises in the morning. But she was not badly injured. She was not defiled. *Thank you, Father.*

Suddenly her knees felt weak, and her limbs

began to shake. Fresh tears slipped down her cheeks as she slowly backed away from Rob, her emotions spinning. Fear, relief, anger were all jumbled inside her.

For a moment she thought she might faint or be sick. More than anything she wanted to run, to put as much distance between them as she could. But her legs would not carry her yet. And there were things she had to say.

"You must leave at once," she told him, her voice raw with pain. "Not only Bell Hill. Not only Selkirk. You must leave Scotland and never return."

She heard nothing but the wind, whipping the grass round their feet.

Then he spoke. His words were low, broken, and filled with remorse. "I niver meant for it to happen, Bess. I niver meant to hurt ye."

She believed him. But it changed nothing.

"Listen to me, Rob." She lifted her head, feeling a bit stronger. "I'll not tell Lord Buchanan until you are well away. But I will tell him. And he will hunt you down unless you are beyond his reach."

Rob slowly turned, his face haggard. "Why, Bess? Why would ye spare me?"

"Because you were my friend once. And because the Lord spared me when I foolishly worshiped another."

The rain began at last. A few large drops, then more. In another minute they would both be soaked through.

"Go," she urged him, raising her voice above the steadily increasing patter. "Go to the Americas just as you planned. Start a new life."

He shook his head, not meeting her gaze. "I canna live without ye."

"But you must, Rob." She collected her hat and basket, her thoughts fixed on Halliwell's Close, on home. "You'll not be alone. The Lord will be with you."

He looked at her at last. "Are ye sure, Bess?"

"I am." She lifted her face to the heavens, letting the rain wash away her tears.

Sixty-Two

Cling to thy home! If there the meanest
shed
Yield thee a hearth and shelter for thy
head.

Leonidas of Tarentum

Marjory had never cared for thunder. Lord
John had often found it soothing, especially
at night when a low rumble traveled across
the hills, lulling him to sleep. But a hard rain
had followed this evening's thunder, and
Elisabeth was not yet home.

Glancing toward the window, Marjory fretted, "She should leave earlier now that
September is here."

"Aye, and start later in the morn," Anne
agreed, never looking up from the lace work
she'd brought with her.

Though Marjory did not have a candle-
stool to offer her, she mimicked the effect
with clear glasses of water on either side of a
tallow candle, allowing the women to work

into the evening hours. The glasses belonged to Jane Nicoll, who resided in one of the better houses on Back Row. A widow without issue, Jane had many more glasses on her sideboard and assured the Kerrs that two would never be missed.

Marjory had accepted them as graciously as she could, still learning how to receive instead of give. At first, feelings of resentment and shame had welled up inside her. But she was beginning to understand that those with plenty found joy in giving to those in need. And so she welcomed their generosity and reminded herself that every good gift came from the Lord. Had she not begged the Almighty to provide for her loved ones? To guard them and keep them safe? Well, here was Anne, newly married to a prosperous tailor. And Elisabeth with her eye on a wealthy admiral. And herself with the stalwart love of a good man.

Every day the Kerrs had eaten breakfast, dinner, tea, and supper and wanted for nothing because of God's provision. Aye, she could accept the gift of Jane's two glasses without embarrassment. If her pride was gone, was that not just as well?

At the sound of footsteps on the stair, Marjory sighed, relieved to have her daughter-in-law home. Elisabeth was moving slower than usual, Marjory noticed. Who wouldn't be weary after walking two miles in the rain?

She gave her turnip soup a final stir, then moved toward the entrance, calling out a cheerful greeting.

But as the door creaked open and Elisabeth entered with her head bowed, Marjory knew something was wrong. "What is it, Bess?"

When she looked up, Marjory nearly fainted at the sight. One of Elisabeth's cheeks was red and raw, and her lips were badly swollen. "My dear girl! Did you fall?"

Elisabeth shook her head and quietly closed the door, then lifted the white linen kerchief tucked round her neck

"Bess!" she cried softly. "Who did this to you?"

Tears spilled from her eyes. "R-rob," she managed to say.

Marjory gasped. "Rob MacPherson?" When Elisabeth nodded, Marjory's hands began to tremble. "I knew it, I knew it. Did I not say he was dangerous, Annie?"

Her cousin nodded, too shocked to speak.

"He did not violate me," Elisabeth said in a low voice. "But . . . he meant to."

"My poor, sweet Bess!" Marjory swallowed hard, her stomach lurching. "This is my fault. I should have told Lord Buchanan what sort of man he'd hired."

"Do not punish yourself, Cousin," Anne said gently, helping Elisabeth ease out of her gown. "None of us could have imagined such behavior from the man."

531

"I could have," Marjory said darkly, "and should have." She quickly filled the wash basin with hot water and added her treasured bar of lavender soap.

Still dressed in her chemise, Elisabeth began to dab at her body with a wet cloth, wincing everywhere the linen touched. Her arms, her chest, her neck, her shoulders. "By morn," she said in a thin voice, "I fear my bruises will look far worse. I pray my clothing will cover them all."

Marjory cautiously touched her cheek. "And what happened here?"

Elisabeth looked away. "His beard was . . . rough."

"Oh, Bess . . ." Marjory could hold back her tears no longer. She sank onto the nearest chair, then clasped Elisabeth's hand and stroked it over and over, rocking as she did. "I am so sorry . . . so very sorry . . ."

Anne sniffed, attending to her damp eyes and runny nose. "Come," she said at last, "let me dress you for bed." She slipped a clean nightgown over Elisabeth's head, then lightly draped a plaid round her shoulders. "Can you eat something?"

Elisabeth shook her head. "Tea perhaps." She sat beside Marjory at the oval table. "I was much . . . stronger . . . before. But on the walk home . . ."

"Of course," Marjory said. "We can only be brave so long. Still, you must have been very brave to make him stop."

" 'Twas the Lord's doing," Elisabeth said, "not mine." In halting words she described her terrible encounter, taking long drinks of tea whenever her throat grew parched.

When Elisabeth ran out of words, Anne stood and reached for her wool cape. "I shall call upon Reverend Brown tonight," she declared. "He will summon the sheriff in the morn and inform Lord Buchanan. By noon Rob MacPherson will be locked in the tolbooth —"

"Nae." Elisabeth's tone was quite firm. "I sent Rob away. Told him to leave Scotland and never return."

Anne looked at her aghast. "But he deserves to be punished!"

"Aye, and he will be," Elisabeth assured her. "Every time he thinks of me. Every time he remembers what he did. Every time he aches for his Highland home. Every time he sees my bruised face in his mind's eye. As to further chastisement, I leave that to the Almighty."

Anne fumed, "But Lord Buchanan —"

"Would kill him," Elisabeth said without hesitation. "And I cannot bear to have that on my conscience. Or on his lordship's. I'll stay home tomorrow and see to my wounds. That will buy Rob one day before I must explain to Lord Buchanan what happened to his tailor."

Marjory plucked at her apron strings, uncertain of her feelings. Proud of Elisabeth on the one hand, fearful for her on the other. "How do you know Rob MacPherson will not come looking for you again? The man cannot stay away from you, Bess."

"Where he is bound, a return trip would be difficult." Elisabeth rose, her tea having grown cold. "Just now sleep might be best."

Marjory was on her feet at once, shaking out the sheet on the hurlie bed. She smoothed it in place, then plumped up the thin feather pillow. "Come to bed, dearest."

When Elisabeth stretched out on the small bed, her long legs did not fit until she drew them up, knees to chin. Marjory draped first one plaid, then another across her daughter-in-law's bruised body and gently tucked her in like a child. And she *was* a child — her child — whom she loved with all her heart. "Sleep well, dear Bess."

"I will," she murmured and closed her eyes.

Marjory tiptoed away, motioning Anne to follow her. Their supper was brief, their exchanges mere whispers, and they parted company earlier than expected.

Standing at the door, Anne confessed, "I wish I could be there when Bess tells his lord-ship."

Marjory shuddered. "Not I. Whatever Bess may think, Lord Buchanan will not rest until justice is done."

Sixty-Three

He who tries to protect himself from
deception is often cheated, even when
most on his guard.

PLAUTUS

Jack paced the length of his drawing room,
staring out at the gray, wet morning. Rain
had fallen through the night and showed no
signs of abating. Last evening Elisabeth had
said, " 'Tis an easy walk." But now she was
climbing uphill in the rain. However accustomed she might be to traveling about in
any weather, her discomfort weighed on him.
Should he send the carriage for her? Or
would she fuss at him for worrying too much?

When he heard a brief knock at the doorway, Jack turned, hoping to find Elisabeth
standing there. Instead it was Roberts.

"Lord Buchanan, I've some rather unfortunate news for you. Unexpected as well."

Jack heard the tension in his voice. "Go on."

"I'm afraid our tailor has quit Bell Hill.

Without a word."

"Mr. MacPherson is . . . gone?" Jack frowned, uncertain whether to be concerned or grateful. "I trust he has not taken anything."

"Only what he brought with him, milord."

"Which was very little." Jack recalled Rob MacPherson arriving at his front door less than a fortnight ago with only a small bundle in his hands.

"He left his workroom tidy and his bed made," Roberts informed him. "The unfinished garment he was sewing is draped over a chair."

Jack exhaled, not knowing what to make of it. "Strange business, aye? I suppose I must see to another tailor. Someone from town." When the weather cleared, he would dispatch a letter to Michael Dalgliesh and seek a recommendation. For all his talents with a needle, Rob MacPherson was easily replaced.

His conscience prodded him. *Admit it, Jack. You're glad he's gone.* If it meant Mr. Mac-Pherson would no longer pursue Elisabeth, then aye. He was very glad.

Jack arranged to have breakfast in his study, then started for the hall. "And do let me know the moment Mrs. Kerr arrives."

Breakfast came and went. His mantel clock chimed eight times, then nine, then ten. Still no sign of Elisabeth. Jack tossed aside his household ledger with its rows of dull numbers and strode into the hall, thinking she'd arrived some time ago and Roberts had simply forgotten his request.

"Mrs. Pringle," he called out, catching sight of her at the far end of the corridor. "Kindly send Mrs. Kerr to my study."

The housekeeper hastened toward him, her expression troubled. "She's not here, milord."

"Not here?" He couldn't hide his dismay. "Do you imagine the ill weather has delayed her?"

"I cannot say, milord, though Mrs. Kerr has walked to and from Bell Hill on many a rainy day."

"You will let me know the minute — nae, the very second — she appears?"

Mrs. Pringle offered a nervous sort of nod, bobbing her head many times before she hurried off to her tasks.

Jack returned to his household accounts, only to abandon them a short time later, his powers of concentration having vanished. Just as Rob MacPherson had vanished. And now Elisabeth.

He stood at the window, willing her to come running up the walk, full of apologies, none of them necessary. Anything might have happened, he reminded himself. A crisis at Halliwell's Close. An ailing family member. A neighbor who needed her.

He refused to consider the possibility that Elisabeth too had quit Bell Hill without a word. Yet with each passing moment, the facts pointed in that direction.

Please, Bess. You cannot have run away with this man.

The thought made Jack's blood run cold. To lose her would be devastating enough. But he could not bear losing her to an ill-tempered, ill-mannered tradesman.

Then another possibility came to him, even more disturbing than the first. What if Elisabeth had not gone willingly? What if Rob MacPherson had simply taken her? Clansmen of old had abducted brides against their will. Who was to say this Highlander was above such a heinous crime?

Undone, Jack pressed his forehead to the window glazing. *Come to me, Bess. Let me know you are safe and well and nowhere near Rob MacPherson.*

When a man behind him cleared his throat, Jack spun round and was surprised to find Roberts standing in the doorway with Gibson.

Jack crossed the room to greet him in record time. "Have you news for me?"

"Aye, milord. I beg yer pardon for not being free to come sooner. I bring ye a message from Halliwell's Close. From Mrs. Kerr."

Jack steeled himself, preparing for the worst. "Mrs. Elisabeth Kerr?"

"Aye, milord. She's not weel this morn and

begs yer forgiveness for missing a day o' wark."

Relief washed over him like the rain falling on his gardens. "She's at home, then. She's . . ." *Safe. Bless you, Lord.* "But not well, you say?" Jack didn't like the sound of that. "Shall I summon a physician from Edinburgh?"

"Nae, nae. A day o' rest will set her to richts."

Jack studied his expression. "You are sure of this?"

"Verra sure, milord. Leuk for her early on the morrow."

"And have you heard our news at Bell Hill, Gibson?" Jack glanced at Roberts, who shook his head. "We've lost our tailor. Rob MacPherson took his leave rather abruptly. Mrs. Kerr might wish to know that."

"Aye." A light shone in Gibson's eyes. "She weel might."

Jack was awake, bathed, and dressed by seven o' the clock on Friday, anticipating Elisabeth's arrival. He'd sent Gibson home with an assortment of jams and teas from Mrs. Tudhope's stillroom, along with a brief note: *Wishing you well.* Not particularly clever, but at least it was sincere.

To keep his mind occupied, he worked on a stack of correspondence, signing each letter with a flourish. When he heard Elisabeth's voice in the hall soon after eight o' the clock, he left his quill on the blotter and quickly stood.

"Mrs. Kerr," he said, not caring if he sounded elated to see her. He *was* elated. "Come and tell me how you are feeling."

Elisabeth moved as gracefully as ever, though she kept her head bowed as she sat on the chair opposite his desk. "We must speak, milord. In private."

He closed the door after sending Mrs. Pringle off with strict orders not to tell the others. "I will not have my household thinking ill of Mrs. Kerr."

"Certainly not, milord."

When Jack returned to his desk, Elisabeth was seated with her gloved hands in her lap, still wearing a light wool cape draped round her shoulders and a cloth bonnet he'd not seen before. He didn't much care for it since the wide, protruding brim nearly covered her lovely face.

He considered sitting in his desk chair, then decided against it and instead sat next to Elisabeth. Whatever she had to share, a large wooden desk between them would not make it easier. He thought of a dozen questions, all of them inane, and so he simply waited for her to speak.

"Lord Jack," she began, "I am the reason you no longer have a tailor."

"Oh." He'd not expected that. "Why, Bess?"

Her voice was low, yet filled with conviction. "I asked him to leave Bell Hill."

A knot began forming inside him, twisting like a midshipman's hitch. "When did you last speak with Mr. MacPherson?"

"Wednesday eve. He was waiting for me on the road, not far down the hill, behind the large boulder."

The knot inside him drew tighter. "Did he intend to walk you home?"

"He did not."

Jack leaned closer, fearing what he could not see beneath her cape, beneath her hat. "Please, Bess. Please tell me he did not harm you."

She said nothing for a moment. Then she tugged on the ribbon that held her bonnet in place and let it slip into her lap. "He did not mean to hurt me. But he did."

Jack stared at the scarlet mark on her face, rage building inside him. "What . . . caused . . ."

"The stubble of his beard."

"Nae!" Jack shot out of his chair, startling them both. *"How . . . dare . . . he!"* He ground out the words, fighting for control, knowing Elisabeth needed his compassion. He forced himself to sit, to breathe, to think only of her. If he thought of Rob MacPherson, he would hurt everything he touched.

"Bess, Bess . . ." He took her hands in his,

though he could not look at her. "Forgive me."

"You are not to blame, milord." Her voice was low, the words broken.

"I am entirely to blame. I should never have engaged his services. I should never have allowed him to stay —"

"You couldn't know this would happen," she was quick to say. "In truth, I never saw him behave as he did Wednesday eve."

Jack swallowed with some difficulty. "Men are capable of terrible things when they do not get what they want."

"Aye," she said softly. Though her eyes glistened, she held her tears in check.

Jack was grateful, knowing her weeping would unleash his anger afresh. "Why did you not come to me at once?" he asked as gently as he could. "Surely you were not ashamed?"

Her eyes cleared, and her voice grew stronger. "Nae, Lord Jack. I was in pain."

He gripped her hands, then realized he was holding them too tightly. "I am no help at all," he said, frustrated with himself. Twenty-odd years on a ship filled with men had ill prepared him to comfort a woman. " 'Twas courageous of you, Bess, to ask him to leave Bell Hill."

"I did more than that," she confessed. "I asked him to leave Scotland."

Jack straightened in his chair, feeling the

knot tightening further. "Is there something you've not told me?"

"There is."

He could not form the words. "Did he . . ."

"He did not. Though he tried."

Jack closed his eyes, overwhelmed by the images flashing through his mind, each more terrible than the one before. *My poor Bess.* "What the man did is no less a crime."

"I know." She swallowed. "So I sent him somewhere you could not find him."

He looked at her, his every feature knotted in confusion. "Why, Bess?"

"Because you would have killed him."

Her words shocked him. Not because she said them, but because they were true.

Elisabeth held him with her gaze. Her clear, warm, blue gaze. "It was not Rob Mac-Pherson I wanted to spare, milord. It was you."

Oh my sweet Bess. He bent forward and kissed her gloved hands. "How is it you know me so well?"

"I know you are an admiral," she said softly, "and therefore well accustomed to thrusting swords into the hearts of your enemies."

She knew him very well indeed. When he rose, a new resolve filled him like wind swelling a topsail. "No man will ever threaten you again. I will keep you safe at all hours and at all costs."

Elisabeth tipped her head. "But how —"

"Belda is now at your disposal. Ride her to and from Bell Hill and anywhere else you choose. I will see to her upkeep in a stable near Halliwell's Close."

For the first time that morning, hope shone in her eyes. "Truly, milord?"

"Truly." It felt good to offer her more than sympathy, though she deserved a large measure of that too. "Every man in my employ will be sworn to protect you —"

"As well as the other women of Bell Hill," she insisted.

How like you, Bess, to think of others. "Aye," he promised her. "Another tailor will be engaged, though he'll not reside here."

"Not all tailors are like Rob MacPherson," Elisabeth said gently. " 'Twas his obsession, not his profession, that made him dangerous."

"Indeed." Jack exhaled, as if breath alone might drive out the fear, the anger, the guilt that lingered inside him. "Yesterday morn I imagined you might have gone with him."

"Never, milord," she whispered. "My heart is here at Bell Hill."

He lifted her hands and lightly kissed them once more. "I am glad, Bess." *More than you know. More than I can say.*

Sixty-Four

There is a secret drawer in every woman's heart.

VICTOR HUGO

Elisabeth's fingers trembled as she tried to pin another cuff in place. *My heart is here at Bell Hill.* Without meaning to, she'd all but confessed her fond affection for his lordship. No wonder he'd responded as he did. The tenderness in his voice, the warmth of his touch, the attentiveness of his gaze left little doubt of his mutual regard.

But 'tis too soon, milord. Much too soon.

She'd retreated to her workroom in haste, needing time to sort through her feelings. *Keep thy heart with all diligence.* Aye, she must. The only two men who'd ever professed to love her had also wounded her, savagely. She'd not offer her heart again until she was sure — *very* sure — he was not simply a good man but also the man of God's choosing.

Elisabeth looked up at the window, a golden yellow square spilling light into the room. *Is Lord Buchanan that man, Father?* Silence was all she heard, though deep inside she knew the answer: *Wait, my daughter. Wait.*

She pressed on with her sewing, grateful to have work that occupied her hands if not always her thoughts. At least in her quiet workroom she was free to abandon the too-large bonnet, on loan from Mrs. Tait. In another day or two the unsightly mark on her cheek would disappear. Certainly by the Sabbath, or she'd be forced to wear the borrowed bonnet all day.

"Och!" Sally flung open the door unannounced, eyes and mouth gaping. "He *did* harm ye! That *scoonrel.*"

Elisabeth rose to her feet even as her heart sank. If Sally knew, so did the entire household.

Still catching her breath, Sally blurted out, "His lordship called us a' into the dining hall. Told us ye'd been accosted by a man on the road hame and that we were to watch for strangers." The maidservant drew closer, studying Elisabeth's cheek. "Comfrey leaves," she said. "Mr. Richardson can pluck ye some."

"Such a remedy would be most welcome." Elisabeth sat once more, then tugged on Sally's apron, drawing the lass into the chair next to hers. "Did Lord Buchanan tell you anything else?"

Sally nodded vigorously. "Said we were to treat ye with respect. And to leuk oot for ye. Which I'm happy to do."

"Bless you," Elisabeth murmured. He'd not mentioned Rob's name, then.

Sally went on, "The men o' the hoose were vexed whan they heard what happened. A' the lads have sworn to protect ye and keep ye safe." She sighed dramatically. "I wouldna mind if Johnnie Hume did the same for me."

Elisabeth pictured the young blacksmith on Water Row, his muscular arms wielding sledgehammers with ease. "Perhaps you'll have your wish someday, lass."

"Aye." Sally winked at her, then jumped up from the chair and quit the room as swiftly as she'd arrived.

Elisabeth watched her go, then resumed her sewing, wondering if other visitors might come by to assess the damage. However embarrassing to have the household see her thus, Elisabeth was grateful they knew of her injury. Better to have such things discussed openly than whispered behind doors.

The path to her workroom was soon well trod. Mrs. Pringle brought a large flatiron. "A fine weapon, should the lout make another appearance." Mr. Richardson did indeed find comfrey growing in a shady spot not far from the gardens and produced an abundance of fresh leaves to press against her wound. Mrs.

Tudhope came in for a brief commiseration, leaving one of Elisabeth's favorite apple tarts in her wake. And late in the afternoon, Hyslop stopped in to assure her that Belda would be saddled and ready promptly at five o' the clock.

"Five?" Elisabeth asked, wrinkling her brow. "Not six?"

"His lordship's orders," the head coachman said.

When the hour came, Lord Jack himself arrived to escort her to the stables. He was freshly shaved and dressed in his black riding clothes, which fit his long legs and broad shoulders to perfection. Sewn by a tailor in London, she supposed. Or Paris. How easy it was to forget that Lord Jack had traveled the world.

"You'll be home well before sunset," he assured her, leading her across the grassy expanse north of the house. Though the air was clear and dry, the ground beneath their feet was still spongy from two days' rain. "I've arranged for the mare to be boarded each night in Mr. Riddell's stables on Kirk Wynd."

"You're most kind." She looked up at him as they walked, his rugged face framed by the rosy orange sky. "The household has been quite . . . understanding."

He slowed his steps, his gaze locked with hers. "You did not mind, then? Perhaps I should have asked your permission first."

" 'Tis best they heard the truth from you," she told him, longing to say more. *Because you are trustworthy. And because you are respected by all who know you.*

A stone's throw from the stables, Lord Jack stopped altogether, then turned toward her. "I think you'll find the men of Bell Hill eager to guard your safety, Bess."

She'd already witnessed their loyalty in action. "I cannot step into the servants' hall without a footman watching over me," she admitted, lifting her face, no longer caring if he saw her wound. "However can I thank you, milord?"

His answer was swift. "By riding home without delay." Then he leaned closer, capturing her hands. "And by letting me take care of you, as I should have from the first."

Elisabeth paused, her skin warming beneath his gaze. "I've always felt safe here," she finally said. "Though I am not a woman who needs looking after. Truly, I can fend for myself —"

"Can you?" His voice was low, but she heard the faint edge of frustration. "Had I insisted you ride home in my carriage on Wednesday eve, you'd not be hiding behind this ugly bonnet." He released her hand long enough to pull open the ribbon and lift the bonnet from her head. Then he examined her cheek, the touch of his gloved finger exceptionally tender.

"Would that I might remove his mark as easily as I dispensed with your hat," he murmured. "Time and the Lord's hand will manage what I cannot."

Oh, Lord Jack. With him standing so near, his clean, masculine scent overwhelmed her.

"Come, Bess," he said softly, "or we'll lose our light."

She moved forward, following his lead. "You are riding with me?"

"I am." He was already waving over the stable lad, who had Janvier in hand. Hyslop was not far behind him, bringing Belda. Lord Jack lifted Elisabeth into the sidesaddle with ease, then mounted Janvier in a single sweeping motion. "Shall we?"

They trotted side by side along the tree-lined drive, a warm breeze moving through the branches, fluttering the leaves overhead. In another month the elms and maples would exchange their green garments for yellow ones, the oaks for bright reddish brown. Summer would truly be at an end. But not yet.

As they neared the road to Selkirk and the massive boulder loomed ahead, Bess gripped the pommel more firmly, aware of Lord Jack watching her. Without a word he moved slightly ahead of her, blocking her view until the road straightened again and the boulder, with all its grim memories, was well behind them.

She rode on, feeling her heart ease its

frantic pace and her breathing return to normal. *You're not alone, Bess. The worst is over.*

Lord Jack waited until she was beside him again, then asked amiably, "What can you tell me of Michaelmas? For we paid scant attention to such festivals aboard ship."

She offered him a shaky smile, releasing the last of her fears. "Michael is the patron saint of the sea and of horses as well, yet you've never paid him homage?"

"Nae, madam. Though for the sake of Janvier and Belda, I might reconsider. What rituals must I endure?"

"I cannot say what the good folk of Selkirk may do, but Highland women gather carrots on the Sunday afternoon before Michaelmas."

"Laboring on the Sabbath?" he said dryly. "Won't Reverend Brown be pleased to hear that?"

"Since Michaelmas Eve falls on Sunday this year, the hearth will be put to use too," she informed him. "While the women are baking into the wee hours of the night, the men are lifting horses from their neighbors."

"Lifting?" Lord Jack frowned at her. "Do you mean they pick them up?"

"I mean they steal them," Elisabeth said matter-of-factly. " 'Tis an ancient privilege but lasts only 'til the afternoon of Michaelmas itself, when the horses are returned unharmed."

"You are certain about that part?"

"Have no fear, milord," she assured him. "This is the Borderland. If the old rituals ever took root here, they've long been forgotten." A sad truth, she realized, suddenly missing home. Would her mother ride round the kirkyard on Michaelmas with Ben Cromar's thick arms holding her tightly to his chest? Would they give each other gifts according to the custom? And sing the Song of Michael?

As they neared the foot of Bell Hill, Elisabeth recited the words she knew so well. "Jewel of my heart, God's shepherd thou art."

"Beg pardon?" Lord Jack's question brought her back to the present.

" 'Tis a song for Michaelmas," she hastened to explain. "Offered as folk proceed on horseback round the kirkyard, following the course of the sun."

"Shall we revive all the old traditions for our Michaelmas celebration, then?"

"Not all, milord," she said, trying very hard not to blush. The Night of Michael was known not only for its dance and song but also for its merrymaking and lovemaking. Elisabeth intended to keep such scandalous details to herself. "I know you do not care for dancing, but I hope you'll not mind a lively night of music."

"On the contrary," Lord Jack replied, smiling rather broadly. "I am counting on it."

SIXTY-FIVE

Those move easiest who have learn'd to
dance.

ALEXANDER POPE

"Tis better if you do not count aloud,
milord."

Jack shot the dancing master a murderous
look. "Would you prefer I stepped on the
lady's toes?"

"I would not," Mr. Fowles agreed, "though
women are rather accustomed to it. But
counting aloud will mark you as unrefined,
and we cannot have that, milord."

Jack grumbled under his breath, keeping
the numbers to himself. *One and two and
three. Four and five and six.* At least he'd
sworn the dancing master to secrecy. No one
but Dickson knew of his thrice-weekly visits
to a drawing room in Galashiels where Mr.
Fowles, a small man with a large, beaklike
nose, offered private instruction on the

country dances most Scotsmen were taught as lads.

However old he might be, Jack was determined to learn the steps in time for Michaelmas. A fortnight remained. And still he was counting. *One and two and three.*

A lone fiddler perched in the corner of the sparsely furnished room, and the thin carpet was rolled back to reveal an unpolished wooden floor. While the fiddler sawed away, Mr. Fowles served as Jack's partner, mirroring each step. It would be challenging enough to dance longwise, with men on either side of him, but to cross to the women's side and then progress down the row behind them — well, boarding a Spanish vessel with a sword in one hand and a dagger in the other was child's play compared to this.

"Bow, if you please, then step forward," Mr. Fowles intoned. "Take your partner's hand and circle round. That's it, milord. Now switch hands and circle the other direction."

Jack followed his commands to the letter, resisting the urge to gloat. *Pride goeth before destruction,* he reminded himself, silently counting in time to the music. *Four and five and six.*

Mr. Fowles continued, "Process to her side of the line as she returns the favor, then walk behind the woman who was standing next to her."

The woman in question was a wooden chair. Perhaps that was for the best.

"Meet your partner again in the center," the dancing master said, "then circle round her, this time without taking her hand."

"But what am I supposed to do instead?" Jack demanded.

"Nothing, sir. Let your hands hang loosely by your side. Now step to the center, lift up on the balls of your feet, and step back."

One moment Jack was dancing with another man's partner, circumnavigating the stiff-backed chair. Then he was promenading his own partner, the diminutive Mr. Fowles, as they walked between two imaginary lines of dancers, who were surely laughing up their sleeves. Jack could almost hear them. Or was that the fiddler?

Mercy finally prevailed, and their hourlong lesson ended.

Mr. Fowles was in a generous mood. "You are improving, milord. A few more sessions, and you'll be the talk of the ball."

Jack snorted. "I fear that is certain to be the case." He paid the man, then reached for his hat. "Wednesday noon?"

Mr. Fowles nodded, a twinkle in his eye. "I shall have a surprise for you."

Jack did not care for surprises. Well, except for the ones he sprang on others.

When he found a half-dozen maidservants

waiting for him in Mr. Fowles's drawing room on Wednesday, he was more than surprised. He was mortified.

Jack drew the dancing master aside. "I am not ready," he insisted. "Furthermore, I thought our lessons were to be a secret."

Mr. Fowles glanced at the bevy of wide-eyed lasses across the room. "You're not known in this parish, milord. I told them you were a Frenchman who spoke no English. As long as you do not count aloud, they'll be none the wiser."

Jack had no choice but to join them in forming two lines and let the music begin. After each awkward misstep, each wrong turn, he thought of Elisabeth and tried harder. The maidservants were kind to him, guiding him through the precise movements of each dance, until by hour's end he felt a flush of confidence. Might he manage it after all?

He rode the five miles home in record time, relishing the bright September weather. If Michaelmas were half so fair, the evening would be a success. *Might you throw convention to the wind and dance with me, Bess?* He could hardly wait to see her face. Of course, that was true on any occasion.

At three o' the clock Jack found her workroom vacant. A finished gown hung on the wall, but there was no sign of Elisabeth. Even

Charbon wasn't curled up in his usual spot by the hearth.

Jack strode through the house, glancing here and there, not truly concerned. If Elisabeth was on his property, she was safe. Had he not made it clear to the entire household, and the menservants in particular, what he required of them?

"As a widow and a Highlander, Mrs. Kerr is particularly vulnerable," he'd told them, then outlined the measures he wished them to take. Keep an eye on her by day. Bolt the exterior doors at night. Question any strangers who wander onto the property. Note who bothers her at kirk and at market. Listen for ill news on the wind. "She is never to feel imprisoned here, but I do wish her to feel secure."

At the moment Jack simply wished to find her.

When he heard her voice floating down the stair from the upper hall, he took the steps two at a time. Rather noisily, it seemed, for she was looking his direction when he emerged into the hallway.

"Mrs. Kerr," he said with a gallant bow. "And Mrs. Pringle. I can only assume you two are making plans for Michaelmas."

"We are, milord." Elisabeth held out a rough sketch of the drawing room. "With so many guests coming, I'm afraid your furniture will need to be relocated. I know you are not partial to dancing —"

"Oh, but there must be dancing," he protested. "Isn't that what Michaelmas Night is known for?"

Elisabeth smiled. "Among other things, milord."

Friday's dancing lesson was a revelation: Jack forgot to count yet still remembered all the steps. The following Monday he almost enjoyed himself. *Almost.* And on Wednesday next, Mr. Fowles broke into spontaneous applause.

"You are ready, milord. And with five days to spare."

Jack paid the man his due and bade him farewell. Ready or not, Michaelmas was nigh upon them.

He returned home from Galashiels to find Bell Hill all but dismantled. The drawing room was reduced to long rows of seats and a vast expanse of bare floor. The dining room had more chairs than he could number at a cursory glance, with freshly polished silver displayed up and down the long table. Every maidservant had a dusting cloth in hand and every manservant a broom as they worked their way from room to room, cleaning a house that was already spotless.

"They mean to bless you," Mrs. Pringle explained, a look of satisfaction on her face. Then she nodded toward his desk. "Two letters arrived in your absence, milord."

He had only to look at the handwriting to know the correspondents. "Have Mrs. Kerr come to my study in a quarter hour."

"Very good, sir." His housekeeper almost smiled. "Aren't you pleased I brought her to your study last May?"

"Aye, Mrs. Pringle." *Very pleased.*

He was downing a cup of tea when Elisabeth appeared. She glanced over her shoulder, perhaps to make certain the door was ajar, then sat in front of his desk and folded her hands in her lap. "What is it, Lord Jack? You've a rather serious look on your face."

"I've news you'll want to hear," he confessed, reaching for the two letters sent by men well paid to do his bidding. "You ordered Mr. MacPherson to leave Scotland, aye? You'll be glad to know he did precisely that. On Monday last he boarded a ship in Liverpool bound for the Americas."

When a flicker of surprise did not cross her features, Jack wondered if Elisabeth already knew of Rob's destination. "He told you his plans?"

"He did," she confessed.

"And he expected you to join him?"

She lowered her gaze. "Aye."

Jack longed to reach across his desk and touch her cheek, now fully healed. "I thank God you refused him, Bess." *For your sake. And for mine.*

"I could never have done otherwise," she said softly, then lifted her head. "Does the second letter concern me as well?"

"It does." He glanced at the correspondence in his hands. "According to Archie Gordon, the fellow I dispatched to the Highlands, Ben Cromar has not harmed your mother in any visible way since I last saw her. Furthermore, the Sheriff of Aberdeen has been alerted, and a few of your old neighbors, Mrs. MacKindlay, the midwife, among them, have been discreetly charged to watch over her and guard her safety."

"For which, no doubt, they've been generously compensated."

"Indeed, they have." Jack studied her for a moment, uncertain of her meaning. "Does my wealth offend you, Bess?"

"Nae, it astounds me." Her expression was sincere, her words more so. "You are more generous than any gentleman I have ever known."

Then marry me, Bess. The words were on the tip of his tongue. *Say it, Jack. Go on.*

Youth and beauty were easily found among the gentlewomen of the land but to also find godliness and charity? Wisdom and purity? Strength and humility? He would gladly wait for such a woman. Though the new year did seem a very long way off.

Jack walked round his desk, eying her mourning gown, thinking to test the waters.

"When the seventeenth of January comes and you are free to wear any color you like, I am curious what you'll choose."

She rose, the soft contours of her face glowing in the afternoon light. "I'm rather partial to lavender."

He stood as close as he dared. "Both the scent and the shade?" When she nodded, he tucked away the information for future reference. "A feminine color, signifying devotion. I shall look forward to seeing you wear it."

A smile played at the corners of her mouth. "Shall you indeed, milord?" At the sound of footsteps in the hall, she stepped back. "Then I hope you are a patient man."

"Oh, very patient," he assured her, mentally counting the time that remained.

Three months and twenty-four days, Bess. And then, if you'll have me, if God wills it, you'll be mine.

Sixty-Six

Sowe Carrets in your Gardens, and humbly
praise God for them, as for a singular and
great blessing.

RICHARD GARDINER

Marjory blinked at Elisabeth. "We're to pick
carrots? On the Sabbath?"

Her daughter-in-law laughed, slipping on a
pair of tattered gloves suitable only for
gardening. "If Mrs. Thorburn will not mind."

"And if Reverend Brown will not notice,"
Marjory added rather sternly.

Once Elisabeth convinced her the Michaelmas Eve tradition was embraced by Highland
ministers of old and would in no way dis-
honor the Lord, Marjory gave in. "But have
not all the root vegetables been harvested by
now?"

"There's always a stray or two among the
weeds, waiting to be yanked free." Clasping
Marjory by the hand, Elisabeth pulled her
out of the upholstered chair.

"Now *I* feel like a carrot," Marjory chided her. Since they had no proper spade for digging, she dropped a wooden fork into her apron pocket, then led the way down the stair, feeling rather ridiculous. Still, if it pleased Elisabeth, what harm was there?

The afternoon sky was pale gray with a thin layer of clouds stretched from east to west. Marjory did not sense rain in the air, though it felt cooler than when they'd hurried off to kirk that morning. She'd thrown a cape over her shoulders for their outing and was grateful for it now as they headed for Mrs. Thorburn's garden.

"Not much here, I'm afraid." Marjory treaded gently round the vegetable beds, looking for the telltale foliage: a frothy burst of tiny green leaves.

"Ah." Elisabeth crouched down, then began tugging at a neglected carrot, grasping it with both hands. " 'Tis a custom meant to assure a woman will have children," she said, then smiled as an enormous carrot was unearthed. "See? Chubby as a wee bairn."

Marjory eyed her lumpy harvest. "Is such a thing ill luck or good?"

"Very good," Elisabeth assured her, "although children are a gift of the Lord and not of the garden."

Now that she understood the purpose, Marjory ceased her digging. "Bess, I'm far too old to bear a child."

"But the perfect age to help raise one someday," her daughter-in-law insisted. "Come, see what your bit of foliage yields."

Wanting to be agreeable, Marjory dug and yanked and dug some more until a forked root with not one but two sturdy carrots broke through the soil. They could represent Donald and Andrew, Marjory supposed. Or would she hold Elisabeth's children when the time came?

She glanced at her daughter-in-law, bursting with health and vigor. Aye, if Elisabeth were to remarry, she might well bear a child or two, though she'd not conceived during the years she was married to Donald. Still, Marjory could not find fault with Elisabeth. Not after all the lass had done to care for her, provide for her. Nor could she blame the Almighty, who knew best in such things — nae, in all things.

Michaelmas carrots in hand, including one for Anne to present to Michael, Elisabeth planted pennies in the soil for Mrs. Thorburn's children to discover, then walked Marjory home, chanting a rhyme that made them both laugh.

It is myself that has the carrot.
Whoever he be
that would win it from me.

"I daresay Lord Buchanan would gladly

claim your carrot," Marjory observed.

"Unless Rosalind Murray offers him one first." Elisabeth placed their harvest on the dining room table, her smile fading. "The Murrays are on his lordship's guest list for tomorrow night's Michaelmas feast. I can only imagine the gown Rosalind will wear. And the jewels. And the fine perfume."

Marjory heard the resignation in her daughter-in-law's voice and hastened to assure her, "Lord Buchanan is not a gentleman whose head is turned by pretty clothes."

Elisabeth lifted her cape from her shoulders. "But Rosalind is quite clever and has traveled the Continent."

"Elisabeth Kerr," Marjory chided her, "I've never met a lass more clever than you. Now suppose we get on with Michaelmas Eve and leave Michaelmas Night in God's hands, aye?"

"Very well." Elisabeth tied on an apron. "To our bannock, then."

She moistened ground oatmeal with ewe's milk, then added berries, seeds, and wild honey, and formed it into a circle. "For eternity," she explained before beginning work on two smaller bannocks. "These are to honor the loved ones we've lost since Michaelmas last. Come, Marjory, and help me prepare the dough as we say their names."

Marjory pressed her hands into the mealy mixture. "Donald," she whispered, kneading the dough as she remembered the babe, the lad, the young man, the gentleman whom she'd loved almost more than her own husband. Her throat tightened further as she named aloud her second son. "Andrew," she said, thinking of her little soldier marching about the nursery, then round Tweedsford's gardens, then up and down the streets of Edinburgh, and finally across the battlefield at Falkirk. Elisabeth spoke their names with her, kneaded the dough beside her, and helped her give them each a unique shape.

"I am not sure I can eat them," Marjory confessed.

"Not to worry," Elisabeth said, brushing the flour from her hands. "They're meant to be given to the poor who have no bread of their own."

While the bannocks browned on the hearth, Marjory prepared a rich mutton broth for supper, eying their fat carrots. When she asked Elisabeth if the vegetables might be added to her soup pot, the answer was swift and sure.

"Nae!" Elisabeth pretended to be shocked. " 'Tis a Michaelmas gift for your beloved."

A carrot? Marjory hid her smile. *Won't Gibson be delighted?*

Under Elisabeth's watchful eye, Marjory coated their Michaelmas bannock with a caudle of flour and cream, eggs and sugar. "Three times," Elisabeth said, "for Father,

Son, and Spirit."

After the bannock was placed back on the fire to finish baking, Elisabeth washed her hands, then slipped on her cape. "I am off to Mr. Riddell's stables to be certain Belda is safe."

"Safe?" Marjory echoed. "Why would you worry about a mare?"

" 'Tis Michaelmas Eve," Elisabeth reminded her. "Anything might happen, especially where horses are concerned."

She was gone before Marjory could offer any objection. Not that she would have. The stables were a two-minute walk up Kirk Wynd. If Elisabeth would sleep better knowing Lord Buchanan's mare was secure, Marjory was happy for her to go.

But the house was suddenly very quiet, and she was left with nothing but her thoughts.

Marjory walked from one corner to the other, as she had on the night they'd arrived, when she'd measured Anne's small house and fretted over their living arrangements. *We shall all live in one room.* Aye, so they had.

Come Martinmas, when accounts were settled, the rent for this house would become Marjory's responsibility. Until then she would make a home for Elisabeth, guarding her from the Rob MacPhersons of the world.

Wasn't that what Donald would have wanted?

Marjory sank onto the upholstered chair,

no longer sure what her late son expected of her. He'd played the part of the doting heir, all the while sullying their family's name in the closes and wynds of Edinburgh. He'd also broken his wife's heart, reaching for other women who couldn't hold a candle to her. Yet when he'd departed Edinburgh, Lord Donald had made one wish quite clear: *May I count on you to look after Elisabeth?*

Marjory stared at the dying coals in the hearth. *What can I do for her, Lord? How may I see her well cared for?*

The answer rose in her heart like the sun. *Let her marry Lord Buchanan now.*

"Aye," she breathed into the quiet room.

What possible advantage could there be to waiting until January? Out of sheer necessity young widows often remarried mere months after losing their husbands. Such haste was frowned upon only in the very highest levels of society. And hadn't Saint Paul himself said of widows, "Let them marry"?

"Then let them marry," Marjory said aloud. There were no impediments she could think of. Lord Buchanan was rich and surely desirous of a family. Elisabeth was beautiful and in need of a husband.

The only thing required was a proposal. Gentleman that he was, Lord Buchanan would never cut short Elisabeth's time of mourning. But *she* could.

And stop Rosalind Murray in her tracks.

Marjory couldn't bear to sit, so eager was she to spill out her plans. She darted to the window, then the hearth, then the door. Might she seek out her daughter-in-law returning from the stables? Nae, such details could never be discussed on the street. No one must know until the deed was done, lest Lord Buchanan refuse Elisabeth.

Marjory blanched at the very idea. *Nae, nae, he loves her.* She was certain of it.

Moments later when Elisabeth crossed the threshold, Marjory practically dragged her to a chair beside the dining table and plunked her down without ceremony.

"Now then, Bess," she said, sitting across from her, "it is time you found a home of your own."

Elisabeth looked round. "But this is our home."

"More than a home," Marjory said firmly. "A husband."

Her eyes widened. "Whatever do you mean? I cannot think of marriage when I am in mourning —"

"Listen to me, Bess." Marjory clasped her daughter-in-law's hands in hers. "You have more than honored my son's memory these many months."

"Aye, but, Marjory —"

"We must look to your future now. God has surely brought Lord Buchanan into your life for a reason."

"Lord Buchanan?" Elisabeth tried to stand, but Marjory held her in place. "Dearest, he has not asked for my hand —"

"Only because he wishes to honor the rules of society."

Elisabeth shook her head. "I believe he means to honor you."

"Well, then." Marjory released her and sat back, triumphant. "If *I* am the only impediment, you have my permission to marry as soon as ever the banns may be read in the kirk three Sabbaths in a row."

Elisabeth shook her head, disbelief written across her features. "How can I tell Lord Buchanan such a thing without seeming presumptuous? The man has never even mentioned marriage."

Marjory couldn't keep from smiling. "That is why *you* must be the one to broach the subject."

Sixty-Seven

'Tis expectation makes a blessing dear.

Sir John Suckling

Elisabeth stared at her mother-in-law, trying to grasp what she was suggesting. "You want me to *propose* to Lord Buchanan?"

"At the very least, present yourself to him," Marjory said, her hazel eyes aglow. "Let him know of your willingness to end your time of mourning. He will not move forward until you do."

Move forward. Elisabeth looked down at her plain black dress. Was she ready to drape herself in blues and greens, reds and purples, telling the world she no longer mourned the man she'd once loved with all her heart?

Oh, my Donald, if only I might ask you.

But her husband was gone. Her heart alone held the answer.

Elisabeth met Marjory's gaze and prayed for the right words to say. "You must know how I cherish the memory of your son," she

571

told her, wanting to dispel any doubt in her mother-in-law's mind.

Marjory touched her cheek. "I do, Bess."

"And yet you are willing to let me go?"

"How can I not? You've been so very faithful. To Donald and to me." Marjory's lower lip began to tremble. "I cannot imagine the last year without you by my side."

"Nor can I." Elisabeth leaned forward and gathered her mother-in-law in her arms. "Whatever happens, I will see you well cared for, dear Marjory."

"I know, I know . . ." The rest of her words were muffled against Elisabeth's shoulder.

After a quiet, tender moment, they eased apart. "There's something I've not told you," Marjory confessed. "It is about Lord Buchanan."

Elisabeth's heart skipped a beat. "Oh?"

"According to Reverend Brown, his lordship is a distant relative on Lord John's side of the family."

Elisabeth let the words sink in. "Lord Buchanan is our kinsman?"

"Not by blood," Marjory assured her, "but certainly by marriage, however long ago. Because of that slender tie, Reverend Brown thought we might prevail upon his lordship to provide a small income for us. But I'd hoped for more than mere silver." She stood and moved to the hearth. "I asked the reverend to keep this discovery to himself. Even

Lord Buchanan may not yet be aware of it."

Elisabeth watched her measure the tea leaves, then pour hot water into a crockery pot. "You've had your eye on him from the first, haven't you?"

Marjory smiled. "Not for myself, of course. My heart has been engaged elsewhere for some time. But for you, aye." She rejoined her at the oval table, bearing a wooden tray with cups and spoons, honey and milk, and the steaming pot with its fragrant brew. "I've given this some thought, Bess, and have decided the very best time to approach his lordship is tomorrow night after the Michaelmas feast at Bell Hill."

Overcome, Elisabeth sank back against her chair. "So soon?"

"Remember the words of Shakespeare," Marjory cautioned her. "Delays have dangerous ends." She stirred honey into her tea, frowning. "What if Rob MacPherson leaped from the ship before it sailed and is even now bound for Selkirk? Or what if Lord Buchanan decides Rosalind Murray would make a fine wife, especially since she is free to marry him at once?"

Elisabeth didn't like the sound of either one of them, the second especially. "What have you in mind, Marjory?"

Her mother-in-law's response was swift and decisive. "When the festivities are drawing to a close, slip down the stair to your workroom and bathe from head to toe, using my lavender soap. Brush your hair until it shines and place Annie's silver comb where it will show to best advantage. Then dress in the lavender gown my son bought for you —"

Elisabeth gasped. "Marjory, I couldn't!"

"Aye, you could," she insisted. "Lord Buchanan has never seen you wearing anything but black. 'Tis time he viewed you as a beautiful and marriageable young lady. Not as a poor widow who sews dresses for his servants."

Elisabeth glanced toward her leather trunk, picturing the folded gown inside. " 'Twill need to be aired and ironed . . ."

"Easily managed," Marjory promised. "Gibson and I will wrap your gown in a sheet, lay it out in a cart, and deliver it to your workroom tomorrow, such that none will be the wiser."

In spite of her qualms, Elisabeth smiled. "You really have thought of everything."

"The hour matters most of all," Marjory told her. "Long after supper, when his lordship is well sated and his guests have departed for home, you must speak with him in private."

Elisabeth's eyes widened. "You cannot mean in his bedchamber?"

Marjory paused, as if considering it, then agreed, "Nae, 'twould not be proper. But you must approach him in a secluded spot where you are not likely to be interrupted."

Elisabeth knew the very place. "His study," she said. "Sally once told me Lord Buchanan often ends his evenings seated by the fire."

Marjory sipped her tea in silence. "Aye," she finally said. "Once you're certain he's alone, quietly enter the room and present yourself to him. A deep curtsy and your lovely gown will speak volumes. Once he understands you are no longer in mourning, he will surely propose marriage in short order."

Can it be as simple as that? Elisabeth pressed a hand to her fluttery stomach, imagining what she might say, what he might do, how things would end.

Do I want this? 'Twas the greater question. Better a peaceful widow than a heartbroken wife. Yet Lord Jack was surely different than Donald or Rob. He'd never gazed at other women in her presence, let alone seduced them. Nor had he raised his voice against her, let alone his hand.

If he welcomed her proposal, they might soon be married. But if he misunderstood her, if he refused her, if he preferred Rosalind Murray, with her title and her wealth . . .

Elisabeth's courage began to falter. "Oh, Marjory, are you certain?"

"I am," she answered without hesitation. "With Rosalind in the wings, we cannot wait until January."

Elisabeth nodded, finally convinced as well.

"I shall follow your instructions to the letter."

"And may God bless you for it." Marjory glanced at the window, hearing voices on the street below. "Until then, not a word to anyone, Bess."

Sixty-Eight

Oh, thou art fairer than the evening air,
Clad in the beauty of a thousand stars.

CHRISTOPHER MARLOWE

Jack stood at the edge of his rose garden, smiling up at the twilit sky, waiting.

Behind him in the dining room, Mrs. Pringle was giving orders. He could hear her firm, steady voice floating through the open windows, putting everyone and everything in its place. By the time his first guests appeared in the entrance hall, Bell Hill would be ready to welcome them.

"She's here, milord."

Jack turned with a grateful nod, then strode past the footman, hoping he might have a moment alone with her in the drawing room. He'd not seen her since yesterday morning at kirk, when she'd promised him a Michaelmas surprise. Of course, his own surprise for her would come when the musicians struck the first note.

Jack swept through the open doors with a jaunty step. *One and two and three.*

When he entered the drawing room, Elisabeth turned before he said her name. "There you are, Lord Jack." She smiled, curtsied, and stole his heart, all in a trice. "The Dalglieshes will be along shortly."

Even now he did not have Elisabeth to himself. Marjory and Gibson were standing with her, the women neatly if soberly attired in black, and Gibson wearing a proper coat and waistcoat. Borrowed from his employer perhaps. "You look very well, Gibson," Jack told him, though Marjory was the one who beamed at the compliment.

Elisabeth appeared to be hiding something behind her back. "If you'll excuse me, I must speak briefly with Mrs. Pringle," she said, then swept round him such that he could not see what she held in her hands. "I'll not be a moment, milord."

How very mysterious. Though he did not care for surprises, this one held some promise.

"Will you have your monthly supper tomorrow eve?" Marjory inquired. "Or shall your Michaelmas celebration suffice for September?"

"Mrs. Tudhope would serve my head on a platter if I required large banquets two nights in a row," he admitted, "though I shall make it up to the household at Yuletide."

When Elisabeth returned, her cheeks were flush with color. "You are wanted in the entrance hall, milord. The Chisholms of Broadmeadows have arrived."

Jack offered his arm, hoping she might join him. "As Bell Hill has no mistress, I'd be honored if you would stand beside me to greet my guests."

Elisabeth exchanged glances with her mother-in-law, then boldly took his arm. "If you wish it, milord. After all, it *is* a special night."

If any visitors were shocked to see Elisabeth by his side, they hid their disapproval, smiling and bobbing and fluttering their fans. But he steeled himself when the Murrays of Philiphaugh stepped through his door.

Last week Sir John had reminded him of the generous dowry that would accompany Rosalind's hand in marriage. "Even you, Admiral, must admit 'tis a worthy sum." Jack had agreed that it was, then quickly changed the subject. His heart was not for sale at any price. Did the Murrays think of nothing but wealth, property, and advancement?

They stood before him now, dressed like peacocks, right down to the feathery plumes in Rosalind's hair. "Admiral," she said demurely, then sank into a deep curtsy. Yet for all their fine manners, none of the Murrays acknowledged Elisabeth. And when Charbon made an unexpected appearance, Rosalind lifted her hem with a look of dismay, then gave the cat a none-too-gentle nudge with her foot and hissed, "Be gone."

Jack felt Elisabeth stiffen, even as he clenched his teeth, lest he say the same to Rosalind Murray. *Be gone, madam.* Only when she followed her parents into the drawing room did Jack relax enough to greet his next visitors, the Currors of Whitmuir Hall, who not only spoke warmly to Elisabeth, but also reached down to pet Charbon.

"They may stay," Jack murmured, bringing a smile to Elisabeth's face.

Not every woman needed a dowry to make her appealing.

The sky was black and the candles blazing when the supper hour arrived. Jack escorted Elisabeth into the dining room with some three dozen friends and neighbors following in their wake. Laughter and conviviality filled the air as they found their seats up and down the long table, the place cards neatly lettered in Mrs. Pringle's hand.

When he reached the head of the table, Jack glanced down at his plate, then looked again. *A carrot?* Gibson had a large forked one. Michael Dalgliesh had one too. All three were tied with red ribbons. A swift perusal of the table provided no clue, for none of the other plates were so decorated.

Very odd.

Still, solving the carrot question would have to wait.

Jack stood before his guests, arms open. "Ladies and gentlemen, if we might join in giving thanks." He prayed earnestly for the hours ahead, for the meal and the music and the dancing, keeping his eyes closed lest he catch sight of the enormous carrot and laugh aloud.

The moment he took his seat, Elisabeth leaned across the table. " 'Tis a gift for Michaelmas," she said softly. "I plucked it for you from Mrs. Thorburn's garden."

He stared at the root vegetable, scrubbed clean but uncooked. "Am I meant to eat it?"

"You are meant to keep it. For good luck." She blushed when she said it, then hastily reached for her napkin, putting an end to the discussion.

If this was her surprise, Jack was not about to disappoint her. He dutifully placed the carrot to the side, then signaled to his footmen to commence serving the first course.

Carrot soup, as it turned out. Seasoned with coriander.

The evening's feast was a great success, with a dozen tantalizing aromas competing for their attention — among them, pan-baked trout, stewed lamb with mushrooms, and baked apples stuffed with currants. The Michaelmas goose was given pride of place at the center of the table, surrounded by smaller fowl, necessary to feed so many mouths.

"Do you know the saying, milord?" Elisabeth asked him when the poultry course was served. "Eat a goose on Michaelmas Day; want not for money all the year."

"Is that so?" He noted the small serving on Elisabeth's plate, the substantial one on Marjory's. "You don't believe in such things, do you?"

Elisabeth smiled. "Of course not, milord. Every blessing comes from the Almighty. But then, so do carrots."

By the time plates of rich almond cake were served, the Michaelmas feast was declared a success. Jack stood, eager to get on with things. "If you will kindly repair to the drawing room, you'll find our musicians waiting for us."

As the guests rose and headed for the door, Jack offered Elisabeth his arm.

"Milord," she said, leaning close to him, "perhaps you might prefer to retire to your study."

He arched his brows. "And miss the pleasure of dancing?"

Her shocked expression was worth every painful hour with Mr. Fowles.

"*You*, milord?"

Jack merely smiled as he guided her into the drawing room, where two lines were already forming. Since the young Widow Kerr was not permitted to dance, he needed her mother-in-law's approval and so sought out Marjory.

"Mrs. Kerr," he said respectfully, "I wonder if I might request a very great favor. In honor of Michaelmas, would you allow your daughter-in-law, just this eve, to —"

"Aye!" Marjory said, grinning at him.

Had the woman sipped too much claret? "You'll not mind, then, if we —"

"Nae!" Marjory assured him, standing opposite Gibson, waiting for the opening notes.

Elisabeth blinked at him, clearly astonished. "Am I to understand you wish to *dance* with me?"

"If you'll have me, madam," he said with a bow.

She took her place at once. "Depend upon it, milord."

Sixty-Nine

Night was drawing and closing her curtain up above the world, and down beneath it.

JEAN PAUL FRIEDRICH RICHTER

Elisabeth hastened down the empty servants' hall, the candle in her hand flickering wildly. Her heart too was doing a merry dance, though not nearly so merry as Lord Buchanan's clever footwork on display earlier that evening.

"I engaged a dancing master," he'd said blithely as they'd spun round the polished floor. His invited guests were unaware of his newfound talent, but his household staff had watched him in astonishment.

How the admiral had looked at her as they'd moved in tandem! His brown eyes gleaming, his mouth curled into a permanent smile. Elisabeth had heard him counting his steps now and again, but that only made his efforts all the more endearing. Not once had he landed on her instep or swept her into another dancer's path. For a man of his stature, he was surprisingly graceful, like a skilled fencer or an expert horseman. As it happened, his lordship was both.

"I did this for Michaelmas," he'd insisted.

Elisabeth knew better. *You did this for me, dear Jack.* She'd complimented him profusely and thanked him at the end of each set, urging him to choose other partners, though he never did. Rosalind Murray had shot daggers at her whenever she swept past. Elisabeth almost felt sorry for the young woman. *Find another,* she wanted to say. *This one is mine.*

Now the clocks were creeping toward midnight, and a hush had fallen over Bell Hill. Lord Buchanan had retired to his study after the last guest had departed. Eyelids drooping, his smile still in place, he'd entrusted her to Marjory and Gibson, then murmured in parting, "I shall see you on the morrow, Bess."

"You shall indeed, milord," she'd answered. *Sooner than you know.*

Breathless, she darted into the workroom. Her satin gown was precisely where she'd left it, hanging on the back of the door with a bedsheet draped over the pale, shimmering fabric. Marjory had promised to join her in a half hour but presently remained in the servants' hall to guard the door while Elisabeth bathed her body and brushed her hair.

Aye, and prayed.

She closed the door, then lit a few candles, brightening the room. Hot water simmered on the hearth — Marjory's doing. Elisabeth quickly undressed, dipped a clean linen cloth in the water, then rubbed it with her mother-in-law's fragrant soap. Would his lordship even notice the scent? She bathed in haste, grateful for the warm fire, then pulled on her chemise and laced her stays as tightly as she could. Marjory's silk stockings felt like feathers against her skin, and her brocade shoes, dyed to match the gown, slipped on her feet as if she'd worn them every day.

Standing near the fire to keep from shivering, she groomed her hair with slow, even strokes, waiting for Marjory to tap at her door. *Let me not be afraid, Lord. Let me speak from my heart. Let him not be dismayed.* A moment later Elisabeth ushered her mother-in-law into the workroom, then bolted the door once more. "What news from upstairs?"

"Everyone has retired for the night," Marjory informed her in a low voice, "including Mrs. Pringle and Roberts. I overheard Dickson saying he'd left Lord Buchanan nodding over a book in his study. All is in readiness for you." Marjory smoothed a hand down Elisabeth's hair. " 'I will even make a way in the wilderness.' So the Almighty promised, and so he has done for you this night."

"You are certain this is his will and not ours?"

Marjory did not hesitate. "Have we not prayed for his leading? Have you not searched the Scriptures and your heart, seeking an answer? I have no doubt Lord Buchanan is the husband God intends for you."

Buoyed by her mother-in-law's faith, Elisabeth swept her hair onto the crown of her head, then let Marjory add the silver comb where it might best be seen.

Last of all, her gown. When the lavender satin brushed against her shoulders, Elisabeth reveled in the cool feel of the fabric against her skin. She touched the bodice, with its tiny gold sequins, and the sleeves, trimmed in fine Belgian lace. "Your son was very generous with me," she said softly.

"You were far more generous with him," Marjory reminded her, slipping the matching satin reticule over her wrist. "Now go, my bonny Bess." She kissed her brow. "Gibson is waiting in the entrance hall to walk me home. I'll trust his lordship to see you safely to town or provide a bedchamber for you here if the hour grows too late. My prayers are with you, dear girl."

Moving on tiptoe lest her heels clatter against the flagstone floor, Elisabeth navigated the long servants' hall, then the turnpike stair, lifting her gown to keep from stepping on the hem. So far she'd not seen or heard a soul. More to the point, no one had seen her. The first-floor hall was bathed in shadows with a single sconce to light the way. As she neared Lord Jack's study, she lifted up a silent prayer of thanks. No footman stood at the entrance. And the door was slightly ajar.

Please be with me, Lord. Guide my steps. Guard my words. Keep my thoughts and actions pure.

She knew not what else to pray and so took a deep breath to calm her nerves, then approached the door, prepared to tap on it, announcing her presence. But when she peered into the room, she discovered Lord Jack was sound asleep. Seated in his favorite chair by the fire, he'd propped his feet on a cushioned footstool with a plaid draped across his long legs. She waited while her eyes adjusted to the meager firelight, then moved across the study, grateful for thick carpet to muffle her steps.

Then she heard a loud purring. Charbon jumped down from Lord Jack's chair and padded toward her, greeting her with a plaintive meow.

"Hush," she whispered, scratching his head, which only made him purr louder. She scooped him up and held him close, hoping he'd not give her away until she'd done as her mother-in-law had instructed. *Present yourself to him.* She carried Charbon into the hallway and, with a whispered apology, left him there, quietly shutting the door behind her.

With the curtains closed, not even the waning moon shed its light on the scene before her as she tiptoed to his lordship's side. Surely he would hear the loud beating of her heart or catch a whiff of her perfumed soap or feel the warmth of her presence and so awaken. But his breathing was steady, and his rugged features relaxed. She smiled down at him, secretly glad she'd found him sleeping. Even in repose, his physical strength was evident.

Elisabeth eased to the floor, spreading her elegant gown round her in a circle of silk, then rested her head on the large footstool. She'd wait until he roused. Surely it would not be much longer. Whatever the hour, and no matter the consequences, she was determined to speak the truth.

Seventy

The calm, majestic presence of the Night,
As of the one I love.

HENRY WADSWORTH LONGFELLOW

Jack vaguely heard the first chime of the mantel clock, as if from a distance. *Two. Three.* His limbs were too heavy to lift, and so he remained in his chair, not stirring, still counting. *Five. Six.* What had he been reading that he'd drifted off so quickly? *Eight. Nine.* Perhaps his need for sleep had more to do with the feasting. And the dancing. *Eleven. Twelve.*

Midnight, then. Later than he'd expected.

In the darkened study he felt the weight of something beside his feet. Charbon, no doubt, curled up on his footstool. Jack lifted his head to see the creature, then froze.

A woman. At his feet. Not moving, not speaking.

His heart began to thud in his chest. Who

was she? Not Elisabeth, for this woman's gown was pale, colorless. And Elisabeth had never worn so flowery a scent.

"Who are you?" he finally asked, his voice rough from sleep. Or from fear.

" 'Tis Bess, milord."

He abruptly sat up, exhaling in relief. "Madam! What sort of mischief are you up to, sneaking into my study at night?" To think, he'd supposed her some shameless lass among his Michaelmas guests come to tempt him at this gloomy hour.

Instead it was his own dear Elisabeth, seeking his company.

"Do forgive me for startling you," she said softly. "I wished to speak with you. Alone." When she rose to her knees, he could see her gown more clearly, as bits of gold caught the firelight. An exquisite costume, the sort only someone of means could afford.

Jack cast aside his plaid blanket and stood, lifting her up as well. "Come, let me have a look at you." He turned her toward the fire, then lit a candle, holding it aloft. His plainly garbed dressmaker was gone. In her place stood a vision in lavender. "Is it yours, this fine gown?"

"Aye." She glanced down, smoothing the wrinkles from her skirts. "Since I've not worn it in a twelvemonth, I was afraid it might no longer fit."

Oh, it fits, dear lady. To perfection. He averted

his gaze, yanking his wayward thoughts in line. "Forgive me for asking, Bess, but . . . what has become of your mourning clothes?"

She lifted her chin. "I am no longer in mourning for my late husband. That is what I came to tell you."

Only then did he notice the door to the hallway was closed. "What of your mother-in-law?" he asked, feeling a certain uneasiness. "Does she know about this . . . , eh, decision of yours?"

A slight smile. " 'Twas her idea."

He let that rather astounding fact take root. "So Mrs. Kerr will not mind if you enter into . . . , well, a courtship with someone? With . . . me?"

"Nae, she'll not mind," Bess assured him. "Reverend Brown has recently learned that you are a distant relative of Marjory's late husband. Which means you are a kinsman of ours."

Jack nodded, the picture growing clearer with each waking moment. "No doubt the minister thinks I should provide for the two of you. And I should. Nae, I *will*. Gladly."

Bess took his hands in hers. The warmth of her skin surprised him.

"I am grateful for anything you might do for Marjory," she admitted. "But provision is not what I seek from you, milord."

He drew her closer, longing for an honest answer. "My dear Bess, what *do* you seek?"

"A future." She looked up at him, her blue eyes hiding nothing. "Lord Buchanan, if your feelings for me compare in any measure to the fond affection I have for you, then I believe the Almighty intends for us to be together."

Jack couldn't quite believe what he was hearing. "You wish . . . to marry me?"

She lifted his hands and gently kissed them. "I do."

"Lord bless you," he whispered, swiftly pulling her into his embrace. "You might have chosen a younger man, Bess. A richer man —"

"Nae, there is only one man for me." Elisabeth nestled her head in the hollow of his neck as if she belonged there. And she *did* belong there. By the grace of God and no other.

He mustered his courage, knowing there was no turning back now. "You say you have a fond affection for me, Bess? Then I'll be bolder still and confess I adore you. And everything about you." He kissed her hair, like silk beneath his lips. Then the soft plane of her brow. Then the tender curve of her cheek.

"Lord Jack —"

"Jack," he murmured. "In this room titles mean nothing."

She smiled in the darkness. "Jack, then."

He eased her from his embrace, then lowered her into his chair and drew up the footstool for himself. "No one must find you here," he said firmly, keeping his voice low. "And no one must see you depart."

She eyed the door.

He understood. Even now someone might be listening between the cracks.

"You've nothing to fear," he assured her. "I'll protect you and your good name as well. You are much respected in Selkirkshire, Bess." He claimed her hands, then kissed each one. "At Bell Hill most of all."

They sat in companionable silence for a moment, barely touching, simply breathing. He had a thousand things he wanted to tell her, but one issue prodded his conscience at the moment. "Bess, we must speak of a subject that will not be pleasant for you." He inched closer, praying for wisdom. "Every wedding begins with the question, 'Is there any impediment to this marriage?' Alas, there is one for us."

Her eyes widened. "What is it, milord? Have you been married before? Is there some other woman who —"

"Nae, there is no other woman," he said firmly. "But there is someone who could destroy the very future you seek. A powerful man, who rules us all."

SEVENTY-ONE

Daughter of hope, night o'er thee flings
The shadow of her raven wings,
And in the morning thou art flown!

ANNE HOME HUNTER

Elisabeth's hands turned to ice. "King George."

"Aye," Jack said grimly. "Because you and your mother-in-law supported the Jacobite rebellion, you can never be truly safe without the king's pardon."

She stared at him, hearing the words, yet not understanding. "You've known this all along."

His skin took on a ruddy tint, visible even in the dimly lit study. "I have, Bess. But I could not say anything until . . ." He looked down, clearly distraught. "Until now. Until the possibility of marriage was raised."

"The . . . possibility?" Elisabeth felt herself sinking into the chair. Her shoulders, her body, her heart. "Might the king withhold his mercy?"

"He might," Jack confessed, then looked up to meet her gaze. "But I've been preparing your case for months. Since the Common Riding, when Reverend Brown informed me of your treason."

"I see." Elisabeth did not know what to say, how to respond.

"As a retired admiral and peer of the realm, I am in . . . shall we say, a unique position to seek the king's mercy on behalf of my bride."

His bride. Elisabeth closed her eyes, overwhelmed. With her bold proposal, she'd now forced him to defend her. "Jack, I should not have —"

"Aye, you should have." He bent forward and kissed her, his mouth warm against hers.

When he slowly pulled back, she saw in his eyes the answer to every question that mattered. He loved her. And he meant to save her.

Jack was still holding her hands, more firmly than ever. "I need only travel as far as Edinburgh," he explained, "where I will meet with the king's representative at Edinburgh Castle." He paused before adding, "Dickson and I shall depart at noontide."

Elisabeth hesitated but a moment. "There's something I must do before you go." She ran her fingers along the hem of her gown until she found the row of white silk rosettes stitched inside the hem of her petticoat. "Have you a pair of scissors, Jack?"

He retrieved a paper knife from the table beside them, the slender, curved blade designed to slice open the folded pages of bound books. "Will this do?"

"Aye." She gripped the ebony handle and, using the sharp point of the knife, began picking apart the stitches holding her hidden roses in place. "If you are willing to stand before God and king to seek my pardon, then 'tis time I put aside my past."

Elisabeth sensed his gaze on her as she removed the roses one by one. She felt no sorrow, no regret, only relief. When all her flowers were in hand, she tossed them into the nearby fire. The flames quickly consumed the silk, leaving not a trace.

After a quiet moment Jack said, "No tears, Bess?"

She looked up at him so he might see that her eyes were dry and her soul at peace. "No tears," she assured him, "for I've a whole new life ahead."

"Indeed you do." Jack slowly stood, then pulled her to her feet. "At the moment we must get you home before someone sees you and sends rumors flying."

They crossed the room together, then she stepped to the side while Jack checked to see if the hall was deserted. He opened the door no more than a crack before closing it again, just as quietly. "Footman," he whispered.

Elisabeth's heart quickened as Jack drew her back into the recesses of the room.

He explained in a whisper, "Roberts stationed one of his men outside my study in case I might have need of him in the night. He's fallen asleep, I'm afraid, with his shoulder against the door. We've no choice but to tarry here until he wakes and finds his way to bed."

She looked about the study. "Do you mean for me to spend the night in this room . . . with you?"

"Can you think of another solution?" he asked.

In truth, she could not. "Perhaps I might sleep over here," she said, standing to consider an upholstered chair by the window.

"I can do better than that." He quickly gathered a dozen plump, down-filled pillows from round the room, then built a tidy nest for her next to his reading chair. "Will this suffice?"

She sank onto them, knowing very well she'd not be able to sleep. In this gown? At his feet? Not for a single moment. "Very cozy," she assured him.

Jack added a fresh log to the fire, extinguished the only candle in the room, then settled into his chair with its thick, rounded upholstery. Unfolded, his plaid blanket draped over them both. "Perhaps we might take turnabout," he said softly, "so we do not both oversleep. If we rise well before dawn, we can be halfway to Selkirk before the household stirs."

Elisabeth propped her head on the footstool, looking up at his shadowy form. "You first, milord."

"Jack."

"Aye." She smiled in the darkness. "Jack."

He shifted round a bit, trying to get comfortable. Then again. Yet a third time. " 'Tis more challenging than I'd expected," he murmured.

"Because of the chair?"

"Because of the company." His hand found hers beneath the plaid. "Have I told you why I love you, Bess?"

She clasped his hand more tightly. "Not yet."

"Ah." His voice caressed her like the firelight. "I love your kindness, Bess. Your generous nature. Your courage. Aye, and your sense of humor."

Elisabeth closed her eyes, undone by his words. She'd not thought it possible to be loved for herself and not merely her appearance. Still, she could not resist teasing him. "All well and good," she said lightly, "but what about my hair? My face? My form? I thought that was all men prized in a woman."

"Some men, perhaps. Not this one." He drew her hand close enough to brush his lips across her skin. "Though I have taken note of your beauty. By the hour, truth be told."

"I see." She did not mind that so much.

Jack changed position once more. "Come, Bess, we must sleep while we may."

"I shall try," she promised, her eyes wide open.

With muted chimes the mantel clock marked each quarter hour through the night.

Elisabeth heard them all.

Jack slept off and on, for which she was grateful. He had a long ride ahead of him that day and much to prepare for. Whoever the king's man might be, Jack would have no easy task convincing him the Kerrs were worthy of his pardon.

In those long, quiet hours, Elisabeth remembered something Donald had said to her on their last night together, promising he'd return from battle a changed man. *A different husband will cross your threshold. A husband who is faithful.* Donald did not return. But he did speak the truth, without knowing how God might bring it to pass. Lord Jack Buchanan was entirely different than Donald Kerr. And utterly faithful.

At half past five she heard the scrape of a chair at the door and footsteps fading down the hall. With dawn only an hour away, Elisabeth quickly rose and smoothed the wrinkles from her gown. Jack was awake as well, pulling on his riding boots.

"Have you no other shoes?" he asked, frowning at her brocade slippers.

"Aye, with my gown in the servants' hall."

He nodded, his expression intent. "Make haste to the drawing room and leave by the outer door. I shall stop by the workroom for your clothing, then meet you beneath the tall oak near the stables. Do you know the one I mean?"

She nodded, her pulse quickening. "And if I am seen? If I am questioned?"

"Pray you will not be." He bent down and kissed her again. A brief touch but so very tender, warming her to her toes.

They were almost at the door when he caught her wrist. "Give me your reticule, Bess."

She slipped it over her hand, not questioning him for a moment. It contained all of a ha'penny, and he was welcome to it.

Jack unlocked his desk drawer, pulled out a fistful of bank notes, stuffed them inside her reticule, and returned it to her, bulging at the seams. "For your mother-in-law," he explained, then slowly opened the door to the hall and looked out.

She held her breath until Jack beckoned her forth. *Be with me, Lord. Cover me with your wings. Let me not be seen.*

Without a word they hurried down the turnpike stair, then went their separate ways, he to the servants' stair, she to the drawing room. The house was utterly dark and absolutely silent. She took off her shoes, tiptoeing as quietly as she could, and still she felt like a Highland coo stomping through the halls, so loud was the swish of her satin.

A minute later Elisabeth entered the drawing room, watching the door to Mrs. Pringle's private office. If anyone would be up at this hour, it would be Bell Hill's loyal housekeeper. Lord willing, the servants would soon be informed of their marriage plans. But not now, not like this.

The well-oiled hinges did not protest when she unbolted the door and pushed it open. A damp, chilly breeze rushed over her bare skin, making her shiver. Her warm wool cape and sturdy leather shoes would be most welcome. She closed the door, thanking the Lord for safe passage thus far, then hastened across the lawn, hearing the whinnying of horses in the stables. Hyslop would not question his master, not even when Jack claimed both Janvier and Belda at this early hour.

When Elisabeth reached the oak tree, she leaned against the rough trunk, catching her breath, calming her heart. In all her five-and-twenty years, she had never known such a night nor encountered such a man as Jack Buchanan. *I adore you.* He'd spoken those words with such conviction, leaving no room for doubt or fear.

And I love you, Jack. More than I realized. More than I could possibly imagine.

By the time he'd crossed the lawn with their mounts and reached her side, she was trembling all over.

"Cold?" he asked, sweeping her wool cape round her shoulders.

"A bit," she admitted, pulling on her gloves. He lifted her onto Belda's saddle with ease, then exchanged her slippers for sensible shoes before draping her black wool gown across the back of the saddle.

"You'll need new attire," he said, "now that you're no longer in mourning."

She hadn't thought of that. Hadn't thought of a great many things. "I shall have time to sew a new gown for myself, now that I've finished dressing all your maidservants."

"So you have." He threw himself onto Janvier's back, then sent both horses trotting forth with a simple command. They were soon through the park and onto the drive leading them away from the house and toward town, the sun still a half hour below the horizon.

Jack looked at her beneath the velvety blue sky, riding as close as he dared. "I've been meaning to talk to you about your employment, Mrs. Kerr. I'm afraid I must dismiss you as my dressmaker."

She pretended to be greatly offended. "Lord Buchanan! Is this how you repay my many hours of service?"

"Even worse, madam, I insist you marry me within the month."

Elisabeth laughed softly. "I believe I was the one who proposed marriage."

"So you did, my dear."

The night was drawing to a close by the time they reached Mr. Riddell's stables. Jack tarried some distance away while Elisabeth turned over the reins to a sleepy lad with hay sticking out of his hair. Once the groom tottered off with Belda, Jack joined Elisabeth once more, letting Janvier poke his nose in a bucket of water, while the two of them stood in the deserted street.

Elisabeth looked up at him, finding it hard to bid him good night. Or was it good morning? "How long will you be in Edinburgh?" she finally asked.

"If all goes well, I shall be home Saturday afternoon."

"And if it does not go well?"

His response was long in coming, and his gaze did not quite meet hers. "Bess, I need to know that you trust me."

"*Trust* you? Jack, surely —"

"Listen to me." His voice was low and rough with emotion. "You've trusted men before who threatened you and frightened you, who betrayed you and lied to you, who bruised you and tried to violate you." When he looked at her, the intensity of his gaze stole her breath. "I am not like those men, Bess. I could never hurt you. And want only what is best for you."

"I know." She touched the strong line of his jaw, felt the faint stubble of his beard. "That is why I trust you completely. Did I not lie at your feet through a long, dark night?"

"Indeed you did." He placed his hand on hers, holding it against his cheek. "Though I wonder if you actually slept."

"Not a wink," she confessed.

Seventy-Two

Uncertainty and expectation are joys of life.

WILLIAM CONGREVE

Marjory clutched the letter in her hand, having read it so many times the creases were beginning to wear. But what else was there to do when she could not sleep? The box bed felt very strange indeed, large and solid compared to the narrow hurlie bed she'd known for months. And the house was entirely too empty without her cousin or daughter-in-law to keep her company.

Anne was happily settled in her new home.

As for Elisabeth, Marjory was beside herself with worry.

You must speak with him in private. She'd not given her daughter-in-law much choice in the matter. Had she asked too much of Elisabeth? Too much of his lordship? Their warm regard for each other was clear. Never more so than in the drawing room last evening when they'd danced together for hours. With Elisabeth's mourning ended, however prematurely, Marjory felt certain Lord Buchanan would make her his wife.

Please, Admiral. 'Tis God's will, I am certain of it.

With a sigh Marjory unfolded Neil's letter once more, if only to cheer her. He'd pressed it into her hand at last evening's Michaelmas feast. "Dinna read it 'til ye're hame," he'd insisted.

Amid the excitement of helping Elisabeth dress, Marjory had all but forgotten his missive until Neil had delivered her to Halliwell's Close sometime after midnight and reminded her of the letter in the pocket of her gown. "I vowed to surprise ye with a praisent at Michaelmas, aye?"

"You did," she'd agreed, pulling out the letter, suddenly curious.

"Not 'til I'm gane," he'd cautioned her, kissing her cheek. Well, *both* cheeks. Her brow too. Each one felt like a promise of things to come. And the *words* Neil had spoken! "I will aye want ye by my side," after the first gentle kiss. "I will aye need ye in my life," after the second. Then, "I will aye luve ye, Leddy Kerr."

Naturally, she'd returned the favor. With her own kisses. And her own words.

The memory of their parting made her sigh even now, hours later. Lingering at the door like two young lovers. Whispering endearments old as time yet fresh as spring water in their mouths. Holding hands in the quiet sanctuary of her wee house.

Marjory read his letter once more, though she already knew every word by heart.

To Lady Marjory Kerr
Halliwell's Close, Selkirkshire
Monday, 29 September 1746

My Beloved Marjory:

She swallowed, hard. *Beloved.* Lord John had never addressed her so ardently. *Dear,* aye, but never *Beloved.*

I hope you will be pleased to find this letter written in my hand.

Pleased? Marjory had burst into tears.

Of all the ways Neil might have blessed her, honored her, this was the finest: he'd spent the summer learning to read and to write, keeping it a secret until now, until he was ready. *My sweet Neil.* She pictured him sitting at Reverend Brown's parlor table, laboring over each letter, each word.

I wished to be more worthy of you, milady. And so I asked the minister to teach me, which he kindly did.

608

Clearly Reverend Brown was more supportive of their courtship than he'd once put forth. Else why would he have helped Neil Gibson become a literate man, lifting him to a higher station, opening the world of books to him?

Oh, Neil, 'tis only the beginning.

Marjory vowed to be nicer — nae, *much* nicer — to the minister henceforth.

I pray each day for the Almighty to provide a larger income so I might ask for your hand in marriage. Until that day comes, my heart is yours to keep.

And mine is yours. Marjory touched his signature, neatly drawn.

Helen Edgar, their housekeeper at Milne Square, would be so proud of her old friend. Even Janet, her nigh-forgotten daughter-in-law, might have applauded Gibson's efforts. And Elisabeth would be ecstatic.

Marjory looked toward the window. *Hurry home, lass.* The sky was already growing lighter, a warm pink nudging the midnight blue toward the western horizon.

When she heard footsteps on the cobblestones below, she swept aside Anne's lace-trimmed curtains. *Bess!* Marjory tucked Gibson's letter in her hanging pocket for safekeeping, then flung open the door and stood at the top of the stair, anxious to greet her daughter-in-law. Whatever had happened last night at Bell Hill, breakfast would wait.

Elisabeth opened the door from the close, then looked up. "Shouldn't you be in bed?"

Marjory waved her up impatiently. "I've not slept all night, worrying about you." She pulled her inside, then closed the door, noting her daughter-in-law's damp wool cape, her wrinkled satin gown, her muddy leather shoes, and the mourning gown draped over her arm. "So," Marjory began, all but crowing, "who are you, then? The next Lady Buchanan?"

A look of surprise lit Elisabeth's features. "I'd hardly considered it, but, aye, if we marry, I would bear the title 'Lady' again."

"*If* you marry?" Marjory's breath caught. "Please do not tell me things ended badly."

"Nothing has ended. Not yet." Elisabeth laid aside her satin reticule, then pulled off her gloves. "If there's hot water in the kettle, I could do with some tea."

Marjory had never prepared tea with such haste. A minute later they were seated at the oval table, a plate of oatcakes and cheese before them, teacups in hand. Marjory held hers to keep warm, not bothering to take a sip. "Tell me everything," she begged.

Elisabeth patiently described her night in Lord Buchanan's study, though on occasion Marjory sensed her daughter-in-law skipping over a few details. When she came to the pardon his lordship intended to seek from the king, Marjory gripped her hands. "Can this be true, Bess?"

"No more fear of the dragoons," Elisabeth assured her. "Nor of Cumberland or the tolbooth or the gallows."

Marjory could barely take it all in. " 'Twas the Lord's plan all along," she breathed.

"Aye." Elisabeth touched her hand. "Of course, you will be pardoned as well, which should relieve Gibson immensely."

"Oh!" Marjory fished out his letter, ashamed at having forgotten. "I have something you must see, Bess." She placed it in her daughter-in-law's hands and watched her closely as she read.

"Gibson wrote this?" Elisabeth stared at the paper. "Marjory, 'tis wonderful!"

She smiled, proud as any wife. "His hand *is* quite accomplished."

"Nae, I mean 'tis wonderful to know money is all that prevents you and Gibson from marrying."

Marjory was taken aback. "How can that be good news?"

"Because of this." Elisabeth reached for her discarded reticule and tugged open the drawstring. "Lord Buchanan filled this just before we left Bell Hill."

Marjory watched a stream of bank notes spill onto their battered dining table. "The admiral *gave* these to you?"

"Nae, he gave them to *you*. His lordship clearly stipulated, 'For your mother-in-law.' Is it very much?"

Marjory began to count, her hands shaking. "One hundred pounds. Two hundred. Oh, Bess, this one is five hundred . . ." Speechless, she laid down each bank note, one after another, never losing track of the number, however unfathomable.

When she finished, Marjory looked up. " 'Tis fifteen hundred pounds."

Elisabeth gasped. "I had no idea —"

"But God did. Aye, he most certainly did."

Marjory could not stem the tears that flowed from her eyes or the joy that poured from her heart. *You have dealt kindly with me after all, Lord. You have, you have! I came home empty, and you filled me to overflowing.*

Dazed at his boundless provision, Marjory straightened the Royal Bank notes into neat stacks, trying to make sense of it all. But there was nothing sensible about so vast a sum. And this sum in particular. "Bess, did I ever tell you how much I gave to the Jacobite cause?"

"I know 'twas a great deal."

Marjory lightly touched each stack, her fingertips still wet with tears. "Fifteen hundred pounds."

"Fifteen hundred . . ." Elisabeth stared at the table full of money. "Is it possible Lord Buchanan knew that?"

Marjory turned to her. "Let me ask you this. Did he count the notes, as I did just now?"

"Nae," Elisabeth admitted. " 'Twas dark in his study."

"Then this gift is from the Lord." Marjory was more certain than ever. "Though it passed through the admiral's hands, it came from above."

Marjory quietly put the bank notes in the only safe place she could think of: rolled inside a stocking at the bottom of her trunk. She need not worry about paying for her lodgings now. Or shopping at market. Or offering her tithe.

"I wonder . . ." Elisabeth quickly crossed the room to join her. "I wonder if Gibson might agree on the source of this blessing. Because if he did . . . , oh, Marjory, if he did see this as a gift from God . . ."

"We could marry," Marjory realized, her mouth falling open.

Elisabeth laughed. "Aye, you could. At once."

Marjory threw her arms round her clever daughter-in-law for a brief hug. "Oh, but, Bess, Gibson must come to that conclusion himself. I would never want him to suffer a moment's doubt."

"Can you live on such a sum?"

Marjory clapped her hands like a child at an entertainment. "At our age? Neil Gibson and I could live out the rest of our days in this fine little house, dine on meat and broth daily, and still have money left to share with grandchildren." She glanced at Elisabeth. "Though I suppose they will not truly be *my* grandchildren —"

"Any babe I might ever bear shall be nestled in your arms," Elisabeth assured her. "Though I have no promise of that, do I? Not unless the king is merciful."

"Blessings come from the Lord, not men," Marjory insisted. "Do not fret, my dear. His lordship will not rest until this matter is settled. Is he not heading north this very day?"

"He is." She sighed. "And you are right."

Thinking to find some worthwhile diversion for her, Marjory eyed Elisabeth's black gown, heaped on the chair. "You have an important matter to attend to as well, Bess. Since you're no longer in mourning, your attire must reflect that. What say you to adding a bit of trim round the neckline? I know a fine lace maker in town."

"An excellent plan," Elisabeth agreed, "though I thought *I* was the dressmaker."

"Not for long," Marjory reminded her.

"True. Lord Buchanan informed me that my services are no longer needed at Bell Hill."

"You see? You'll be Lady Buchanan well before Hallowmas Eve." Marjory shook out the black gown and laid it across the hurlie bed. "Did his lordship say whom he'll be meeting with in Edinburgh?"

Their tea grown cold, Elisabeth began to clear the table. "He didn't mention a name. Only that he was the king's representative in the capital."

"Nae!" Marjory dropped onto the hurlie bed, crushing Elisabeth's mourning gown. "Bess, that can only be one person. 'Tis the Honorary Governor of Edinburgh Castle, General Lord Mark Kerr."

SEVENTY-THREE

The resolve to conquer is half the battle in love as well as war.

GEORGE STILLMAN HILLARD

With Dickson by his side, Jack trotted across the Ettrick bridge, fighting the urge to look back. However much he longed to bid Elisabeth farewell, he and Dickson could not tarry in Selkirk. Not if they were to arrive in the capital at noontide on Thursday, giving him sufficient time to shave, dress like an admiral, and sail into battle.

He'd sent a hired messenger ahead to make sure the governor was in residence yet with strict orders not to inform the man of their imminent arrival. Jack intended to use the element of surprise to his advantage. Having once offered a cool welcome to General Lord Mark Kerr at Bell Hill, Jack could only imagine the icy reception he would find at Edinburgh Castle if Lord Mark knew he was coming.

Still, for Elisabeth Kerr, he would do whatever was required.

He'd not told her Lord Mark would be the one acting on the king's behalf, knowing it would only add to her fears. He could still hear the plaintive note in her voice, still see her downcast expression. *Might the king withhold his mercy?*

Not if God is with us, Bess.

Before leaving Bell Hill, Jack had taken Mrs. Pringle and Roberts into his confidence, explaining the reason for his journey north. "I care little whether or not Lord Mark finds her worthy, but I would know your thoughts," he'd said. "Will you honor her as Lady Buchanan? Or will she remain a dressmaker in your eyes?"

Their response was swift and heartening. "Your lordship has chosen well," Roberts said emphatically, while Mrs. Pringle beamed. "You already know of my regard for her, milord." Jack was certain the rest of the household would follow their good example.

Only Lord Mark needed convincing.

"Mind your mount, sir," Dickson called out when a large brown hare darted across Janvier's path. "Mrs. Tudhope would happily throw that one in a pot."

Jack calmed his horse with ease, grateful for any benign subject to occupy his thoughts. "I recall a decent plate of hare soup when we last supped at the Middleton Inn. We shall see what they have to offer us come Wednesday eve, aye?"

"Venison and pheasant," Middleton's cook said proudly, ladling a second helping of game soup onto Jack's plate.

He could barely hear the woman above the din, or taste her soup with the pungent aroma of tallow candles filling his nostrils. One stage out from Edinburgh, the Middleton Inn welcomed travelers from all levels of society to sup and drink in the low-ceilinged room with its broad, soot-stained beams and sanded floor.

"I found your messenger," Dickson announced, steering a gangly young man into the chair across from Jack. "Waiting for us, as requested, though he was hanging round that large bowl by the hearth. The one with the hot whisky punch."

Jack frowned at the lad. "You'll not be paid unless you've done your duty."

"Oh, I have, milord." His eyes were a bit glassy, but his words were sober enough. "Went to the castle this morn and learned from one o' the dragoons that the governor is at hame 'til Friday."

"Good," Jack told him. "What else did you hear?"

"Meikle ado about Lords Balmerino and Kilmarnock. They were Jacobites, ye ken, beheaded in the Tower o' London for treason."

Jack grimaced, having read a detailed report in *The Gentleman's Magazine.* "That will do," he told the lad, then drew a handful of coins from his purse.

While the messenger stumbled off toward the punch bowl, Dickson resumed his seat, a troubled expression on his face. "Is your lady still loyal to the Jacobites, milord, or is she all for the king now? 'Tis the one question the general is sure to ask."

"Aye." Jack picked up his soup spoon, though he'd lost his appetite. "When he does, I'll be ready with an answer."

With a blustery wind roaring down the High Street, Jack walked uphill toward Edinburgh Castle, the paving stones slick beneath his boots. On the day of the Common Riding, his heavy admiral's uniform had been an encumbrance. But with October upon them, the dark blue wool coat, as well as the scarlet waistcoat beneath it, provided much-needed warmth.

Dickson had spent two hours grooming him. "Like a thoroughbred, milord," he'd said.

Jack had offered no protest, knowing he would need every advantage his military standing might offer. His mission was twofold that noontide. The first would require gold;

the second, humility. Though Lord Mark had a reputation as a duelist, Jack had no intention of touching his sword.

They passed beneath the portcullis of the castle with little resistance, the dragoons easily spotting his rank and deferring to him accordingly. Climbing the cobbled road round to the left, past the cart sheds, they were directed toward the governor's house, clearly the newest building in the castle compound.

"Fine prospect," Dickson commented, nodding at the splendid view of the capital and the North Sea beyond it.

"Aye," Jack agreed, giving it a cursory glance. On the way down, when he held two signed agreements in hand, he might admire the scenery. But not now.

Judging by the number of dormers and chimneys poking through the slate roof three stories above, the governor's residence housed a full complement of officers, deputies, constables, and the like. Jack approached the center entrance, shoulders squared, head high, all the while reminding himself he'd need more than his own strength to see him through. "The LORD strong and mighty," he said under his breath, "the LORD mighty in battle."

"Praying, milord?" Dickson asked.

"Always," Jack replied, then lifted the brass knocker. A moment later they were ushered into the entrance hall where they found enough weaponry mounted on the walls to give any visitor pause.

The lieutenant who greeted them was polite but wary. "Is General Kerr expecting you, sir?"

"He is not," Jack informed him, "though he'll know my name. Tell him Admiral Lord Jack Buchanan wishes to meet with him. At once."

SEVENTY-FOUR

Gold loves to make its way through guards,
and breaks through barriers of stone.

HORACE

Seated among the high-backed chairs lining the entrance wall of the governor's house, Jack crossed his legs and brushed a fleck of dirt from his boots as if he had all the time in the world. Letting his impatience show would not serve him well. General Lord Mark Kerr might leave his visitors cooling their heels for a half hour, but he could not ignore them forever.

Finally the governor strode into the hall, a thick stack of papers tucked under his arm.

Jack was on his feet at once. "General, a moment of your time."

"I always have time for a peer," the older man said, though he did not smile, and his tone was cool. "In my office, shall we?"

"I should think a larger room with a table might better serve," Jack told him. "I am here on business of some importance to His Majesty. Others may be required to serve as witnesses."

The governor's slender mustache twitched. "This way, then."

They traveled through a warren of rooms until they reached one of sufficient size to feature a table with a dozen chairs, empty and waiting. Jack nodded, pleased with the arrangement. "If you might summon ten honorable men of high rank to observe these proceedings?"

"I could summon ten times that number," the governor said evenly. A threat, however subtle. He turned to the lieutenant hovering behind him and rattled off a list of officers.

Within minutes various gentlemen began striding into the room, each one taking his own measure of Jack. He expected it and did the same. Once all were seated, Lord Mark claimed his place at the head of the table, dropping his papers with studied indifference, while Jack took the opposing end. Dickson sat behind and to his right, a heavy box at his feet, the necessary documents in hand.

As Lord Mark made obligatory introductions round the table, Jack observed how the others responded to the general. Begrudging deference at best but not genuine admiration. That would make things easier.

"Tell me, Admiral Buchanan," Lord Mark began, "what business might be of such interest to His Majesty that you've summoned us from our duties?"

Jack stood, not only as a show of respect to the others, but also to gain a visible advantage. He was the tallest man in the room and of equal rank with the general. Above all, he had the Almighty on his side and so spoke with authority.

"I have come here to discuss a certain property," he declared. "The king's property. Though at the moment, General, it is in your possession."

He arched a single brow. "You are referring to . . ."

"Tweedsford in Selkirkshire."

Lord Mark waved his hand dismissively. "What of it?"

"I believe you referred to it as 'a poor prize.' "

The others began to murmur, as Jack knew they would. When the king rewarded one of his subjects with a house and lands, the recipient was expected to be, at the very least, grateful.

"In my presence," Jack continued, "you expressed your intention to leave Tweedsford unoccupied for an indefinite time, stating, 'Another ten years would hardly matter.' Is that correct, General?"

"Aye." Lord Mark glared at him, his color mottled. "I might have said that."

"Then I have a proposal, sir, which will

provide a handsome income for you and a home for a widowed gentlewoman. Should you agree, the king will consider his award duly appreciated, and you'll no longer be encumbered with a property that does not suit you."

Jack glanced at the others, gauging their response. As for Lord Mark, he appeared relieved, even interested.

To force his hand, Jack took a different tack. "Or I could inform the king of your dissatisfaction and offer His Majesty the income instead. You know as well as I do how eager King George is to fill his coffers."

"Nae, nae," Lord Mark swiftly protested. "I would be pleased to entertain your offer. What terms would you suggest for the lease of this property?"

"Forty years would suit." Jack paused as the murmuring rose in volume. It was an extraordinary length of time, requiring a vast sum to match it. "General, I am prepared to pay the full amount in advance." He shrugged nonchalantly. "In gold."

The room nigh to exploded. Paper bank notes could not compare to the indisputable merit of guineas.

Jack nodded at Dickson, who began walking the length of the room, bearing a wooden box they'd claimed from the Royal Bank not an hour ago.

Lord Mark watched the gold moving toward him, his eyes glowing, his greed showing. "Perhaps I am acquainted with this widow. Surely she must be a woman of means."

"You once knew her as Lady Kerr, a distant cousin of yours." Jack paused, anticipating a response, but Lord Mark's attention was riveted elsewhere, just as Jack had hoped it might be. He continued smoothly, "You and I are related as well, General. It seems a Kerr and a Buchanan were wed in the Borderland a century and a half ago."

"Very fortuitous," Lord Mark agreed as Dickson placed the box of coins before him. "Upon my word, Admiral, consider the bargain struck. I shall have a lease drawn up at once."

"No need." Jack started toward him, legal documents in hand. "I've taken the liberty of preparing one for you so as not to delay the possession of your gold."

"Very thoughtful," the governor murmured, his guineas gleaming in the candlelight.

Jack chose the side of the table opposite Dickson, forcing Lord Mark to shift his gaze from one to the other. "If you might kindly review these papers and affix your signature, the gold will be yours, and Tweedsford will no longer remain your concern."

Lord Mark called for more candles, as well as pen and ink. Two lieutenants scurried about, bringing all that he needed. Jack willed his hands not to shake as he laid two papers, one on top of the other, before the governor. The gold had done its work. Now humility must do its part.

Drawing a candle closer, Lord Mark looked over the lengthy document on top, reading bits aloud as he did, confirming the terms of their agreement.

"Everything in order?" Jack asked, holding out the quill pen and holding his breath as well.

Lord Mark caressed the gold with his gaze once more, then dutifully signed the lease. He could not put the pen down fast enough before he pulled the box closer. "Now then, Admiral Buchanan, have you other business of interest to the king? For you have my full attention, I assure you."

"There *is* another matter." Jack paused long enough to pray. *You know my heart, Lord. Yet, thy will be done.* "I am weary of the bachelor life and wish to marry."

"Indeed." Lord Mark smoothed his fingers across the coins, not bothering to look up. "And what good lady have you chosen for your bride?"

Jack lifted the first document to reveal a second one. A marriage agreement.

"She is a widow without issue from a Highland family with no title and little property."

Lord Mark snorted. "Well, Admiral, the

lady certainly hasn't much to recommend her." The others round the table seemed amused as well.

Jack smiled too, though his heart was pounding. "Nevertheless, we are well matched. The king can hardly object to a beautiful woman among the peers."

"Hear, hear," one of the officers said, banging the table. His compatriots soon joined in.

Jack steeled himself, knowing what must come next. "There *is* one impediment to our future happiness, which only the king can remove."

Lord Mark cocked his brow. "Oh?"

"If you might act on his behalf, General, I would be most grateful." Jack flicked his gaze at the box of gold, a reminder of his generous provision.

The gesture did not go unnoticed. "How may I assist you, Admiral?"

"Last autumn His Majesty extended a general pardon to all who might renounce their support of the Jacobite cause." Jack paused, wanting to be certain the general recalled the king's offer of clemency.

The others ceased their murmuring. Lord Mark said evenly, "Go on."

Jack could delay his bold confession no longer. "My betrothed, Elisabeth Kerr, and your new tenant, my future mother-in-law, are in need of His Majesty's mercy."

Lord Mark's features drew into a fierce

scowl. "You mean to say these women are Jacobites?"

"They are no longer so," Jack quickly amended, "for I have seen for myself their complete devotion to the Crown. In my presence Elisabeth Kerr burned her Jacobite rosettes in demonstration of her fealty to the king."

Lord Mark eyed his gold at length. "I remember Marjory Kerr now. Her sons foolishly threw away their inheritance to follow the Young Pretender." His stern tone softened. "She wrote asking for my assistance."

Jack knew but asked him nonetheless, "Did you help them, milord?"

"Nae, I did not."

A beat of silence, then two.

Jack slowly knelt before the general, praying for a strength beyond his own. "Then I am asking for a royal pardon on behalf of Marjory and Elisabeth Kerr. Indeed, I am pleading for their very lives."

Jack bowed his head. *Please, Lord.* There was nothing else to be said, nothing else to be done.

Finally an answer came. "Very well."

Jack looked up to find the general dipping his quill in the ink. A miracle, and nothing short of it. *Thy mercy endureth for ever.* Jack stood, though it was all he could do not to leap to his feet and shout with joy.

Lord Mark signed his name with a flourish,

then sanded the document with a careless flick of his wrist. "You're as good as married, Admiral. Though I doubt you'll thank me for it in a year."

The ten men round the table chuckled in agreement.

Jack smiled but for a very different reason. *You are safe, Bess. And you are mine.*

With steady hands and a calm voice, he held up both documents and announced, "You are witnesses this day that I have leased the land that once belonged to the heirs of Lord John Kerr and his widow, Lady Marjory Kerr, who will reside at Tweedsford for the next forty years or until she stands at heaven's gate."

The officers nodded in approval.

"Moreover, I have hereby obtained permission to marry Elisabeth Ferguson Kerr, widow of Lord Donald Kerr." *My beloved Bess.* He swallowed, hard. "Upon our marriage Lady Buchanan will reside with me at Bell Hill in Selkirk, the parish of her late husband, without fear of the king's reprisal for her former allegiance to the Jacobite cause." Jack whisked the last traces of sand from the documents, then bowed. "So you have witnessed, and so it is done."

Men on both sides of the table applauded, their duty dispatched, while General Lord Mark Kerr attended to his gold.

Jack took his leave and quickly, lest the

general change his mind. Only when the two men reached the portcullis gate did Dickson slap him on the back. "Well done, milord."

"Well . . ." Jack exhaled. "Done, at any rate."

SEVENTY-FIVE

Thinkest thou that I could live, and let thee
go,
Who art my life itself? — no — no.

THOMAS MOORE

"Cousin, you *must* tell him."

Marjory saw the determined spark in Anne's eye and knew any argument would be offered in vain.

Even Elisabeth, whose every thought now centered on Lord Buchanan in Edinburgh, told her, "Gibson deserves to know, dearest."

Marjory had little time left to make a decision. Neil was coming for dinner at one o' the clock, with all three Kerr women waiting to greet him. Two of them were convinced he would accept Lord Buchanan's provision as a gift from the Lord, allowing the couple to marry without delay. Marjory was less certain.

What if, presented with this clear opportunity, Neil suddenly balked? Some men, after all, were more in love with the idea of marriage than the fact of it.

Or what if, when she suggested they wed, her boldness offended him or wounded his manly pride? She couldn't bear to think of hurting him.

Distraught, Marjory poked the mutton simmering over the hearth, then jabbed the potatoes baking in the grate, hoping if she turned her back toward her family, they might let the subject rest.

They did nothing of the sort.

Anne sidled up to her first, flashing the silver band round her ring finger. "You could have one of these," she said smugly. "Once the reverend has read the banns three Sabbaths in a row, Gibson would be yours."

"You make it sound so simple," Marjory fretted. Which upset her even more, because she *hated* fretting. Even the Buik said, "Fret not thyself." Yet, here she was again, fretting.

Then Elisabeth appealed to her heart, which was patently unfair. "Gibson loves you, Marjory," her daughter-in-law said, circling a hand round her elbow, tugging her away from the hearth. "Think how grieved he would be if he heard the news of this blessing from someone else."

Marjory spun round. "Bess, you wouldn't —"

"Never," she assured her. "I only meant

that Lord Buchanan might say something in passing, certain Gibson already knew. And what will happen when you start spending this money? Gibson is a canny man, Marjory. He will guess its source and be heartbroken you didn't tell him."

Marjory sighed. "But it amounts to a proposal of marriage."

"Precisely!" Anne cried happily. "Elisabeth insisted I propose to Michael, and look how well *that* turned out."

Elisabeth squeezed Marjory's arm. "And weren't you the one who suggested I present myself to Lord Buchanan? Although we cannot be sure of the outcome, I'm most hopeful."

Marjory could not dispute their claims. Perhaps it *was* her turn.

"All right," she said with a groan. "But I cannot do this with an audience —"

"Certainly not." Anne took Elisabeth by the sleeve, pulling her toward the stair. "We'll take Peter for a nice, long walk. 'Tis a dry day, and his father will be glad for an hour's peace."

"Dinner will keep," Elisabeth assured her, opening the door, "but Gibson will not."

"What willna I keep, lass?" Neil Gibson stood on the landing, wool bonnet in hand.

"Oh!" Elisabeth blushed to her roots. "Well . . . I believe Marjory has . . . good news that will not keep. We'll be back shortly."

Both women quickly skirted round him, then hastened down the stair, leaving an awkward silence in their wake.

Marjory dried her hands on her apron. *Give me the words, Lord. Give me the courage.*

Neil entered the house, an expectant look on his face. "Will they not be staying for dinner, then?"

" 'Tis just us," Marjory said, stretching out her hands to welcome him.

Neil, it seemed, would not be satisfied with handholding.

He crossed the gap between them in three strides and took her in his arms. "Marjory, my luve." His voice was rough, his kiss tender. "I canna wait 'til I have mair money. Say ye'll marry me, lass. We'll make a go of it somehow . . ."

"Oh, but, Neil, I . . ."

He kissed her again, then pressed his brow to hers. "I ken ye should be the one asking, Leddy Kerr, because o' yer station. But I must do the asking, because I luved ye first."

"I'm not sure that's true," she managed to say round the lump in her throat. "I loved you before I could put words to it." She stepped back so she might look into his eyes. "If you are the one asking, Neil Gibson, then I am the one answering. Aye, a thousand times, aye!"

Then she kissed him, giving him her whole heart, her whole self. He responded in kind, throwing prudence to the winds.

When at last she tucked her head beneath his chin, Marjory said with a smile, "Have I told you how much I love you, Neil Gibson?"

"Ye have. But I'll not mind hearing it again."

So she told him several times. And kissed him several times more. And then she remembered the news that would change everything and drew him to her table.

"I've nae appetite for dinner, Marjory, if that's what ye're thinking."

She laughed. "I mean to serve you something other than mutton."

After putting an empty wooden plate before him, she hurried to find the stocking in her trunk, then returned with a bank note in her hand and hope in her heart. "The Almighty has sent a generous gift our way." She served up the note, worth far more than her meat dish, however well seasoned.

He stared at it, eyes and mouth agape. "Five hundred pounds? How did . . . Whaur did . . ."

Then she told him the truth. About her foolish gift to Prince Charlie, to a lost cause. And about Lord Buchanan's generosity. "I believe with all my heart this is from the Lord's hand."

Neil shook his head in disbelief. "Ye say there are . . . mair?"

She brought out her stocking and poured

the rest onto his plate, thinking if he saw it all, he would understand.

" 'Tis a miracle," he finally said. "And those only come from God."

Marjory sighed. "What a wise man I am marrying."

He curled his arm round her waist and pulled her onto his lap. "And I get a rich woman in the bargain."

"Not rich, but we'll not starve." She looked about the house. "When Bess and Lord Buchanan marry, which surely they will, we can live here, if you like."

"We can indeed, but I still must wark at something," he cautioned her. "I canna be a kept man." He kissed her, lightly this time. "The reverend will read oor banns on Sunday. And marry us three weeks hence, aye?"

Three weeks. She nodded, overwhelmed by the thought.

"On the Sabbath," Neil said firmly, "in the manse. If the Almichty means for us to marry, then let us honor him from the start."

"Aye," she said without hesitation, then stood, remembering dinner. "Might I offer you meat before you return to your labors?"

"Ye may." He let her go, though he did not take his eyes off her.

She felt him watching her closely as she went about her tasks. Slicing the juicy meat. Cutting open the hot potatoes. When a moment later she joined him at table with their plates in hand, she asked, "Are you imagining what it will be like, day after day, seeing me cook?"

His mischievous smile told her otherwise. "I was imagining ye all richt. But not at the hearth."

"Neil Gibson!" she exclaimed, pretending to be shocked, though she was secretly delighted. They were not young, but they were not dead.

"I must think of a praisent for ye," he said, then bit into his mutton with a satisfied groan.

She brushed the hair from his brow. "You love me, dear Neil, with all my faults and weaknesses. That gift will last me a lifetime."

"I mean it to, lass. A lang life, full o' a' that is guid."

She watched him now, as he'd watched her, and forgot everything she ever knew about fretting.

SEVENTY-SIX

Gifts come from above in their own
peculiar forms.

JOHANN WOLFGANG VON GOETHE

"Will you be finishing that, milord?" Dickson
eyed the large cut of beef that sat untouched
on his master's plate.

Jack pushed the remains of his dinner
across the table. "I thought you left such poor
manners aboard ship."

"Oh, I did, mostly." Dickson cut into the
meat with relish. "But I brought my appetite
with me. And 'tis a shame to waste good
meat."

Jack gazed out the inn's small-paned windows into the Grassmarket, eager to quit the
capital and start for home. But when they'd
returned to the inn to change into riding
clothes and claim their belongings, Dickson
had reminded him he'd eaten little for breakfast that morning, and they'd be some hours
riding to Middleton. "We'd best dine now,"

Dickson had said. So here they sat on hard wooden chairs while the clock ticked round.

When Dickson had consumed everything on both their plates and began gazing longingly at a stranger's meal, Jack pushed back from the table. "Time we were off."

"Lord Buchanan!" a voice called from the entrance. "Can it be ye?"

Jack turned to find Archie Gordon, the bearded Scotsman charged with looking after Fiona Cromar's welfare, lumbering toward the table. Jack had chosen the man not only for his honesty but also for his size. Even the fiercest Highlanders might think again before they'd take on Archie Gordon.

The man lowered his bulk onto a tottery chair and planted his elbows on the table. "Are ye lodging here?" he asked.

"We were," Jack told him, "but are now bound for Bell Hill."

"Weel, that's whaur I was headed." Archie wagged his head, his thick red hair tied back with a bit of leather. "A coincidence, aye?"

"I prefer to think of it as divine providence," Jack told him. "You must have news of some import, Archie, to bring it to my door rather than post a letter."

The man's jovial expression faded. "Aye, milord."

Jack's stomach knotted. "Good news or ill?"

"I'll let ye be the judge o' that." Archie rubbed his hand over his beard, then waved over the innkeeper and ordered a pint of ale and a kidney pie before finally relaying the news. "Ben Cromar is deid."

Jack stared at him. *"Dead?"*

"Aye," Archie said, frowning. "Got into a brawl with a neighbor after they both had too much whisky. Cromar fell and hit his head on a rock sticking up from the ground. Folk were there as witnesses. 'Twas an accident and naught else."

Jack sank back in his chair. "I am very sorry to hear it."

"Is that a fact?" Archie looked at him in amazement. "I thocht ye micht be pleased, cruel as the man was."

"Relieved," Jack admitted, "but not pleased, not at another man's death."

"Aye, weel." Archie took his first sip of ale and sighed. "To be sure, Fiona Cromar is alone noo, with none to provide for her."

Jack stood. "That I can remedy." He sought out the innkeeper, then returned to the table shortly thereafter with quill, ink, paper, and wax. "In a moment I'll have a letter ready for Mrs. Cromar. When you return to Bell Hill with her answer, I'll reward you for your labors. Will that suit?"

"Aye, milord. If ye'll not mind, I'll have my dinner while ye write."

Jack nodded, his pen already moving across the paper. He did not know Elisabeth's mother well enough to guess how she would respond. But he knew Elisabeth. *Say you will, Fiona. For your daughter's sake.* Jack added a few pieces of gold, then sealed the letter well.

Dickson looked at him askance, then said in a low voice, "Are you certain about that, milord?"

"Aye." Jack had no qualms entrusting Archie with his gold. Unlike the young messenger tarrying round the punch bowl, Archie Gordon was not prone to drink and had shown himself to be an honest and honorable man.

Archie dropped the sealed letter in his coat pocket with a nod of assurance. The delivery was as good as done. "Sorry to bring ye bad news, Lord Buchanan. Ye leuked quite happy whan I first saw ye."

"Indeed I am, for I'm to marry this month." Just saying the words made his heart leap.

"Weel, then," Archie said, "ye're in the richt city. Walk up to the Luckenbooths in the High Street and find a silver brooch for yer bride. 'Tis an auld Scottish custom."

Jack was not keen on delaying their journey any longer. But if it meant taking home a gift for Elisabeth, something that might have a special meaning to her, he'd make time for it. "Come, Dickson. It seems we're going brooch hunting."

The two men climbed the West Bow, a steep, winding street that carried them up to the main thoroughfare where the Luckenbooths, a series of market stalls kept locked at night, sat in front of the High Kirk of Saint Giles. Weaving his way through the jostling crowd, Jack headed for a shop with a promising sign painted above the lintel: *Patrick Cowie, Merchant, Jewelry and Silver Bought and Sold.* Surely this Mr. Cowie would have a silver brooch or two to choose from.

Jack and Dickson ducked inside the small, dimly lit shop and were greeted by Mr. Cowie himself. "Guid day to ye, gentlemen," he said, waving them toward a glass case brimming with jewelry. "Whatsomever might ye be leuking for?"

Jack began, "I am to marry this month —"

"Then I've just the thing." The merchant quickly produced a small silver pin with two hearts intertwined. "Ilka bride in Edinburgh langs for such a praisent."

When Jack saw several more brooches like it, the item lost its appeal. Elisabeth deserved a unique gift, meant for her alone. "Perhaps something else," he said, studying the other jewelry on display. "Might I see that one?" He pointed to a large, oval-shaped cameo bearing a woman's likeness.

"Verra guid, sir." Mr. Cowie lifted out the wooden box and placed it in his hands. "Carved in Paris for a leddy in toun."

Jack touched the peach-and-ivory shell, the delicate silhouette done in relief. "I know 'twill sound odd, but this woman is the very image of my bride."

Dickson looked round his shoulder. "You are right, milord."

Jack was already reaching for his leather coin purse, certain he'd chosen well.

Once the merchant had money in hand, he admitted, "Bit of a sad story with that one. But it's aff to a guid hame and will nae doubt come to a blithe end."

Dickson stayed Jack's hand. "Do you mean to say this pin is unlucky?"

"Weel . . ." The flustered merchant waved his hands about. "I wouldna say *that* . . ."

"I don't believe in luck," Jack assured him, "so it matters not." He tucked the wooden box in his waistcoat pocket and turned toward the street. "Come, Dickson. However fine this cameo, I'd rather gaze at the woman herself than study a likeness carved in shell."

"We've two days' ride ahead of us," his valet reminded him, hurrying to keep up.

Jack was already striding toward West Bow, his mind fixed on the stables in the Grassmarket below, where Janvier waited to carry him home.

To Bell Hill. To his bride.

SEVENTY-SEVEN

Every delay that postpones our joys is long.

OVID

"But whan will we see his lordship?" Peter cried, a decided pout on his freckled face. "Oor picnic will be ower afore lang."

Elisabeth eyed the heaps of cold duck and beef, the mounds of hard cheese, the willow basket brimming with crisp apples and succulent pears — all fresh from yesterday's market, now spread across a plaid blanket. "We have plenty," she promised the lad. "Enough to feed Lord Buchanan *and* Dickson."

"I'm not so sure o' that," Michael said, reaching for an apple. "I've watched Dickson eat."

Elisabeth was glad for such sanguine company on a day when her future hung in the balance. General Lord Mark Kerr was not a man of mercy. Had Jack found some way to convince him? Knowing very well it was not the king, nor the general, nor the admiral who could save her, she glanced at the heavens. *I have trusted in thy mercy.* Then she remembered the rest of the verse and was comforted by it. *My heart shall rejoice in thy salvation.*

The Kerrs woke that morning to unseasonably mild weather. Elisabeth had suggested they take their dinner out of doors and bring the Dalglieshes with them. Gibson, too, if the reverend might allow it.

The rolling meadow at the foot of Bell Hill seemed a worthy spot for a picnic.

"So you can watch for a certain admiral?" Marjory had guessed.

Elisabeth could not pretend otherwise. Jack had said, "Look for our return on Saturday afternoon." So she was looking. And waiting. And praying. Of the three, waiting was the hardest.

With a sigh she stretched out on the blanket and lifted her face to the sun, drawing strength from the warmth of its rays. They'd not have many days like this left in the year. Even the occasional breeze had no bite to it. At least the road should be dry through the Moorfoot Hills. Though anything might delay them. An injured horse. An injured man . . .

Elisabeth sensed someone's shadow blocking the sun and opened her eyes to find Peter leaning over her, arms akimbo, chubby fists at his waist. "Must ye take naps, like I once did?"

She sat up and pulled him onto her lap, hugging him close. "Aye, sometimes."

Elisabeth rested her chin on his curly head and watched the two couples who'd each claimed a corner of the blanket. Anne and Michael, playful and teasing, still rather shy round each other, at least in public. Marjory and Gibson, tender and gentle, with an undercurrent of passion that charged every glance.

In three weeks the older couple would wed. Elisabeth wished them only joy, yet she longed to join them at the altar with Jack by her side.

When Peter wriggled free to chase a leaf that blew temptingly near, Anne turned to watch him, her eyes filled with maternal affection. Elisabeth looked away, ashamed at the stab of envy that pierced her heart. Aye, she wanted that as well. *Am I being selfish, Lord? Am I being foolish? Dare I hope?*

Michael was soon up and chasing after the lad. A good father to his son, as Jack would surely be someday.

Then Anne turned to her with a question Elisabeth had not even considered.

"Will Lord Buchanan come directly to Bell Hill, do you suppose? Or will he stop in Halliwell's Close?"

Chagrined, Elisabeth looked toward the

mansion hidden in the trees. "I cannot say. If 'tis good news, surely he would come find me at once. But if 'tis ill news . . ."

Nae. She would not dwell on the possibility.

Another hour or so passed. None of them had a pocket watch, dependent on the moving sun to mark the time. Elisabeth eyed Belda, nibbling on the grass. Might she ride out to meet Jack?

"I can wait here no longer," she confessed. "Mr. Dalgliesh, will you kindly help me with the mare? I've decided to meet Lord Buchanan on the road approaching Selkirk."

Her brow knitted with concern, Marjory called out to her, "Are you certain 'tis wise to go alone?"

"On Belda? In broad daylight?" Elisabeth heard the note of impatience in her voice and quickly curbed it. "Truly, I'll not go far. No more than a mile or two out the Edinburgh road. I would hate for him to look for us in town and be disappointed."

"Very well, though I do not approve," Marjory said, sounding like the mother she was.

Elisabeth did not tarry, lest anyone else object. With a lift of her hand in farewell, she guided Belda across the meadow's many hillocks, grateful when they reached the road without mishap. As they trotted toward town, she noted a few clouds starting to move in from the west. But they were neither thick nor dark, and the air was calm. An hour or more of sunlight remained and then the gloaming. Plenty of time.

Jack was drawing near. She knew it absolutely, as if his scent traveled through the air, though she did not find him at Halliwell's Close.

Riding through town, Elisabeth noted many a curious glance. Her neighbors had often seen her on Belda but not in a gown adorned with buttons and ruffles. If she did marry — *Nae! Not if, Lord, but when* — the gossips of Selkirk would blether about it for months. A small price to pay for the blessing of being a good man's wife.

Elisabeth guided Belda through the East Port, then down to the bridge across the Ettrick, before turning north toward Edinburgh, toward Jack. She rode one mile, then two, passing only the occasional rider, until she eventually reached the gates of Tweedsford. Odd to see the place again. Though not a soul was in sight, Mr. Laidlaw and the other servants were assuredly within.

The sky was grayer now and the sun lower. *Hurry, Jack.* This was the only road to the north; he had to come this way.

Belda pawed at the ground, clearly wanting to continue. "We must wait here," Elisabeth said in a firm voice. Beyond Tweedsford the road grew more winding, with lonely stretches between properties. As it was, Jack might not be pleased to find her abroad unescorted.

I do not approve. Was that Marjory's voice, or was it Jack's?

Elisabeth looked through the open gates, wondering if she dared seek shelter at Tweedsford should rain or nightfall come before Jack appeared. *Nae.* Though General Lord Mark Kerr was not in residence at the moment, she could not look to his servants for help.

She started forward, then turned back, started forward, then turned back, frustrating Belda and herself in the process. Should she ride home? Ride to Bell Hill? Now that she'd come this far, she longed to greet him on her own, without the others present, however much she loved them. She imagined waving to Jack from a distance, catching him by surprise, welcoming him home with a kiss . . .

Aye, she would wait a bit longer.

Though the rain did not come, the gloaming finally did. Each time she heard hoofbeats on the hard dirt road, her head and heart lifted with anticipation. When instead a stranger trotted by with a tip of his hat, she offered a faint smile, relieved when he moved on.

Are you certain 'tis wise to go alone? Marjory's voice again.

Elisabeth knew the answer now.

In the fading light Belda whinnied at the sound of another rider approaching. More than one, judging by the hoofbeats. Elisabeth eased a bit farther down the road, moistening her lips, trying to swallow. She could not see them round the bend in the road, but she heard voices. Male voices.

Mustering her courage, she called out into the dusky air, "Lord Buchanan?"

SEVENTY-EIGHT

Thou bringest the sailor to his wife.

ALFRED, LORD TENNYSON

Bess? Nae, it couldn't be her. Not on this road and not at this hour. When he heard his name called again, all doubt was erased.

Jack spurred Janvier forward, with Dickson riding close behind. A moment later they came round the curve and found Elisabeth waiting by the gates of Tweedsford as if a gentlewoman riding alone at twilight was of no concern.

He quickly brought Janvier to a halt beside Belda, then reached for Elisabeth's hand. His own was shaking. With frustration, with relief, with joy. "Beloved, whatever are you doing here?"

"Welcoming you home." When her gaze met his, nothing else mattered.

He could not kiss her as he wished, but he kissed her nonetheless, bending forward

652

across the saddle, fitting his mouth to hers.

"I'll be going on, milord." Dickson trotted past him. "Shall I have the household prepared to greet their master?"

"Aye." Jack lifted his head only slightly. "And their future mistress."

Elisabeth's eyes widened. "Do you mean . . ."

"I do." He kissed her again, taking his time.

"Very good, milord," Dickson called over his shoulder, riding off.

A sudden drop of rain splattering on the back of his neck brought their tender reunion to an end. "Follow me," Jack told her, aiming for the leafy shelter of a maple tree inside the gates of Tweedsford as more drops began to fall.

Once they were well beneath the branches, Jack dismounted, then lifted her down, taking her in his arms without a word.

"Should we be here, milord?"

"Jack," he reminded her, "and, aye, we should. Lord Mark will not be arriving anytime soon, I assure you." He carefully took the two documents out of his pocket and placed them in Elisabeth's hands, showing her the marriage agreement first, with Lord Mark's bold signature. "You need never fear the dragoons knocking on your door, my love."

"Oh, Jack." She kissed him again, then read every word aloud. "Pardoned," she whispered, gripping the document. "Safe, forever."

He gazed down at her. *May it always be so, Lord.* "You'll be interested in the second document as well," Jack promised, unfolding it.

Holding the lease close to her eyes in the twilight, she scanned the words. "Marjory is to live *here?* At Tweedsford?" She looked toward the grand house at the other end of the drive. "Jack, does she know this?"

"Indeed not, for I didn't want to make a promise I couldn't keep."

Elisabeth carefully folded the lease, still gazing at the property. "Marjory lost so much. Everything, really. Yet God has restored her heart, and you, dear Jack, have restored her home."

He could think of no other way to broach the subject, and so admitted, "There are some things I cannot restore. Ben Cromar is dead."

A host of emotions crossed her features. Shock, then dismay, and finally acceptance. "If my brother were alive," Elisabeth confessed, "he'd not shed a tear for the man."

Jack had heard some of the grisly story. "Will your mother mourn Ben?"

Elisabeth took her time answering. " 'Tis hard to say. I've not seen my mother for many years . . ."

When her voice trailed off, Jack longed to

share the contents of his letter to Fiona. But since he could not guess when and how the woman might respond, he held his tongue.

Elisabeth glanced at the property lease again as if she didn't quite believe it. "Much has happened since you left for Edinburgh. Marjory and Gibson plan to marry on the nineteenth of October. Their banns will be read in the morn."

Jack smiled. "Won't the parishioners get an earful this Sunday?" Then he remembered the small gift in his pocket and quickly fished it out. "I've a present for you. Archie Gordon tells me women in Edinburgh expect such things from their betrothed."

"Is it a Luckenbooth pin?" She fumbled with the lid in the growing darkness. "How wonderful!"

Jack watched her closely, fearing he'd erred in choosing something else. " 'Tis not a silver pin," he cautioned her, "but I do hope you'll like it."

"How could I not?" she said, her voice light. Then she opened the box.

Silence.

"Bess, what is it?"

She slowly lifted out the pin and held it to her breast. In a moment a tear slipped down her cheek, then another.

Jack wasn't certain what to make of her response. Was she pleased? Overwhelmed? The brooch was expensive, aye, but still only a piece of jewelry. "I thought it a good likeness, but if you do not care for it, 'tis easily sold."

"This cameo . . ." She tried to speak, her voice breaking. "You couldn't know . . ."

"What is it, Bess?" He kept his voice low, not wanting to upset her further, smoothing his hand across her hair. "Can you not tell me?"

She nodded but did not meet his gaze. "You found this at Mr. Cowie's."

"I did." A wave of uneasiness swept over him. How could she know that? Had she seen it there months ago?

Finally she told him. "Donald had this made for me in Paris. It arrived in the shop after he . . . after Falkirk."

Then Jack remembered the merchant's words. *Carved in Paris for a leddy in toun.* "You were the lady," he breathed. "Cowie never mentioned your name."

She opened her hand. " 'Tis a beautiful pin."

"Bess, if you'd rather not —"

"I rather would." She slipped off her gloves, then with trembling fingers unbuttoned her cape and pinned the cameo to her gown. "Don't you see? I was always meant to have this but could not afford it." She brushed her lips against his. "My dear Jack, however can I thank you?"

"Marry me, Bess." He kissed her, harder

than he meant to.

She responded without hesitation, matching her passion to his. "I will, Jack," she whispered. "I will."

Dickson would have made an able town crier.

Not only was the household waiting at the entrance to Bell Hill, but also the Kerrs, the Dalglieshes, and some of their close neighbors were gathered on either side of the walk.

"Think of it as a gauntlet," Jack murmured in her ear as he lifted Elisabeth down, then handed the reins to a grinning stable lad. "A test of faith for the knights of old. The idea is to reach the other end unscathed."

Elisabeth straightened her cape. "If you are ready, milord, then so am I."

He offered her his arm. "Onward, my dear."

Instead of the usual polite bows and murmured greetings, the couple was welcomed with exuberant handshakes and merry words. When Jack and Elisabeth finally reached the threshold, he slipped one arm round her waist, holding her close, then turned to address the small crowd.

"You will hear our marriage banns read at kirk in the morn," he promised, to which a cry of joy erupted. "All I wish to say is, may the Lord bless you for your kindness. And for recognizing a virtuous woman when you meet one."

"Indeed she is," Marjory said, having hurried to Elisabeth's side.

"Mrs. Kerr, since you're here, I've brought good news for you from Edinburgh." He winked at Elisabeth. "Perhaps you'd like to tell her?"

"With pleasure." Elisabeth leaned forward and whispered in Marjory's ear.

SEVENTY-NINE

And half of the world a bridegroom is
And half of the world a bride.

SIR WILLIAM WATSON

"Tweedsford?" Marjory could hardly say the word. "But how did . . . What of . . . Nae, it cannot be!"

Yet here was her daughter-in-law promising it was true. And the most generous man she'd ever known insisting the lease was signed and could not be revoked.

Marjory clung to Neil's arm for support and peered through the door into the entrance hall, hoping she might spy a chair, a bench, a footstool — anything to prevent her from fainting on the spot. "Mr. Gibson —"

"This way, Leddy Kerr." He steered her firmly into the house and located a comfortable chair within seconds. The man truly was a marvel.

Once seated, she bade him to come closer, then confided, "I'm not certain how I feel about our neighbors learning of his lordship's provision. Though I suppose they would discover the source soon enough, wouldn't they?"

Neil's expression was more somber than usual. " 'Tis the provision itself that concerns me," he admitted. "How am I to hold up my head as yer husband whan anither man has paid for the hoose we live in?"

Marjory begged the Lord for a swift answer. "If the rent is already paid, and we've yet to marry, it would count as one of my few possessions, all of which are entirely yours once we're wed." That seemed to satisfy him, and surely it was true. "Anyway, dear Neil, you've lived there before. 'Twill be like going home." She curled her hand round his elbow, already growing accustomed to the shape and feel of him. "This time, though, you'll be the master of Tweedsford and not its head servant."

His expression lightened considerably as he cocked an eyebrow in her direction. "And how will that be different whan I'll still be serving ye?"

She offered him a coy smile. "For one thing, you'll be sleeping in the master bedroom."

Her words had precisely the effect she'd intended: Neil Gibson was smiling broadly.

"Bess, we cannot plan two weddings at once." Sitting at their dining room table, Marjory

660

frowned at the twin lists of duties to be accomplished, giving serious thought to taking up fretting again. "With my small ceremony on the nineteenth and your large one on the twentieth . . ." She threw up her hands, dripping ink onto the paper in the process. "However will we manage?"

Elisabeth reached for her own list and dusted it with sand. "I shall give this to Mrs. Pringle. Nothing would please her more than overseeing my wedding. All I care about is standing before the bride stool with the man I love by my side."

Marjory searched her heart and realized she felt quite the same. When did such a happy occasion become so complicated? She tore her paper in half.

"My guest list will be as follows," Marjory declared. "Annie and Michael Dalgliesh, Lord Buchanan, and you, dear Bess. My gown will be the one I'm wearing, my flowers will be a single damask rose from Bell Hill's garden, if his lordship will not object, and the wedding supper will be a pot of cock-a-leekie soup, simmering on the hearth while Mr. Gibson and I speak our vows at the manse. To be served with bread, I suppose. And cheese."

Elisabeth laughed. "And cakes."

"Naturally." Marjory found herself warming to the idea. Small, quiet, simple. "This is, after all, my second wedding."

"Mine too," Elisabeth reminded her, taking her hand. "You are quite certain —"

"Elisabeth Kerr," she said rather pointedly, "you were a wonderful wife to my son. Though I did not realize it at the time, 'tis very clear to me now. You did everything in your power to please him. And honored him when he did not honor you. I could not be . . ." Marjory's throat tightened. "I could not be more proud of you if you were my own daughter. You deserve every happiness."

Elisabeth looked up, her heart in her eyes. "I will never forget Donald."

"Nor I. How could we?" Marjory swallowed. "No matter how abominably he behaved, Donald will always be my first son. And your first husband." She dried her eyes with the hem of her apron, then sniffed. "Now, that is *one* thing I refuse to have at my wedding: tears."

Marjory could not look at Anne.

Elisabeth was worse.

'Twas a miracle the manse was not flooded, so copious was their weeping. Happy tears, to be sure, but still tears. Even the weather had confounded Marjory's wishes, with a steady rain that began at daybreak, then continued all through the Sabbath morning at kirk and well into the afternoon.

Neil, at least, was dry-eyed and looking more handsome than ever in his silvery blue coat, waistcoat, and trousers — a wedding gift from the Dalglieshes. Whatever his upbringing, Neil Gibson was a true gentleman. Now he looked the part.

As for Elisabeth, she'd insisted on stitching a new black gown for her — not of wool but of watered silk — with sufficient ruffles and bows to please her without raising too many eyebrows on Kirk Wynd. Since her daughter-in-law would soon become Lady Elisabeth, Marjory agreed such a gown might prove useful on special occasions at Bell Hill.

Tomorrow's wedding, for example.

Marjory glanced over her shoulder, relieved to see Michael Dalgliesh and Lord Buchanan contributing fresh handkerchiefs to the cause. Perhaps by the time the ceremony began and she spoke her vows, not a sniffle would be heard from the seats behind her. Because truly, Marjory could not hold out much longer.

"How d'ye like the bride stool?" Neil asked her, patting the small wooden pew used only for weddings. "The auld one was a sorry thing."

"You made this?" She touched the smoothly planed wood, the neatly matched joints. "I believe you are becoming quite a carpenter, Neil Gibson."

When he smiled, eyes twinkling, Neil looked ten years younger. "Syne ye mentioned it, I

wonder if we might spend some o' yer pounds
—"

"*Our* pounds."

"Aye, oor pounds, on fine wood. Oak or mahogany or whatsomever ye like. I've a mind to make a few pieces o' furniture. For the hoose, ye ken."

Marjory saw through his request. If Neil could work with his hands, if he could make something that pleased her, he would feel he was doing his part.

"You clever man," she told him. "I cannot wait to see what you'll make first."

"Och, I've already started it," he said, "which ye'll see whan we move there come Martinmas."

Marjory blushed, quite certain she knew what he'd spent the last fortnight designing.

At last the reverend joined them, his black robe flapping round his legs. "Shall we begin?"

Neil stood, bringing Marjory up with him, keeping her close by his side.

She dared not turn to him. Already her eyes were growing moist.

Reverend Brown looked about the drawing room as if surprised to see so few in attendance. "Very well, then. First, is there any impediment to this marriage?"

"None," the four witnesses said in unison, then grinned at one another like the children they were. Well, not *children* perhaps, but certainly young.

Reverend Brown spoke of marriage, of its purpose, of its sacredness, then asked for the rings to be produced.

Neil held out a delicate silver band, waiting for Marjory to offer up her hand.

She was embarrassed to find it trembling. Badly.

But Neil was unflappable. He took her hand, calming her at once, then slipped the ring over her finger, stopping at her knuckle, prepared to speak his vows.

The minister said, "Do you, Neil Gibson, take this woman, Marjory Nesbitt Kerr, to be your lawfully wedded wife?"

Neil looked down at her, smiling. And then he seemed to disappear from view as tears pooled in her eyes. Marjory had no choice but to tip her chin and let them cascade down her cheeks. When she looked up, she could see him again. And fell in love with him again.

Beloved. Aye, he was surely that.

Neil's voice was steady, yet thick with emotion. "Even so, I take her afore God and in the presence o' his people." With that, he gently pushed the ring in place.

I am yours, Neil. Truly yours.

Reverend Brown turned to her and asked the same question he'd surely asked hundreds of brides. But on this day, she was the one to answer.

"And do you, Marjory Nesbitt Kerr, take

this man, Neil Gibson, to be your lawfully wedded husband?"

She slipped a thick silver band, newly purchased, onto his ring finger and looked into his eyes, amazed to find she could speak. "Even so, I take him before God and in the presence of his people."

You are mine, Neil. Truly mine.

Marjory did not remember what else the minister said, though he spoke at length and all of it was good and right. What she remembered was the warm hand that held hers and the tender kiss that followed at the door of the manse, when the rain stopped and the sun shone and Neil Gibson swept her into his embrace.

EIGHTY

To marry a second time represents the
triumph of hope over experience.

SAMUEL JOHNSON

"Guid morn!" Sally cried. "And a bonny
wedding day to ye!" Elisabeth turned as the
maidservant entered her new dressing room
at Bell Hill with a breakfast tray laden with
freshly cooked eggs, a rasher of bacon,
toasted bread, and raspberry jam.

"Compliments of Mrs. Tudhope," Sally
explained, placing the tray on a nearby table.
She poured a steaming cup of tea, added just
the right amount of sugar and milk, then offered a cheerful curtsy.

"Such service," Elisabeth praised her, savor-
ing her first, bracing sip. "You know, Sally,
I'll be needing a lady's maid."

Her eyes brightened. "Is that so?"

Elisabeth was not fooled. Sally Craig was a
clever lass who never missed an opportunity

to improve her situation. "Might you be interested?"

"Och!" She spun in a circle. "If ye'll have me and Mrs. Pringle will allow it, I'm yers."

"You must start at once," Elisabeth cautioned her. "This very day."

"Weel, mem, yer lavender gown is already aired and pressed. And ye'll find yer dressing room weel stocked with lavender soap. Provided by his lordship," she added, blushing prettily.

Elisabeth smiled. "I see I've chosen the right young woman."

"Aye, mem," Sally assured her, grinning back at her. "Noo, eat a' yer food afore it gets cauld, and then we'll see to yer toilette." She took her leave, no doubt off to inform Mrs. Pringle of her new position.

Elisabeth obediently nibbled on a piece of toast and jam, thinking how strange it would be to have a maidservant waiting on her again. Bathing her, dressing her, styling her hair. She vowed to be a good mistress to Sally. Teaching her useful skills, encouraging her in matters of faith. She had further plans for the entire household if Jack would allow it. Reading and writing, to begin with. Needlework for the women. Carpentry for the men.

She'd once longed for Donald to lead the Kerr household in a time of family worship each evening after supper, a common practice in devout homes. Might Jack be willing? And include the servants as well?

So much to discuss! And a lifetime to do so, she reminded herself, overjoyed at the thought. Thirty, forty, even fifty more years if God was kind, which he surely was.

She was finishing the last bite of her breakfast when she heard a man's footsteps in the hall, then a light tap at the door. "Mrs. Kerr?"

Elisabeth crossed the room, clasping shut her dressing gown. Speaking through the crack in the door, she told him softly, "I am not dressed, milord, and so cannot invite you within."

"Oh. Might you be prepared to meet me in . . . say, an hour? In the garden?" Lowering his voice, he added, "I should very much like to see you, Bess."

"And I, you." *Very much.* "If you might ask Sally to attend me."

Her new lady's maid soon reappeared bearing hot water, clean linens, and a wide-eyed expression. "His lordship bade me come at once."

Elisabeth smiled. "Then let's not keep him waiting, shall we?"

For her first effort, Sally did exceptionally well with Elisabeth's hair. " 'Twill need to be done again for the wedding, o' course. At four o' the clock, aye?"

Elisabeth nodded, a sudden chill sweeping over her. Not from fear, certainly, or from nervousness. But from sheer delight.

Jack was standing in the garden when Elisabeth hurried through the drawing room doors into a bright October morning. The air was crisp and dry and the cloudless sky a brilliant blue.

"Dickson is dressing you rather smartly of late," she told Jack, admiring the dark brown coat that perfectly matched his eyes.

He shrugged. "My valet insists I look the part of a wealthy gentleman."

"I approve," she told him, "though 'twill be some time before I can sew enough gowns to look the part of Lady Buchanan."

"My dear, you are already a lady." Jack took her hands, tugging her closer. "As to your wardrobe, I hope you'll not be unhappy with me, but I employed two dressmakers in town to create a few simple gowns for you. Nothing like the quality of your own designs, of course. Feel free to pass them on to Mrs. Dalgliesh, if you like."

Elisabeth laughed. "Jack, my cousin is a half foot shorter than I am and a good deal smaller. Any gown of mine would need to be remade completely for her."

"Surely the dressmakers can manage that," he teased her.

"I suppose," she agreed. "When might those 'few simple gowns' of mine be ready?"

He smiled. "You'll find six of them hanging

in your new dressing room when you return."

"Six?"

"The women had only a fortnight," he apologized.

"Oh, I'm not disappointed," she hastened to say. "I'm amazed. Having worn the same gown from September last 'til June, the thought of six new gowns at once is . . . well, 'tis remarkable." Then she eyed him more closely. "However did they manage without taking my measurements?"

"I confess, I had an accomplice. Your mother-in-law employed your measuring tape one night while you were sleeping."

Very canny of you, Marjory. Elisabeth would have to think of some way to repay the woman for being so secretive. Put salt in her sugar bowl, perhaps, or stitch her pockets shut. Or she could thank her profusely when next she saw her. Aye, that seemed best.

"Milord?" A footman came forward bearing a thick letter.

Jack accepted it, then broke the seal at once, though his expression showed some misgivings. " 'Tis from Archie Gordon, the man I sent to Castleton." When he unfolded the letter, another one fell into his hands. He palmed it for a moment, quickly reading through the first letter, then sighed. "This one is for you." He held the second out to her. "From your mother."

Seeing his face, Elisabeth unfolded the letter with misgivings of her own. Had something else happened to her mother, some further tragedy? *Please let her be in good health, Lord.* Then she read the few Gaelic lines and understood.

My beloved Bess,

I received a letter from Lord Buchanan and was pleased to learn of your wedding plans. He is a man of honor and will be a good husband to you.

Elisabeth nodded as if her mother were standing there in the garden. *I believe he will be, Mother. Just as your first husband, my father, was to you.*

Lord Buchanan offered to bring me to Selkirk so I might make my home with you. And a very fine home it is, I am sure.

Oh my dear Jack. Elisabeth gripped the letter, overcome by his kindness. Alas, she knew her mother well. Fiona would never leave the Highlands.

My place is here, Bess, among the friends and neighbors I have known all my life. You can be sure they will take care of me to the end of my days.

A great sadness welled up inside her. *I wish I could see you, Mother. I wish I could tell you about the Almighty and all he has done for me.* Would she never have the chance?

I shall look forward to your letters now that I am certain to receive them. I promise to write as oft as I can.

Elisabeth's sorrow began to ease. She would write her mother every week. Nae, twice a week. All was not lost.

I will anticipate with great joy the news of your first child.

Your loving mother

My first child. Seeing it written in her mother's familiar hand stirred hope anew in Elisabeth's heart. Though she'd not borne a child for Donald, might the Lord still bless her womb? *Please, Father. For Jack's sake.* Aye, and for her own. *A braw wee lad. A bonny daughter.*

Elisabeth slowly folded the letter, then looked up. "You are so generous, Jack. Offering my mother a place in your home."

"Our home," he reminded her.

"Just to be able to write her and know she is willing to write back . . ." She sighed, then drank in the fresh breeze, scented with dried leaves and ripe apples. " 'Tis a beginning,"

"This day is all about beginnings." He drew her to his side as they walked along the garden bed, Charbon leading the way, twitching his gray tail. "Our guests will not arrive until noontide," Jack reminded her. "What say we enjoy this fine weather and discuss our plans for the future. Have you any improvements in mind for the household?"

Her smile returned. "I do."

EIGHTY-ONE

In all the wedding cake, hope is the
sweetest of plums.

DOUGLAS JERROLD

Late afternoon sunshine poured through the
freshly scrubbed windows of Bell Hill as Jack
strode through the halls, stopping only to
confer with the musicians, making very
certain all was in readiness. Reverend Brown
was waiting by the fireplace, and the two
newest brides in the parish, Anne Dalgliesh
and Marjory Gibson, were seated in the front
row with their husbands. Now if he just had
his own bride, the ceremony might begin.

He'd not spied Elisabeth since Sally had
spirited her away. "Ye'll see her in the drawing room at four o' the clock but not afore,"
she had told him. Rather firmly, for a maidservant.

Dickson came round the corner and immediately frowned. "Whatever have you done
to your neckcloth, milord?"

"Nothing," Jack insisted. *At least not on purpose.* He stood still while Dickson righted the thing but kept one eye on the broad, open stair where Elisabeth would descend.

"We've had no correspondence from Lord Mark in Edinburgh?" Jack inquired, expecting Dickson to shake his head, which he did. "And nothing from London?" Jack was not prone to worry, but until Elisabeth spoke her vows, His Majesty could still intervene. Should King George protest a marriage, any Church of Scotland minister, including Reverend Brown, would be required to honor his sovereign's wishes, signed agreement or no.

Is there any impediment to this marriage? Jack could not wait to get past those dreaded words.

"Milord," Dickson murmured, " 'tis your lady."

Jack looked up just as Elisabeth started down the stair. Even with her wide hoops and full skirts, she moved effortlessly from one step to the next. Her dark hair was a crown, piled high on top of her head and studded with pearls. But it was her smile that captured him, pinning him in place until she reached his side.

"Lord Buchanan," she said with a tilt of her chin, "I wonder if you might escort me to the drawing room."

He smiled down at her. "With pleasure."

Jack immediately noticed the scent of lavender wafting from her gown and the quickness of her step. "Madam is in a hurry," he murmured.

Blushing, she tugged him closer. "I'll not deny it."

"I shall be waiting for you," he assured her when they reached the door. Then he slipped into the drawing room and took his place by Reverend Brown.

"Treat her well," the minister said gruffly, "or you shall answer to me."

"We are of the same mind," Jack assured him, never taking his eyes off the massive wooden door, slightly ajar.

When the fiddler struck his first note, Elisabeth entered with a dramatic sweep of satin. Her smile grew with each step until at last she reached his side. *My love, my Bess.*

Reverend Brown offered a word of greeting and a few solemn thoughts on marriage. Jack had heard them yesterday at the Gibsons' wedding yet listened intently.

Then the minister lifted his head and asked, "Is there any impediment to this marriage?"

"None," Jack said firmly, producing the marriage agreement. "By order of His Majesty."

Whispers swept through the room as Reverend Brown examined the paper. "Very well, then," he said, putting it aside. "Do you, Lord Jacques Buchanan, take this woman, Elisabeth Ferguson Kerr, to be your lawfully wedded wife?"

Jack clasped her hands, never more certain of anything in his forty years. "Even so," he said in a clear, strong voice, wishing his words might carry to all the corners of the globe he'd traveled. "I take her before God and in the presence of his people."

He looked down at her, hoping his eyes said the rest. *Oh, sweet Bess, with all my heart do I take you and gladly. You are the one I waited for. You are the one the Almighty chose for me. You are the one I love.*

The minister continued, "And do you, Elisabeth Ferguson Kerr, take this man, Lord Jacques Buchanan, to be your lawfully wedded husband?"

"I do," she said, gazing up at him. "Even so, I take him before God and in the presence of his people." In her eyes he saw the rest. *I trust you, Jack. And I love you completely.*

Reverend Brown finished with conviction, "What therefore God hath joined together, let not man put asunder."

Jack's throat tightened. *Not even a king.* Then he kissed her, sealing their vows, pledging his heart. *No one but you, Bess. Now and always.*

Voices circled round them as the wedding psalm began.

Thy wife shall be a fruitful vine
By thy house sides be found
Thy children like to olive plants
About thy table round.

Amid the joyous clamor, Elisabeth stood on tiptoe to whisper in his ear, "I do hope I might give you a son, dear husband. Beginning this very night."

Her breath warmed his skin; her words warmed everything else. "I will be delighted to do all that is necessary to ensure that happy outcome." He winked at her, then offered his arm. "In the meantime, Lady Buchanan, shall we dance?"

EIGHTY-TWO

What joy is welcomed like a new-born child?

LADY CAROLINE NORTON

Bell Hill
Ten months later
Elisabeth had never heard a sweeter sound.

Not a soft whimper, but a lusty, ear-piercing cry.

She fell back against her pillow, drenched in sweat from the August heat and the hours of effort. "Water," she moaned, and a cup appeared, offered by the women who'd surrounded her birthing bed: Marjory and Anne, Sally Craig and Mrs. Pringle, Elspeth Cranston and Katherine Shaw.

Tradition had brought them to her door. A woman never gave birth without other women present to give counsel and advice and to pray for mother and child. Though at the moment it was the child's father Elisabeth longed to see.

"Jack," she called out, sounding rather pathetic.

The women laughed. Katherine Shaw, who'd borne four daughters, said, "D'ye plan to *gowf* the man for putting ye through a' this? Or shall we take care o' that for ye?"

Elisabeth mustered a faint smile. "Nae, don't slap my dear husband. He's suffered enough, walking the halls of Bell Hill for a day."

Marjory pressed a cool cloth to her brow. "Lord Buchanan only suffered when *you* did, Bess. Now, let Mrs. Scott finish her duties, and we'll tuck your babe in your arms."

Elisabeth glanced down at the sturdy midwife from Back Row, whose kind demeanor and gentle hands had seen her through the long and painful hours. "Bless you, Mrs. Scott," she murmured.

"Ye ken what the auld wives say," the woman answered softly. "There's mirth among the kin when the *howdie* cries, 'A son!' "

A son. Elisabeth would have gladly cradled a lad or a lass with equal affection. But Jack would be pleased to know his heir was born. And when she delivered a daughter into his arms someday, her stalwart husband would surely weep with joy.

When Mrs. Scott was satisfied the lad was fit to be seen, she brought him to Elisabeth, his wee body tightly wrapped in clean white linen, with only his pink features showing.

Elisabeth started to reach for him, then saw the look on Marjory's face. "Let Mrs. Gibson hold him first."

"Nae, Bess," Marjory protested, "he's your son."

"Have you forgotten the promise I made? That any babe I ever bore would be nestled in your arms?" Elisabeth motioned to Mrs. Scott, who honored her wishes.

Marjory received the child with a look of wonder, touching his tiny nose with her fingertip. "The Lord is faithful," she whispered. "And so are you, dear Bess."

Elspeth Cranston looked on with pride in her eyes. "It does me good, Marjory, to see you with a son in your arms. 'Tis like you are one-and-twenty again, holding Donald."

"I remember," Marjory said, her voice thin.

"I do too," Anne said on a sigh, "though I was a wee lass myself."

The others gathered round, admiring the child, declaring him the most handsome baby boy in Christendom.

"I did not know your sons," Mrs. Pringle confessed, "but I do know Lady Buchanan. She has surely been better to you than any mother-in-law could hope for."

Marjory gingerly placed the newborn babe in Elisabeth's waiting embrace. "No one will ever know all that my Bess has done for me."

Marjory bent down and pressed a kiss to her brow, her lips wet with tears. "The Lord bless you, dear girl."

A sudden knock made them all jump. "Lady Elisabeth?"

Her heart quickened at the sound of her husband's voice. "Come in, milord."

Jack was through the door before Sally had time to dry her mistress's face or comb her hair, though he did not seem to notice. "How beautiful you are," he said, fervently kissing her on the lips, dry and cracked as they surely were. When he finally looked down, his strong chin began to wobble. "And who is this fine lad?"

Elisabeth held him up with trembling arms. "Your son."

Jack cradled him in his hands, studying him like a nautical chart, interested in every detail. "I had no idea he would be so small."

Elisabeth laughed. "I confess, I am glad for it. But he will grow, milord. Wait and see."

When the lad began to wriggle, Jack quickly deposited him in Marjory's waiting arms for safekeeping.

"The lad will have his faither's name, o' course," Katherine said.

"Another Jack?" he protested lightly. "Nae, I think not. 'Tis a plain name and too short, like a bark. I hoped we might choose something more royal sounding."

"George?" Elisabeth teased him.

His scowl was answer enough.

"Kenneth," one of them put forth, and the rest quickly voiced their approval.

"He was the first King of the Scots," Mrs. Pringle explained. "You'll not find a name more royal than that." One by one, the women eased away from Elisabeth's bed, allowing the new parents a moment of privacy.

Jack eyed her closely. "What say you to 'Kenneth,' milady?"

"A fine name," Elisabeth agreed, wanting to honor the women who'd supported her. "Though at the moment I have another in mind."

"Oh?" He leaned closer. "And what name might that be?"

She smiled, then whispered in his ear, "Yours."

The Auld Kirk

AUTHOR NOTES

Tears are the softening showers which cause the seed of heaven to spring up in the human heart.

SIR WALTER SCOTT

Readers often ask if I cry while I'm writing my novels. Oo aye! Whenever my characters grow teary, you can be sure I leaked first. With *Here Burns My Candle,* I shed tears of sorrow, and with *Mine Is the Night,* tears of joy. As the Psalmist wrote, "Weeping may endure for a night, but joy cometh in the morning" (Psalm 30:5). Just as Marjory and Elisabeth Kerr deserved a happy ending, I thought you, my dear, were due one as well.

Before I began my Scottish research, I spent months immersed in Scripture, studying the biblical account in a dozen translations. Then I dove into stacks of Bible commentaries to help me understand what God might be trying to teach us through the lives of his people.

Now that you've read this eighteenth-century interpretation, I do hope you'll take a moment to read the real story in Ruth 1–4. God's faithfulness and loving-kindness shine all over the ancient account of Naomi, Ruth, and Boaz. As I wrote, I prayed we might also catch a glimpse of his goodness in the lives of Marjory, Elisabeth, and Lord Jack Buchanan.

Where better to turn for an epigraph than to the words of Sir Walter Scott? He was appointed Sheriff of Selkirkshire in 1799, drew from the ballads of the Borderland for his poems and novels, and was buried in Dryburgh Abbey, where Lord Jack escorted Elisabeth on horseback. Lovely, secluded Dryburgh is my favorite of the four Borderland abbeys, the others being Melrose, Kelso, and Jedburgh. The towns are so close together you can visit all four abbeys in one day and still have time for tea and scones.

In the twelfth century Selkirk had its own abbey until David I moved it to Kelso. A royal castle also came and went amid the fine hunting grounds of the Selkirk Forest, and James V confirmed the town's royal burgh status in 1535. For those reasons and more, Selkirk seemed a fine setting for a novel based on the biblical story of Ruth, the great-grandmother of King David, royal ancestor to the King of kings.

Selkirk is a delicious town, not only because of its famous bannocks, stuffed with sweet currants, but also because of its quaint appearance. All the streets are narrow, hilly, and delightfully crooked, with bits of history tucked here and there. Halliwell's Close boasts a fine regional museum, a plaque marks the spot where the Forest Inn once welcomed lodgers, and the old well still stands in the marketplace.

Stroll up Kirk Wynd, and you'll find the remains of the old parish church on a rise where William Wallace — aye, *Braveheart* — was proclaimed Guardian of Scotland in 1298. My descriptions of the ruinous state of this auld kirk were not exaggerated. After several stones fell into the pews in 1747, the "venerable pile was leveled to the ground," as one historian phrased it. The Selkirk congregation met at the nearby Grammar School while another church was erected on the same site in 1748. Our closing sketch by Scottish artist Simon Dawdry captures what remains of that church — the entrance gate and bell tower — plus a fine view of the surrounding hills.

Two maps of our triangular town plan guided me as I wrote: Walter Elliot's recent map re-creating "The Royal Burgh of Selkirk 1714" and John Wood's "Plan of the Town of Selkirk," first printed in 1823. When I finished writing the novel, Benny Gillies of Kirkpatrick Durham in Galloway created our 1746 map. If you love books about Scotland

as much as I do, visit www.BennyGillies.co.uk for a peek at the shelves of this fine man's bookshop. That's where I found *Flower of the Forest — Selkirk: A New History,* edited by John M. Gilbert, an invaluable resource that Benny insists is now "rare as hen's teeth," though it was published in 1985.

The Scottish Borders Council Archive Service at the Heritage Hub in Hawick also provided answers to questions about Reverend David Brown, a historical figure. Despite their best efforts we couldn't pinpoint a location for the manse, so I placed it across from the church, a likely spot.

While doing on-site research I slept and

dined at various spots round Selkirk, but the Garden House at Whitmuir near Bell Hill holds a special place in my heart. That is where I wrote the last dozen chapters of *Mine Is the Night,* nestled in a cozy room overlooking the garden. Robert made fresh porridge for me each morning, and Hilary delivered suppers to my room, helping me stay on task with my writing. I can still taste her mincemeat tarts, warm and fresh from the oven. *Mmm.* Heartfelt thanks to the Dunlops for their exceptional hospitality.

I am blessed to have given birth to an artist and seamstress, Lilly Higgs, who helped me understand the dressmaking process and created Elisabeth's drawing of Mrs. Pringle's gown, shown above. I have zero artistic ability yet am dependent on visuals to stoke my creative fire, so I have decorated my desk with a pewter plate, horn spoon, paper knife, magnifying glass, and photos of my characters. Ciarán Hinds from the 1995 BBC production of *Persuasion* was my inspiration for Lord Jack. Oh baby.

As for Charbon, I'd no sooner decided the admiral needed a cat than a charcoal gray kitty appeared at our door, desperate for a new home. He found one. Naturally we named him Jack. His fur is like velvet, his purr is prodigious, and Jack the Cat has stolen my heart more thoroughly than any hero ever could. (Cat lovers will find photos on my Web site.)

I am ever grateful for the fine editors who guided me through the long process of bringing this novel to the printed page: Laura Barker, Carol Bartley, Danelle McCafferty, and Sara Fortenberry, you are precious beyond words. I'm also grateful for my dear husband, Bill Higgs, who combed the last draft for grammar glitches and stray typos, and for our talented son, Matt Higgs, who put his B.A. in psychology to fine use, analyzing the words, actions, and motivations of my characters.

Of course, I could never do what I do without readers like you! I'd love to send you my free e-newsletter, *O Gentle Reader!* e-mailed twice a year. To sign up, just pop on my Web site: www.LizCurtisHiggs.com. And if you'd like free autographed bookplates for any of my novels, simply contact me through my Web site or by mail:

Liz Curtis Higgs
P.O. Box 43577
Louisville, KY 40253-0577

I hope you'll also visit my Facebook page or follow me on Twitter — two more fun ways to stay connected.

How I've loved roaming the hills and glens of Scotland with you: first in Galloway with *Thorn in My Heart, Fair Is the Rose,* and

Whence Came a Prince; then on the Isle of Arran with *Grace in Thine Eyes;* next in Edinburgh with *Here Burns My Candle;* and finally in the Borderland with *Mine Is the Night.*

I so look forward to our next grand adventure together. Until then, you truly are a *blissin!*

Liz Curtis Higgs

READERS GUIDE

A woman's whole life is a history of the affections.
The heart is her world.

WASHINGTON IRVING

1. Marjory and Elisabeth Kerr begin their new life in Selkirk as penniless widows, but they don't arrive empty-handed. What practical skills, emotional strengths, and spiritual gifts does each woman bring with her? Even so equipped they still have a great deal more to learn about life and love. How does Marjory's character grow from first page to last? And Elisabeth's? Of the two women, which is your favorite, and why?

2. Anne Kerr is less than happy to find two long-lost relatives at her door requiring food and lodging. How would you handle the situation if you were Cousin Anne? It appears she has lived alone most of her adult life. In what ways might that have shaped

her character? Elisabeth observes, "One moment Anne seemed content to be unwed, and the next she was miserable." If you are, or have been, a single adult, what's your take on the joys and challenges of singleness?

3. Knowing that *Here Burns My Candle* and *Mine Is the Night* are based on the biblical story of Ruth, readers have been eager to meet our Scottish counterpart for the heroic Boaz. Yet this novel has at least three heroes, including Michael Dalgliesh, Neil Gibson, and Lord Jack Buchanan. What heroic qualities do these good men possess? Wealth and title aside, which of the three do you find the most appealing, and why?

4. When Marjory presents Lord John's magnifying glass to Anne, their relationship takes a significant step forward. What unexpected gift have you given or received that deepened your relationship with someone? Marjory is able to share with Elisabeth the chapbook that once belonged to Donald, yet she cannot part with Andrew's toy soldier. How would you explain the difference from Marjory's viewpoint? What possession could you never part with under any circumstances, and why?

5. Novelists add children and animals to a story with care, knowing how quickly they can take over a scene. What does young Peter Dalgliesh bring to the novel? In what

ways does he remind you of a child in your life or of yourself as a child? Four-legged creatures usually reveal something about their owners. What do Charbon and Janvier tell us about Lord Jack? If Marjory were to have a pet, what would it be, and why? And what sort of pet might you choose for Anne Kerr? Reverend Brown? General Lord Mark Kerr?

6. The epigraphs, or opening quotes, for each chapter were chosen to reflect the action that follows. The quote from Robert Southey — "And last of all an Admiral came" — suited chapter 31 since Lord Jack Buchanan was the last of our major characters to be introduced. What was gained by delaying the admiral's appearance? How did your view of the admiral change from your first impression to the final scene? As to the other eighty-some epigraphs, which one did you especially like, and why?

7. After experiencing the tension, drama, and heartache of *Here Burns My Candle,* you may have been surprised to find several lighthearted moments in *Mine Is the Night.* What is gained by adding a touch of humor to a scene and to this novel in particular? Think of one bit of action or dialogue you found amusing or entertaining. Why did it appeal to you, and what did it reveal about each of the characters involved? Since laughter and tears are at one end of the

emotional spectrum — and apathy is at the opposite end — we often move rather quickly from one heightened emotion to another. Which scene in particular moved you, and why might that be so?

8. Restoration and redemption are the twin themes of *Mine Is the Night*. After many losses what is restored in Marjory's life? In Elisabeth's life? When someone is redeemed, he or she may be rescued, set free, delivered, or bought back, depending on the situation. In what ways are Marjory and Elisabeth redeemed? And how do some of the other characters experience redemption? Roger Laidlaw perhaps, or Fiona Cromar? Are there any characters in the novel whom you consider beyond redemption? If so, who and why?

9. Imagine Marjory, Elisabeth, and Anne ten years hence. What might their lives look like in 1756? Where are they living, how are they spending their time, and what is the condition of their hearts? The epigraph chosen for our Readers Guide states, "A woman's whole life is a history of the affections," suggesting women tend to measure themselves by the success or failure of their relationships with others. Do you agree or disagree, and why? What might your own life look like in ten years, particularly in regard to your relationships with those you love?

10. Readers who favor historical fiction are quick to explain their preference. Cynthia from California wrote, "It transports me to another world and enlightens and enriches me while I am entertained." And Christine from Indiana said of historical fiction, "It carries me away to another time and place where people lived, loved, and were finding their way just as I am today." If you prefer contemporary novels, what reasons could you offer? And if historical novels are more to your taste, what do you enjoy about them? When you reach the last page of any novel, what emotion do you most want to experience?

For more about the author, visit www.Liz CurtisHiggs.com.

SCOTTISH GLOSSARY

a' — all
aff — off
ahint — behind
ain — own
Almichty — Almighty
anither — another
atween — between
auld — old
awa — away, distant
aye — yes, always
bairn — child
bethankit! — God be thanked!
blether — jabber, gossip
bliss — bless
blissin — blessing
braw — fine, handsome
brig — bridge
Buik — the Bible
burn — brook, stream
byre — cowshed
cauld — cold

close — passageway, courtyard

coo — cow

creepie — low chair, footstool

deid — dead

dominie — schoolmaster, teacher

doon — down

dreich — bleak, dismal

dwiny — sickly, pining

faither — father

fash — worry, trouble, vex

foy — party, feast, celebration

freen — friend

gane — gone

gie — give

girdle — griddle for cooking

gowf — hit, strike, slap

gracie — devout, virtuous

granmither — grandmother

greet — cry, weep

guid — good

ha' — half

hame — home

heid — head

heidie — headstrong, rebellious

heiven — heaven

het — hot

Hielands — Highlands

hoose — house

hoot! — pshaw!

howdie — midwife

hurlie — trundle, move about on wheels
ilka — each, every
ill-kindit — cruel, inhuman
ither — other
jalouse — imagine, presume
ken — to know, recognize
knowe — knoll
lands — tenement houses
lang — long
leal — loyal
leddy — lady
leuk — look
loosome — lovely
Luckenbooths — locked market stalls
luve — love
mair — more
mebbe — maybe, perhaps
meikle — great, much
mem — madam
mercat — market
micht — might
michty — mighty
mither — mother
monie — many
muir — moor
nane — none
nicht — night
niver — never
noo — now
och! — oh!

onie — any
oniewise — anyhow
oo aye — yes (from French *oui*)
oor — our
oot — out
ower — over
pend — vaulted passageway
praisent — present, gift
puir — poor
richt — right
scoonrel — scoundrel
sma' — small
souter — shoemaker
spurtle — porridge stick
stayed lass — old maid
syne — since, ago, thereafter
thegither — together
thocht — thought, believed
tolbooth — town prison
toun — town
tron — public weighing machine
verra — very
wa' — wall
walcome — welcome
wark — work
weel — well
wha — who
whan — when
whatsomever — whatever
whaur — where

wheesht! — hush!
wi' — with
wird — word
wynd — narrow, winding lane